UNDER THE FULL MOON'S LIGHT

A SHORT STORY ANTHOLOGY

Edited by Emma Nelson & Hannah Smith

OWL HOLLOW PRESS

Library of Congress Control Number: 2018961098
ISBN 978-1-945654-27-5 (paperback)
ISBN 978-1-945654-28-2 (e-book)

UNDER THE FULL MOON'S LIGHT/ Nelson, Smith. 1st ed.

www.owlhollowpress.com

To the authors of these dazzling stories—may you never stop spinning magical tales or howling at the moon.

CONTENTS

Hannah & Emma

UNDER THE FULL MOON'S LIGHT

On a recent camping trip with my family, the stillness of the night seemed to amplify each sound. Every rustle of a branch or scrape of a twig seemed louder than a gunshot. I froze in fear and barely slept a wink all night. I felt exposed and vulnerable, and it terrified me. Knowing that bears often visited this park didn't help matters either. How could I sleep when an attack could come from any direction?

This frightful anticipation reminded me of a scene from one of my favorite TV shows, *Lost*. Survivors from a plane crash hear the metallic scream of an unknown beast that sounds like a dinosaur in the jungle as it draws closer to their safe position on the beach. Palm trees are knocked sideways at an alarming rate as a terror in the night inches closer to their exposed location. Not being able to see the beast heightens the suspense. *What is that thing? When will it strike? How can they survive?*

I wonder how our early ancestors slept outside in the open air. Did they ever feel secure enough to fall into a deep sleep? I think it would be impossible for me. I find security in our houses, towns, and cities. So many horrors lurk in dark alleyways and shelter in deserted corners of the world. Very quickly, my mind pictures vampires hungry for blood or monsters creeping through abandoned buildings on the outside of town.

A fire burning bright in the darkness seems like a beacon of hope. Light seems to drive the fear away and offer a bit of safety, while the dark unknown teems with danger. But adding the lure of a full moon to a night already fraught with fearful shadows, it also becomes easy to imagine all sorts of spooks and specters. The moon adds an element of mysteriousness to the equation. Now, a jaunt in the woods can lead to an unfortunate stumbling upon a pack of werewolves. A blood moon seems the perfect backdrop to human sacrifice.

The moon, despite its beauty and grandeur, has often had negative connotations associated with it. For centuries before humans landed on the moon, little green men and other types of aliens were imagined to live there. Many cultures, like the Aztecs and Greeks, believed the moon was a living organism. Whether as a young girl or a woman who drove her chariot across the sky, the moon played a huge role in creation myths of our world. People once thought the moon caused insanity. Not only was it supposed to affect the body, but it changed a person's mind and drove them to madness. Thus, the word *lunatic* deriving from the Latin word for moon. Beauty and wonder, terror and mystery all surround this one celestial orb.

In this anthology, we'll explore the spells the moon has cast upon humanity since the dawn—or should we say dusk—of time. Come, join us, as we cast our literary enchantments with a delightful menagerie of stories told under the full moon's light.

LUNA'S LURE

Ocher-colored light absorbed into the floorboards of the front porch, bringing a warmth to David's broken home, but not to his weary state. Something was off—in the colors of the sinking sun, in the taste of his cold beer. The orange-yellow light of day faded into a cool gray, bringing with it a warning. A pressure in his chest.

"Full moon tonight," his neighbor Jeff said, and pulled a sip from a chilled amber bottle. "Feels wrong being off duty. Where's your boy?"

David stood up to break away from the threat within him—that admonishing voice inside whispering to him to get out. To run.

"Upstairs," he managed to reply as he leaned against the porch railing, unable to shake off the apprehensive feeling. After all, it was the same feeling he had right before finding out his wife was screwing some other guy.

Jeff nodded with what David assumed was judgment and disappointment.

"Still no clues on a suspect?" David asked.

Four disappearances, once a month on the full moon, had all of upstate New York on edge—Jeff most of all. Being Jeff's only confidante made David privy to information police wouldn't even give to the reporters. The first man's disappearance in Ontario County didn't make big news until they found traces of blood and bone fragments behind his work shed. Then came disappearances in Seneca, Cayuga, and Tompkins Counties. Three men, one woman, all had wandered outside around sunset. The only remnants were pools of blood or bits of hair and bone—the rest of their bodies remained missing. Poor bastards. Jeff said the police in those counties couldn't seem to make any connections between the murders, other than they had all disappeared on a full moon. Then the FBI got involved and took the case from local authorities, leaving Jeff off-duty and sipping a beer with David on a Friday night.

"No clues," Jeff said. "The last woman—there was so much blood. I got to see the photos." He shuddered and set down his beer. "Really feels wrong not working tonight. If this guy is moving from county to county, then he's gonna hit either Tioga or Cortland County next."

A gravitational pull swelled inside David, the kind that made him want to stray from his home.

"Dave!" Jeff reeled him back in. "You there?"

"I'm listening." He turned his attention from the neighborhood, back to his best friend.

"This guy could hit Cortland County tonight. Keep your eyes open."

David scanned the neighborhood as that force yanked at his chest.

"Where the hell did she come from?" Jeff whispered, nodding toward a leggy brunette wearing a flowing skirt and a tight red top. The long, uncoordinated strides of her pale legs carried her up the driveway to the vacant house next door.

The force pulled harder, piercing David's sternum and hooking into his ribs, directing him to *her*. David locked eyes with the stranger as she limped barefoot toward the steps. Feelings of warning drowned in his attraction to her.

Jeff brushed shoulders with him. "I hope she's our new neighbor," he said, letting out a slow, breathy whistle. "Dibs."

"Dibs?" David's trance broke. "What is this, junior high?"

Despite talking big game, Jeff was far too much of a gentleman to ever lay claim to a woman. In high school, he wouldn't even approach Julie Hardy, who couldn't have made it more clear that she wanted him to ask her out. Whereas David—by the age of 18—had mastered the art of making women drop their panties with nothing more than a smoldering stare. Over the years, Jeff worked on his confidence to approach women, but deep down, he was too much of a puppy. Especially for a woman like the one walking up the driveway next door.

Jeff smirked and then got serious. "Miss!" he called out.

The mysteriously charming woman climbed the steps without breaking David's gaze—there was no doubt in his mind that she wanted him.

"You okay?" Jeff shouted. "You injured?" He lowered his voice to a whisper. "Shoot, maybe I shouldn't have said that. What if she has a physical condition or something?"

As she reached the front door, it drifted open, and the gorgeous woman disappeared inside.

"Or maybe she's just rude." Jeff chuckled and poured more beer down his throat.

David released his breath, fighting the silent summoning from behind her closed doors. Plenty of experience taught him to be cautious of beautiful women—they were nothing but trouble. He had been knocked on his ass one too many times. Even his wife, who was the epitome of beauty, kicked him in the nads and left him squirming for mercy. She got paranoid, without any serious proof, then hopped in the sack with the first guy that made her feel special. To top it all off, she walked out on her family, claiming the appetite of a flesh and blood woman—whatever that meant—and leaving David to care for their teenage son.

"Dad!"

Jeff laughed. "That's him calling for attention."

"Don't start, man."

"Just saying you might have to take him outside every once in a while."

"I tried," David said with his hand on the doorknob. "He has no outdoor skills."

"Well maybe if you—"

"Lay off!" David snapped. "You don't know. Travis has no interest in anyone other than himself. I'm done trying to help that kid."

Travis's telescope was perched in the window of his second story bedroom. Gifted to him by his mother before she left, the telescope sat in a box for weeks, right next to the baseball bat that David had bought him.

"Finally decided to try that thing out, huh?" David asked as he stalled in the doorway, eyeing the untouched bat. It burned a little to know the kid chose the telescope over sports. Not that he was surprised. David had tried to teach the kid to play a couple years back—he'd always had a hell of a powerful swing—but it only resulted in strike outs and foul balls. Every week for months, David made an unsuccessful attempt to practice with Travis. Tireless eye-rolls and huffs of derision wore David down, and he gave up on the kid. Only a year until graduation, so all David had to do was try not to screw the kid up too much and keep him alive.

"You gotta see this," Travis said.

David could not care less about looking through the eyepiece of the ex's guilt gift. The $300 shiny black stargazing piece of bribery that she had probably hoped would win Travis back. One hand on a warming beer, and the other in his pocket, David pretended to care and entered Travis's room.

"What are you looking at?" he asked, hovering over Travis's shoulder. His corner bedroom allowed a direct view into the backyard next door. The gorgeous woman in the fitted crimson top stood below, stretching her arms to the sky.

"Supermoon," Travis said. "It's rising now."

David lifted his eyes from the alluring brunette to see the full moon filling the gaps between the houses on the horizon. Of course. Travis was the only teenage boy he knew that would be looking at the moon instead of an insanely hot woman. The kid's eyes were always on the sky, rather than the ladies.

The woman's presence in the yard below lured David's attention away from the moon on the horizon. Twilight turned the grass beneath her bare feet to a lifeless gray. Her flowing, knee-length skirt lifted in the breeze, allowing a flash of her bare thigh, and the gentle wind played in the strands of her hair.

Then, as if she knew exactly what David was thinking, she slid her shirt over her head.

David—needing to set an example for his kid—turned his back to her and dragged the telescope away from the window, fumbling like an idiot. "Whoa."

Travis's face, painted with confusion at first, turned stoic. "I wasn't looking at her. Honest."

David leaned the telescope against the wall. "What's weird about that, is I believe you."

He couldn't help but look again. Topless, she turned her body toward him—eyes lingering on the window for a moment while he sank into the darkness of the room, hoping she didn't catch him gawking.

"Okay, so the neighbor's a nudist," David joked.

"When did she move in?" Travis asked.

David shrugged.

Travis moved his telescope from the wall, fiddling with the parts, while David stole another glimpse of *her*. A flutter in his chest caught his breath. The rest of her clothing had been removed. With her bare backside facing him, she greeted the rising moon in the east.

David forced himself away from the window again. "What's so super about a supermoon?"

"It's a bit closer to earth than usual, and it can look bigger sometimes," Travis said. "Especially when it rises."

David tried to combat his need to look again. Maybe if he were able to control his lustful desires, his wife would not have strayed to the bed of another man. If he had just looked away instead of enticing every gorgeous woman to bed with him, he would still have the one woman that ever meant anything to him. Perhaps if he loved her, and only her, the way she deserved to be loved—if he could have satisfied her needs emotionally—he might still have her. And perhaps Travis would still have a mother living with him.

"Can I set up my scope again now?"

"Go take a shower or something, Travis."

"But the moon's rising *now*," he argued.

"Now is clearly not a good time." David gestured out the window.

"Why should I have to suffer because of her?"

"You'll be asking yourself that about women for the rest of your life."

The compulsion within him to go to that stranger next door ebbed and flowed, but David remained mindful of the warning in his heart. He grabbed a fresh beer downstairs, avoiding the peep show next door—he had *some* class after all. And he had *some* desire to save his marriage, if his wife would ever take him back.

He stepped onto his front porch where Jeff was standing guard, as if the serial killer at-large would stroll into his neighborhood at any moment.

"Feels wrong not working."

"You said that already."

"I should go talk to her," Jeff said with a sly smile, "and let her know to keep her doors locked tonight. I gotta be a good neighbor and all."

"I wouldn't strike up a conversation now," David said. "She's naked in the backyard."

Jeff's eyes bulged. "You're full of shit."

"Nope," David said, and took another swig of beer. "But it's weird. She was staring at me through the window. Like she knew I was there and she didn't care."

"In the nude?" Jeff asked, brows furrowed.

"Yep."

"That's an invitation if I've ever heard of one," Jeff laughed.

David held his breath, considering the idea. "No. I'm off women for a while."

"That's no woman," Jeff smiled. "That's a goddess. You don't turn that down. If a woman like that is eye-screwing you, you offer her a drink."

David leaned on the porch post and sipped from his beer, withholding his lecherous thirst for the woman next door, along with the contrasting yearning for his wife's love. The warm summer breeze skimmed his arm hair as the force of *her* calling pulled at him again.

Jeff straightened up his stance, took a swig from his bottle, and tucked in his shirt. "If you're not going to talk to her, then I will."

"She's naked, man."

"I know that." Jeff cringed. "I'm not some perv. I'm gonna knock on her door, let her put some dang clothes on, and then introduce myself. Let her know she's safe in this neighborhood. Maybe I should put my uniform on. Women love that." He paused for a moment and shook his head. "No time for that. I gotta do this now while the mood is right."

Jeff strolled next door with his hands in the pockets of his cargo shorts, climbed the steps, and knocked.

After a few seconds, the door opened to the tall, enchanting woman—no longer naked, but draped in a red satin robe. The sight of her welcoming smile captivated David all the way from his porch. She turned away from Jeff and faced David's house, imprisoning his gaze again.

Then the unexpected—she turned back to Jeff and allowed him inside. The front door shut behind them. David kicked himself for not calling dibs on her first, but found comfort in knowing he did the right thing.

As he headed upstairs, the intense sensation to go to her ceased. Released from her grasp, David stalled by Travis's room where the hiss of his shower grew louder. The moon crept higher against the darkening sky, spilling light through his window. Despite trepidation within discouraging him from going to the window, David edged closer anyway, taking in the glow from the supermoon.

Travis's shower cut off.

David peered into the darkening yard below as Jeff and the woman stepped outside. With her back to David, she stood before Jeff's silhouetted frame in the moonlight and opened her robe to him. David leaned closer to the window, stunned. "What the hell?"

Jeff stood still—what a dumbass. A gorgeous woman in front of him, and he freezes. David would have known how to play her.

Jeff's arms dangled by his sides as she drifted closer. Pale hands slithered across his chest. David leaned against the frame of the window, drawn to her. She pushed Jeff to the ground with a violent jolt, and David jumped, ready to help his friend. But Jeff wasn't exactly fighting her off. He lay on the grass as she crawled over him on her hands and feet.

That's when David should have turned away, but his eyes were trapped. The high contrast between her pale skin and dark shadows created an illusion of some inhuman form. She crawled over him with the awkward mechanics of an insect.

David squinted through the darkness trying to make sense of the contorted shape of her limbs.

Her robed body writhed and rocked over Jeff. David pulled his eyes away, toward the light beneath Travis's bathroom door to be sure his son wasn't coming. Despite his conscience insisting he look the other way, he was drawn back to the window.

Her back hunched over Jeff.

A darkness grew beneath them. A black shadow crept outward from under their bodies, so dark—like a void in the earth could swallow them whole.

The air shifted in the bedroom as Travis opened the bathroom door, stealing David's attention for only a moment.

The woman crouched over the growing black shadow. And Jeff was gone.

Her shoulders jerked in a violent, seizure-like episode. Still hovered over the black void, with her back to David, her head twisted in pulses as if being cranked by a wrench. The woman's eyes locked on him through the window. Impossible for her to see him through the darkened room, but her lips stretched into a sinuous smile inviting him to come to her.

Stumbling over Travis's books, David scrambled away from the window, unsure if his eyes were betraying him. All the possible explanations rushed through his mind. Weird lighting and shadows. Alcohol. An elaborate prank—knowing Jeff, it was the most likely of the scenarios.

"What happened?" Travis asked.

"Stay here," David urged. "Keep away from that window!"

The side yard, deep in the shadow of the house, provided cover while David went looking for Jeff. His heart hammered against his breastbone, bruising him from the inside, while he called for him.

"Jeff," he whispered as he stepped around the back of the house. Trying to remain calm and sensible, he walked into the moonlight, expecting Jeff to pop out of some hiding spot, laughing about how he "got him good."

"Jeff?" he called again.

While distracted by the nearly blinding light of the massive rising moon, he slipped. His foot slid in the grass, throwing off his balance, but he caught himself from falling.

"What the—"

Beneath his feet laid the same black shadow where Jeff had been.

He knelt down and placed his fingertips in the dark, slick substance, then raised his hand to the moonlight. A red viscous fluid encased the tips of his fingers—blood.

His pulse sped faster than his icy blood could pump through his veins. David backed out of the carpet of bloody grass. Shaking hands pulled his phone out to call for help.

The woman in the red robe came out of her house with a grin. Moon glow reflected off her skin as she jerked toward him in convulsions that defied physics. The satin robe, open and draping from her breasts, exposed a long, rugged scar from her clavicle to pubis. A scar indicative of some horrible surgery, or some traumatic event that ripped her open from the base of her neck all the way down her body.

David's hands betrayed him as his finger dialed the last digit. The phone fell to the ground.

"911 dispatcher…" the woman's voice faded.

His throat swelled from the inside. He couldn't speak. Gravity pulled at his feet with so much force it felt like the earth would suck him in. Standing petrified, David's body was unresponsive to his desire to flee.

Her pale gray eyes, cratered with dark splotches, captivated him. Mesmerized and paralyzed, he allowed her closer. One delicate hand rested against his chest, radiating an energy that permeated his skin. It surged through his veins, swelling and receding.

"Luna," she said with a voice that hissed and rolled like ocean waves. "She's close tonight. So strong."

With a gentle nudge, she sent him falling backward. Joints fused stiff, David could not break his own fall as he crashed into the grass. Flat on his back, with his arms to his sides, lying only feet from the blanket of Jeff's blood, David struggled to escape his paralysis.

The woman opened her robe, exposing her body. The long, vertical strip of white scar tissue widened, splitting along the length of her torso.

"She must feed again." A gravely breath of pain and pleasure seeped from her parted lips.

The flesh at the scar's seam stretched and separated.

Long, white strands of fleshy tissue thickened and formed into spindly teeth. Unclasping from an interlocked position over her organs.

Ribs fractured. The newly formed monstrous fangs opened, exposing a cavernous abyss within her body.

Terror-ridden and charmed, David remained flat on the ground as she dropped to her hands and feet to scramble over him.

Her eyes eclipsed to darkness.

The spiky teeth of her abdomen dripped saliva onto his belly, and a snarling moan rose from the beast within her gut. The fanged pit widened like the unhinging of a snake jaw, prepared to devour him.

Unable to close his eyes, he was forced to watch as it lunged upon him, delivering a fate he probably deserved. A flash of Travis smiling. A glimpse of his wife dancing. The memory of his young son laughing hysterically after an epic swing of a wiffle-ball bat that busted the plastic ball in half. As the moments of his life filled his heart, David snapped back to reality as the beast screeched and jerked to the side.

Travis towered over him with the baseball bat on his shoulder.

It squirmed in the grass, squealing from the blow.

Travis heaved, trembling, panting. David—shocked by his son's bravery—shifted an arm beneath him. As his vision pulsed with his heartbeat, he tried to break from his petrified state to help his son.

The woman's arms and legs buckled and snapped. She unfolded herself into an upright position.

David manipulated his numb legs to a standing position, but he could barely lift them for a simple step.

Her blackened eyes revealed a glowing crescent as they came out of their eclipse. She moved toward Travis. Surely the kid didn't have it in him to fight it off again.

The atrocity in her belly hissed and drooled as it closed in on the boy.

"Travis!" David shouted, lunging his torpid body between them, knees weak, crumbling beneath the weight of his body.

The scream of a thousand voices howled from the creature, and police sirens joined in from down the street.

"You'll be all right," David said to his son as something caught his breath.

A pressure in his chest.

Travis's eyes widened with panic. A fleshy, bony tentacle exited David's sternum. The creature pierced him from behind and wrapped the segmented extension around his waist.

Travis struck at her abdomen again, cracking one of its teeth, as red and blue emergency lights flashed across the fencing.

"Over here!" Travis screamed for help.

The pale beast on all fours backed against the fence with David in tow. His son's image shrank as David was pulled into the shadows of the yard.

"Dad!" Travis called, but his voice was distant—safe.

Tingling numbness sparked through his circuits as David allowed the monster to take him far away. His body tore through the woods, dragged by the demon to be consumed later. Relief blanketed him, knowing that Travis was safe from the beast's appetite for flesh and blood.

Katie Sherman

CAST IRON CORNBREAD

NEVER start something new on a full moon, her nonie had said the last time Elodie saw her, a few yellowing teeth peeking through bright red gums and oversized glasses slipping from the bridge to the end of Nonie's nose. She wore a blue and white striped housecoat, and her white hair curled naturally over the tips of her elfish ears. She had always been short but, in her old age, she'd shrunk like laundry left too long to dry. Elodie preferred to think of Nonie as compact, a big personality stuffed aggressively into a tiny body. Still, sometimes she worried all that attitude would ooze from her, leaving slimy puddles on the black-and-white-checkered linoleum.

Elodie hadn't spoken to Nonie in weeks. Not since the tour started. Nonie's hearing aid buzzed loudly into the cordless phone and Elodie was forced to holler throughout the conversation. The whole thing left a bitter taste in her mouth, one that reminded her of sucking dandelion roots. Now, with the steady beat of the opening band thumping through the field and a straw fedora perched on the crown of her head, Elodie wished she could summon her cell phone. Nonie would be in the kitchen making Luna cookies. It was her ritual during every full moon. Elodie could almost taste the almond milk, the slightest hint of salt within the dough.

New beginnings are for the crescent moon, Nonie would claim, working the tines of the fork through flaky dough, her hands little more than an intersection of blue-green veins and knobby knuckles. Then Nonie would list all the things in her life that happened on crescent moons.

Meeting Elodie's grandfather, a wide gregarious man who had a laugh for most things and a cuss word for everything else. Giving birth to her mother, a puckered pink baby who rarely cried. Finding the plot of land where they built the ranch-style brick house.

It wasn't until Elodie was a teenager that she realized the great tragedy of Nonie's life, losing her only son, happened during a full moon. He'd been taken as they stood at the edge of a festival in the park.

Nonie's back had been turned momentarily as she gathered the picnic basket and blankets. His too-small body had been recovered nearly a year later at the bottom of a ravine three miles from the park. His killer was never found, leaving Nonie to imagine him around every corner. Under every bed.

Was that why Elodie had suggested the concert? The park? Was she testing her nonie's theories?

Recently, Elodie's life felt like a surreal dream interspersed with hallucinogenic mushrooms, crowded concerts, and assertive sex. She hadn't imagined her bluegrass band, Cast Iron Cornbread, would've been anything other than a hobby. Her voice was mediocre. The lyrics were trippy and arguing with the band's lead guitarist, Milo, was relentless. Still, an undeniable chemistry radiated from the group. Their song was on the radio, signaled by Milo's piercing whistle in the opening bars.

Elodie pulled her knees to her chest, resting her chin on their peaks. The ground was damp beneath her, seeping through the thin floral kaftan. The "backstage" was a rudimentary tent. Milo had set up a tea kettle and a small fire. The flames licked the black sky and damp logs, crackling angrily.

"Odie," Milo called and Elodie cringed at the nickname.

Elodie meant French royalty. Milo thought this was pretentious and refused to say it, despite Elodie telling him Nonie named her. Elodie liked her name. She didn't like Milo. She watched him walk across the open field, barefoot and wearing a hat that matched hers but with a broader brim. He was shirtless and pale, his jeans torn fashionably at the knees.

"Odie," he yelled again.

She crawled from the tent. Her muscles were sore from setting up and her biceps ached with effort as she pushed herself to her feet. The thongs of her flip flops left deep red indentions and she wished she shared the tough skin on the underside of Milo's soles. He reached her in a few quick strides and his hands traced the outline of her face. Elodie stared at the contours of the moon. She wished he wasn't high and that he would stop touching her.

"I'll make you some tea," he said.

He used a small outdoor knife and a flat board to slice the shrooms, poured a bottle of water into the empty kettle, and removed a tea bag. Herbal mint to cut the earthiness of the drugs. Unlike Nonie, the band didn't have rituals. No superstitions, but they did perform high. Weed. Acid. Shrooms. Only once had they done coke before a concert, but the energy was wrong. Too manic. Too Wall Street.

Elodie would've liked to say no. She would've liked to let the crowd's vibe carry her through the evening. But as he handed her a tin mug, she couldn't refuse. Milo had spiked the tea with honey and the sweetness bit at the enamel of her teeth. The drugs washed down Elodie's spine. They sent a tingling sensation around her wrists and ankles, cuffing her gently to the ground. A banjo in the distance picked its way up an A Major scale before transitioning into a G-Chord progression, fretting energetically to the beat of the crowd's feet.

Tiny goose pimples formed on the nape of Elodie's neck. She missed her long hair. She used to tie it back in a fishtail braid, allowing the free wisps to lash her forehead. Elodie was always cold, shivering beneath vents in restaurants. Rubbing circulation into her arms on planes. When she was chilly, she would shake the hair loose, letting it stream down her back and warm her. Milo had asked her to cut it in a short pixie. More bohemian. More in line with the band's image. Now, Elodie wished she could draw the thick mane like a curtain over her face and hide behind the grapefruit-scented strands.

Milo sat on the ground next to her. "The Zeroes sound like shit tonight."

His hands were tight fists that made nervous circles in the dirt. His hair was about the same length as hers now. He pushed it back, revealing a forehead lined with deep wrinkles.

"I think they sound great," Elodie said. Her voice cracked in the middle and she hated herself a little.

She wanted hair to hide her embarrassment.

She wanted a voice that spoke louder, willing to articulate disdain.

She wanted Nonie to watch her on the stage, track her movements, without fear of a moon's curse.

Milo propped his feet in Elodie's lap and she traced a line of black sludge between his toes. He flung his head back, stretching his neck to one side, then the other, undoubtedly looking for comfort.

"We need an opener with some teeth," Milo said.

He slipped a clove cigarette from the front pocket of his jeans, balancing it in the corner of his mouth without lighting it. Elodie wondered if he bought the jeans with pre-torn holes.

"The music's solid though. It's damn good," Elodie said, humming along to the song they played.

Milo scoffed. "We need to play bigger. Get out of this shit town."

Milo had grown up in a wealthy Chicago suburb. He spoke with a southern accent on stage, drawing out long a's and calling fans y'all. He'd never understood the hills. Or moonshine. Or the way a banjo's rhythm could call you home. Elodie bent her arms behind her head, lying in her own hands.

Once, when she was sick, Nonie brushed her hair while Elodie lay like this on the cool cotton sheets of the guest room. Once, when she was tired, Nonie sang Italian lullabies, her tongue cradled around rich Rs. Once, when Elodie was excited, she introduced Milo and Nonie. Staring across the room at one another, they looked like mismatched bookends. He was tall and broad. She was short and thin. His arrogance and ambition counterbalanced her homey earnestness. At the end of the day, Nonie drew her aside, fingernails slicing through the skin on Elodie's forearm. "He's handsome but terrible," Nonie said. She sounded like a child, unwilling to diagnosis his terribleness. Unable to articulate the problem. She shook her head. It looked like she was trying to free water from her ears. "Terrible," she repeated.

The music slowed, and the lead singer of the Zeroes spoke softly into the microphone. The sound was seduction. The moon cast a strange glow over the park, catching checkered picnic blankets and kissing couples. Its light pried apart the secrets of the evening, stretching them thin. Nearly translucent. Elodie rubbed her arms. She pushed on an aging bruise, willing it to vanish. The fire looked cartoonish in its orange, flared brilliance, and Milo breathed so heavily Elodie wondered if he was asleep.

"This was a good idea," Milo said, apparently not asleep, fiddling again with the cigarette without lighting it. "Everyone loves a night like tonight."

Elodie took another long drink. The tea had grown cold and bitter, the heavy honey coating the bottom of her mug.

"Everyone doesn't love anything," Elodie said. "Nothing's one hundred percent."

Milo stared at her. Then he leaned forward and flipped the hat from her head, most likely angling to see her more thoroughly.

"God, you're brooding," he said. "It's a bad look."

Elodie shoved Milo's feet from her lap. She wanted to storm away, to run into the darkness. To find her baby uncle, scared and alone, and wrap him in the floral kaftan she wore. Instead, she slid her knees to her chin, making herself smaller. Elodie's eyes bulged and retreated, shifting from the sky to the blades of grass to Milo. The knife he'd used to slice shrooms lay exposed without its sleeve, bright and sparkling outside the fire. Milo continued to complain, his voice a nasal wail that grated her high. He scratched his rib cage, leaving red track lines on his waxy skin. Milo smelled like moist leaves on a fall day, as if he'd been buried and dug up hours later.

Elodie would rather be the remnant ashes from the flames, blown into the wind and carried over the mountains. Over the elm trees. Into the ocean. A cello's deep G belched like a bullfrog in the dead of night.

"Nonie lost her son on the night of the full moon," Elodie said.

Milo sighed, air gushing from his lungs in great puffs.

"His body was found the following year on the crescent."

"What do you want me to do with that?" Milo asked, a giggle creeping into his voice. He splayed his fingers, pinching the excess skin between the thumb and pointer. "Do you ever think about how big the world is? What are the odds something so horrible would happen to your nonie?"

Elodie bit the inside of her cheeks. A small, pocketed ulcer formed in her mouth. How many phases of the moon had Nonie waited for her son to return? How many Luna cookies had she baked and eaten?

"The weather had worn his clothes to threads."

A whooping ring of applause echoed through the park and Milo stood, dusting himself off. He handed Elodie her hat.

"Time to charm them, Odie," he said with a wink.

Elodie pulled her violin from its case, carrying it in one hand and Milo's ukulele in the other. She trailed him onto the stage, her feet a sluggish shuffle. Normally the shroom tea made her feel fluid, like the pelting river rapids that skimmed rocks and reeds alike. Now it felt like she was drowning within it.

"Mushrooms," she said to herself, elongating the Os.

Elodie touched her face as she walked onstage, accounting for both lips. Both nostrils. Both eyelids. The lights came on and a few people in the crowd whistled. The bass drum laid a steady beat, and Elodie bounced on the balls of her feet. She raised the scroll of her violin toward the crowd, making it sing. The horse hairs from the bow peeled back as she sawed faster and faster. Back and forth and back again.

"I been locking myself in my room for some time now," Milo crooned the Avett Brothers lyrics. "Reading and writing and reading and thinking and searching for reasons and missing the seasons."

He and Elodie did a synchronized dance on the stage, stepping around one another, then facing each other. Sweat stuck on Elodie's brow and Milo reached over to brush it from her.

"He's terrible," Nonie had said, not willing to elaborate.

But she's never seen this energy, Elodie thought. *She's never watched him perform.*

The drugs were now no more than a slow buzz against her temples. Elodie picked out faces in the crowd, singing directly to them. Once, she thought she saw a little girl among the couples. Her hair tied in sweet pigtails and her face drowsy. Then, she couldn't find her again. *Poof! Vanished!* The rhythm of the group slowed, and they slipped into their popular song. A few people stood, swaying in makeshift dance to the awkward beat. Elodie gripped a microphone, looking at Milo. There was a part in the middle of the song when he called out to her and it always felt intimate. The first time he'd talked to Elodie on stage, she'd wanted to kiss his face. Run her tongue gently over the soft, salty bend of his lips. Sometimes that reaction returned, surprising her. The first time Milo had said he loved her was on a rickety stage in a smoky lounge during those twelve bars. She still wondered if he'd ever meant it or if it was for the crowd.

As the group neared the conversation in the middle, the crowd leaned forward in anticipation. Elodie felt like she was floating in a florescent bubble. Maybe that's what they'd needed the night her uncle was taken. Maybe they'd just needed to climb higher. Search harder. Hadn't her nonie warranted that?

The band repeated a few bars, and she knew she'd missed her cue. *Amateur hour*, Milo would say. She could sense his frustration like a bumblebee in her back pocket. It stung her again and again.

"Odie," he said-sang.

"Yes, Milo." She fluttered her eyes like a cartoon princess.

Here he traditionally went into a story that embarrassed her. He talked about her tripping from a second story window, smoking a cigarette as she wailed through the pain. He was falling in love with her in that moment, he would say. *But, how?* she thought. *It wasn't just that she was hurt. She was vulnerable. She was a mess of mascara smudges and bruised limbs and bro-*

ken toes. Now, though, something was different. His eyes said the story tonight would be original. Unique. Another piece of them.

"You remember that time you told me about your uncle who went missing as a child?"

A few minutes ago? By the fire?

"I sure do," she said, positing a normal response. "You came over to hug me."

"Well, you started crying. Snot running down your face. You said he was taken on a night like tonight. That this concert was to honor him. I pressed your head to my chest—you remember that?"

"Yes I do," Elodie said, her standard response this time delivered in a robotic tone.

"There's something I didn't tell you about tonight."

"What didn't you tell me?"

She was flat, wanting more than anything for this exposure to be delivered and finished. She wanted to lie beneath the moon until it freckled her skin. She wanted to wither in the heat of Nonie's kitchen and eat her uncle's favorite cookies.

"You were sipping that tea like you couldn't get enough, and I was falling deeply in love with you. I just wanted you to know!"

The band pounded on with Elodie holding the microphone far from her mouth. She walked toward the back of the stage and took a drink of water to calm her trembling hands. The drummer stared at her in sympathy. This was too far. Too much. This felt like an operation conducted for a crowd. A chance to shimmy her organs from their cavities. To slice apart innards. Milo was jumping up and down, energized by the crowd's support and Elodie's real reaction. His Cheshire Cat smile was taunting. Elodie took another breath as the song wrapped up. They would traditionally play two or three more, but she stood at the edge of the stage and gripped his hand, swinging them both into a deep bow. Then she tripped off stage, trying hard to catch her breath. Milo followed, grabbing her hand and pulling her toward the crowd. She shot timber through her veins, so unwilling was she to move. She walked quickly.

"What the fuck was that?" he asked, following her to the tent. "You're out of your god damn mind!"

Elodie turned to face him. The fire had fizzled into a few glowing wands. The cutting board and the knife and the drugs were a disheveled heaping mess. Elodie stepped backward. The crowd had been surprised but accepting. It was Milo's face that frightened her. It looked like a deranged mask. His eyes wide, white circles. His mouth a thin straight line. His hands curled fists of fury.

"That wasn't for everyone," she said, staring into the sky. The moon laughed back at her. "That was between us."

Milo grunted, a snort of such knowing disdain that Elodie wanted to crawl from her own skin. She wanted to hide her face in the deflated flesh and blood.

"We're Cast Iron Cornbread," Milo said, stepping closer, he and Elodie doing a two-step dance where he advanced and she retreated.

"Nothing's private anymore. They loved every minute of that."

Elodie shook her head, trying to stop the buzzing. Trying to free herself from the drugs and this night. She tripped over the log they once sat on, twisting her ankle slightly. Milo's finger was so close she could bite it. He waved it in her face.

"You're replaceable. We could find better, cheaper," he said cruelly.

A moonbeam caught the edge of the knife, still gleaming brilliantly against the grass now puckered with dew. Milo didn't reach to help her up. Elodie leaned toward the knife. The red handle felt cool in her hand. She squeezed it, reminding herself that Nonie had said not to start something new on the full moon. But this was an ending, a completion. A closure. What would Nonie say about that?

Madison McSweeney

TELL ME AGAIN HOW YOU KILLED THE WOLF

"Tell me again how you killed the wolf," Mona asked the old hunter, gently stroking the grey pelt that was draped over the work bench.

Skinned, stretched, and splayed across the wooden bench in the hunter's living room, the beast's form was mostly intact. Four narrow flaps of skin hung from its shoulders and hips, ending in long black claws. At one end of the pelt, the wolf's tail was thick and lush; the opposite end narrowed into a flattened snout, two vacant holes marking where its eyes had once been.

Mona reclined farther in the tattered armchair, shifting to avoid an exposed and rusted spring. Her uncle Ed sat across from her, rocking slightly in an old wooden chair. A fire burned from the woodstove, bringing heat to that corner of the room only; the rest of the house was cold.

"Well," the old man said, as a cat wandered idly by, "You don't see a lot of wolves around these parts. That's important to know."

She nodded, continuing to run her fingers along the fur of the vanquished beast.

"So, when we got word about all the livestock getting killed, we didn't know what we were dealing with at first. It was Marty who first got a glimpse of it. Caught the thing in his henhouse—

said, 'Sure enough, that's a wolf we got there. No doubt.' And from that night on, we started going out looking for it."

Mona had first encountered the hunting party on the outskirts of Lakesedge. It was dark at the time, the sky black and the moon all-but-obscured under greyish clouds. The men were walking along the shoulder of the road, and had her uncle Ed not been wearing a reflective vest, her truck might have plowed right into them.

In reality, there was no lake bordering Lakesedge; the closest thing to it was a clammy, self-contained body of water a kilometre or so past the Silver Moon Trailer Park, supposedly created when a meteor crashed into the earth millions of years prior, leaving a crater the size of several dozen football fields. Developers had briefly tried to make the lake a tourist attraction: clearing the foliage around the shoreline to create a narrow beach, building docks and adding outhouses. But the tourists had never come, and now the lake was predominantly used by drunken teenagers at unholy hours of the night. There had been four drownings in as many years.

Bruce was already there by the time Mona pulled up to the beach, leaning against a browning evergreen and staring out over the unsettled water; if he heard her pull in, he didn't show it. She flashed her high beams at him before pulling her key out of the ignition. An ice wind blew across the lake, sending the trees swaying wildly.

"No truck tonight?"

Bruce shook his head; a strand of black hair fell from behind his ear. "Close enough to walk."

Mona didn't reply, and he didn't follow up. She wondered if she should have come here at all, or if she should have insisted on meeting somewhere public, in the daylight.

"You said you had something to show me?" she asked, finally, reluctantly.

"Yes," he said. There was a certain wariness in his eyes, intermingled with lust. She unconsciously started to edge backward.

"And you couldn't have shown it to me in the daylight?"

He shook his head. A smirk crossed his lips. "This ain't the kinda thing you can show someone in the daylight." He angled his head towards the sky, his face twisting into an unsavoury grin. She followed his gaze. The moon was high above them, its cloak of cloud drifting away with the wind.

Before Mona could ask him what he'd meant, he was on her.

His right arm snaked around her lower back while his left hand travelled up her shirt, and she had no choice but to yield as he lowered her to the ground. She protested meekly: "Bruce, we're outside—"

"Think anyone's here to see us?" he replied.

An electric shock rippled through her body as he climbed on top of her. She raked a hand through his long hair and put her lips on his, tracing the roof of his mouth with her tongue. He pulled away from her embrace, lifted her shirt and kissed her breast, his teeth grazing her nipple. His left hand fumbled its way to her waist and started undoing her jeans; he paused just long enough to let her nod in assent before sliding his hand through the gap. She let out a cry.

As she unbuckled his belt and slid it from its loops, Mona glanced at the moon again. It was large and round, shining brighter than she'd ever seen it before, as the last wisps of cloud were blown away.

Suddenly, Bruce released her and clambered to his feet.

She pushed herself up and saw his body framed by the moon's glow, his limbs twitching with the effort it took to restrain himself. He must have seen the glint of fear in her eyes, because he laughed, tossing his hair back and flashing a set of long, sharp teeth. As the flesh on his muscular limbs started to writhe, Mona finally understood what he'd wanted to show her.

"And how did that go?" she asked.

"No luck, the first few nights," Ed replied. From the corner of the room, a clock chimed. Mona jumped. Ed laughed. "Not used to that clock by now, Moaner?"

"I forgot about it," she replied. "Anyway, you were saying?"

"Oh yeah. Where was I? We had no luck for a while, but we kept going out. We knew we'd get 'im eventually."

"And the killings?"

"The livestock, you mean? Oh, it was a chicken here, a pig there. One night the thing stuck its teeth into Art Mask's favourite guard dog. Art sure didn't like that."

Mona cringed. "Did the dog make it?"

Her uncle shook his head. "Yes 'n' no. It made it through the night, but paralysed. Art had to shoot it. Any-who, after that, things died down for a month or so. But we knew the wolf was out there somewhere."

"Weird," she replied.

He nodded, then looked at his feet. "You know, Mona, it's nice a'you coming to see me like this. I know things ain't been good between us, since you moved back in with your mother."

Mona looked at her knees, fidgeting with the gaping holes in her jeans, fighting back the flashbacks of that time. "Yeah. I mean, you know I appreciated you taking me in back in the day. I'm sorry things got rough when I left."

"How is your mom, anyway?"

Mona didn't look up. "She's okay," she replied, twirling a frayed thread of denim around her ring finger. "You know how she gets."

Over the next few months, Mona spent less and less time at home, and more time at Bruce's trailer. Soon enough, the waning of the moon mellowed him, and he was uncharacteristically attentive as she re-hashed her family history.

"It was a nightmare living with Ed," she complained, her head resting on Bruce's shoulder. "I mean, Mom's not great, but Ed was such a control freak, it was like being in prison." She shivered and curled up closer. Bruce kissed her on the forehead.

"My old man was an asshole," Bruce remarked. "But he got killed when I was fourteen, so I guess that worked out."

"Accident?" she asked.

"Mauled."

Mona stiffened. She was about to ask, "By what?" when there was suddenly a loud clatter from across the room. She yelped in surprise.

Bruce hopped up and walked the few steps to his kitchen. "Sorry, that window's been half-off its hinges." He began to crank it shut. "It's usually fine until the wind gets going like this."

"No worries; I'm just a bit jumpy is all. Loud noises." She squirmed into an upright position. "That was another thing about Ed—he had this antique clock that chimed every fifteen minutes. All day, all evening, it was all I heard."

"That would drive me crazy," Bruce replied, wrenching the window into place. "I would've probably smashed it."

Mona raised an eyebrow.

Bruce returned to the threadbare sofa. "So, is living with your mother any better?"

Mona shrugged. "She rags on me a lot. You'd think she'd be happy to have me around. But I don't think she's ever truly happy about anything."

"That's her problem, babe," Bruce replied, planting a kiss on her forehead.

"I know." Mona lifted her head and smiled at him. "She doesn't like you either, you know."

Bruce grinned. "That's also her problem." He started to kiss her. Coming up for air, she tried to whisper, "I love you;" if Bruce heard, he didn't react.

"Anyway, I was telling you a story there, wasn't I?"

Mona smiled and nodded. "You were saying the killings died down for a while?"

Ed leaned back in his rocking chair. "Yep. But not for good. Soon enough, things got real bloody again."

The night of the killing, Mona paid an unwelcome visit to Bruce's trailer. He didn't answer at first, so she banged on the thin metal door until he had no choice but to let her in.

"What were you doing making out with that motorcycle gang slut?"

Bruce didn't react. He looked her up and down for a moment before remarking, "You're drunk."

She scoffed. "Don't change the subject, Bruce—you fucked up. I mean, I know you can't control your urges when it's getting near your 'time of the month,' but I'd at least expect you to have better judgement. That chick's been passed around like a bong—"

"Mona—"

"I wouldn't touch that bitch with a ten-foot pole."

Bruce's expression was hard. "It's the full moon, Mona. I suggest you leave before something bad happens."

"Like what?" she scoffed. "You're gonna turn into a little puppy and kill some chickens, huh? Mr. Big-Fucking-Wolfman." She shoved him. He grabbed her by the shoulders and pushed her up against the wall. She yelped as a light-switch jabbed her in the back.

Bruce's hands were around her throat. "What, I'm not dangerous enough for you, bitch? You wanna see me do worse?"

Her eyes widened, and in that instant she truly believed he was going to kill her. Then he let her go.

As she struggled to catch her breath, Mona started to giggle. "'Bitch.' Nice word choice. Hate to break it to you, Brucie, but I'm not the one here who's literally a dog."

"Get out, Mona." Bruce's voice was level but strained. She looked up and saw his skin start to ripple.

She laughed again. "Why, are you gonna kill me? You can if you want. That's what you *really* want, isn't it?"

"I'm serious. Get the fuck out *now*."

"Fine." Mona grabbed her purse and threw open the door. "I hope you get fleas!"

He snarled, and she darted down the steps, slamming the door behind her.

She was halfway to her truck when she heard the sound of a screen being wrenched open. She turned to catch a glimpse of Bruce climbing out his kitchen window, landing on all fours, and breaking into a hunched-over run in the direction of the woods.

"If yer interested in hunting, I have a treat for you."

Ed jumped up from his chair and beelined to the oak cabinet that leaned against his back wall. He unlocked the cabinet with an antique key, bent down, and pulled out a rifle.

Mona's eyes widened. "Is that…?"

Ed grinned. "Darn right. This is what I shot 'im with." He laid it down on the coffee table for her to admire.

She stopped herself from asking what type of bullets he'd used.

Mona drove home slowly that night. The road through the forest was unlit and poorly paved, and she was in no state to be operating a vehicle. "Sorry, Officer," she said aloud to no one in particular. "I know I shouldn't be driving, but I'm fleeing a werewolf."

She felt her front wheel veer onto the shoulder and swerved to avoid sliding into the ditch. As she turned, her high beams glanced across something reflective and orange.

The hunting party was out.

"It was maybe ten o'clock at night when we caught sight of him," Ed continued, his voice becoming more animated as he made his way toward the climax.

"How'd you track him?" she broke in. "Footprints?"

Ed shook his head. "Too dark for that. We heard the rustling in the branches and followed the sound."

Mona found the footprints almost immediately upon entering the woods. Deep treads from heavy work boots. Unmistakeable.

About twenty metres in, she found the boots discarded. A black t-shirt hung from a branch nearby, and a pair of faded blue jeans were crumpled underneath a protruding root.

She shone her flashlight along a line of ever-shrinking prints heading deeper into the trees. Goosebumps prickling her bare arms, she followed, watching as they warped and shifted, becoming less human with every step. Above her, the moon was bright and full.

The ground became firmer as she travelled, the footprints fainter. Just when Mona was convinced she'd lost the trail, she heard snapping branches somewhere in underbrush. She threw her light in the direction of the noise; the beam landed on grey fur and glowing eyes. Deep in the trees beyond, there was a flash of orange.

In the sky, a cloud drifted over the moon.

"How were you able to see the wolf, if it was so dark?" she asked, trying to quell a mounting hysteria.

Ed didn't reply for a moment. "I think Art had a flashlight. It was a full moon, too; things were lit up pretty bright."

"No clouds?"

Ed looked puzzled. "No."

"Why did you always go out so late, anyway?"

Was there a hint of suspicion in his expression? "Wolves are nocturnal."

"Oh. Of course."

Ed stood up again. "How about I go make you another cup of tea?"

"That'd be great," Mona replied. She watched as he turned his back and walked into the kitchen. Her eyes drifted to the rifle. "So, this is what you shot him with?"

"Yes, ma'am."

She gulped. "What type of bullets?"

She heard a clatter from the next room, as if he'd fumbled and mishandled a mug. "Bullets? The regular kind. Why do you ask?"

"No reason."

"Say, I hope you're not going all 'animal rights' on me."

She laughed. "Of course not. I was just wondering—well, was it instant, or did the wolf put up a fight?"

He chuckled from the kitchen, and walked back in carrying two mugs of hot tea. "Oh, the thing thrashed and writhed a bit, but it was as good as dead, the second I—"

Ed stopped in his tracks and let go of the mugs. Dark tea stains spread across the carpet. The clock chimed again.

Mona was standing by the stove with Ed's rifle aimed squarely at his chest. He opened his mouth in protest but didn't get a word out before she pulled the trigger.

She ran her fingers across the wolf pelt as she watched the light leave her uncle's eyes. As he shuddered and twitched on the floor, she remembered Bruce bleeding on the ground in the woods, moaning and howling, his pale body convulsing as he withered back into a dog.

She remembered running away before the hunting party could see her, lest they turn their guns on her to prevent her from revealing what she'd seen them do.

And she remembered the moment just before the shot, Bruce naked and fully illuminated by her flashlight, the shadow on the moon bringing him back to his human form. And the bullet penetrating him regardless, her uncle determined to capture his prey, be it human, animal, or both.

Ed lay still. Mona lifted Bruce's pelt from its spot on the workbench and planted a kiss on the thin flap of skin between the two empty eye sockets.

Her lover in her arms, Mona walked out of the farmhouse and closed the door behind her.

Tony Evans

THE BONE LADY

"Come on, Mom! Are you serious?" Dan said, furiously. "It's just gonna be Mike, Jerry, and me. We've been planning this for weeks!"

Mary stood, her arms crossed as she stared at her feet. "I know, but I didn't realize it was this weekend. I'm sorry."

"What do you mean you didn't realize it was this weekend? I've been talking about it for forever." He walked over to the calendar hanging on the wall and slapped his hand over it. "Look! It's circled in bright red marker *and* highlighted."

Mary closed her eyes, took in a deep breath, and raised her hand in front of her. "I know, Dan. I knew it was this weekend; I just didn't realize it was a—" She hesitated, her hand found her chin as she struggled to find what she wanted to say. "Well, I just didn't realize it was gonna be here so soon. Now, you all can go next weekend or the weekend after that. But you are *not* going out into those woods *this* weekend. Do I make myself clear?"

"But, what's wrong with this weekend?" He looked to the date on the calendar, finally making the connection. Like a gear catching in a cog for the first time, something clicked. "Wait…is it because it's a—it is, isn't it? It's because it's a full moon! Are you serious, Mom?"

Her sternness suddenly losing hold, Mary's eyes began to twitch from side to side. Her breathing accelerated, became shallow and quick.

"You really believe those old stories you used to tell us? About witches and spooks?"

"You're not going, Dan. Make the plans for any other time, just not this weekend."

"You've got to be kidding me!"

"Those woods are not the place for a bunch of sixteen-year-old boys to go off by themselves, anyway. Especially during a full moon."

"It's not real! There's no way that stuff was real. They're stories to keep kids from running off and getting lost. Folk-tales, Mom. Jesus! You probably still believe in Santa Claus too, huh?" He laughed, condescendingly.

"They are *not* just stories. You weren't there. It was…*is* real. And it doesn't matter what you think or what I believe. I'm your mother, and I say you're not going. If you don't believe me, ask your dad when he gets home. End of discussion."

"But Mom, the guys—"

"I said, end of discussion."

Dan sat in his room and waited on his father to get home from work. Surely, *he* could talk some sense into his mom. He watched the clock with the attention a heart surgeon gives his most fragile patient. Each click of the second hand seemed to echo a deep vibration through the air as Dan thought about the whole situation. He remembered back to the stories she'd told him and his friends when they were little. Stories of witches and demons, people making pacts with Satan for eternal life and love and wealth. Stories of talking snakes and panthers in the woods that turned into beautiful women to lure in their prey.

She's losing her mind. Monsters don't exist. The monsters we think we see as children are just products of our imagination. Mom just had a very vivid imagination. That's all.

He was deep in thought when the sound of a car door slamming jerked him back to reality. He ran downstairs and waited at the door.

"Dad!"

"Well, hey there, Dan. Excited to see your old man?" Brent chuckled.

"Oh, uh-y-yeah, I guess."

Brent laughed and looked at him, unconvinced. "Yeah, thought so. What's up? Must be something good for you to meet me at the door."

"It's about the camping trip with Mike and Jerry."

He stepped to the side and dropped his briefcase against the wall. "What about it? Should be good for you boys. Why, I remember my first camping trip away from my par—"

"Mom said I can't go."

He loosened his tie as his brow furrowed. "Said you can't go? Why?"

"Because it's this weekend, Dad."

"O-okay. And?"

Dan ran to the kitchen and grabbed the calendar. He held it up and grinned with sarcasm. "It's a full moon."

"Aaaah, I see. Yeah, that's a pretty serious topic for her."

"I mean, what is it she's so scared of? The full moon?"

"She's just…what's the word to best describe it? Cautious. She's cautious, that's all."

"She's nuts, I think," he said, half joking.

"And I'm guessing you want me to talk to her for you?"

"If you could?"

He laughed as he slapped Dan on the back. "I'll see what I can do."

Dan had just dozed off when he heard a knock at his bedroom door. He jerked his head up, a small string of spit clung to his pillow. "Huh-a-wha?"

"Come on down, Dan," Brent called. "We'll talk about the trip this weekend."

When he reached the bottom of the stairs and turned toward the living room, he saw his mother and father sitting on the couch. His father seemed calm and normal. His mother, anything but. Her hands were shaking, feet fidgeting, and her forehead was covered in a light coating of sweat.

"Hey, guys. So…how about that camping trip?" Dan said, hopeful.

Brent smiled. "Well, I've talked to your mom, and she really doesn't wanna budge on this one."

"What? Seriously? Why?"

"Now, Dan, calm down."

"Calm down? Ha! I've been planning this trip for weeks, for *months*. Now I can't go because Mom's afraid of a full moon? This is ridiculous, Dad. You have to agree, right?" He looked his father in the eyes.

"Well, to be honest, I'm not sure this time."

"What?"

"Let's just listen to your mom for a minute. She's got something to say about the whole situation, okay?"

Dan's jaw dropped, his eyes widened. Was he hearing this correctly? Had he fallen into another dimension? Was his mother, his *father*, going to let months of planning fall apart, all because of his crazy mother and a full moon?

Mary took in a deep breath, steadying herself. Her unease was obvious; an air of fear and nervousness clouded the room. "Do you remember the stories we told you and your friends when you were younger?"

He rolled his eyes, shook his head. "Yeah, I remember."

"Well, you probably know that they weren't true. They were just stories to keep you boys entertained. Stories to keep you from going into those woods alone."

"Right. They're not real! So, what's the problem?"

His mother hung her head, stared at her knees. "*Those* stories aren't real, but the one I never told you is."

Dan shifted back, surprised. "Huh?"

"Long ago, there was a man who lived in a cabin up on the ridge behind us. His name was Mr. Caldwell. He was the man who owned all of Caldwell Junction. He also owned a large majority of the land surrounding it, including Caldwell's Mountain."

"Okay," Dan said. "Somebody had to own it. What's that got to do with us camping?"

"Well, one day, when your great-grandpa was a little boy, a coal company came in and made Mr. Caldwell an offer on all this land. There was a large coal seam that ran under it, and there were millions to be made. Mr. Caldwell wanted nothing to do with it, so he turned the offer down. They really wanted that coal, though, so they kept pushing. They offered more and more money, sure that Mr. Caldwell had a price, but he kept saying no."

"Good for him. I'd have done the same thing," Dan said, with conviction.

"Things weren't as simple as that back then, Dan. The company *really* wanted that land, and they were willing to do whatever it took to get it."

"What happened?"

"It was his family they went after; his wife and young daughter. They hired a small group who went into his house one night and murdered his wife while making him watch. Then they took his daughter and held a knife to her throat, telling him they'd kill her if he didn't sign over the deed to the land. So, he signed it."

"Man, I don't blame him. That's pretty serious."

"Right. But after he signed it away, they slit her throat and forced him to watch as she bled out in front of him."

"Is this for real, Mom?"

"Yeah. Go to the library and look up the newspaper article. Ask anyone around here that's old enough. They all know the story. It was a real tragedy."

"Okay, so is the mountain supposed to be haunted now or something? Is that what we're getting at here?"

She cleared her throat and looked up at Dan. "Mr. Caldwell wanted revenge. So, he called on…her." Her eyes twitched, nervously.

"Her? Her who?"

"It's just an old superstition around these parts, that's all. It's just that, your mother would feel more comfortable if—"

"The Bone Lady," Mary interrupted. "He called on th-the Bone Lady."

"Mary, you're not supposed to say her name."

"It's okay. He's old enough to know."

Dan's brow furrowed, and he leaned back in his seat. "What's the Bone Lady?"

Brent started to pace the floor. "It's nothing, Dan. J-just, you're not going camping this weekend, and that's final. You understand?"

"She doesn't have a name, not a real one anyway. Everyone just called her the Bone Lady. In times of extreme need, when nothing else seemed to work, legend said that she could be conjured."

"Mary!" Brent yelled in protest, his eyes wide, hands shaking nervously.

She continued. "She was a sort of fixer. Some people believed she could fix things that couldn't be fixed any other way."

Dan's interest was genuinely piqued. It reminded him of when he and his friends were little, listening to spooky stories before bed. "What kinds of things? Was she a doctor? Like, some sort of natural healer or something?"

"I refuse to stand here and listen to this. I-it's not, it's just not supposed to happen!" Brent stormed out of the room.

Dan looked at his mother, waiting for her to respond.

"Something like that. Some people believed she had…powers. That she could bring people back from the dead." She laughed, quietly. "She couldn't, of course. Once you're dead, you're dead. But that didn't stop people from talking, and you know how people are. Some even said that she sold her soul to Satan himself."

"Seriously? So, is that why Mr. Caldwell called on her then? To see if she could bring his family back?"

"He was a smart man, Dan. He knew that would never happen. He called on her for the worst possible reason. Revenge. He wanted that group of men to pay for what they'd done."

"Revenge? How would she do that?"

"Whether or not she sold her soul is something only she knew, but she most certainly had ties in with *them*."

"Ties with *them*? Who's *them*?"

Her head cocked to the side, she took in a shallow breath and held it. "The dark side, Dan. Demons. She was a collector of certain…*things*. People said she never aged, and it was believed by most that she kept her youth by acquiring these things. If you could give her what she needed, she would use her connections to bring about justice for those who felt they deserved it. And Mr. Caldwell felt he deserved it."

A sly grin crept across Dan's face, amusement beamed from his eyes. "This is getting interesting."

His mother frowned, her eyes narrowing to thin slits. "Interesting? You look like you're enjoying this. It's not a laughing matter."

"I'm sorry, Mom, but you're sitting here telling me some story about a half witch half demon lady who made deals with the devil to keep her youth? Really? That's just crazy! And besides, this still has nothing to do with me going camping!"

"They called her the Bone Lady for a reason, and it's not funny! Those things that she collected? They were the bones of children. She ate the flesh off of them to stay young."

"Uhhh—"

Mary jumped to her feet, enraged, arms flailing. "And Mr. Caldwell summoned that *witch* to his house and fed her the body of his slaughtered daughter so that she could unleash a demon straight from Hell to get revenge on those men!"

"Okay, Mom. Calm down. It's just a stor—"

"No, it's not, Dan! You think you know everything? You think you're so smart? There are things in those woods, boy. Things you wouldn't believe are real. And every full moon, that godforsaken *thing* comes back, roaming the mountains and protecting Mr. Caldwell's land from trespassers. It doesn't know the difference in good and bad. It was conjured to protect what was his and what threatened him and his family, and that's just what it'll do, without prejudice."

"Mom, listen, please?"

"That's enough!" his father screamed, bursting back into the room. "Too much has been said already. This discussion is over. No more about...*her*, and you are absolutely not going camping this weekend. Is that clear?"

"Dad!"

"I said, is that clear?"

"But what about Mike and Jerry? I bet their parents let them—"

"I don't care, Dan. They can go if they want to, but you're staying home. You can be mad if you want. One day, maybe you'll understand."

Looking to his mother for support, a frown stretched across Dan's lips.

"I'm sorry, honey. Any other time, but not this weekend."

"I hate this! Mike and Jerry are gonna go have fun, and I'm stuck here all weekend because of some stupid children's story!" Dan jumped to his feet and ran upstairs, slamming the door to his room.

Mary looked to Brent. "I hate that he's mad."

"Me too, but you know it was the right decision."

"But what about his friends? Do you think—"

"I hope not, Mary, but they're not our responsibility. Their parents know the story. For Dan's sake, I can only hope they stop them from going."

On Friday morning, Dan broke the news to his friends. He'd explained how his parents wouldn't allow him to go, but when asked why, he made up an excuse about how his mother was sick and his father would be out of town, so he had to be there to help her. If his friends found out he wasn't allowed to go because his mom was crazy, he'd never hear the end of it.

"Sorry, guys, I'm a good son. What can I say?" he joked.

"Dude, you're gonna miss out. Gonna be a hell of a weekend," Mike replied.

"Maybe next time," Jerry said. "Just too bad you had to puss out."

"Whatever, guys. Sorry I'm the nice one in the group."

"Yeah, it's gonna be fun, though," Mike said. "Mom and Dad said something about an old ghost story in the area. One I'd never heard before."

"Man, it was ridiculous. My dad told me about it too," replied Jerry. "Something about an old lady who eats kids? I don't know. It was weird."

"I'll bet that's why Dan's not goin'," Mike joked. "I'll bet he heard the story and pissed his pants." He snickered. "That's it, huh? I'll bet that's it."

Dan stood before his friends, caught off guard. He couldn't let them know he'd heard the story, and he damn sure couldn't let it slip that it was the reason he wasn't going. "N-nah. I don't know what you're talking about. What story?"

"It's just a dumb local ghost story, right Mike?" Jerry punched Mike's shoulder. "We were gonna try and find some old cabin. Supposedly, a murder happened up there years ago. You know, see if it's haunted. Just too bad you can't go."

He wasn't sure why, but his heart began to beat faster. It was all just make believe, just a dumb urban legend. "Since when did you guys become ghost hunters?" He shuffled his feet, trying to hide his anxiety. "You don't actually believe that stuff, right?"

"Ha! Are you kiddin' me? Hell no, we don't believe it. Still gonna be fun though, findin' an old cabin and trashin' it." Mike snickered.

"Well, maybe you—"

Jerry put his hand on Dan's shoulder. "Wait a minute. *You* believe it, don't you?"

Dan placed his hands in his armpits. He wasn't scared of ghosts and demons; he didn't even believe in them. But there was something about the whole situation, especially the way his parents reacted to him going, the way they told the story with fervent belief, that made him nervous.

"No, of course I don't believe it. I just think trashing someone's property is wrong."

"Relax," Mike said, stretching his arms above his head. "That place is probably rotted to the ground by now." He looked to Jerry and winked. "But we'll be sure to tell everyone that you didn't go because you're afraid."

Dan's face turned red, embarrassment radiated from his skin with a heat that could have boiled water. "I-it's not like that, guys," he pleaded. "I-I just don't wanna, you know, don't want you all to get in trouble."

"Don't worry, Dan. We'll be just fine."

That night, Dan ate dinner with his parents. Tension filled the air like a thick southern humidity. The only sounds were teeth scraping forks with each bite of food taken. Dan kept constant watch on his phone for texts or updates from his friends, and his parents kept their heads down, avoiding eye contact.

Finally, Dan decided to give it one last shot. There was still time to grab his pack and head up into the woods. If he hurried, he would be able to cut them off where the old logging road above his house ended. Besides, what did he have to lose?

"Mom, Dad?" The sound of his voice broke the silence like thunder cracking throughout a quiet summer sky. "I-I just wanted to say, I'm sorry. You know, about before, about the story and the camping thing."

They both looked at him and smiled.

"It's okay, Dan. We're sorry, too," Mary said.

He looked to the window. The sun would be gone down in half an hour, so if he was gonna make a move, it had to be soon. "You know, I was talking to Mike and Jerry this morning. They said their parents told them a similar story, too."

They looked at him, their smiles replaced by looks of concentration.

"They're still going. I guess their parents weren't too concerned. Do you think, maybe, I could go meet them? There's still time, if I go now."

Brent took in a deep breath as Mary hung her head and began tapping the table with her fingernails.

"Dan, we told you the matter was closed. Now, their parents know the same story that we told you. Everyone around here knows it. What they decide or allow their children to do is out of our hands, but *you* will not be going up on the mountain tonight."

"Dad, come on!"

"That is final."

His father stood and slammed the chair into the table before walking into the kitchen. His mother, head still facing down, began to cry.

"Jesus, what a messed-up family!" Dan jumped from his chair and ran to his room. He threw himself onto the bed and stared out the window in time to catch the last glimpse of the autumn sun fall behind Caldwell's Mountain. He checked his phone and sighed. There were several unread texts, all from Mike and Jerry asking if he was coming or if he was too scared. He'd be made fun of forever for this.

Damn! Of all the parents, why do I have to have the craziest ones?

He looked at his pack, fully loaded and ready to go, then to the window. He could get out without being seen, he was sure of it. But something held him back, a feeling in the pit of his stomach. Guilt? Loyalty? Whatever it was, he knew he shouldn't go. He swiped his phone screen and replied to Mike and Jerry in a group text.

'*Nah. I'm out on this one. I gotta stay in and look after my mom, remember? Be sure to text me pics of the Boogeyman, though!*'

Dan woke to a constant vibration in his ear. His eyes opened, slowly at first, as his brain tried to play catch up and remind him of where he was and what was going on. Groggy, he raised his head.

"Huh-wha-whas going on?"

The sensation continued. He wiped his face and fumbled his arm around, feeling for the source of the vibration—his phone. There were thirteen missed calls, all from Mike and Jerry. He looked at the time. It was Midnight.

"Jesus, I must've fallen asleep." His phone began to vibrate again, as his friends made another attempt at calling. "Hello?"

It was hard for Dan to make out, but it sounded like heavy breathing on the other end, as if someone were, or had been, running.

"Hello? Jerry? You there?"

More breathing, broken up gurgles, chokes.

Dan's eyes widened, the taste of pennies finding his tongue. The room began to spin as a feeling of trouble filled the air. "J-Jerry? You guys okay?"

"Dan," a whisper replied. "Y-you gotta help. We…I don't know where else to go. I-it's coming."

Dan jumped to his feet and ran a hand through his hair. "What? What are you talking about?"

The sounds coming from the earpiece were low and quiet, a combination of whines and almost silent coughs and mumbles.

"I-I'm at th-the, la-large rocks." He whined again, holding back crying. "You know, the ones where we always go? I'm close. Please?"

"I can't hardly hear you, man. Sounds like you been running or crying. Speak up. Is everything okay? Did one of you get hurt?"

A long silence fell over the receiver. Deep, heavy breaths. A low, muffled growl, then an eerie, forced grunt.

"Please, Dan? You gotta help. I-it's real. The stories, that, that *thing.* I-it killed him, Dan. It ate Mike."

"What?"

"No! It hears me, Dan!"

Heavy crunches filled his ears; a whisper of wind kissed the phone. He heard screams growing more distant, and he heard his friend's voice yell.

In a panic, Dan wasn't sure what to do. It wasn't far from the rocks to his house, and it was mostly downhill, so he knew Jerry would be there soon. He froze for a moment, his imagination flowing with images of monsters, carnage, and death. Was it real, or just some crazy joke they were playing on him? It didn't matter. If it was real, he had to help.

He ran down the hall and threw open his parent's bedroom door. "Mom, Dad! Jerry just called. H-he sounds like he's in some kind of trouble! W-we gotta help him!"

His father raised his head and rubbed sleep from his eyes. "Wh-wha?"

"Jerry called, Dad! He said—"

"There's nothing we can do to help him, Dan. It's best to let things take their course." His mother was standing by the window staring into the sky. The moon was large and full, appearing to take up a full quarter of the otherwise empty blackness above. Its light shined into the room, forcing shadows from places they didn't belong.

A confused look fell over Dan's face. "What? It sounded bad, Mom. It sounded like someone was after him!"

"It's not someone. It's *something*. I told you those stories were true, and you wouldn't listen. Nobody ever listens. Now you'll see I'm not crazy."

"But Mom, we have to help!"

She pointed to the moon. "The only time that place is forbidden is during a full moon, and they wouldn't listen. I tried to tell you boys. They woke it, and now they'll see. It'll take them, then it'll go back to sleep. We'll be safe here. It only takes those that get in its way. It won't leave the woods unless—"

"He's coming here, Mom. He wasn't far when he called. I-he needed help!"

She turned to look at him. "He's what?"

"He can't come here, Dan!" Brent yelled.

"Wha-where is he?" Mary turned to look out the window again. There was a beam of light darting back and forth in the woods above the house. "That's him. It has to be. He *is* coming."

Dan ran to the window. "Where? I-I see him! We gotta help him, guys. I'm gonna go let him in." As he turned, he felt a tight grip wrap around his wrist.

"You'll do no such thing, boy. You don't understand what he's done, what you've done."

"Mom, let go! He's my friend. We can't just let him die."

"He should've just stayed up in those woods. By coming here, he's brought *it* with him, and if we help him, it won't stop until it kills us all. There's only one thing we can do, and it's something that should've been done long ago." She looked to

Brent. "Something that nobody in this godforsaken town has been willing to do."

"You don't mean it."

"It's the only way, Brent, and you know it."

"But, you know what she's like, Mary. She'll need a—"

"I know," she interrupted. "And now we'll have one."

A series of loud thumps accompanied by screams echoed throughout the house. They were coming from the front door.

"Mom, we gotta help him!"

"Go let him in, Dan. We'll make all of this stop tonight."

Dan smiled, finally relieved that his parents were going to do something. As he opened the door, Jerry fell to the floor and crawled inside.

"Close the door!" he screamed. His body was covered in dirt. Tears, sweat, and blood coated his face and hands. "M-Mike!" he said, sobbing. He clawed at Dan's legs to help himself to his feet. "H-h-he's dead!"

"Calm down, Jerry." Dan said, trying to comfort his friend. "It'll be okay, now. You're safe here."

"It's coming. That thing. It's going to kill everyone!"

"No, it's not. You're safe here. I promise."

Mary and Brent ran into the room and grabbed them both by the arm. "Did it follow you, Jerry?" Mary asked.

"Yeah, I think. I-I heard it the whole time. It's going to kill me."

"You both need to come with me. There's something we need to do, now." She led them to the back door. As she opened it, a scratching noise began to rap at the front.

"Jesus, help us! It's here!"

Thump! Thump! Thump!

Jerry cried hysterically, his body going nearly limp with fear. "No!"

"Drag him out here, Brent. Help him, Dan." Mary said.

They grabbed Jerry and drug him out the door. They watched as Mary marked a large circle in the grass, digging out a thin, shallow trench with her foot and pouring table salt in it as she went.

"Stand inside the ring."

Dan drug Jerry into the circle, and he heard the door crash apart as if a stick of dynamite had exploded next to them. From where he stood, he saw it, pushing its way through the house. It was so tall that it had to duck to fit through each doorway. With slow, deliberate swipes, its long, black, bony fingers tore through the walls like a saw.

"Jesus Christ!" Dan exclaimed. "What in hell is that thing?"

"We told you, Dan," Brent said.

Mary grabbed Jerry and tore a piece of his bloody shirt from his body. She rubbed it in the salt and began to chant an incantation.

"Bone Lady, Bone Lady, come again. Bone Lady, Bone Lady, come take my sin."

The monster made it to the back porch. Dan stood, mouth hanging open in awe. He noticed its eyes, black and shiny, like polished gems. Its skin was coal black, its texture appearing rough. Its shape almost human, offset just enough to show it was not of this world.

It started toward them and Mary threw a handful of salt outside of the circle, causing the beast to wince back. She repeated the phrase two more times.

"Mom, what's supposed to be happening? We gotta do something!"

"She's coming. Trust me."

"Who's coming? This is crazy!"

Dan felt something at his feet. A poking and prodding feeling, like someone was stabbing at his soles. He looked to his mother who was smiling now, her expression one of crazed excitement. He could feel pressure around his toes as something grabbed his foot. He looked down and lost his breath.

It was a hand, coming up from the very soil they stood on. Like a zombie in a bad horror movie, the hand used his foot as a hold, forcing itself up, inch by inch, until a thin, frail figure stood before him. Long gray and matted hair covered the face, and he could tell from the shape that it was a woman.

He staggered back, dropping into the grass. "What the hell is that? A-a fucking naked hag just shot up out of the ground!"

"It's *her*, Dan. I told you." Brent said.

Dan lay there, crying hysterically. His mother continued to laugh, clapping as if some parlor trick had come full circle.

The figure raised her hand, slowly, and the monster behind her steadied. She opened her mouth to speak and a foul, rotten smell filled the air. "Who summons me?" a raspy, high pitched voice hissed.

"I did," Mary replied.

The Bone Lady cocked her head to the side, gestured with her hand. "For what reason didst thou call?"

"This monster, the curse over this town, its gone on long enough. It needs to end. My family has done nothing to deserve its wrath."

The Bone Lady pointed to Jerry, who was now clawing at Dan's legs like a dog begging for comfort. "Thy children trespass on sacred ground during the full moon. A pact was made years ago, and it will be honored with blood from all who stand with thee."

Dan began to scream.

"It took one boy. Leave it at that. There doesn't need to be any more bloodshed. Its pact has been honored."

"One doesn't amend a pact with *darkness*," the old lady hissed.

Mary looked to Dan, to Jerry. She hesitated, then with an odd certainty in her voice, she responded. "I conjure you to offer a deal."

The Bone Lady chuckled, took a step forward. "A barter? What dost thou offer?"

"What do you want? What will it take to send this creature back to Hell for the rest of eternity?"

The beast let out a shriek, shaking the house.

"For a price the same as the conjure, so shall it be returned to darkness." She smiled, revealing jagged, yellow stained teeth. "It has been too long," she said, as a long, pointed, black tongue caressed her upper lip. "That is the price."

A look of sorrow and apology filled Mary's eyes.

"Mom? Wh-what's going on?"

"Hold him, Brent. Hold Dan back."

"Mom! N-no, you can't seriously be doing what I think you're—Mom!"

Brent tackled him to the ground, forcing all his weight on Dan, restraining him. "It has to be this way, Dan! It's either one of us, or all of us."

"We have made a trade?" the Bone Lady hissed.

"Yes," Mary said. "The boy for the end."

Jerry began to look back and forth from Mary to the Bone Lady to the creature. His fate becoming apparent, his screams growing more frantic and helpless. "N-no! Please! Dan, you've got to help me! Don't let them do this!"

"Take him. He's yours now," Mary offered.

"No! Mom, Dad, you can't do this!" Dan fought to free himself, but the weight and strength of his father was too much.

The Bone Lady's laugh grew deep and fierce. Her mouth began to expand as large, pointy teeth grew from her gums. Like a snake dislocating its jaw to consume its prey, the Bone Lady grasped Jerry's arm and swallowed it whole, stripping it clean of flesh and blood as if it were a chicken wing. He couldn't scream anymore, his voice too hoarse. His struggles became less frantic as the Bone Lady consumed him piece by piece, until all that was left was a pile of clean, polished bones.

Dan was too weak to fight. He closed his eyes and cried as his friend was torn into pieces in front of him.

"Now, take your beast and leave!" Mary shouted. "Honor your deal."

With a sinister smile across her face, she responded, "It shall be completed." The Bone Lady collected the bones in a sack, and with one loud, thunderous clap, released a shockwave with a force so powerful that it left Dan and his parents unconscious on impact.

Dan awoke with a sudden jerk. Sweat covered his body, and his mother sat beside him in his bed. He took a deep breath and let it out, slowly. "Jesus. I-it was all a dream."

"Calm down, Dan. Just calm down."

"Mom, you won't believe the nightmare I just had. It was crazy! Where's my phone? I gotta text Mike and Jerry about it. I dreamt that some monster killed them!" Looking for his phone, he glanced at the window. The moon was still full, piercing the darkness with a light unlike any other. It was a sight that sent a chill deep into his spine.

His mother sighed, placing her hand on his shoulder. "I-I'm sorry, Dan. It wasn't a dream."

Dan's stomach dropped and the room began to spin. "Y-you mean, they're—"

"I'm sorry. It was the only way."

He lay back down, tears streaming from his eyes.

"You need to calm down, Dan. The police will be here in a little while to ask some questions."

Dan wiped the tears from his eyes and sniffed. "Wh-what am I supposed to tell them? They'll never believe the truth."

His mother smiled. "Yes, they will, son. You tell them the Bone Lady came. That's all they'll need to hear."

Rob Francis

THE KING IN REPOSE

This late at night the museum is like a morgue, an observation I keep to myself, instead acting impressed at everything Charlotte points out as we walk the crepuscular corridors. I need this evening to go well.

"Down there is our Chilean collection. I'm not sure I agree with grouping the paintings by provenance, but I have no say over that. We have two Altamiranos and a Matta with pride of place."

"Really? Very nice."

Charlotte looks sideways at me and her mouth lifts at the corners, though I don't *think* the smile is at my expense. She raises the rainbow rose I brought and twirls it so the petals brush her nose.

"The room on the left houses our Barrai collection. I imagine you haven't heard of Barrai. She's a Bolivian artist. Mostly oils but very experimental."

"Bolivian, eh? Wow." I am racing for something sophisticated to say. I've never had much interest in art—real art anyway, the kind wealthy people like—but I want to make a good impression. It's my first date in a long time. I try to turn the conversation away from the museum and toward Charlotte.

"Do you paint yourself? I mean, do you, yourself, paint?"

She smiles indulgently at my nervousness, which gives me a little shiver of pleasure but also makes me feel more than a bit jejune.

"Only if I need to do minor restoration on an exhibit. That's quite rare, though." We turn down another silent, half-lit corridor. Even the cleaning staff have finished and gone home, so that it seems we are the only people in the building. Moonlight slants through a window and our shadows break it as we pass. "You're not an art lover, are you?"

"Not really. Sorry." I'm not sure why I'm apologising, but I do it a lot. Desperate to please, perhaps. Or just desperate.

Charlotte pats me lightly on the arm, which I take as a good sign at first but then start to worry at. Was the pat affectionate or just reassuring? Is there any deeper meaning to it?

"Thanks for coming to the museum, Daniel. I thought it might make for an interesting date; less forced than meeting in a cafe or restaurant, and not many people get to see behind the scenes, as it were. I'm sorry it had to be so late, but I often don't finish until well after closing. It makes it hard to meet people."

We pass into a series of small halls dotted with modern art sculptures that are somehow disconcerting without any illumination. They seem to brood.

"To be honest, this is my first date in a while. I'm not much for the websites. I was really happy when I got your message, though I'm not sure why you picked me. I don't get a lot of interest." I stop, aware that I am already harming my chances and that my face is flushed with embarrassment. I almost consider making an excuse and leaving, but that would be even more awkward.

"I liked your profile. And I've always found the idea of data management interesting."

"Really?" I can't tell if she's joking. "It's just a job, really."

"I'm lucky there. This is a calling. I can't think of anything I'd rather do."

We walk in silence for a few moments, and I admire how confident Charlotte is. I'm impressed that she would invite a stranger into her museum when there is no-one around. I wouldn't have dared to. For a moment, I am tempted to spill out my insecurities, to tell her how lonely and afraid I am, how the world is so awful and meaningless that to face it alone is torture. But the moment passes, as it always does, and we carry on.

She stops at a steel door and taps at a keypad on the wall. Something clicks in the mechanism and then we are through and into a small workshop, half of which is covered with boxes, canvas, sheets of paper, cloth, brushes, notebooks. It's all very creative and artistic, and the complete opposite of my regimented workspace. The other half of the room is clear, apart from an easel on which rests an oil painting almost as tall as me.

"This is what I'm currently preparing for display. A new acquisition. No-one has seen it yet."

I make a show of examining the artwork and nod politely, wondering what the best response would be.

Then I actually *see* the painting.

There is a man reclining on a throne of pale wood. He must be a king or prince, as he wears a band of dark silver around his head. He is naked, legs splayed, one draped over an arm of the throne. His arms dangle listlessly, one hand touching the floor and another covering his groin.

My eye is drawn to the unusual patterning on the king's body, which I slowly realise is patches of missing skin, the muscles shining raw and red beneath. One eye is a gaping hole. As I step closer I can see small nails protruding from the crown, and that the hand resting over the king's genitals is soaked red with blood, some of which is creeping down the legs of the throne. Behind king and throne is a dark stone wall, each block marked with white letters from a language I haven't seen before.

The painting is truly hideous.

"Amazing," I say. "Very…evocative."

"Yes. *The King in Repose*. Painted in 1811 by Rudolf Kuennsberg, a rather obscure artist from Bavaria. Almost nothing is known about him, and it seems he did little beyond paint and compose a handful of unusual treatises. I have a small collection of his personal correspondences. It seems that in his late thirties he moved to the Orient, or at least intended to. Then all records of him stop." She smiles. "This is one of his final paintings. I was lucky to find it."

"I see." I reach for something to say. "The king doesn't look too well."

"No. He suffers but is not dead. Kuennsberg is telling us something of the human condition. The artist was very attentive to detail, getting all the nuances of emotion and feeling just right. Suffering is a recurring theme for him."

There is something else disturbing me about the painting, but I can't quite decide what it is.

"What do the letters mean? Anything?"

"They are Enochian. Dee and Kelley's language of the angels, from the sixteenth century. Easy to translate now, less so back when the painting was completed. Kuennsberg had an interest in angels and anything antediluvian, and his letters clearly show that he was influenced by Dee's writings."

"It certainly has character." I'm lining up a series of noncommittal observations I can use to avoid any awkwardness. Hopefully we'll move onto something else soon. I start to work through different ways to suggest that we go for a drink nearby, without seeming too forward or giving offence.

"It's a wonderful piece, very special. For decades it's been in a private collection. I only managed to acquire it because the original owner recently passed away, and his next of kin were keen to get rid of it. Some people have no taste at all."

I finally realise what has been bothering me. The king has thin blond hair, a Roman nose, full lips. Like me.

"Oh."

Charlotte puts her hand on my arm. "There is a faint resemblance, isn't there? I noticed that from your profile photo."

"How odd."

"Yes."

The silence grows to become uncomfortable, but I am not sure how to break it. I keep my eyes fixed on the painting out of embarrassment, but the more I look at it, the more familiar it seems. I start to wonder if perhaps I have come across it before somewhere, in a book or on TV. But it is more than that.

Yes, much more. I can feel the king's pain. Not just the sensation of blade on skin and the ache of missing flesh, but the tendrils of despair that strangle him, squeezing so tight that he longs for oblivion. I can hear him pleading, telling me of his desperation, warning me of what is to come. The king is as lost and lonely as I am. And he is waiting for something.

"You may be surprised to learn that this isn't just a work of art." Charlotte is speaking next to me, but I can't tear my gaze from the painting.

"It is a guide, an instruction. The message on the wall reads that only the King in Repose and a 'passionate observer' can welcome angels into the world and command them. Specifically, the angel Levanael."

"Levanael?" I whisper the name, but it seems impossibly loud.

"The guardian of the moon. A bright and beautiful soul."

Charlotte turns my head and kisses me, her lips warm and wet against mine. My body is suffused with lightness, as if I am no longer fully contained within it. I can't stop imagining the king's suffering, the feel of the flaying knife. Charlotte's fingers brush my hair.

"I don't understand. Is it possible?" I am not sure who I am talking to. "An angel?"

"A *perfect* angel. The moon is for lovers, after all."

She steps back and looks at me with cool green eyes that promise wonderful things. I think of the king on his bloody throne. I want to run. And yet.

"Let me show you my studio." She takes my hand and leads me to a door and another room beyond, in which stands a heavy wooden chair that looks identical to the throne the king is sprawled across. A band of silver sits on one arm. On a desk against the wall is a set of steel knives and other implements.

Charlotte turns to me and smiles, radiant with excitement. "Can you imagine, Daniel? We can bring forth an angel. Together. We can create an endless moment of love and beauty for everyone. It would be magnificent."

The world is distant and I move through it numbly, feeling only the enchanting lightness. Is this how the king feels? Tranquil, despite the agony?

I sit on the throne, but Charlotte beckons me up.

"You are not ready yet. Over there." She motions to a large black sheet spread across the floor before turning away. I float to the sheet as she slips off her clothes. She turns to the desk and carefully places the rainbow rose in a jar of blue ink. I start to undress, somehow knowing that it is the right thing to do, that it is expected of me. I am not ashamed or afraid. When Charlotte finally approaches she holds a flensing knife, its blade gently curved with a piercing hook at the end.

She looks at me appraisingly. "I like you a lot," she says. "I want this to be special."

Charlotte's work is done, and I am in repose. The world burns with a bright agony that has been waiting for me all my life. Didn't some philosopher once say that pain is what gives life meaning?

How right they were.

With my one eye I can see Charlotte preparing for Levanael's arrival. Her skin is slick with sweat, hair clinging tight to her face while she works on herself with a razor. She becomes more beautiful with every stroke of her hand.

She sings as she cuts, a song of the divine written in words that I don't understand. Every syllable rings through my body to set my nerves on fire.

The lights dim. Darkness gathers in the room.

The moment is close now. Charlotte and I smile at each other. I am satisfied at last, at peace with myself and the world. I have found my soul mate, and together we have done something wonderful. Nothing else matters.

The darkness is absolute, apart from the luminous glow of the moon captured high in the skylight.

Charlotte moves in the blackness, her footfall soft and wet on the floor. Her breath catches in her throat.

The room is suddenly cold as the night sky.

And we are not alone.

Jennifer R. Donohue

BREAD AND MILK

You've never followed somebody before, but when you see them at Walmart you have to know. Yes, the fringes of a hurricane are slouching too far north, but a man and a woman have four carts clogging the self-checkout with gallons of milk and loaves of white bread, and what kind of people do that?

In the parking lot, they load their bounty into a pickup truck. The night is still, crystalline clear, each star so sharp as to cut you, but the air is starting to feel sodden around the edges. There's a storm coming, but it isn't here yet.

You follow them too closely in the parking lot before you control yourself and hang back a little. It seems impossible for them to not notice you, and you wait at every stop sign to be suddenly confronted by the angry driver in his work boots and camo coat, or for them to take a sudden turn in order to shake their tail, but none of those things happen. Maybe they're too busy peering at the sky, watching clouds roll in, praying for disaster to miss them one more time.

You make a mental list of where you think they might live. One of the little towns without a post office tucked in the hills here, in part of a green-roofed brick row house. A cultish trailer park off the highway, sign burned out. A white-paint-peeling farmhouse in the middle of dead nowhere. You've begun to regret your decision, started to look for a place to turn around, when their brake lights flash sudden red ahead and they swing off onto an arced, gravel driveway leading up to a large A-frame house.

You drive past without slowing, then find a chained-over driveway with enough room to nose your car into and turn around. You cut the lights and the engine and roll in neutral back down to the soft shoulder across from the house, pulling the emergency brake to stop. Trees stand in huddled pairs throughout the field next to you, POSTED signs gleams of orange in the moonlight. You stay in the car; it seems safest. You won't wait here long.

The whole front of the couple's house is made of glass, and it's like a set stage. The living room takes up the whole front of the house, no wall between it and the kitchen, a banked fireplace of big flat river stones, a large dark-colored couch which seems, even from your remove, as though it would be very comfortable. You watch as they carry the bread and milk from the truck, straight through to the kitchen island, the woman pausing briefly to transfer some bone-white logs to the fireplace, stepping back as the sparks dance up. They're just a blur of features, blue jeans, her shirt red and his yellow. He slams the tailgate of the truck when he goes inside with the last bags straining in his left hand.

The wife sorts the bread and milk out of the grocery bags, bundling them into that bag of bags every household in America seems to own, and the husband gets out two big bowls, like the kind you'd put popcorn in for movie night. Though you can see the fireplace, you can't see a television, or a computer.

The clouds roll in with silent purpose, slowly blocking the stars and stretching cotton wool over the moon. The husband and wife bring the bowls to the big front windows, opening their gallons of milk to fill them. The wife opens a bread bag first, pulling out a handful of slices that she mashes into the bowl like it's laundry on an old fashioned washboard. Then, dripping, she packs the resulting sludge against the bottom of the windowsill. The husband does the same. They both peer through the window from time to time as they work, pale faces tipped skyward.

Sometimes they chew the bread instead of pummeling it into the milk, spitting it directly onto the growing mass.

Before long, though longer than you meant to stay, they're standing, bowls on end tables so they can reach the milk without bending. You can't see the floor any longer, but it has to be adrift with bread bags and milk jugs, caps and twist ties skittering like bugs as the couple moves back and forth. When they can't reach any farther, they climb up onto the end tables, still visible through some gaps not yet closed. When there's only a broad strip left at the top through which light still escapes, the man's head pops up and he works solo. You hope he's on a ladder, because the window is far taller than those tables would accommodate. You think, maybe, that he isn't on a ladder.

Finally, the entire front of the house is closed off with the bread, glowing gold with the firelight and lamps burning inside. The smoke from the chimney mixes with the cloud cover, solid white now as well. You shake yourself as though from some horrible dream, not quite a nightmare, as nothing bad has happened. Just profoundly strange. Inscrutable. Is it insulation? You struggle to put a mask of sanity on the couple, on their frantic decoupage. The first fat raindrops are starting to fall as you reach to turn the ignition key and bring your engine back to life. It has grown cold, and turns over slowly with a complaining growl before catching. You put it into gear before movement catches your eye.

Silhouetted against the golden light is the stocky frame of the man, a shotgun held unmistakably in his hands. He stalks down his hill as you put the car in gear and try to drive, remember the emergency brake is still up, drop it and then stall the car. The engine catches again, faster this time, but there's a thump on your bumper and you press back against the seat when the wife crawls up over the hood, bringing her face in close to the windshield.

"I'm sorry; I'm just trying to leave," you call. The car's building speed doesn't deter the woman as she holds onto the hood with one hand, metal visibly bending in her grip, and she brings her fist around and punches the windshield once, twice. It holds at first. The closed windows only barely muffle the shotgun blast, and the tires lose purchase on the rain-slicked road, wheel jerking out of your control. The third strike buckles the windshield.

Safety glass is a funny thing. It seems like it won't break and then it does, slowly, with a sound like putting milk on rice crispies. The pieces of glass are uniform, square, edges green-tinted. Safety glass or no, it still draws blood when it scratches bare skin. Your hands sting with tiny cuts and the cold wind as your car veers left, pulling toward your flapping rear tire, and off into the ditch on the opposite side of the road. The woman reaches in and takes you by the scruff of the neck, dragging you out through the windshield, pulling you painfully against the steering wheel, the taut seatbelt. She pauses in irritation, shouting something at the man. He comes into view, pulling a gleaming blade from his belt, and chops down until you're free of the seatbelt.

With the cloud cover everything is terribly dark except for the weird half-light from your remaining headlight, reflecting up through the sheets of rain. The couple each takes you by an arm and brings you up the hill, your toes dragging. You can still feel the woman's fingerprints on your neck, but the rest of you is pins and needles, limbs failing to respond to your trapped-animal thoughts of escape.

It's very warm inside and smells sweet and smoky and like a half-finished bowl of cereal. They drop you on your back just in front of the fireplace; the floor is honey-colored hardwood with a satiny finish. You're losing the ability to move your head, and the woman turns your face to look up at the exposed beams of their cathedral ceiling.

"Why are you doing this?" you whisper through stiff lips.

"A storm's coming," she says in a quavering voice. They have strange eyes now that you see them up close, black and shiny, reflecting the firelight, and you wonder how they can go into public, shop in Walmart. The man brings the bowls over, milk still sloshing in them. You hear the rustle of plastic as the woman opens another bread bag and pulls some slices free, plopping them into the milk. After a moment of kneading, she takes the soggy mass and presses it against your ankle. The man opens his own bag and shoves bread into his mouth, kneeling on the other side of you as he begins to chew mechanically.

You don't know if it's worse or better that they start at your feet. Your breathing slows. Your eyes are dimming. You try one last time to scream as the woman reaches your neck, packing the bread in carefully, gently, but your mouth will no longer open. Before everything is dark and your thoughts slip away, you take note that they leave your nostrils uncovered.

PLANNING FOR RETIREMENT

"Aren't you a little young for retirement?" Michael had been staring at the couple next to him since the initial awe of the journey had worn off and he'd grown tired of looking out his window at the stars. He also knew that the trip would be over soon and had always been a little too curious for caution. He recognized a lot of old faces like his, but this pair was an anomaly, and he had given up on ignoring it. They shared a quick glance into each other's eyes and smiled.

"Yes. A lot of people were surprised when the government granted our filing for retirement, but here we are. My name is Alice," The woman replied in a sweet voice.

"And I'm Ben." He reached over for a quick handshake. "I guess we just got lucky."

Michael smiled in return, but he couldn't let it go. He had just had his 55th birthday, which was the minimum retirement age at this point. He had been scanning the other 30 or so men and women in their seats and most were about his age, if not a little older. He knew he had been lucky to be allowed retirement so early, but this couple must have been in their mid-40s.

"I was actually rejected for retirement initially." Michael swiveled in his seat to face them and look at their relatively un-lined features. "I guess you could even say that when I get there, I will still be on probationary retirement."

"What does that mean?" Alice asked. "I've never heard of that before."

"Well, it is a special case, and I wasn't aware of it until I was contacted and interviewed by my retirement coordinator." Michael lowered his voice. "I couldn't pay for retirement, but after they said they had a special job related to the systems work I did for the military, they made sure I was approved as soon as possible. How about you two? What kind of jobs do you have?"

"Oh, well, we haven't had to work in a while." She giggled, and the man looked uncomfortable with the admission. "Our parents were two of the first pioneers for the retirement program, and we had been living off that inheritance. We can't wait to see them again. We have kids, too, that will live off what we left behind after paying for our retirement and hope they'll make the same choice as we did."

At this, the man did speak up and interject "Absolutely, but it's also been a lifelong dream for both of us to go to the moon."

He and Alice both turned to look at the front of the passenger area. Michael looked forward as well and saw the shuttlecraft on a screen, artistically filled with galaxies and occasionally shooting stars, but more importantly, an image of their ship with a solid line behind them leading to Earth and a dotted line leading to the moon.

The screen suddenly zoomed in to focus on the remaining distance to be covered, and a large, green circle appeared in front of them.

"Five minutes until arrival protocol," a soft, feminine voice announced. "Please prepare for deceleration."

"Have a safe landing," Michael intoned, and several of the people around him chuckled lightly.

"Safe landing," Ben replied, and he and Alice held each other's hands.

On the viewscreen, their shuttle separated into a rectangle representing their passenger area and an outline of the shuttle as it continued its course to slingshot around the moon. A few people were startled enough to gasp when they felt the directional and retro rockets fire. The screen shifted to show the bright, full moon growing quickly to fill the entire viewpoint.

Michael couldn't help but feel giddy. He forgot about the couple that had simply paid their way to the moon early when he had been working for this for a long time. He had given everything he had to buy this seat and had turned his career around from decline just to try and be accepted here. While Earth continued to boil over with war and congestion and pollution, the moon was pristine. Mostly untouched by construction, craters and slopes abounded. He was in awe.

As they descended to an open area that Michael guessed was the spaceport, he could make out the bubbles—large, geodesic domes with frameworks like cells in a beehive—spread out in all directions. At certain angles, the domes went from clear to rainbow iridescence, and he couldn't help but be impressed by the spectacle. Easy to see in contrast to the white and gray, he could make out distinct sections with colorful mansions, large lakes, and wide sets of fields. Some of those fields looked freshly planted with gold and green and some empty with brown, but there were many more than he had expected.

The attitude of the passenger compartment shifted so that their line of windows was parallel to the ground. The screen changed to show their gradual descent to an empty landing pad. Michael couldn't detect any vibration; their landing was so smooth. A tubular walkway extended to connect the front of their craft with the central bubble of the spaceport. The front viewscreen dissolved to gray, and the center slid out and up to reveal the same door where they had initially boarded.

There was a short hissing as the front airlock equalized, and they could see down the extended space jetty. Cheering erupted and couples shared hugs. Handshakes were given between friends made during the journey to the moon.

"Please line up as you are called and proceed forward for your complimentary transportation to your appropriate relocation. Please enjoy your retirement." The soft voice enunciated last names, and Michael watched couples rise and walk out. Ben and Alice walked out still holding hands, as did many of the other pairs. Once the last few people were walking to the front, Michael felt anxiety rising because his name still hadn't been called. Without any remarks, the last people in lines did look back but smiled and shrugged or waved as they moved onto the jetty, leaving Michael alone.

"Mr. Bradley, please proceed forward. Meet Shepherd 7."

Michael leapt out of his seat and stopped himself from running down the jet way. He walked quickly, trying not to strut, and also trying to look excited but not frantic. Just going through the jet way, he felt younger. He felt more purposeful than he had in years. He chuckled as he caught up to the tail end of the departing group. The door to the shuttle slid shut behind him.

Inside the building was a grand display of illuminated holograms surrounded by balloons and rainbow-colored streamers. Projected between the scaffold-like honeycomb, the signs read, "Enjoy your retirement!", "Welcome to the best part of your life!" and "Thank you for your sacrifice!" There were bright yellow happy faces painted on the borders as if by children's hands. Bach's 'Air for G String' eloquently played in the background from unseen speakers.

In the center of the room stood tables filled with fluted, half-filled champagne glasses. Michael could detect the sweet smell easily after having been in the shuttle cabin with everyone who, like himself, had gone through a quick sterilization shower before getting dressed in their neutral gray suits for the journey. Two squat, cubic-shaped robots on wheels flanked the tables. An older woman in a black suit played hostess behind the tables.

"My name is Emily. The moon is lucky to have you here. Please help celebrate your arrival," she said and beamed at the newcomers. Some took a few sips and others finished their drink with a single tip of their glass. A few quietly said they didn't drink, but the greeting woman continued to beam. "These glasses over here are sparkling water. Please enjoy!"

Michael stepped toward the group, the airlock to the jet bridge sliding shut behind him, but Emily flashed her eyes and looked directly at Michael. Her smile slipped to become pursed lips for only a fraction of a second, but Michael stopped in midgrasp before touching a glass. From her side, she produced a simple plastic bottle and pushed it into his hand.

"You'll have to go to the side of the room and wait." Her eyes flicked to the left.

Michael was tempted to ask questions, but her lips pursed again, and involuntarily, he felt himself walk over and stand by a metal pillar.

Behind Emily the walls slid open. Michael noticed that above the doors were only two symbols, a "1" and a "0," and now the "1" was glowing.

"Please make your way into the transport. You will be able to watch a brief orientation video while you are taken to begin your retirement. Just relax and everything will be taken care of for you."

The group quickly made their way toward the elevator, except for Michael. The robots moved on silent locomotion and seemed to drift across the floor, moving into positions on either end of the group of people. As soon as the elevator was filled, the doors slid shut silently. Alice looked from her husband to Michael, smiling, and waved as the doors sealed. Michael looked from the elevator to Emily and saw she was bringing several glasses toward him.

"Don't just stand there; grab some so we can get out of here." There was now an alcove with a tray extended behind him where she was putting them.

"Hi, my name is Michael—"

"Of course, I know," she interrupted and went to grab more glasses. "But you are also now Shepherd Nine. Better get used to that."

He picked up some glasses and copied her movement. "I'm really excited to be here, Emily. I can't tell you how much—"

"Seven," she said.

"What?"

"Just call me Seven; we're done with the Emily nonsense. My name was never even Emily. I hate that name."

He stopped in his tracks before picking up more glasses. "All right…Seven…what's your problem?"

"The moon is full," she replied simply.

"What?" he said again, standing still.

"The moon's been full for a while. You and I are only here as a courtesy for the—" she sighed heavily and paused "—Moon Lords." She tipped her head quickly back and to the side. Michael's eyes noticed the glassy lens of a camera pointed at the center of the room.

"What?" He felt like an idiot, but he couldn't think of any other way to respond to a statement like that.

"Fine. You and I are only here as a courtesy for Sudhir and Chang, but they really get petty when they think you're being disrespectful. They rarely have to deal with that these days and everything goes more smoothly if you just play along."

"Play along with what?"

"You knew this was a one-way trip, right?"

"Yes, of course. Fork over your retirement for an all-expenses paid, one-way passage to the moon. Be a guinea pig for the next colonization. No guarantees."

"None of that sounded too good to be true?" Emily put the last of the glasses away and pushed on a corner of the tables, causing them to lower to the floor. The music clicked off. The hologram signs winked off all at once.

"I know I'm lucky to be here, despite the circumstances."

Emily had a long laugh, and in the silence, it echoed inside the dome. "You are lucky, but not the way you think. You're a shepherd now."

"If I'm a shepherd, where's my sheep?"

Now Emily did smile, and with the room cleared, she stepped toward where the elevator doors had closed. The alcove closed and the arrival room was empty and shadowed. The elevator doors slid open, and Emily waved impatiently for Michael to join her.

"The moon's been full for a while, but everyone still dreams it's somehow bigger than it is. Or that it could sustain everyone that the earth no longer has a use for. Do they still show orientation videos of cozy little cubicle neighborhoods to people before they sign up for retirement? Tending the moon fields?"

"Yes…a hard life but still a way for people to contribute."

The elevator doors opened to another domed room but without the sunlight streaming through like above the ground. This time the center of the room had bodies laid out in rows.

Michael had taken a single step before he could comprehend what he was seeing. He was surprised, but it only took a second for him to be more curious about the orderliness of the scene. In front of the bodies, two parallel rail lines led into two circular airlocks. The sentinel-like robots had moved to the opposite side of the room and sat motionless by the wall. A claw extended from a track in the ceiling. With its many curled arms, it gently descended to pick up the body of an old man. It lifted slowly and placed the body neatly on a line of flatbed carts already loaded with several inert bodies.

Wary of the claw's movements, Michael walked forward and stared down at the people with whom he had spent their last journey from Earth laid out like corpses.

"Don't you need to do anything? Can I do anything?" he asked, seeing Ben and Alice lying together in the remaining group. "Are they dead?"

"No, no, and no," Emily replied and folded her arms to stare at Michael.

Michael crouched down beside an old woman, but hesitated before touching her. He stood back up and very carefully stepped in between the bodies to kneel beside Alice. She looked peaceful and asleep. He tapped her shoulder, but she didn't move or even flutter an eyelid. He looked up from her where the claw had halted over a body and then resumed its action to scoop up another body, seemingly at random in the group.

"I don't understand. Why did you drug them?"

"Because they're not going to be helping the moon exactly the way they were told. That should be obvious by now."

"They were brought all this way to die?"

"Damn near everything up here is automated. They can't afford to generate enough oxygen for that many people, so robots do the bulk of the work. And the people running the show don't want to get their hands dirty— that's why you're still alive."

Michael didn't answer but got up and walked outside of the group of prone bodies to focus on their transportation. He watched as belts snaked across the bodies on the carts and smoky glass lids came down to seal the bodies inside. The right airlock opened, and the carts immediately began to pick up speed and left the room. The left airlock then opened and a small singular cart rolled in and the tracks shifted it to the right set of rails.

"You all thought you were very special, didn't you? Finally your hard work had paid off?"

Emily beckoned and Michael left the bodies to board an adjacent cart with seats for four people. He was tempted to sit as far away from her as possible, but when she patted the seat next to her, he sat beside her in the front.

"Maintenance," she said simply.

"Confirmed," the pleasant robotic female voice responded from beneath them. A clear canopy covered the top of the cart, and the side swung shut behind Michael. The left airlock opened again and another set of carts entered. The claw began doing its work again as the airlock in front of Michael opened and they sped through.

"You want to know why bother to even send up those people at all?" Michael nodded. "Well, those farms need organic matter to continue running, and what is a more bio-diverse set of living materials to satisfy that requirement?"

"But why not just take them after they die?"

"As soon as you die, all those wonderful bacteria working alongside your body start to die as well. Freezing them doesn't work quite as well. Kills some of the stuff they need. Also, the energy and chemicals to keep them frozen for the trip takes just enough weight to be less economical. And besides, for the biggest reason of all, it's just easier to lie to people," Emily said as the cart sped through tunnels lit only by lights on the front of their cart.

"All of those people back there, they were going to be worm bait anyway. And go to waste. Just like you said, there's still a way for those people to contribute. The pads will take them to the farms where they will be added to the—" she hesitated "—stock."

"What about just shipping dirt? Animals? Some other manufactured organic material?"

"Dirt is heavy, also mostly polluted these days. And you know well the decimation that has gone through every animal, fish, and insect species and how much genetic modifications they maintain just to try and keep a balance. Except there's no balance. You are old enough to know that. What was balance is now just mistake after mistake, tipping from one end of environmental chaos to another. These people had the funds to keep themselves clean and healthy for their entire lives. You didn't see any of the unwashed masses on that shuttle, did you?"

Michael just looked down at his hands.

"Not to mention, they helped pay for their trip!" Emily was smiling again; she seemed to really enjoy the storytelling. "They won't suffer growing old. They are sleeping like little babies even now, dreaming their last dreams without any pain. Once they are sorted and used in the fields, they will be separated and tilled into the soil. Nothing will go to waste. We have healthier plant life and ecosystems than any on Earth now that go to feed our merciful masters as well as ourselves."

"But those people's families…how do they not find out? There are calls home to friends, sons, daughters, grandchildren?"

"You're an expert with computers. Why don't you tell me?"

Michael turned to Emily. "Computer generated?"

Emily's smile didn't waver, but she turned forward as the cart slowed and another airlock lit up and popped open.

"I guess there's even a built-in delay for communications." Michael thought of movies where actors who had been dead were still present, their features mapped onto someone else and rendered lifelike. He also thought of the voice-activated computers that could carry on regular conversations. It seemed a rather trivial exercise now that he thought about it.

Past the airlock was a switching station with different rails ending in airlocks leading in every direction. Their cart reached the central turntable and spun clockwise. At the third rail, it locked into place and they accelerated again through a separate airlock.

"Who is doing this?"

"I only know a few, and I never have to deal with them directly. It doesn't really matter, does it? You and I, shepherds, are kept in our own berths. We follow directions. We can live until we are actually ready for retirement. We have a choice. The 'sheep' are mostly tended by automation, but we need to be on hand to keep everything running efficiently and clean up any messes."

"What kind of messes do you get here on the moon with robots and dead bodies?" Michael asked, but Emily did not answer.

"If you're ever out in the moss fields in sector 5 or olives groves in sector 6, you can see their domes and their mansions. Very impressive…"

"What if we tried to go to them? Talk to them? Stop them?"

"What's to stop? They are only taking what is no longer useful on Earth and making it useful here. Hell, maybe the moon will see expansion some day for real people. But for now, it's just another rich neighborhood where the best take care of our own, and we try not to get in their way. No one will hurt us here. We breathe one hundred percent clean air. We eat the freshest food. Sometimes we can even be escorted to the zoo or the aquarium tanks below. We won't be robbed or hurt. You wouldn't have a chance of living this sweet a life on Earth! What's not to like?"

"But you're killing people!"

"I don't hurt them and neither will you. We're giving them exactly what they asked and paid for: a blissful, useful retirement without any more cares or worries. And the system has been in place for a decade. It works."

"Can we talk to them? Can we talk to anybody?"

"There are a handful of other shepherds, and of course, as the new guy, everyone will want to meet you. But as for 'them'? The Moon Lords? Ha! Everything is locked down. We have limited access to the transports, as you can see, and no one else cares about us on the moon. Definitely no one cares about us on Earth. Everything is taken care of."

Another airlock lit up and opened for their cart, which slowed to the end of its rail in another meeting room. Emily and Michael exited and a small elevator door opened in front of them. Michael's mind was racing, and he didn't know what else to say. He felt like a sheep himself getting walked along the path.

After a short elevator ride, a smaller room of similar dimensions to the arrival dome opened up before them. Emily walked to one of two doors on opposite sides. The door slid open. Michael, following, walked into a small suite appointed like a hotel room.

"As I said, you have a choice, just in case you want that early retirement, Michael. There is some champagne there for you beside the bed. If you are ready to help, then get dressed in the black uniform on the bed and finish drinking your water. But if you're still not convinced, there is always the champagne. Take your time." Emily backed up a step and the door shut immediately.

When Michael walked up to it, the doorframe glowed amber but would not open. Voice commands did not work, and there were no handles or buttons. However, Bach began playing again. Inside the room, the bed did have the folded black uniform. And beside the bed on a small table was the glass of champagne. Michael touched it, and it was still chilled. Bubbles still rose to the surface.

A single, floor-to-ceiling window showed a view of the moon's pockmarked surface. It was beautiful and serene, the only sound being Bach's musical accompaniment. Sitting on the edge of the bed, Michael could see the earth's small blue and white marble, sitting off the moon's horizon.

He closed his eyes and lay back on the bed, listening as the orchestral violins played.

Laura J. Campbell

18 DAYS

"Of all things visible, the highest is the heaven
of the fixed stars."
Nicolaus Copernicus

Copper, yes, that was her honest-to-goodness real name, was lying on the floor. She had been named after the element, her hair a copper color even from birth. Her father used to call her "29" after the number copper occupied on the Periodic Table. That was about as personal as he ever got with his daughter. He was a man's man and could not relate to a girl child, not even to call her by the name he gave her. Now she wondered if she would ever reach the age of twenty-nine.

She had not spoken to her father in over a decade.

He didn't approve of her being an addict.

Copper looked up through the gauzy curtains of the sunroom windows into the night sky. She could see the moon clearly, its seas and rays shining crisp and clear in the cool night air.

She was in the deep stupor of her drug. She remembered the first time she had used it. It had made her feel two hundred thousand miles tall. She had embraced the moon, holding it close, feeling its cold, rocky surface pressed against her breasts.

She had tried again and again and again to feel like that. But it never happened.

Maybe if she just kept chasing the feeling, she would find it again. Maybe next time.

For now she just lay there, captivated by the oblivion that owned her. Watching the moon and thinking about James coming home. He had messaged her that he would be home in eighteen days.

She had received that message today. She pulled his blanket, the one with his unit's patch embroidered on it, over her. It was very cold in the room. Winter was making no secret that it had arrived. There had even been snow a few days ago.

She had forgotten that the door to the sunroom locked automatically if you didn't disable the lock before closing the door behind you. The drug had made her forgetful. And now she was locked in the back room. Not that it was too bad. There was a bathroom and a small bar in the sunroom, loaded with water, beer, and snacks. And she had his blanket on the soft sofa.

It was a hundred times better than sleeping on the cold concrete of the street.

The moon arched over her gaze. She knew the names of the places of the moon; when she was little, she had wanted to be an astronaut. To walk on the moon and pick up the flag that had been knocked over when the Apollo 11 lunar module *Eagle* departed the moon to reunite with the orbiting *Columbia*. She remembered details like that, but couldn't remember much else.

She looked at the moon.

The Sea of Crises was so clear to her. She wondered why anybody would name an astronomical feature something so dire. It was such a sad name for such a beautiful place.

She tried to remember what it had felt like to hold the moon.

Of course, she couldn't remember.

Oblivion was like that.

The woman had fake breasts and oiled legs. She smiled too much. She wore high heels and a mini-skirt and lots of jewelry. She looked very high-maintenance.

Copper watched the woman and the couple through the glass-paned door that separated the sunroom from the rest of the house. She didn't know who James had told about her being in his house. She didn't want to cause him any embarrassment or trouble. So she stayed hidden.

"It's a little dirty," the false woman stated flatly. "But it won't take too much elbow grease to clean up."

"We're up to the challenge." The woman part of the couple smiled. "This house sure has history."

"There's a separate key to the sunroom, as a security measure. I'm getting a copy of that key made so you can get back there. I recommend replacing the lock, anyway. It locks automatically if you don't leave it unlocked—from either side. It may take a week or two to replace, with the holidays and all. Is that okay?"

"Sure," the man part of the couple said. "Let's have it replaced. There's plenty of other stuff to do in the next few weeks."

They all left together.

He had obviously ordered in house cleaning before he returned. That made her a little sad; that he knew he couldn't rely on her to clean the house up before he came home.

She didn't have much time to dwell on the disappointment. The sleepiness that accompanied no real sleep dragged her down again into the darkness.

When she awoke, it was nighttime again. She could barely see the moon in the sky.

James had said eighteen days. A day had passed. That meant seventeen days now.

She smiled, or at least she hoped she smiled.

All she felt was a teardrop roll down her cheek.

A few days passed. Copper had heard noises that managed to burrow into her intoxicated mind. Heavy, scraping noises, like the moon was being raked by meteors.

She opened her eyes to the night. The moon was shining. It seemed to sparkle.

The house smelled like phenol-based disinfectant cleaning. She remembered cleaning her own house with a similar product, back when she had her own place. James had taken her in when she couldn't handle that anymore.

He had made her a comfortable spot in the sunroom and told her he was going to get her better. Then the base called; he was going off to fight a war. Her battle would have to wait.

"Promise me you'll stay clean," he had ordered.

She had promised.

But promises meant nothing next to the embrace of the drug. The drug promised her it could make time go by faster. That she would not even notice time passing until he came home.

Eighteen days would seem like one. Besides, she could quit again right before he came home. This time for good, she promised herself.

How many days now? She needed to know if she had to stop using today.

She tried to do the calendar math in her head, but her mind didn't work. So, she used her fingers for the arithmetic. "Fourteen days," she said to herself. "He'll be home in fourteen days." It strained her mind to have to hold the number ten in her memory as she ran out of fingers; then to add four…but she managed. It was a small victory.

She looked at the window, noting the frost. It was coming close to Christmas. She remembered that the city workers were putting up the municipal holiday decorations around town when she went to get her supply.

"I should do something," she whispered to herself. "When I wake up. I'll make the place look pretty. I'll put up a tree. James will be so surprised!"

She imagined the pretty lights strung all around the house, the shining-haloed angel atop the tree. It would be glorious.

And all she had to do was wake up.

"I can't believe you brought that in here first," the man said.

Copper lurched out of her preferred coma, peering out of the sunroom. She didn't want them to see her. Not like this.

"It's thirteen days to Christmas, Alan," the girl-woman replied.

"Teri, Teri, Teri." He beamed. "It is a beautiful advent calendar. I like Jolly Old Saint Nick peering at us over his glasses. Have you been a good girl this year?"

"The best." She grinned. "I put up with your shit."

He slapped her ass. "Maybe you've been a little bad," he said. He looked around the house. "Well, we have plenty of opportunity to deep clean now that the furniture is out. I say we bug bomb the place tonight. Let it settle for a day. Come back and get the place ready."

The woman—Teri—approached the sunroom and tried to open the locked door.

Copper gasped and jumped back, hiding herself behind the gauzy curtains.

"Candace says she's arranged for the lock to be replaced. After the holidays," Alan said. "Her locksmith is on winter vacation."

"Between the freeze and the poison, the bugs should be greatly reduced," Teri observed. "We'll get some air fresheners, too. There are some nice smelling pine scented fresheners that I smelled the other day. And some nasty ones—one brand smelled like bad curry. This place has a little funky smell to it anyway. Old houses. They all seem to smell like absinthe, mildew, wood shavings, and grandmas."

"I like curry," Alan replied. "I'd be hungry all the time if the place smelled like curry. Stick with the pine."

The couple set up little canisters of poison and released the tops. They left, leaving the toxic fumes to work their way into the spaces in-between

Copper covered her face with the blanket, the one with James's unit insignia on it. The room was secure, but she worried about the poison. For a fleeting moment that struck her as ironic; she poured poison into her veins all the time—now she was worried about a slight seepage of insecticide into the large, open room?

She hated thoughts like that.

Moments of lucidity sucked.

Copper woke briefly and looked around. It was night again, the moonlight shining through the naked windows. The bug bomb canisters had been picked up.

The advent calendar had been opened; December 15 had slipped away.

"Less than ten days until Christmas," Copper said. She looked at the moon. The Sea of Crises looked so deep and serene. "James will be home in ten days. Less than, now. Single digits."

She sighed, sat down, and pulled her knees to her chest, watching the moonlight dance through the gauzy curtain. It was very cold outside; the frost was forming a thin sheet of ice on the window panes.

The room began to get dark again.

"Wow," she thought. "I got hold of some powerful stuff."

She didn't want to go to sleep. Not anymore. She wanted to help get the house ready for James's homecoming. She only had nine days left to get clean and really decorate his house. Not the half-assed job the couple had done. All they had put up was an advent calendar and a few strands of inexpensive multi-colored lights.

Copper cursed herself for ever taking the drug. That one party years ago, that one offer, that one moment of acquiescence. A friend of hers had told her not to: "*Close your eyes,*" the friend had said. "*That's all you'll have if you take the drug.*"

But Copper knew better. She always had.

And now the fatigue rushed over her; the old familiar lack of pain.

The lack of everything.

The darkness of the Sea of Crises was a bright light in the heavens. Copper tried to fixate on it, to keep herself awake.

But the darkness knew no mercy, and it snatched her away again.

"Nine days," Teri said. She swept the floor with a broom while Alan wiped down the surfaces of the house.

"Candace said it will be Boxing Day before we get the key to the sunroom."

"Who talks about Boxing Day here?" Teri smiled. "That vacation you and James took to England a few years ago obviously impressed you both. He loved those fish 'n' chips with the malt vinegar, and you keep talking about holidays like Boxing Day and celebrating Guy Fawkes."

"We had a jolly time in Jolly Ole." Alan nodded, remembering.

"It's not a big deal about getting into the room," Teri said. "It's too cold outside to use a sunroom, anyway. It can wait. There's nothing much back there anyway, from what I can see through the curtains over the door."

Copper hid from the couple and the sunlight that beamed into the sunroom. Her eyes were no longer friends with the light of day. And she needed to stay hidden, for James's sake.

She thought back to the last time James had seen her. Her eyes were yellow with jaundice. They probably were yellow now.

James wouldn't be happy to see that. She had promised him she would stay off the stuff.

One hit. I just needed one hit, she thought. *Just to get me through the eighteen days.*

She closed her eyes, ashamed. Maybe when she opened them next they would be bright again.

Night seemed darker and colder when she roused into consciousness again. She looked at her arm. The tourniquet was still wrapped around it.

"Dammit," she said, as she released the grip of the plastic band. Her arm was black and deep purple. *Had she really left it on for days? Or had she taken another hit and not remembered?*

James could not see her like this. He deserved better.

She remembered him holding her one night. His legs wrapped around her, holding her in a tight grip, as if he was worried she would escape.

He had lost everything else in life. Perhaps he was making sure she wouldn't leave, too.

She had hated the way he held her at the time. One of his legs weighed heavy on her bladder. Now she missed being held. She looked at the advent calendar. December 20. Eighteen days had turned to five. James would be home so very soon.

Alan and Teri had brought in new furniture and put up a pretty tree. It wasn't an opulent tree, like they had at the shopping malls and the wealthier churches, but it was festive. It was a five-foot tree with strands of multi-colored lights and round glass ornaments made of red, gold, and silver colors. There was an angel atop the tree, her arms outspread with joy.

Copper remembered joy. She looked at the moon. Maybe she liked looking at the moon because it had brought her happiness once before.

But she really couldn't remember.

Oblivion was like that.

Teri had lit scented candles. Alan was sitting next to her on the couch.

"We did a bang-up job," Alan noted, pleased. "The place looks great."

"It still smells a little musty," Teri noted.

"A bit more like pine than curry, though," Alan replied with a broad grin.

Copper looked at the advent calendar: December 24. Where had the time gone? Had she been stoned for days?

"And," Alan said, handing Teri a glass of red wine. "Tonight is Christmas Eve. I say we go for a walk and see the lights."

They finished their wine and picked up their coats.

Copper noted the unit insignia on Alan's heavy jacket. Alan belonged to the same unit as James. A gold diamond with a cross made of four leaves of ivy. *Steadfast and Loyal* was written in italics on the back of the jacket. *Fourth Infantry, US Army.*

Alan is a friend of James, Copper suddenly realized. *They belong to the same unit. They must have fought side-by-side. Been stationed together. That was why Alan was making James's house so cheerful for his homecoming.*

She felt happy. And obligated. Now she really had to clean herself up. And by tomorrow morning. It was going to be Christmas Day. She couldn't be strung out on Christmas Day. And not in front of James's friends.

Not again.

The house was quiet. Teri and Alan had left the lights on the tree illuminated. Pretty boxes wrapped in metallic foil paper glittered beneath the happy tree. Copper could hear the local church ringing out its clarion for Christmas Midnight Mass.

Eighteen days, Copper thought. *I have made it eighteen days.*

"Hi, champ," she heard a familiar voice call out to her.

She recognized it instantly. "James!" she shrieked as she ran into his arms. He must have let himself in while she was sleeping.

"I've been waiting. Eighteen days!" she exclaimed.

"I know," he said.

"I didn't hear from you after you said you were coming home," she scolded playfully.

"It was a little difficult for me to communicate," he explained. He was still dressed in his battle armor; he still smelled of dust and gunpowder.

"Alan and Teri fixed the place up real nice for you," she said. She pointed toward inside of the house. There was a picture of James on the mantel shelf, with a white Christmas candle burning beside it.

"I don't have any family," James said. "I couldn't think of anybody but Alan to leave the place to. He and Teri will be happy here. They have a baby on the way—they don't know it yet." He smiled. "Teri just thinks she's a little nauseated from the stress of the holidays and moving. It's morning sickness. Her nose is really sensitive to any odor right now."

"How do you know that if she doesn't?" Copper asked in a moment of clarity.

"I know a lot of things I didn't before," he said. "It's kind of nice, but it kind of sucks. It's like seeing the answer key to a test you will never take."

"But you're home," Copper said.

"Not quite," James replied solemnly. "I'm on my way home—I am here to take both of us home. I really hoped this would be just me saying goodbye to you. It made me sad to learn that I needed to pick you up and take you with me."

"I don't understand."

"You were so determined to wait out the eighteen days," he said. As he spoke his eyes moved, toward the end of the room, where Copper lay, her open, jaundiced eyes locked onto the path of the moon. Her skin had blistered; it looked as if it would fall off with the slightest touch. Her hair and nails were already beginning to fall off her little battle-wearied body.

"I sent the message to you, about my rotating out," James continued, "And then I went out on patrol. There was a land mine in the road. I didn't stand a chance. I heard a noise and darkness covered me. I've been waiting to come and get you out of here. Waiting for eighteen days. I couldn't arrive before you were finished waiting. You were so committed to those eighteen days."

"No," Copper stated. She had waited eighteen days. It was Christmas. The darkness was being unfair.

"You put yourself in the lobby of death every time you took that drug, Copper. I told you to stop."

"I tried, baby, I tried."

He held her. "I know you did. It's time to go. To a brighter place, yes?"

She felt his chest against her cheek and she nodded; she looked up at the moon.

Somewhere in between his embrace and the Sea of Crises, she felt a pang of joy and peace.

And then James and Copper were gone.

Oblivion was like that.

D.K. Mok

THE MOON COLLECTOR

Starlight rippled across the frost-flecked breeze on the night our moon was stolen.

I was deep into my first solitary hunt. Snow caked the intricate mandala trees, and my heart pounded with such force I almost feared the frantic drumbeat would chase away my prey. Returning with the head of a mud wraith, and its precious swathe of ember-twine hair, would mark my ascension into womanhood. But I had different plans.

I would bring one back *alive*.

"Why slay the mud wraiths?" I'd asked Elder Tirago. "Why not tame them like sheep and harvest their hair?"

"Their hair sheds only in death," he replied. "And they do not die unless their head is taken."

"But Librarian Mahira says there are stories—"

"And while you chase stories, will our leather stitch itself? Will our axes haft themselves?"

Perhaps, I'd thought resentfully. *If you hadn't sealed away the grimoires after that isolated theft many years ago.*

Instead, I said, "But what happens when all the mud wraiths are slain? My mother says there are fewer now than in her youth—"

"There will always be more," said Tirago. "They spawn, like fish and flies."

"Then why has no one ever seen baby mud wraiths?"

Elder Tirago had turned a fearsome hue, and my father ushered me away before Tirago could call for the Gavel of Denunciation.

No doubt, there were Elders who hoped I'd perish on this hunt, and I dearly wished to disappoint them.

"Be careful, Ora," my mother had said as I departed that evening. "The mud wraiths may stand barely taller than a man, but their fists strike with the force of a landslide."

However, it was not only my bones at stake, but the honour of my family, and I'd planned this hunt carefully. Tonight, a full moon shone overhead, inking the world in its bright, clear cast. The mud wraiths were at their most sluggish when the moon was full, basking in the otherworldly light as though they were turned from mud to stone.

I'd tracked my target for weeks—a mud wraith no larger than myself. Still young, perhaps. Still pliable. Unlike most wraiths, it had kept to the wooded hills and gullies near our village, instead of retreating to the densely forested mountains—a sign of its inexperience, I presumed. The mudling—the *wraith*, I corrected myself—could surely be subdued, as long as I kept clear of its fists.

Its tracks glittered in the fresh powder, and finally, through the ornate fretwork of boughs ahead, I glimpsed a satin shimmer of red. They called it ember-twine, but it was nothing so coarse as twine. Supple as gossamer, strong as iron, you could put a thread in the forge for a year and a day and it would emerge unscathed. The wraith stood motionless in a patch of moonlight, its lumpy arms and legs like poorly shaped clay, its formless head little more than a sodden ball. But fine, coppery hair flowed from its scalp down to where its waist should be, a mesmerising cascade that stirred gently in the breeze.

Silently, I drew the stone seal from my belt, curling my hand around the weathered grip. A dozen seals had been crafted by the founders of our village centuries ago, when the arcane powers of the librarians were still anchored in raw sorcery. One blow to the neck would paralyse a mud wraith. A second strike would sever its head. For twenty generations, the daughters of our village had wielded these seals and brought pride to their families, while I—

Perhaps it sensed my shifting weight, or my shiver of doubt, but the mud wraith turned towards me, raising its leaden arms—

I sprinted across the clearing, my heart in my throat, motes of ice speckling my vision. I leapt at the wraith and dodged a rocky fist as I wrapped one arm around its neck and swung behind it, twisting my legs across and letting the momentum carry me around, wrenching the wraith off its feet. Gravity slammed it hard onto the ground, and I straddled it, plunging the seal towards its neck.

"Wait!" cried a voice.

I halted, my own inexperience now betraying my limbs. I stared at the creature beneath me.

The mud wraith had a face.

Or, rather, it had two uneven sockets the size of clumsy thumbs, and as I watched, the wraith hurriedly pressed a furrow into its visage and beamed a lopsided smile.

"Hullo?" it said. "Please don't hurt me."

The creature's voice undulated wildly in pitch and volume, as though it had learned to speak by reading books and listening to donkeys.

I managed to recover my own voice. "You can…talk?"

"Yes! You see, I found this magic book—"

My mind raced. "The stolen grimoire? You're the one who took it?"

"Yes! I mean, no. I mean, what's the penalty for not returning a library book? Is it a fine?"

"It's stoning."

"That seems excessive." The wraith nervously reshaped his furrow into a frown.

I privately agreed, but appropriate library penalties were not foremost in my thoughts. I tried to focus on my training, on all my imagined scenarios, of which, this had not been one.

"Mud wraith, I have defeated you. You will return with me—"

And *that* was when the world went dark.

There was no clap of thunder, no flash of infernal light. Just a sudden, silent darkness, as though a candle had been snuffed.

"What did you do?" I hissed, my fingers tightening around the seal.

The wraith looked past me, and his empty sockets seemed to pool with fear. "It's gone."

I risked a glance over my shoulder and felt a tremor of confusion. It had been a cloudless night, and yet the moon had disappeared behind a—

No, it had just *disappeared.*

I could see faint stars glimmering where the moon should have been, and over the hills and valleys, an eerie, unseen pall was falling.

The mud wraith shuddered. "What have you done?"

"Me? Infernal sorcery appears to be your domain—"

"I was minding my own business when you jumped out of nowhere and pushed me over. If anyone's engaged in suspicious behaviour, it's you." His indignation barely masked the genuine fear in his voice. "My people will die without the moon."

That shook me from my panic. "What do you mean?"

"We feed on starlight, but we need moonlight to make more of us." The mud wraith stared at the unnatural sky, his downward furrow now achingly forlorn. "Without the moon, my people will fade away."

My heart roiled with fears for my own people. What possessed such power as to vanish the moon? My own ambitions now seemed appallingly childish. I'd wasted my time reading wild tales, remaining ignorant to the true dangers that haunted this world. It had been the height of hubris to think that I knew better than my elders, and yet—

My hands shook, the earthy scent of the mud wraith tingling in my nostrils. Two quick strikes and the deed would be done. I'd return home to praise and a handsome feast, the glint of grudging respect in the eyes of all who'd doubted me.

I stared into the creature's misshapen face, the furrow a wobbly line of woe.

I pushed myself to my feet, tucking the seal back into my belt. "Go."

The mud wraith rose unsteadily and took a few steps towards the tree-line, then turned back to me, his expression perhaps a fraction less woeful.

"Do I still have to pay the library fine?"

"Go!" I roared, and the wraith scrambled away into the moonless night.

It was a small mercy that the shame of my failed hunt was overshadowed by the catastrophe of our missing moon.

"An omen most terrible," said Seer Virek to the assembly. "Did I not warn you that we hadn't sacrificed enough cats this year?"

My mother's tone was clipped. "Not everything is solved by sacrificing cats."

"Agreed," said Elder Tirago. "Our enemies have grown in might with their armies and weapons of war, while we've become meek and drowsy with our sheep and our fields. And now, without the moon, the wolves close in on our shepherds, assassins roam with a bolder stride. We must rise to meet our foes, or all will be lost."

My father crossed his arms. "Librarian Mahira says the tides might change and some moths might get confused, but the absence of the moon is unlikely to deal our world a fatal blow. And there's been no clear indication that any territory is massing armies."

Tirago's eyes caught slivers of lamplight. "Such complacency is why you do not lead our people. You would have our village ravaged by barbaric hordes—"

"Elders." A crisp voice lanced through the frightened murmurs of the crowd, and Librarian Mahira stepped into the circle of lanterns. Her brown curls were held neatly in place by a small legion of bronze pins, and her woollen robe cloaked her muscular frame. A heavy tome lay open on one arm, abstruse images swirling on the vellum. "Before we march to war, we may yet remedy the situation. Our moon has not been extinguished, but stolen from our skies. And every thief leaves a trail."

Mahira swept her free arm towards the constellations, and golden sparks danced across the heavens in a pattern resembling the powdery plumes cast up by an owl plucking its prey from a snowdrift. "Comets have been swept from our skies, the very stars disturbed by the passage of an ancient force. Legends speak of the Galliyar, spirits awoken before the first dawn, possessing unfathomable power and inscrutable intentions. I believe one of these has taken our moon. They dwell in realms that rarely touch our own, but there is a way to reach them. Examining the grimoires, I've uncovered references to leviathan nomads—the Raivi—who traverse the galaxies, following the call of distant suns. They covet enchanted trinkets, and while our offerings would be meagre, I believe we can summon one and plead for a trade. Our charmed artifacts, in exchange for safe passage for a party of brave souls to retrieve our moon from the lair of the Galliyar."

There fell a silence so thick I felt I could hardly breathe. Ancient spirits, leviathan nomads. To hear these words, not in the secretive shelter of the story nook, but on the public stage of the village council, prised at something within me that I hadn't realised lay sealed.

Elder Tirago spoke first, contempt cloying his voice. "You speak of unseen spirits and fanciful beasts. I speak of real armies advancing in the darkness, real tyrants seeking to use this omen as a pretext to seize our lands and slaughter our people. Childish stories have no place in stratagems of war—"

"They're not just stories—" I faltered as dozens of firelit eyes fixed upon me. "You declared the mud wraiths incapable of thought, but tonight, a mud wraith *spoke* to me. In our own tongue, just as the legends said was common long ago." I saw the worry—the doubt—in my mother's eyes, and my moment of courage wilted.

A smear of anger coloured Tirago's cheeks. "Your lies will not deflect the disgrace you've brought upon your family. Your failure to complete the hunt surprises no one. Your cowardice is clear."

Quiet fury burned in my veins, but the indignity paled in comparison to the clear-eyed fear growing within me. Fear for my family under the reckless, unjust reign of Tirago. Fear that the moonless sky would indeed spur other reckless, unjust tyrants to turn their hungry eyes towards my village. And, in an odd flutter of sorrow, I thought of the mudling staring forlornly at the impoverished sky.

I slowly uncurled my fists and strode from the crowd. I would not waste my strength on men like Tirago. I would need my strength for what lay ahead.

It was almost dawn when I slipped into the library, the scent of old leather and fresh ink evoking memories of bitter winters made warm by fantastic tales. Thimble lanterns illuminated the central desk, where a glut of scrolls and manuscripts formed crests and valleys.

Mahira sat on a drum stool, her fingers tracing the air above the texts, as though the words radiated a layer of meaning that could only be felt. Her hand stopped at my presence, and the words I came to say clung to my throat.

If this were a normal night, moonlight would have streamed in through the circular windows. Instead, only the feeble glow of the lanterns battled the oppressive dark.

"I'll go." I held out my hand, the stone seal resting on my palm. "It may not be enough to summon a Raivi, but we have to try."

My family's seal was carved from humble soapstone, not like the marble and garnet seal wielded by our village champion, Peregrine: a hunter so ferocious we'd restrung the entire northern fence from the heads she'd brought back last year—

Mahira's gaze was full of tender sorrow. "You have nothing to prove, Ora, daughter of Ena."

"I'm not going for pride. You know that." Sensing her hesitation, I tried to smother my own misgivings. "I know I'm neither the strongest nor the wisest of warriors, but I'm willing. Elder Tirago's hold over our village will not ease soon, and if we idle, he may decide that the grimoires should not only be locked away, but destroyed. And then, our moon will truly be lost."

I couldn't tell if it was hope or defeat that clouded her expression; perhaps a little of both. "I cannot protect you on this journey, and I have no guidance to give on how to recover our moon from the Galliyar."

"You've counselled me well over the years. That is all the shield and sword I need."

A melancholy smile flickered across her lips. "Before you set your heart on this course, you must know one more thing. Time turns on a different spindle when you travel the celestial realms. It is almost certain you will not return within my lifetime."

A triptych of visions knifed through me: Mahira's grave, tangled with weeds; my parents, growing old and frail; a pair of cairns, untended and forgotten.

"How long will pass here?"

"It depends on where you go, and how you return."

I tried to shake the visions from my mind, but a sensation remained, like a fishhook caught in my ribs. To leave would be to abandon my family, but to stay would damn us all to a moonless fate. And the promise I'd made the day my mother passed her seal to me was not only to those who lived now, but to all who would come after. I might not be here for my village, but I could give them hope. Hope that, one day, their children's children might sleep beneath their moon once more.

I replied before my voice or courage could fail. "Then I had better leave now."

Feeling slightly numb, slightly electric, I collected provisions from my family's larder, loading dried fish, pickles and cheese into my pack. I unhooked a coil of rope from the shed, trying to suppress the unease gnawing at my conscience. For over five hundred years, my family's seal had been passed from mother to daughter. It was more than just a tool—it was a symbol of trust. It was a promise that you would protect your family, just as those who'd come before had done.

My hand paused over a reel of ember-twine. I couldn't predict what might befall our village in a moonless world, but I was certain it would not be solved by slaying mud wraiths. I left the twine, hefting a bedroll from the shelf before stepping out into the silvery pre-dawn.

"Hullo!" gurgled a voice.

In the shadow of the mandala trees, the mud wraith stood in wait. "Are you going to fetch the moon?"

"I am."

"I'll come with you. No disrespect intended, but it could be a long voyage, and your people have a habit of decaying. I mean, really quickly. A mere six-hundred full moons pass, and your people go—" He mimed something that could only be described as explosive decomposition.

"We don't—" I mirrored his gesture. "And six-hundred moons is a very long time."

The mud wraith shook his head. "Not to the mountain. Not to the sea. And not to me."

His reasoning was irritatingly solid.

"Do you have a name?" I said gruffly.

"You can call me Book."

"Only criminals and ten-year-olds use made-up names."

"In the time it would take for me to say my genesis name, you would have turned to mulch. Your people sometimes name themselves after things they like: Lily, Basil, Pie."

"No one's called Pie."

The wraith shrugged. "I like books."

"Too much, apparently. Will you be returning the one you took?"

"I gave it to my brothers, so they can learn human-speak. But I think they're mostly learning the cuss words."

I suspected that Mahira wouldn't entirely disapprove of this use of her enchanted texts. Somewhat hesitantly, I extended both my fists towards the wraith. "My name is Ora, daughter of Ena."

Book's expression brightened, and he raised his fists to meet mine, gently bumping our knuckles in greeting. His hands felt surprisingly dry and slightly yielding: not unlike a pouch of honey.

My neck prickled at the sensation of being watched, and I turned to see a figure standing in the nearby doorway. My mother's eyes slid from me to the mud wraith to the pack on my shoulders. Guilt sliced my heart, like ember wires drawing tight. My mother backed away into the house.

"Ma!" I raced after her and nearly crashed into her as she rushed back out.

She pressed a woollen coat into my hands, her lips trembling. And wordlessly, she embraced me. I held her tightly in return, trying to commit to memory the warmth of her slight figure, the scent of pomegranates in her hair.

"Don't worry about me," I whispered. "Don't wait for me. I love you, always."

My last memory of my mother was a stoic figure on the crown of a snowy hill, silhouetted against the coming dawn.

Twenty days' march took me and my sedimentary companion far beyond the borders of my village, beyond the safely bounded world I knew. Tidy fields gave way to unkempt woodlands, which yielded to rocky canyons. We endured twenty moonless nights that simmered with confused cries and ominous silences before we reached the base of Defiance Rock. The summit of the sandstone spire pierced the veil of clouds, and at its peak, a sweeping plateau jutted like an eyrie altar.

If there is a place on this earth the Raivi will hear your plea, it will be at Defiance Rock, Mahira had said.

We climbed for days, taking rest in the wind-carved hollows. Here, the heart of the rock was revealed in rainbow bands of pink and grey and umber. Book stroked his fingers gently down a curving wall.

"These are the libraries of my people. Here, a flood. Here, a fire. Here, an ocean. I've read these tales a thousand times."

"Is that why you broke into our library? You were searching for new tales?"

"'Broke in' sounds very judgemental—"

"You left a six-foot hole in the wall."

"To be fair, I made that on the way out, when I was—"

"Fleeing?"

"—departing promptly." He fell silent, and I wondered if he were pretending to be asleep. Finally, he said softly, "I was looking for answers." And he said no more for the rest of the day.

The evening stars were just peppering the sky when we reached the plateau. Scraps of cloud swept past our feet, and it felt as though we could see all the world from our altitudinous perch: jagged mountain ranges, vast barren deserts, endlessly shifting seas. And our ever-spreading villages and cities, a multitude of hearths and furnaces burning like a challenge to the heavens.

With Mahira's diagram to guide me, I etched the sigils of the Raivi across the stony stage. Thick, crumbly lines of charcoal; spirals and domes of pale sand. The sallow air chilled the sweat on my face and neck as I struggled to finish the convoluted inscriptions. Arcane circles within arcane circles, and finally, only one element remained incomplete.

I withdrew the stone seal from my pouch, and it lay heavy in my hand like betrayal given form. Without the seal, my family's honour would be gravely diminished among my people. How would they stitch their leather and mend their fences? My fingers closed around the rough stone. I had to trust in their resourcefulness, their resilience, and hope that the kindness they had sowed among their neighbours would yield harvest in their time of need.

With painfully stiff fingers, I placed the seal in the centre of the innermost circle. Out of the corner of my eye, I saw Book shudder faintly as the seal touched the rock, and a strange sense of relief washed through me, as though the guilt I felt now for my family had lifted a deeper sin.

I stepped back from the summoning circle, taking a breath that felt somehow cleaner, somehow lighter, than I'd ever known.

"Don't worry about your parents," said Book kindly. "You'll probably disintegrate before we return, so I asked my brothers to take care of them."

"You did what?"

"You know, just asked them to check in on your family now and then, to see if they need human things done."

"Human things," I said flatly.

"Like digging holes. Or crushing cows."

"Who the hell crushes cows?"

"Well, your parents can, now."

Without warning, the world swayed, the ground seeming to surge towards us before plunging away again. The charcoal lines beneath us darkened, deepened, until they cut into the rock itself, and shadows rippled outward, smothering the fading cusp of the sun.

The Raivi rose from below the plateau like a dark-mirror moon, a circle of midnight, before she rippled and we beheld her true form. She had the semblance of a stingray the size of a village, and her back and fins were a lustrous black, flecked with luminous constellations. Her pale grey belly was the colour of winter skies, and her mouth curved into a delighted "ah" as she slowly circled our position.

Breathlessly, I struggled to recall the rituals from my childhood tales. "Honoured Raivi, we seek the Galliyar who stole our moon. We beg safe passage to the realm of the ancients, in exchange for this ensorcelled artefact."

The Raivi swooped slightly as she passed again, her fin ruffling over the seal, investigating its curves and nicks before she rippled it up onto her back, where it presumably joined her other treasures. She turned ponderously, her fin running curiously over Book before he too was rolled up and out of sight.

"You know I'm not a trinket, right?" he called urgently. "I'm a passenger. A passenger!"

If the Raivi understood, she gave no indication, wheeling as though to leave.

"Ahoy!" I cried. "I'm a passenger too!"

The Raivi didn't slow as she steered away, and I raced across the plateau, chasing Book's startled cries before I took a desperate leap across the widening gulf. I landed on the Raivi's back and tried to find something to cling to as she abruptly plummeted, as though in freefall.

"Shouldn't we be going upwards?" I said.

"I'm sure she doesn't need a back-fin driver," replied Book.

I gasped as the ground loomed closer, and pressed my eyes shut as I braced for impact.

There was a soft hush, a sensation of floating, of passing through sunlight and shade. When I opened my eyes, Book and I were still clinging to the back of the celestial ray, but all around us, above and below, was an unbroken night brimming with stars. The Raivi's fins undulated slowly as she continued on her course through the unseen realms, apparently unconcerned by her new passengers. Or acquisitions.

Across the gentle slopes of her back, mounds of trinkets and treasures formed esoteric hills. Geodes of blood-plum quartz, gold amulets inlaid with pearl, brass orreries arrayed with unfamiliar worlds, and, for some reason, the occasional giant pumpkin.

I found a patch of clear hide on which to pitch my tent, anchoring the ropes with wads of resin. I was pleasantly surprised to find that the skin of the Raivi was neither cold nor damp, but warm and slightly napped, like the worn velvet on a favourite chair. The tent I'd brought was the only one not stitched with ember-twine—a draughty child's cubby, patched with canvas and string. But for now, it would be home.

I glanced at Book, who stood nearby, head tilted, as though listening to a faraway song.

"Why don't your people build things?" I asked.

Book seemed genuinely puzzled. "Why would we need to? Everything builds itself: trees, corals, stalagmites, people. Your people build lots and lots of yourselves. I mean, *lots*."

I quickly steered the conversation to more constructive territory. "Do you think the Raivi understands us?"

"Too well, perhaps."

We stood, for a while, side by side, with the countless stars illuminating the way ahead, and, if time proved kind, lighting the way back home.

We sailed through glistening strands of nebulae, past the silent maw of collapsed novae. We watched the bright white fire of newborn stars and the dim red forge of dying suns. At times, towering plumes of cosmic dust rose around us like the phantom ruins of a behemoth's city. We braved storms of icy comets—the occasional stray rock scattering a pile of trinkets into the void.

I'd relocated my tent to a more sheltered valley, and Book and I huddled inside during a particularly fierce barrage. I tensed at the clamour of whistling rock and shattering ice, wincing at every *crash.*

"I'm not used to hiding from the weather," said Book.

"I don't think comets count as 'weather'."

"You know, once, back home, it rained continuously for twelve million moons."

I cocked an eyebrow. "Are you sure about that?"

"I was there," he said solemnly.

Over the passing months, his voice had settled into a more appropriate rhythm and volume and developed a musical cadence that, now, carried a wistful air. "When I was just a clod, monsoon phoenixes used to sweep across the skies every summer, their amethyst plumes trailing fresh mists carried in from the snowstorms of the southern pole. Your people hunted them for their feathers until there were none left.

"There used to be giant wombats the size of full-grown baobabs, carving tunnels through the impassable mountains. And there were singing serpents with scales like spattered gold and lapis, and little jewel frogs that caught the morning light like rainbow glass. They're all gone now. The world used to be a carnival of colour, song and scent. It's much quieter now. The colours more muted. And the air smells of dust and memories." He bowed his head in quiet mourning. "You wanted to know what I sought in your library. Long ago, my brothers from the river glades conversed with your people on many occasions."

"Why did they stop?" The question was a penance, for I already knew the answer.

"Your people slew them all."

I had no words to heal a wound that deep. No measure of remorse could bring absolution for what my people had done. Yet what Book sought was not apology, but answers.

"Our people never hurt you," he said. "Why do you kill us?"

I knew that a soul as steadfast as his could not understand the urgent, frenzied and solipsistic existence we lived, but he desired an explanation, and I offered what I could. "We think we're protecting our families, our communities. We feel that's more important than anything else."

"But you know that once everything is dead, there'll be nothing left to eat?"

"We assume things will grow back. That there'll always be more, because there always has been."

"You can't see that it's not coming back? You can't see the deserts spreading further, the forests growing frailer? Is it because your brains are so small and so squishy that they can't think big, long thoughts?"

"Partly, yes." I lowered my gaze to the living velvet beneath us, the muscles of the Raivi rhythmically bunching and releasing as she navigated the storm. "I know it makes little difference now, but I am truly sorry."

We sat in aching silence for what felt like an age, the bubbling sorrow within me slowly crystallising into bright needles, the pain no longer amorphous, but clear and precise, like spears of quartz.

Finally, Book lifted his gaze, listening intently. "I think the storm has passed."

Outside, the field of comets had given way to an expanse of stifling darkness littered with tiny pinpricks of red. A massive world, dwarfing anything I could have imagined, hung motionless in the night, an orb of fetid browns and greys.

But even more arresting was the colossus who loomed beside it, rendering the alien world a miniature in her presence. Tendrils of ebony hair drifted like tentacles from her head. Her skin was black, with rivulets of mercury tracing the muscles of her back and belly. Where her legs might have been, she possessed a massive fish-like tail, the ragged iron scales shifting with a susurrus of haunting *clanks*.

I felt like a mote of dust demanding the attention of a volcano.

"Honoured Ancient, I am Ora, daughter of Ena. I seek the Galliyar who stole our moon."

I wondered if a being so powerful would even register the existence of a human speck like me. Our answer came almost immediately.

The Galliyar leaned down towards the trembling Raivi, and her silver eyes were each the size of a moon.

"I am not the one you seek. I am the Galliyar of Forgotten Seas." She drew away and dropped the end of a gigantic chain into the silent brown waters. She twisted the chain and heaved it back up, a huge sunken galleon now tangled in the links, cascades of water pouring from the sightless portholes. "I salvage wrecks from the seas of long-dead worlds. To find your lost moon, let a piece of her guide you."

"What do you mean?" I called.

But the Galliyar was already moving on, swimming through the primordial dark, trailing a chain of ships behind her like a string of broken toys.

"That wasn't particularly helpful," I muttered.

"Actually, I think I know what she means," said Book. "The moon left fragments of herself with us when she kissed our world, long before the seas were formed. Our mountains and deserts carry pieces of her within them."

"Please don't tell me we have to double back."

Book placed his hands across his chest. "I have pieces of the moon within me. You might have tiny bits of the moon within you, but it probably comes and goes. Your people are very unstable. I mean physically—and mentally—but mostly physically. You're made of mush, and you always have mush going in and mush going out. Whereas my rock has been essentially the same since the mountains went up."

I eyed Book dubiously. "Then why do you look less muddy than when we left?"

"It's the different humidity," he said primly. "Oh, I have a surprise for you!" He rifled through a nearby mound. "I made these from the comet that broke your fort of telescopes last month." He pulled out two prehnite cabochons and pressed them into his eye sockets. "Now I have googly eyes, like you."

"I don't have—" I stopped, and allowed myself a smile. "They suit you. But you look fine without them. And you were right: the Raivi knows where she's going. Or, at least, she's not too proud to ask for directions."

Book seated himself on the ground and placed one palm on the Raivi's back, and one palm on his own chest. I didn't know if I had any moon within me, but I sat beside Book and adopted the same pose.

"Please," I said. "Take us to our moon."

I had no measure of time, or at least none that made sense to me. My hair grew longer, but my fingernails did not. My hands became rough and lined, but Book assured me that my face remained the same. Although, I suspected that all humans, regardless of age, looked the same to him. I sipped icy water captured from passing comets and was thankful for the Raivi's penchant for giant pumpkins, telling myself she wouldn't miss a few from her ever-growing stockpile. As recompense, I helped her sort her collection into more orderly themes: gemstones, talismans, textiles, perishables.

"I think she has a hoarding problem," I once told Book.

"It's only a problem if it makes you or others unhappy. Or if it becomes a fire hazard."

"It gives the asteroid mites more places to hide. I had to dislodge three of them from her fins last week. One almost broke my crosier."

Book himself did not remain unchanged. His hair had grown to astonishing lengths, like that of the abyssal maidens of myth, riding their chariots of jellyfish. His muddy complexion had progressively hardened and dried until he moved with the stiff, pained gait of a frail elder. Soon, his hair began to fall out, strand by strand, and I spooled them onto wands and staves, in case he had need of it later. At my persistent, worried queries, he'd finally mumbled "diagenesis" before curling up into the boulder-position, and he remained that way for several weeks. Or perhaps it was years.

I covered him with my woollen coat to keep the dust at bay and fended off marauding mites tempted to take a bite of this peculiar rock. Over time, I regaled his motionless form with stories from my childhood. I told him all my favourite legends, followed by the ones I considered acceptable. I left out the ones I'd always thought unhelpful or steeped in questionable values. After I'd expended all my tales of myth and adventure, I recounted the history of my people, my family, myself. That story hadn't found its ending yet, but the middle was…less lonely than I'd expected.

When Book finally re-awoke, the brittle clay flaked off his skin to reveal smooth sandy boulder matrix, shot with lightning veins of vivid opal. I marvelled at the rich tiger's eye hue of his new incarnation, and the blue-green fire snaking over his chest and limbs.

"Why don't more of your kinfolk look like that?" I asked.

"Among my people, diagenesis is the transformation of one kind of rock to another. We only metamorphose to maturity after twelve million moons. Your people haven't been around for one generation yet."

The scale of time pulled my mind into tortured strands, and I was momentarily dizzied by the sense of history, the sense of loss. I swayed on my heels, then realised that Book was also catching his balance.

The Raivi had stopped.

Although I could feel the stillness of the Raivi beneath my feet, the stars around us seemed to shift and waver, and in a giddy visual trick, the space before us drew aside like a curtain.

In the space between realms, in the place after time, there hung a gargantuan castle rimed in stardust. Turrets of smoky green glass rose in twisting spires, and encircling the base of the castle were concentric rings of sapphire shards, spinning in slow, eternal devotion. We glided through glassy gates that yielded like panes of water, and as we drew near the fortress portico, Book refracted a paler shade.

He nodded to a hanging mobile I'd taken for a string of wind-chimes. "Are those moons?"

As we passed beneath the dangling orbs, I could see the craters pocking each sphere. Voices of reason within me urged me to flee, but those old, familiar voices had grown fainter over the years, and other voices had taken their place. Voices I was only beginning to understand.

With wordless awe and dread, we entered the cavernous halls of the Galliyar's lair. Feeble diminutive suns hovered in brass-lattice lamps that occupied alcoves along the walls, illuminating the cabinets that lined every room.

And every cabinet was filled with moons.

Ice-encrusted baubles, glittering with diamond frost; spheres of roiling scarlet gas and caramel clouds, the colour of hibiscus tea at the moment milk is poured; striated balls of coppery light, pluming with ethereal geysers. A myriad of sizes, shades and compositions floated in their glass prisons, but I could not see the moon I sought.

"So," said Book nervously. "What do we do? I'm not good with fast-moving things or complicated, twisty minds."

I dragged my gaze slowly over the arsenal of talismans and enchanted weaponry that lay neatly arranged across the Raivi's back, and I took a deep breath.

"Honourable Galliyar, I am Ora, daughter of Ena, and I have come for our moon."

"Have you, now?" The voice rumbled like the tide of time manifested. She appeared before us as though the entire universe had moved to take its place around her. A halo of malachite beads framed an opaque white face, and her eyes were tourmaline skies from edge to edge, drifting with wisps of white clouds. Jade spines extruded from her back like skeletal wings, and her skin from the shoulders down was a shifting sea of blue, the shadow of giant placoderms skating beneath the waves.

Book pressed in close beside me, the force of so many moons twisting within him. I squeezed his hand and raised my face to the Galliyar.

"Are you the Galliyar who stole our moon?"

"Stole?" The physical force of her word rattled the halls of glass. "You have no greater claim to it than I. I am the Galliyar of Abandoned Moons. What are *you*?"

"I am of the world that captured that moon. We still need it, and we have no others." I risked a pointed glance at the overfilled cabinets.

"Your world captured it from passing debris, and I captured it from you. As for *need*, your people no longer need it."

She raised a watery hand and a vision floated at her fingertips. My heart fluttered at the sight of familiar constellations, a familiar world—

But no, instead of a blue-green globe streaked with white, there was too much grey, too much orange, and black—why were so many of the rivers black?

The Galliyar slowly spun the ghostly globe. "Your people are long gone. Two thousand years after I collected your moon, they finally consumed their world to the marrow. And before you accuse me of triggering their fall, your people were already drawing their final breaths, the decisions that would doom them already made. What's two thousand years, in the grander scale of things?"

Shock and rage scoured away my grief. "The moon was not yet abandoned when you took it. You don't *know* that my people would have continued on their fatal course—"

"And yet, I do. I have seen a billion worlds just like yours, lapping up their own poison, prying at their world until it breaks. Not unlike a mindless infestation that eventually kills its host. And it's true; your people *could* have averted it. Almost every world like yours *could* have averted it. But none of them *did*. All of them knew what lay ahead, but none of them stopped. None of them changed. Not in time."

"You could have waited. You could have asked." The futility of the exchange, of our entire venture, burned away what was left of me. My family, my village, my world, all lost. Hope fleeted away, and I wondered if it had ever been more than mere illusion.

The Galliyar's eyes deepened to twilight, lashed with spokes of lightning. "Do you wait for the tree to fall in its own time before you carve it into timber? Do you parley with the beasts you slaughter?"

I felt Book's hand hold mine a little tighter. "Yes," he said quietly. "She did. I asked for mercy, and she showed it. And we ask for your mercy now."

We stood together in silence, facing down the Galliyar.

Her twilight eyes threw a lidded gaze towards us. "An offer, then. If you have such faith in your people. I cannot reverse time, but I can open a window, a sliver of a gap for you to pass through." She flicked a finger towards the ghostly vision, and an emerald thread snaked towards the globe. Where it touched the mottled grey surface, the world suffused with colour, once more a blue-green sphere. "I can send you back to the day your moon was taken. You can do what you wish, try to convince your people to defy their nature and avert their fate. But in exchange, your moon stays with me. Your people won't need it."

There was a time I would have wept with relief, with frustration, with all the emotions a human frame could cage. But that girl was gone, the voices of doubt and ambition within her transformed into voices of stillness, patience, and—perhaps—the occasional big, long thought. Time turned on a different spindle here, and I, too, had undergone a diagenesis.

I'd made a promise, lifetimes ago, to protect my family. And now, I understood that one's family was more than mere blood. More, even, than one's own people. It was your world and all who shared it, from the slumbering dust to the blazing stars, and all the glorious, heartbreaking mess in between.

"My people are gone," I said. "But there's a chance that some life persists. And they need their moon."

"Would you call it 'life'?" said the Galliyar.

"They do," I replied. "Our moon, please."

In the end, the Galliyar had tipped our sad little moon from a silken pouch containing other moons, as though it were a set of marbles. With a rope woven from the scarlet strands shed by Book during his metamorphosis, we tethered the moon to the Raivi's tail and towed it behind us like a kite.

"I thought you might try to fight the Galliyar," said Book. "Or steal the moon back. Or trick her with riddles."

We sat beside a mound of knitted octopuses, which I suspected were charming rather than charmed, but the Raivi wanted what she wanted. "Why didn't you fight me, the night I hunted you?"

"A rock is a library of all the things that came before. We remember every drop of rain, every fall of ash, every friend made, every life taken. Some stories are drenched in blood and victory. I am not that kind of book."

"Is that a pun?"

"What's a pun?"

"Never mind." I watched as the glow of a passing pulsar swept over Book, his skin like polished copper, but his arms and legs as lumpy and mismatched as they were that first night among the mandala trees. "The Galliyar believed my people to be thieves and butchers, undeserving of mercy. Hubris fuelled our downfall. Perhaps humility would be our redemption."

"I'm sorry about your people," said Book.

"So am I."

Defiance Rock had been shattered millennia ago, felled in the war that created the Infinity Wasteland. So, instead, the Raivi deposited us on the sloping sands of the desert, which didn't seem as desolate as it had from a distance. Rotund kangaroo rats hopped across the dunes like ginger pom-poms, and bleary frogs peered out from the sands, disappearing again when the false cloud of the Raivi's shadow departed.

"I'm sure she won't keep things sorted by category," I said as we waved farewell.

"She might," said Book. "You gave her a very educational lecture about the dangers of mange."

We had released the moon in what Book assured me was the appropriate position, and if it were slightly misaligned, there was no helping it now. We made our way across the hazy desert, the air cooling as the night breathed closer. We had no clear destination, but one didn't feel necessary.

The surface of a nearby dune rippled and shifted, and a lumpy figure rose from the sands, his skin the colour and texture of sandstone. Two thumb-sized sockets were pressed into his face, and these, he turned towards Book.

"Hullo, brother. We missed you." He then turned to me. "Hullo, sister. Welcome home."

Twilight painted the sky in pastel shades of lavender and periwinkle, and the moon shone like the smile of a long-lost friend, casting a silvery wash over the dunes and beyond. My people's story has ended, pressed between pages of earth and rock, but the story of the mud wraiths continued. And, in time, my own volume would join the library of this world, a tale of mud and stone and starlight.

I smiled at the sand-encrusted figure. "Hullo."

SWAMP MALLOW

A retelling of the recently rediscovered fairytale, The Girl and the Pond

Once upon a time there lived a girl named Mallow who, craving adventure, read as many books as she could and wore a dagger strapped to her leg. She lived with her mother and father in a grand house next to a swamp. Her father was a businessman and landowner who turned swampland into sellable real estate. Her mother, a beauty, held the most lavish parties in all the land and was, according to the cook, rumored to be the daughter of a mysteriously absent *gris-gris* woman.

Any time Mallow brought up the subject of her grandmother, Mama would exclaim over the limpness of her curls in correlation to the humidity. Everything unpleasant correlated to humidity, Mallow realized from a very early age.

On Mallow's sixteenth birthday, her parents threw a party so extravagant, it surpassed all except for her mama's sixth thirtieth birthday party earlier that year. As the guests poured through the massive oak doors, Mallow suspected they were all her parents' friends—no one else below the age of thirty-five except a horrid little cousin. And her mama, of course.

When standing next to her father, conversation was less about Mallow's ability to balance water droplets on her fingertips—a trick she was delighted to discover just this morning as she overturned a fingerbowl after breakfast—and more about the rich farmland her father discovered under a particularly odorous bit of wetland. So she accompanied Mama and her court for a jaunt around the ballroom. The talk here was the fluffiness of the meringues in direct correlation to the humidity. Mallow attempted to interject with the fluffiness of the underskirts of her seersucker birthday dress, but her mama rapped Mallow's shoulder with her fan.

Oddly, Mallow found it difficult to open her mouth.

"These are *birthday* meringues, darling. Stop sulking. Not everything must be about you *all* the time."

Mallow thought a little something should be about her—her name being on the invitation and all—so she disappeared into the kitchen to feel sorry for herself. Here Mallow discovered two things:

1. The meringues had indeed collapsed because of the humidity and
2. this was far more interesting—the cook, Betty, had an alligator tail peeking out from the hem of her calico dress.

Mallow smoothed the bodice of her own dress and wondered the most polite way to bring this up.

"Betty, I believe there is a burnt biscuit behind you," Mallow finally said, thinking—correctly—that alliteration was the best way to proceed.

The cook glanced behind her and whisked her skirts over the not-baked-goods. "Thanks, *chère.*" She gave the girl a sideways glance.

The look, as Mallow interpreted, contained a battle within the cook. Can-she-be-trusted verses she's-the-Grandsir-and-Granddame's-daughter-so-absolutely-not. Mallow showed Betty her new water trick and was much more pleased with Betty's reaction than her parents'.

All too soon, Mallow was called to blow out the candles on her birthday cake.

"I'd rather stay in here," she told Betty and the maid who came to fetch her. "Mama will just lean in at the last minute and steal my birthday wish again."

Betty patted her hand. "I baked that cake just for you, *chère*."

So Mallow left the comfortable kitchen to join her parents' guests. The birthday song was sung, a bit unsteadily by those closest to the open bar, and only one-third of the attendees got her name correct. Cake slices were divvied out. Mallow was pleased to discover her piece was topped with a beautiful sugared flower composed of delicate white petals and a deep red center. A marsh mallow, her name flower. She placed it on its own napkin in front of her, thinking it too pretty to eat.

She looked around at all the party-goers, grimacing when she noticed her frosting-coated cousin bee-lining for her. The little horror pulled on her skirts as he begged for the rest of her slice. Mallow could see in his eyes the exact moment when the sugar took over his mind. He yanked harder. Mallow winced as a seam ripped. She snatched the fabric back and the brat lost his balance, screaming like a bobcat. Her aunt, flustered, rushed up to the table and popped Mallow on the cheek.

"Picking on a child. How dare you!" The feathers on her headpiece shook with indignation.

"He's had enough sugar, Auntie." Mallow's cheek stung and her eye watered.

"Give him your piece and stop acting so selfish. Your poor mama told me you've been in the most difficult mood all day. Puttin' on airs like you're all grown up…"

Mallow sighed and slid the plate toward her cousin. Now she *was* in a mood and the cake would taste like cardboard.

The slice demolished, her cousin pointed to the napkin where the pretty sugar flower bloomed. "Give me that."

"You can't have it." Mallow pushed her chair back to escape but bumped into a guest, the lady's red punch sloshing all over Mallow's birthday dress.

"My toe! You're ruining my slippers!"

"Sorry, but could you please move so I can get out of my chair?" By now, Mallow noticed what a crush the party was. She found it difficult to breathe. The noise from too many competing conversations buzzed like hornets.

"I want that candied flower!" Her cousin stamped his foot.

"Give it to him," her auntie commanded.

"No, Betty made it just for me."

Her auntie shrieked. The brat screamed. Mallow covered her ears and her cousin seized the opportunity to snatch the flower off its napkin. In his haste, it fell to the floor, shattering, and was stepped upon by the red punch woman with a horrifying crunch.

"See what your selfishness caused?" Auntie screeched.

Mallow felt tears scrambling up, their hot claws digging into her throat and eyes. She ought to feel silly for crying over a candied flower, but it was much more than just that. She fought her way through the crowd, eliciting more "owws" and "clumsy girl" and "What's gotten into her?"

"The humidity, I'm afraid," murmured her mama to a gentleman Mallow bumped.

She ran out the oak doors into the day turning to dusk, unsure of where to go. The kitchen—and Betty—was on the other side of the ballroom. Going back through that circus was out of the question. Of course, she could go around the house and through the servant's entrance, but she felt unfit for company. Even the bluebird watching from a nearby post looked as if it would prefer she moved her presence elsewhere.

So she ran down the circular oyster-shell drive, and into the dark green swamp, keeping just enough wits about her to stay on the dry pathways. Tears managed to scrape their way out and Mallow wiped at her eyes, accidentally veering off the path. Her foot immediately sank into the ground. She stumbled but caught herself on a log before falling face first into the swamp muck.

"Excuse me, but that's my eye," the log said in a gravelly voice.

Mallow yelped, knowing full well that logs have *hollow* voices or *wooden* tones. Not gravelly. Gravelly was more suited for low crawling things such as—yes, alligators. Mallow confirmed her suspicions with a closer look. She scrambled backward, her foot coming loose with a wet *sploch*, sans slipper.

"Are you going to eat me?" She knew she couldn't outrun it but was mildly puzzled as to why it hadn't moved. Her day was going along terribly as it was, so she may as well stick around to appease her curiosity.

"My leg is stuck in an otter trap." Metal clanged as if he was shaking his leg for her to verify.

Mallow followed the body to where it was hidden by the underbrush. Pushing swamp lily leaves to the side, she saw that the gator's leg was indeed clamped tight. She winced.

"Do you think you could release me? Otherwise, I'll have to gnaw off my leg."

"If I do, you'll chase me down and eat me."

"You have my word, I will not. If you're lost, I can help you find your way home as payment for releasing me."

Mallow considered the transaction. Nighttime in a swamp was dangerous. She studied the trap. "I'm not sure I know how to spring it."

"There's a lever that must be depressed."

Mallow located it and realized she could stick the tip of her dagger in to open the trap. She reached under her fluffy skirts that no one had mentioned, but were ruined regardless, and withdrew it.

Or she could leave him here and wander by herself. Perhaps die of exposure or bear mauling. She recalled Betty's gator tail and hoped this one would have a similar disposition. She would feel horrible if the gator turned out to be as nice as Betty and she left it to chew off its own foot.

Mallow stuck the blade in the metal and the trap's jaws sprang open. The alligator whipped around so fast, Mallow couldn't follow with her eyes, thinking only *I hope it doesn't hurt terribly* as she slipped back into the muck.

But when she sat up, she looked into round human eyes rather than slitted reptilian ones, though still the same green-gold color. "Oh," she sighed for the gator had turned into a young man. He held out his hand and helped her up. Mallow was now very conscious of her frosted and ripped and punch-soaked and mud-smeared dress, lack of shoe, and tear-streaked face. Her hair, she suspected, contained twigs acquired from her mad swamp dash and more than likely resembled Spanish moss which she was sure her mother would tell her was decidedly *not* the trend this season.

"Much better," he said. "My name is Alcide. Thank you for saving me from your father's trap."

"My daddy? You know who I am?"

"Yes, and you know my mother, Betty, your cook. She's told me much about you."

"So that *was* an alligator tail under her dress! But—why does she have that tail and you…that body?" Mallow blushed; his human form was decidedly handsome.

"Your father stole magic from a *gris-gris* woman. He holds onto his servants by transforming us into swamp animals as we leave the premise. It's how he clears the swamplands so efficiently. I don't know how you could see *Maman*'s tail though, if she was still on the property."

"Daddy enchanted y'all?" Mallow was horrified but just the teensiest bit fascinated by the thought of stolen magic. An idea bloomed as an old story once told in her nursery tapped at the edges of her memory. "Could you take me to the *gris-gris* woman?"

"Wouldn't you rather go home?"

Mallow looked around at the growing shadows on the evening glory-draped trees and lacy cedars and cypresses. Swamp lily flowers curled like question marks. A full moon rose through the treetops, as white and shimmering as the sugar flower on her cake. The glow stirred something wonderful and daring inside her.

Here was an adventure. Potentially as grand as the ones she'd read about for years. She rubbed her thumb along the dagger's handle.

"No. You shall take me to the woman immediately, or I shall trap you again," she commanded. The words felt too serious, as if they came from her mother's mouth. Mallow spoiled the effect of sternness by grinning. "Please." There. Now her lips felt her own.

He bowed and extended his arm. "As you wish."

The moon lit their way as if summoned by magic. Its reflected light dipped below the dark western woods by the time they reached the cottage. With its luminosity straining through the trees, Mallow's courage suddenly waned. She looked at the warm, yellow glow spilling from the curtained windows.

What if this woman wasn't her grandmother? Or she was and, angry that her son-in-law stole her magic, took it out on Mallow. Her daddy wouldn't pay a ransom, Mallow was sure. So what if she was turned into a gator, too? Or worse, a mosquito. Mallow bit her lip. Scratched a bite on her arm. Dug into the dirt with the soiled toe of her remaining slipper.

Alcide took her hand and squeezed. On the walk there, they had discovered a shared love of books and adventure and Betty's Cajun cakes, the more pecans the better. It felt like she had known him her whole life. Why had Betty never introduced them? Her childhood would've been a lot less lonely with a friend nearby. She was a prisoner of Daddy's just as Alcide was, she realized.

"Whatever happens next, I am better for having met you. I'm not even counting the fact that I would lack a foot."

Mallow's toes curled and her confidence bubbled up. She stepped onto the porch and knocked on the door.

From inside there was a crash followed by very witchy cursing. Mallow looked at Alcide in alarm, but before they could jump off the porch, the door was wrenched open and an older version of her mother stood there. Where her mama held her shoulders and head stiffly, this version carried herself like she might spontaneously break into dance. Her mother's face was creased with discontented frown lines. This version had gloriously deep laugh lines.

"Grandmother?"

"My word. Little Marsh Mallow? Come in, come in." The *gris-gris* woman beckoned them to enter. "Please, call me Gram."

Certainly nothing this cheerful could be bad, Mallow told herself. Yes, Gram's magic had cursed Alcide and his mother and all the other servants, but she had no choice in the matter much like Mallow with her father's draining of the swamps.

A cauldron bubbled above a crackling fire. The cottage smelled of honeysuckle and gumbo.

It was a lovely reunion. Mallow hadn't eaten since her disastrous party and that had been a few bites of cake. Alcide had eaten only a frog the day before and was famished.

"Your mama made my magic her dowry," Gram explained as Mallow and Alcide ate their gumbo. "She wanted your daddy to be powerful, so they bound my magic in a pig's bladder."

"You can't get it back?"

"It's complicated. I fear it would be bad for your mama and especially for you. But let's talk of something more pleasant. Today's your birthday, is it not?"

"Yes, ma'am."

Gram's eyes sparkled like lightning bugs. "I remember turning sixteen. Wake up with any special abilities?"

"Oh, yes!" Mallow tipped the water pitcher over and the spilled water floated like a bubble, following the tip of her finger. Alcide looked impressed.

Gram leaned forward. "Your magic eye."

"I have Daddy's eyes, everyone says. Green."

"Your right eye is blue," Alcide said.

"I think I know my own eye color," Mallow replied.

"Close one eye," Gram said.

Mallow closed the right one. "Why?" She hoped she didn't look too foolish.

"Now close just the left."

Mallow did so and immediately jumped out of her chair, backing away from the table, toward the door. "Gram? Alcide?" For at the table, in their places, sat a *roux-ga-roux* and an alligator.

"Mallow, it's still us," the *roux-ga-roux* said in a voice very much like Gram's though the face was dark and twisted, ears pointed and snout elongated in a wolfish way.

The girl looked at the alligator more closely and recognized the green-gold eyes. She opened both of hers, and it was as if she peered through a stereoscope with two illustrations merging into one as they returned to their human forms. Mallow was at a loss for words.

"I have the gift, too. Your blue eye sees how things really are, while your human—green—eye is confused by the *gris-gris* curse," Gram explained.

Mallow looked at them again with her blue eye. "This won't do. How can I break the curse?"

"Darling, it'll upset your mother."

"It doesn't seem right though." Alcide's face, as he stared into the fire, made Mallow realize that her mama being upset weighed little compared to being trapped in an alligator's body. "I'll get your *gris-gris* back. You can break the curse if I return it to you?"

Gram nodded and looked at her with pride. Alcide watched her with fire in his eyes.

And wouldn't it be nice to have someone who understood her in her life?

Though they left before the sun burned the fog off the swamp the next morning, it was late afternoon when she and Alcide pushed open the heavy oak doors of the great house. Her pile of presents sat in a corner, forlorn and unopened. She heard voices from her father's study and burst into the room. He and the gentleman seated before his desk turned to look in shock.

"Mallow. What on earth! You're filthy."

"Where's the pig's bladder?" she demanded.

Her father glanced at his business partner in embarrassment. "What are you talking about, you silly girl?"

The confusion on his face looked real. To be sure, Mallow closed her green eye. She snorted. For sitting in her father's massive leather chair was a bullfrog. He blew out his throat pouch. "Are you daft?" he croaked. "What's wrong with your eye? Primrose! Come get your daughter!"

"Sorry to bother you, Daddy," Mallow said with a grin. She shut the doors behind them before whispering to Alcide, "Mama must have the *gris-gris* because Daddy's bewitched, too."

"Your mother is very powerful if she has both her and your grandmother's magic. Are you sure you want to do this?"

Mallow nodded. Then sucked in a breath when it looked as if he wanted to kiss her.

A maid approached, and he straightened. Mallow squinted and saw that the girl's lashes were really glossy cormorant feathers. "How pretty."

The maid looked startled, then afraid. She covered her eyes. "Grandsir wishes for me to escort you to Granddame in the rose garden."

Alcide reached for Mallow's hand as the two of them followed the cormorant-maid. The warmth from his palm snug with hers gave her that same wonderful, daring feeling as the moonglow from the marsh. Yes, even though Mallow was the teensiest bit afraid of her mama, she'd go through with it.

Mama fluttered her fan in her typical annoyed fashion as she frowned at Mallow's appearance.

"You stole Gram's *gris-gris*!" Mallow had failed to prepare a speech so indignation took over her mouth. "And turned her into a *roux-ga-roux* and Betty and her family into alligators."

Her mother gave a crooked smile and reached for Mallow's free hand. She touched Mallow's fingertips and Mallow felt an odd pull that reached to her naval. "I think you have something for me? I've only been waiting sixteen long years for it. I've built a family fortune with Mother's and mine. With yours, I'll have more than this dirty swamp in my power. Think of the possibilities, my little bayou rat!"

"Not likely," Mallow snorted as she pulled her hand away. "I've come to get Gram's back."

The thunderous look on her mother's face lasted only a moment before it softened, much to Mallow's bewilderment.

Her mother merely flicked open her fan, causing Alcide to spin down to his alligator form. Mallow blinked each eye but saw no trace of Alcide except for the green-gold irises.

"Turn him back!"

Her mama, or more aptly, the witch—for that was what Mallow's blue eye saw—sighed. "This humidity seems to have made you quite dense, darling. Give me your sweet little *gris-gris*, and I won't turn your pet into a new pair of boots." She looked appraisingly at Alcide. "I desire a new pair, and his skin is quite lovely."

Horrified, Mallow looked from her fingertips to Alcide. His face, as all alligators', was expressionless.

The witch huffed and flicked her fan again. "You always were so indecisive. One of your many flaws. Perhaps I should make this easier for you?" She snapped her fan shut and Alcide let out a surprised bellow as he was hoisted in the air as if by an invisible grappling hook.

"Let him down!" Mallow screamed as he roared a terrible alligator roar and thick blood dripped down his belly.

"I'm sure this is the precise reason his mother kept him hidden from me."

Mallow had undone what Betty tried to protect. Tears clawed their way up her throat again.

"I can't spell it out any clearer." The witch tapped her foot, twirling lazy circles with her fan that caused Alcide to spin mid-air. "Your magic—that you don't even know how to use—for his *life*."

Of course Mallow would choose his life. Even though they'd just met, that didn't mean she could be so throw-away with it, with someone who actually cared about *her* and not what they could take from her. A tear dripped onto her cheek. She went to wipe it away when an idea bloomed.

She reached into her new, untried *gris-gris* and grabbed hold of every tear in her body. Absorbed all the humidity that her mother hated so much. Brought them to the surface. She let go, thinking only of protecting her magic *and* Alcide from her mother. Then she was expanding past her normal girl body, and suddenly, water was everywhere. She was the water and Alcide, still in alligator form but no longer bleeding, floated beside her.

Where are we? his reptilian eyes seemed to blink.

Mallow didn't know how to answer. Her head swam.

It seemed she turned herself into a pond. *Still waters run deep*, she thought with uncertain pride and a hysteric sort of amusement.

Were they hidden enough in this bewitchment? She touched Alcide's snout, wondering at the tingling in her fingertips. They enjoyed a few moments of bemused silence until Mallow felt an odd suction.

Her mother drank up the entire pond, swallowing the girl and gator. Shortly, they found themselves in darkness.

Mallow felt shaking and realized it was her mother laughing. This helped her throw off the mantle of despair that had crept onto her shoulders. With the mantle gone, a thinking cap, as they are wont to do when despair is discarded, settled on her head. If Mallow were going to hide something extremely valuable—like a pig's bladder of stolen *gris-gris*—wouldn't she keep it somewhere close to herself? As in, *in* herself, if she could?

Mallow's eyes adjusted to the dim lighting and using her blue eye, quickly found Gram's magic hidden behind a number of land deeds. No wonder her mother always had indigestion. "But how shall we escape?"

Alcide stuck his snout into her not-so-fluffy petticoats.

"Beast!" Then Mallow realized what he had nosed. "The dagger?" She was horrified at the idea, but when an odd sensation pulled at Mallow, she saw something effervescent wisping from her fingertips.

The witch was stealing her *gris-gris*.

Mallow unsheathed the dagger. She was wonderful. She was daring. She held the moonglow inside her.

Alcide clicked his massive jaws.

A bluebird chur-leed on a trellis while hunting lunch. It was a regular bluebird, not a bluebird-gardener or bluebird-maid, so it paid no mind to the witch cackling to herself among the roses.

Until a peculiar look came over the witch's face, much like the time the bird had swallowed a devil's horse. It cocked its head as a girl with a knife in one hand and bladders in the other burst forth from the witch, followed by an alligator who soon stood on human legs.

The bluebird dropped his earthworm in astonishment as the two embraced, then it flew off to an open field where things were quieter and less astounding. It did hear later from a mockingbird that the two restored the *gris-gris* to the woman in the swamp, and everyone lived happily ever after.

But really, one can't believe everything a mockingbird says.

Jennifer Lee Rossman

THE WOLF MOTHER

Mother and child huddled in the corner of the church as the things beat at the door, stained glass moonlight bathing their fear in soft blues and reds.

The baby cried. The mother cried. The man standing between them and the barricaded door did everything in his power to keep all emotion from his face. It was a skill mastered over decades of this kind of work—people felt safer when they thought their guard was brave, even if he wanted to run screaming for his life and leave them to fend for themselves.

"Why me?" Her whisper was barely audible through the sounds of the many claws digging into the wood.

Osmund glanced at her over his shoulder before returning his gaze to the door. He tightened his grip on his laser. "I don't know," he said under his breath, afraid the things could hear him. "My typical wards are rich, powerful. Influential."

"Important," she translated, only slightly bitterly. She had no delusions about her status as a poor farmer's daughter, but people usually tried to be tactful about it.

"Yes," he agreed. "There are a hundred people in town I'd have guessed I was sent to guard before I would even think of it being you." He winced. That sounded rude. "I only mean, the beasts have a taste for kings and senators. People who matter."

In the cold silence that followed, he winced again. This was why he kept his mouth shut.

"You should take their interest as a compliment." He gave Candace an apologetic smile. "It means you're important. Or he is."

She held the baby protectively to her chest and wrapped the end of her skirt up over him to keep him warm. Next time they had to flee for their lives in the middle of the night, she would remember to bring a shawl. "Are they gone?" she asked, indicating the lack of chaos coming from outside.

Osmund shook his head but allowed himself to relax for the moment. "Resting," he said, going to sit on the stone floor beside them. He poked the baby's hand and smiled when the tiny pink fingers curled around his own. "You got a strong handshake, little man." To Candace he continued, "They were designed for short bursts of violent fury, not prolonged attacks."

If the word "designed" surprised her, she didn't let on. "And why don't we take advantage of this and sneak out?" Her big, brown eyes darted to the church's ornate candlesticks, and she suppressed a smile at the thought of using them as spears.

The sound of massive bodies slamming against the door answered her question—the beasts took incredibly short naps.

Osmund didn't get up. His old back ached, and the heavy pews piled in the doorway would fall in as a signal if the doors even began to give way.

He tried not to stare at the young mother, but he liked this one. In his line of work, too many clients acted as if they deserved his protection—once, the man who'd created the beasts demanded he kill a pack and didn't give him so much as a nod of gratitude.

But she appreciated it in a way he couldn't even fathom, and rare moments such as this made his hard life worth it.

"What do they look like?" she asked suddenly. "I only got a glimpse as they broke through my window. Are they like wolves?"

What did they look like? Words hadn't been created to accurately describe the hideous, twisted features, the utter lack of light in their hollow eyes. What did they look like? They looked like death. Death with teeth.

"Yes," Osmund said. "They're like wolves, if wolves had been designed by an evil man to inflict maximum death and given the ability to travel through time to kill their master's enemies. Six feet tall, fur like razors, and so many teeth that he had to give them a second mouth."

"Oh, so exactly like wolves. Except in all the ways." Candace almost smiled, but a thunderous crash somewhere in the bowels of the church wiped it from her face. "They're inside," she breathed.

In an instant, Osmund was on his feet and disappeared around the corner. His echoing footsteps grew softer until they fizzled into nothingness. There was the sound of electricity as his laser discharged, then silence.

When he didn't return, Candace gathered up her dress and stalked down the corridor after him. Moonlight failed to penetrate the twisting halls, and at times she found it difficult to tell whether her eyes were even open.

Heavy breathing and grunting wafted on the air, and the sound of needles scraping on stone. The baby fussed, but she kissed his head and pushed through the fear, feeling along the cold wall with her free hand.

A triangle of light cut across the floor, and the sounds became louder. Candace quietly pulled a crucifix from the wall and held it aloft in anticipation of an attack. Though she was quite sure its power only worked on vampires, its heft gave her confidence in its usefulness for bludgeoning.

She paused only briefly at the open doorway, cursing whatever it was that made her important enough to be killed, and then she charged in with a primal scream.

Osmund looked at her in surprise and amusement from where he stood, trying to slide the dead beast in front of the jagged hole in the stone wall. Several others lay sleeping outside.

"I appreciate the help," he said with a genuine smile, "but you can get the next one."

Candace lowered her weapon awkwardly and got her first good look at the things that wanted her dead as Osmund used its body to block the hole made by its entrance.

The word "horrible" didn't begin to describe it. It was a

nightmare come to life, a disfigured mass of black and red fear disguised as something vaguely animal in nature. Even in death, its fur dug deep grooves in the stone floors, and it did indeed have two sets of jaws, though she hadn't imagined them to be on top of one another.

What had she done to deserve the wrath of these hideous things? She looked at her son. His father, maybe. She'd hardly known him; maybe he was important and the beasts' master thought it would destroy the father to have them killed. Good luck, she thought with a bitter shake of her head. She hadn't seen him in months.

"More will get in," Osmund said grimly, wiping the sweat from his brow. He picked up a massive, pointed tooth that had been dislodged when the beast fell and carefully handed it to Candace. "If one goes for you, jab it with this. The fool made them venomous but forgot to make them immune to their own venom. Take care not to touch the pointy end."

She laughed despite the dire situation as she slipped it into her pocket. "What on earth are you?"

The area around his eyes crinkled in a smile. "Oh, just an old mercenary, raised by an even older mercenary. No one else likes hunting these things down, so I do it. You could say it's in my blood."

"Your parents did this, too?"

"Never met them. I'm told my mother died a hero, though, so there's that." He turned over his left hand and showed her a round scar surrounded by a nasty discoloration on his palm. "No, it's really in my blood. Lucky I didn't die, being so young, but it gave me their powers to travel—"

Chaos erupted in the main room, the pews falling from in front of the door.

Taking Candace's hand, Osmund nearly dragged her from the room and down the twisting halls. Like the things, he must have been able to see in the dark.

Up a flight of unseen stairs they went, their footfalls and breaths obscuring any sounds of further entry by the wolf beasts. Another flight, and Candace felt their escape routes flitting out of reach like dandelion seeds.

They reached the landing and Osmund pushed open the door to the widow's walk leading to the belfry. The cool night breeze chilled her tear-streaked face, and she covered her baby to spare him the discomfort.

Beside the ancient bell that once tolled the hour but now only rang for weddings and funerals, they stood and watched the wolf beasts break into the church.

The pack writhed in the moonlight as one massive creature, and indeed it was. A hive mind, they called it in the future, each individual acting selflessly for the good of the queen. It was her, one of several breeding females made with higher intelligence and bloodlust, that the master sent through time to find his victim. The packs followed her, merely doing her bidding as she lurked somewhere out of sight.

Osmund thought it best not to tell the poor girl about the wolf queens and managed to keep his mouth shut this time.

"Will they ever stop?"

He shook his head. "Not until we kill them or they kill you."

She stared blankly at the silhouetted shapes of her town, doing a remarkable impression of someone looking very brave. "And do you have a plan?" she asked. "Other than getting us trapped up here?"

"There…aren't usually this many," he said in weak defense of his poor decision. "I just wanted to buy us time to strategize, maybe find out how your existence becomes so threatening to their master. If we change your future—"

"So there's really such a thing as time travel." It wasn't so much a question as it was a statement. "There's time travel, and creatures from the future want to eat me."

"Not eat." Osmund caught the baby's eye as his little face peeked around his mother's arm, and Osmund gently relieved her of him for a moment. "They are actually vegetarians." He let his voice rise to a comically high pitch and touched noses with the baby. "They just enjoy killing. Yes they do. Yes. They. Do!"

Candace flopped to the ground in frustration, the beast tooth falling unnoticed from her pocket with a clatter. Osmund sat next to her, bouncing the baby on his knee.

"Now think, Candace," he said gently. "Their master has a hatred for the rich and influential, and sends them after kings, leaders of businesses…on one curious occasion, a parakeet who earned Internet fame for whistling the theme to *Titanic*." He ignored her confusion at these terms from the future. "Why would he want to kill you? A farmgirl from an era where women like you—forgive the bluntness—don't become rich or influential?"

She just shook her head as the baby patted at the ground, reaching for something.

"No political ambitions or plans to invent the laptop computer?"

"The laptop what?"

"Good." At a loss and with the beasts now filing into the church, Osmund felt desperation closing in around them. In a last attempt to change the future, he said weakly, "Promise me you'll never do anything with your life."

She laughed and wiped her eyes. "Promise. How do you know they aren't coming for you, anyway? You seem to be his biggest adversary, going through time and saving all of his victims."

"I am." He showed her his scar again. "Beast venom. Their DNA." Realizing this was several centuries ahead of her time, he explained, "They're not too bright, you see; think I'm one of them. Maybe the queens are smart enough to see past it, but I'm not their target."

A new level of fear flashed through her eyes. "What do you mean, the queens? Do these things come in a larger size—"

A shriek of pain cut through the night. Candace grabbed her child and pulled the beast tooth from his hand, watching in horror as his skin began absorbing the coloration of the venom.

"No," she whispered, holding him to her tightly.

The scrabbling of claws and faint howling from inside the church abruptly ceased as the beasts' intended victim became one of them.

"I stand corrected," Osmund said with tears in his eyes as he laid a hand on his mother's shoulder. "I *was* the target."

If she understood the gravity of this statement, she did not give any indication, and sobbed into her son's hair.

A shadow crossed in front of the moon. The pack wandered off toward it, as if drawn by some instinctual force.

The queen, stepping carefully over the houses down in the village. Her footsteps sounded like thunder, and the hairs on the back of her neck rattled like rain on a tin roof. If the beasts were death, she was the horrors waiting in hell. And she was headed for the church.

Candace gave no thought to her own safety. She picked up the tooth, holding it tightly in her fist. “This will kill her?”

“Yes.”

“And they won't come after either of you?”

“No.”

She kissed her son on the cheek and handed him to his older self before climbing down the belfry.

“It occurs to me,” Osmund said to himself, “that she never told me your name. I'll have to name you after myself then, as I always did.”

The baby cried, the queen beast howled in pain, and Osmund's mother died a hero.

Aaron Gudmunson

BONEYARD WATCHDOGS

Ben arrived at the church with the spade slung across his shoulders. Dew squelched underfoot, glazing his Nikes. The funeral was set for one o'clock. They'd be in the bell tower until after dark, which was why Dugan told Ben he'd be well-advised to pack a lunch and a pair of earplugs. Dugan said he'd bring the cards.

"Good boy. Right on time," Dugan said as Ben ambled up.

"Is the church unlocked?"

"Church is always unlocked," Dugan said. "That's the beauty of church." He let the door breathe shut behind them.

The chapel lay tucked in shadow, and the crucifix suspended above the altar was barely discernible until Dugan popped his Maglite on.

Ben shivered. Couldn't help it. Was it sacrilege to be in a church on Halloween? He honestly couldn't remember, but didn't like the idea of pressing his luck.

"Scared of ghouls?" Dugan asked. He held the beam beneath his chin, transforming his face into a death-mask.

"No," Ben said, too quickly. "I just don't like being in church when it ain't church time."

Dugan laughed. "Let's get up in that tower. It's gonna be a long day."

Ben knew it would be an even longer night, but he followed Dugan to an anteroom off the chapel and fixed his eyes on the back of his boss's head to avoid the eyes of the Almighty fastened to His burden.

Dugan eased the door open and played the beam along the walls. A length of cord hung from a trapdoor in the ceiling.

He was a slight man with mahogany eyes and tar-greasy hair. His nose came to a point above thin lips that looked somehow unnatural when he smiled. Now he turned that smile on Ben. "How about you give that string a yank, huh?"

Ben, a head taller and twice as broad, obliged. The trap door gaped open like a hungry maw, spilling out a service ladder like a tongue. Dugan shot the light up the black throat.

"There's an open space. Right above it, you're gonna see one big-ass bell. You're gonna see some wood slats, like vents, ya know, to let out the bell chimes. We'll use it as a sort of duck blind, see? I'll watch the boneyard; you take the road. Got it?"

Ben said he got it and started up the ladder.

The open space Dugan mentioned could be considered neither open nor space. It seemed to be more of a service ledge running around the perimeter of the tower, eighteen inches wide, little more than a perch.

"Holy God," Ben said, crawling onto the ledge. "We got to sit up here *how* long?"

Dugan climbed onto the opposite shelf. "Thirteen hours. Think of it as picking up a double at the factory."

"I get overtime?" Ben asked dryly. He brushed cobwebs from his hair.

"Funny, hoss. Listen, those earplugs I suggested? I'd get to stuffing 'em in." Dugan checked his watch again and glanced up at the bronze bell suspended overhead.

"You got to be shitting me," Ben muttered. The bell began to totter. The clapper, hanging like a giant fist, hammered the hour. Even with the plugs, the sound pounded him flat. Ben squeezed his eyes closed and clamped down on his ears. The bell clanged six times before shivering to a stop. He realized he'd been holding his breath, and he released it in a long, shuddery sigh.

Dugan plucked out his plugs. He dug through his sack and removed a kitchen egg timer, which he wound to fifty-nine minutes. "When this thing clicks, I recommend stuffing your ears again."

Ben moaned.

Dugan chuckled. "It ain't so bad. Just lay back if your handsome end starts to cramp." He demonstrated by flopping onto his side.

"Try being six-four, two-fifty and see how it suits you," Ben said with contempt.

"Quit bitching. Come tomorrow, you're gonna be a hell of a lot richer."

Ben peered through the slats. The sun drew over the horizon. He could see Walnut Road winding back to town. The water tower was a rusty spike in the sky. A block away from that tower, at The Castle Pub, Ben had first met Dugan. Just eighty hours ago, it had been. Eighty long hours.

"Mr. Dugan?"

The small bat-faced man looked up from his newspaper. A glass of whiskey on the rocks sweated nearby.

"You must be Ben."

The larger man confirmed his name and slid into the opposite booth.

"Well, Ben, you've come highly recommended from a trusted associate," Dugan said, folding his paper.

"Thank you."

"Don't thank me yet. Did McDaniels let on about the nature of the work?"

"Outdoor labor, high pay."

"That's the short of it," Dugan said, snaking his thin fingers around his glass.

Ben glanced around. "He also told me it ain't exactly legal."

"McDaniels strikes again. You been in the area long?"

"Month. Been working at the forge."

Dugan squinted at him. "You ever hear of Garret von Cleese?"

"Sure. Rich guy, right? Owns all that land up to the Hollow? Shits in some mansion?"

"Mansion?" Dugan snorted. "You seen that place? More like a fucking palace. His family's lived there since right around the time Moses led the Jews out of Egypt. Our man Garret inherited the whole shebang. Family's got mob ties up the ass. You should see some of the boys he's got working for him. Scary fellas."

Ben whistled. "That's a lot of responsibility for a guy so young."

"He ain't young," Dugan said, still smiling. "He ain't old. He ain't anything." Dugan flipped the newspaper across the table, fingering a small block of copy.

> Garret von Cleese, 38, of Devon's Hollow passed away Sunday, October 27 at his home. He is survived by his wife. A private funeral will be held Thursday at one o'clock at Oak Crest Cemetery in Murdoch, Ill.

Ben looked at Dugan. "He dead?

"He is."

"That's got to be the shortest obituary I ever seen. Hardly says anything."

"You got to read *between* the lines, Ben ol' hoss."

"How do you mean?"

"I happen to possess the knowledge that the von Cleese clan always bury their dearly departed with something they treasured in life. Take Greta, Garret's grandmammy. She was put under wearing her favorite sapphire broach. Thing was worth thirty large. Lloyd, the old man, had his tie clipped with a diamond pin when he got dropped." Dugan's eyes darted around again. "And it just so happens that Garret never in his life took off his 9 karat ruby ring. My gut tells me he ain't gonna start now."

Ben leaned over the table. "We're going to *rob* the grave?"

Dugan flapped a hand. "It sounds so criminal when you say it like that. Think of it as a recycling project. Our subject is no longer in need of his money and we are."

"Why do you need me? Why split the profits?"

"That's the problem," Dugan sighed. "I'm asthmatic. I can't do a timely job. It's a big help when I have someone with meat on his bones to sling the spade. And I can always use a pair of eyes watching my back."

"That's where I come in," Ben said. He gazed out the window at the water tower. "How much?"

"We stand to pull down eighty large on this one. We go halves—forty for you, forty for me."

Ben slumped back, said nothing.

"If you're worried about the pigs, don't. The timing is perfect, hoss. Look at that date. October thirty-first. Where the hell is everyone going to be that night?"

"In town?"

"Bingo," Dugan said. "Families will be trick-or-treating or partying. Cops will be out looking for punks out smashing punkins."

Ben rubbed his chin. "You don't reckon cops'll check on the cemetery? Lot of kids come tip tombstones on Halloween."

"Not out here, they don't. Too close to town. They'll head out to Holy Sepulcher to get up to no good. Anyhow, I have a plan in place to avoid the heat." Dugan extended his small hand. "Do we have a deal, partner?"

Ben shook.

Dugan raised his whiskey. "To your bones."

"To yours."

The egg timer clicked. Ben plugged his ears. The bell clanged nine times. It seemed eternal. When at last the vibrations died, Dugan rewound the timer.

Ben said, "Thought my brains were gonna leak out my ears."

Dugan chuckled, a wet sound. "You got to keep motivated. Just keep telling yourself, 'forty grand, forty grand.' Works for me."

Sweat stood out on Ben's face and he wiped it with his collar. He found his canteen and took a long haul.

"Save some. We got a while yet."

"I know," Ben replied, adjusting his position. His ass hurt already and a low throb had begun at the base of his spine. "Believe me, I know."

The bell rang ten.

Ben had to piss. Dugan reported that the gravediggers were at the site, digging gleefully away.

The bell rang eleven.

The clamor went on so long and loud, he thought he'd lose his hearing. Or his mind.

The bell rang twelve.

It felt as if his insides were being pounded by a sledgehammer. His bladder, stretched at the seams, begged relief.

"Mr. Dugan, I have to take a leak," Ben said. He wiped his slick brow.

"It'll have to wait," Dugan said over his shoulder. He was staring out the slats into the graveyard. "Diggers are gone, but people will be coming soon for the funeral."

"I can't hold it."

"For Christ's *sake.*" Dugan checked his watch. "Back in three minutes. No longer."

The chapel was a welcome reprieve from the tower. Ben found the restroom and relieved himself. Heaven. He washed his hands and refilled the canteen. Out the window lay the cemetery. Ben could see the open ground at the far end, near the fence. A blue canopy flapped above it, looking out of place against the orange elm leaves beyond it. He shuddered.

In the chapel Ben knelt and crossed himself. He prayed everything would go as planned.

In the tower, Dugan watched the dark, oblong hollow in the earth and bit into an apple scrounged from his pack. Something was amiss, but he couldn't pinpoint the source of this feeling. It was more instinctual than actual. He told himself to relax. He'd covered his bases. He'd never been caught before, and he sure as hell wasn't going to start tonight.

There was the issue of Ben. Could he be an undercover cop? No. No way. This guy was too slow to be a pig. Plus, McDaniels had recommended him, and McDaniels would castrate himself before falling under the law's thumb. If not a cop, what then? There was something he didn't like about his new partner.

Didn't matter anyway. Ben was going to get exactly what Dugan's partners always got, and it wasn't half the score. He used a plan that had worked on all his past jobs. It went like this: find a workhorse to dig out the hole where the fresh corpse lay at rest. Then Dugan popped the casket and relieved the departed of his or her treasure. Once complete, while still waist-deep in the grave, he dispatched the partner in one way or another. The partner became a permanent roommate to the grave's occupant. Dugan then simply refilled the grave, tamped it down nice and neat, and went on his merry way a richer man than when he'd come.

The scheme worked every time. McDaniels picked good partners, no one who would be missed. Such was the case with Ben, a drifter with no known relatives. The kind of partner Dugan preferred. Drifters were never anywhere. They were always someplace else.

But still…

He could not shake the feeling that something was not quite right with this picture. He would have to be cautious. He could take no chances. Not this night.

"You were gone seven minutes," Dugan spat when Ben climbed up.

"Oops."

"This ain't no joke," Dugan snapped. "What if someone'd come in while you were down there?"

"Like who?"

"Like, hell, I dunno. The priest or janitor or altar boy or someone." Dugan looked rabid.

"Mr. Dugan, it's cool. Place is a ghost town."

"I hope you got it all outta you. No more breaks till after."

"Okay, Mr. Dugan. No problem."

"You wanna play cards?"

"Sure. What's your game?"

Dugan's thin smile resurfaced. "Spades. What else?"

The bell, mercifully, clanged only once at the turn of the next hour. Their game had been halted twenty minutes prior when mourners began to arrive. Ben watched them wind up Walnut Road from the east, and Dugan watched them gather in the cemetery. There weren't many.

"There's the wife," Dugan had whispered over his shoulder. He was peering through binoculars. "At least, I'm assuming it's her. She got out of a big-ass limo behind the hearse."

"Must be her," Ben said absently.

"Shit, there's hardly anyone here," Dugan muttered. "Is this the right funeral?"

"Got to be," Ben said. "Paper said so." He swigged from the canteen. He still had the cards fanned in his fist.

"Minister just came out. He's behind schedule; he's usually the first one on-site."

"Maybe he was taking a holy shit," Ben offered and was surprised when Dugan chortled.

"Good one, hoss. Now shut up."

Ben did.

"Pallbearers just set the casket down," Dugan reported. "Shit, them guys are as big as you, hoss. Hate to meet them in a dark alley." He fell quiet, peering through the glasses. Then, "You hear that?"

Ben snapped to attention. "Hear what?"

"Listen."

There came a humming, like a swarm of bees. Distant but evident.

"That's the damndest thing," Dugan whispered. "You can't hear that?"

"I don't hear—"

"Okay, shut it. They're lowering him down."

Ben shut it.

By the time the bell sounded two, Dugan reported not a soul remained in the boneyard. The diggers had filled in von Cleese's grave and vanished. "Prolly putting back a few cold ones 'bout now," Dugan said.

"This is hell," Ben said. The tower had grown stuffy, and he inhaled dust with every breath. His spine felt like a rail spike had been hammered into it.

"Hell is probably a place Garret von Cleese is learning a lot about right now." Dugan laughed.

Ben laughed with him, weakly.

The bell clanged three.

And four.

And five.

At last, near six, the sun lost its battle with the sky. At half past the hour, the first shadows slid like oil into the bell tower.

"Not long now, hoss," Dugan said.

When the bell had sounded its seventh note, Dugan pulled his plugs. "Tell me what you see out there."

Ben scouted east. "Not much. Trees, houses, water tower. The moon sure is purty tonight."

"Any cars?"

"Nope."

Dugan slumped against the wall. "All right. Keep your eyes peeled."

"Okay."

"Wanna play another game?"

"Sure."

They quit playing when the bell struck eight. A few stars glittered around a moon fat and orange as a pumpkin. Ben reported no movement on his side of the tower.

"Good. One thing left and then we get to it." Dugan rummaged in his pack and withdrew a cell phone.

"Who you calling?"

"The cops."

Shadows overwhelmed the tower. The bell was a hanging hollow curve above. After calling local authorities to report an accident out on Route 20, Dugan clicked his Maglite on. Seven hours had elapsed since the funeral, and thirteen since they'd first climbed up.

"Ready, hoss?"

Ben's throat felt like crushed gravel. "As I'll ever be."

"Lead on."

Flashlight gripped in one fist, Ben climbed down. Every muscle throbbed. God, he'd better be getting paid as well as he was promised for this.

They made their way out the back door. Dugan made Ben wait while he swept the grounds.

"Clear. Let's move."

Ben shuddered as they stepped onto the new grave.

Dugan took frequent breaks. He was clearly content with letting Ben shoulder the load. His excuse was his asthma was acting up. Or he had to burst a blister. Or he was keeping an eye out for trick-or-treaters.

Nearing the end, Dugan pitched in for a surprising full ten minutes. They were getting down to it. He shoveled in a state of frenzy.

Dugan straightened and whispered, "You hear that?"

"Hear what?"

"*Shh.*"

Ben stood statue-still. He heard it: a humming, seeping up from the ground, as if a beehive had been buried there. It was the sound they'd heard at the funeral.

"What is it?" Ben whispered, keeping a close eye on his boss.

"Dunno. Keep going," Dugan answered. He climbed out of the hole and peered around.

Ben shoveled. Two loads later, the edge of the shovel struck polished wood. The humming stopped.

"Mr. Dugan, pay dirt," Ben said. He chunked his spade twice on the casket lid.

Dugan jumped into the grave, wiping dirt from the lacquered surface. "Give them latches a whack. Let's open her up."

Ben struck each lock until they splintered free.

"Yeah, that's it, hoss," Dugan said, working his fingers beneath the lid.

"Mr. Dugan, why don't I get out of your way? We can't open this thing with both of us down here."

"Yeah," Dugan murmured. "Get outta the way."

Ben pulled himself up, relieved to be topside again. The moon had gone from pumpkin orange to ghostly white since they'd begun digging. Ben watched it because he didn't want to watch what was about to happen behind him.

Dugan pulled the casket open, grit grinding in the hinges. Inside lay Garret von Cleese, arms at his sides, eyes closed.

"Hello, you bastard," Dugan said with a grin, reaching for the hand where the scarlet stone glinted in the moonlight.

"Hello to you, sir," the dead man said. His eyes opened. The hand bearing the ring rose from the coffin. It gripped a .45 caliber revolver.

Dugan blinked. Every cell in his body locked down. His muscles unhinged. His bladder let go. He uttered one senseless syllable. Dugan understood his mistake now; now he believed in ghosts and would believe in them for the rest of his life. Which turned out to be just under half a second.

After the report had faded, Ben turned. Dugan's body—now headless—lay at the foot of the grave, arms flung wide.

"Let me help you, sir," Ben said, reaching down to clasp Garret von Cleese's hand.

"Thank you, Benjamin," von Cleese replied, finding his feet. He adjusted his tie and brushed dust from his sleeve. He rotated his shoulders and rolled his neck. He twisted his ruby ring, and Ben noted how the moonlight turned the stone to blood.

"Are you all right, sir?" he asked, looking away.

"Absolutely," von Cleese said, peering into the grave. "Help me with this, will you?"

They dropped Dugan's corpse into the grave and filled it in. When the last of the sod had been tamped down, von Cleese turned to Ben. "Fine work, Benjamin. You'll receive your payment in full first thing in the morning."

"Don't worry about that, boss. I'm just glad you're all right."

"I was never in any real danger, you know. I had the air tank—noisy bastard though it is—and a flashlight. Tank kept me breathing and flashlight kept it bright. I even got in a much-needed shuteye. Most of all, I now have peace of mind that the places my families are laid to rest shall never again be disturbed."

"I still don't get it, sir," Ben said. "Why didn't you just let me or one of the boys take him out once McDaniels spilled his guts? Would've been easier on you. You could have avoided paying off the cops, setting up the phony newspaper, hiring the funeral actors."

Garret von Cleese sighed. "I don't suppose you'll understand, Benjamin, but a man's family is his pride. His reason for living. There are some things a man must do himself, and this was one of them. And seeing the look in that bastard's eyes. Well, I guess that alone was worth the trouble."

"But, God, lying under six feet of dirt all day?"

"What can I say? I'm a sick man. At least now I know what to expect when the real thing comes. It'll be one long, boring nap."

They laughed.

"Well," von Cleese said. "What do you say we get out of here before we dig up any real trouble? I think the least I can do for you this evening is buy you a drink."

Ben put a hand to his back. "I appreciate it, sir, but I'll have to take a raincheck. All day in a bell tower is hell on your bones."

"I suppose you're right," von Cleese said, as they moved out of the cemetery and up the road to where a Cadillac sat parked in a turnout.

They drove down Walnut Road toward town, and Ben glanced at his employer. "Are you sure you're all right, sir?"

"Fine, Benjamin. Just fine. But I'll tell you this—tonight I'm going to sleep like the dead."

They laughed until they pulled up in front of Ben's cabin, shook hands, and said goodnight.

Liz Delton

RED SNEAKERS

The dark lake water lapped gently against the tip of Wendy's shoes as another tear slid down her cheek. Crouched by the shore, she brushed the tear away with the sleeve of her hoodie, then clasped her arms tightly around her knees.

Stupid shoes. They were the reason she had been locked out of her cabin by her bunkmates, led by the pug-faced Caroline and her cronies. Their counselor had gone to the staff lounge, so no one had noticed when Wendy didn't come back from the bathroom. No one except the girls who had locked her out of the cabin, anyway.

She clenched her eyes shut, squeezing out more hot tears. She let them trail down her cheeks.

Red shoes were cursed, the girls said. Montague Mary would come and abduct anyone who wore red shoes on Montague Mountain.

The girls said Montague Mary and her daughter went camping on this mountain years and years ago, before the camp was even built. Mary's daughter died, though the legends didn't agree on how. One girl said she fell off a cliff, while another argued that the poor girl drowned. No one was really sure what happened to her. What they all agreed on though, was that Mary's daughter always wore red shoes.

Wendy looked down at her bright red Converse high-tops. How was she supposed to know? It was her first summer at Camp Montague, and she had begged her mom for weeks for these sneakers. She had loved them, until now.

It was quiet on the beach by the lake. The full moon's reflection glowed like the beam of a bright flashlight on the nearly still water. Someone in Wendy's archery class had said it was a blue moon, the second full moon this month.

Wendy's stomach growled. She curled tighter around her knees. She hadn't gone to dinner after one of the girls in her cabin had thrown Wendy's sleeping bag and pillow into a tree. Caroline was probably the one who had locked the door on the cabin, too.

A cold wind swept from the trees and across the lake, shattering the moon's reflection and sending a shiver up Wendy's spine. The trees behind her rustled like a thousand whispers.

She wanted to go home, but her mom had just dropped her off yesterday. She didn't want the girls in her cabin to think she was a homesick baby, on top of wearing cursed shoes.

The breeze had dried the tears on her face, and Wendy realized she had finally stopped crying.

She didn't want to go back up to the cabin. Either the door would still be locked, or her counselor would be back and Wendy would have to explain why she had been out of the cabin. Then she'd either have to lie or be branded a tattle-tale.

Maybe she would just stay on the beach all night. She had always liked being near water. Her swim lesson today had been the only good thing about camp so far.

Just as she was pondering breaking into the boathouse to sleep next to the canoes, she heard the gritty sound of crunching sand behind her.

Her breath caught as she turned her head, fumbling for her flashlight. If it was one of the counselors, she was in big trouble.

But the beach was empty.

She flew to her feet, flashlight tight in her grip. Her heart thudded in her chest as she gazed across the deserted beach. With a sigh, she strode toward the path that led back to the cabins.

Reaching into her hoodie pocket, Wendy discovered her toothbrush and was immediately reminded of her ill-fated trip to the bathroom. She would just have to go back to the cabin. She had nowhere else to go. Maybe one of the other girls had taken pity on her by now and unlocked the door.

Her red sneakers crunched along the path as she ascended the steep shortcut their counselor Emily had shown them that afternoon. It was narrow, and she went slowly around the sharp rocks and sharper turns.

The wind rustled the leaves again, and Wendy thought she heard a footstep behind her. She lost her balance trying to get a look at the path and fell, landing on her outstretched hand.

"Ouch," she muttered, bringing her palm to her face to examine the new scrape. A droplet of blood seeped out.

She still didn't turn her flashlight on; she didn't want to get in trouble for being out alone this late. The moonlight was bright enough to see by.

Eventually, Emily would come back from the staff lounge and see Wendy's bed empty. But would Wendy tell her what really happened? She didn't want to be a tattle-tale, but she didn't want to spend any more nights locked out of the cabin either.

A sharp whine came from the darkness ahead of her. Wendy froze.

She peered up the path, but she could see nothing except stones, dirt, and the shadows of the trees.

The whine came again, this time longer, and with a sob at the end. Someone was crying.

"Hello?" Wendy whispered into the dark.

A sniffle came as a response, and Wendy clicked her flashlight on.

A little girl sat hunched on a large rock, one of her knees scraped, and her head in her hands. She looked up into the beam of light, her eyes glinting. Wendy shone it on the ground instead.

"Are you all right?" Wendy asked.

The girl wiped her eyes with balled fists. "I got lost coming back from the bathroom," she sobbed. She looked maybe seven or eight, with long, tangled blonde hair and a thin face.

"You know you're not supposed to go anywhere without a buddy, right?" Wendy asked, knowing the irony in it.

More tears poured from the girl's eyes and her lip trembled.

"I'll be your buddy then. Come on," Wendy said. At least some good would come of getting locked out. "I'll walk you back to your cabin. Do you know which one it is?"

The little girl shook her head, but she took Wendy's outstretched hand. They climbed the path together, Wendy helping the girl around the jagged stones, and even once lifting her up onto a steep ledge. *It was a good thing I found her*, Wendy thought. *The girl would have cracked her head open if she kept wandering by herself.*

Then Wendy led her down the other side of the ridge, instead of up to where her own cabin stood. She vaguely remembered where the younger girls' cabins were from the camp tour.

The little girl was still crying.

"What's your name?" Wendy asked to distract her.

"Connie," she squeaked.

"My name's Wendy," she said, maneuvering the girl around a tree that grew in the path.

They passed the trail that led to the bathrooms, and Wendy smothered a bitter thought about her own cabin. At least she would have a cover story now if her counselor Emily came back and Wendy's bed was empty.

They headed toward the younger girls' cabins, Wendy's flashlight beam bobbing along the path and highlighting the small stones along the way. Emily hadn't exactly shown them the younger girls' area on their tour, just pointed over the ridge in their general direction.

This path must head there, Wendy thought. She knew the other way led down to the dining hall.

She and Connie walked along in silence. The only sounds were their shoes crunching in the gravel and the buzzing and chirping of night insects.

Wendy finally saw a cabin's porch light in the distance and picked up speed. Connie stumbled, going down on her knee.

"Oh no," Wendy exclaimed. "Are you okay, Connie?"

She reached out for Connie's arm and helped pull the girl up. She pointed her flashlight back down to see what she had tripped on. "Oh, your shoe's untied."

Wendy glanced to where she thought the cabins were, but she couldn't see the light anymore. *The trees must be blocking it*, she thought.

Connie made no move to tie her own shoe, just stood there twisting the hem of her T-shirt.

"Here, I'll do it," Wendy muttered.

She crouched down and stuck the flashlight between her knees, aiming at Connie's laces.

"Hey, your shoes are red like mine," Wendy said.

Her flashlight flickered and went out. Wendy let go of the laces and smacked it against her palm.

"Oh, come on; these batteries are brand new," she muttered.

After a last good thwack, the light came back on. Connie was gone.

"What the hell?" *Connie could barely walk without tripping in the light of the flashlight, and she wandered off in the dark without a sound?*

Wendy gripped her flashlight hard, and pointed it everywhere, but she was alone. Her mind flew to the tales the girls in her cabin told, about Montague Mary abducting girls with red shoes. Had she taken Connie?

She whipped around at the sound of gravel crunching. Was Montague Mary coming for her next?

Connie stood in the trees just off the path.

"Connie! You scared the crap out of me!"

Wendy shone her light on Connie's shoes. They were indeed red, but now they looked wet.

"Did you step in a puddle or something?" Wendy asked, going closer.

Wendy sunk down to tie the girl's shoes again, wanting to get back to her own cabin, even if she ended up sleeping on the porch. She picked up the laces, then dropped them as if they had scalded her.

Blood. Connie's shoes were soaked in blood.

"Connie?" Wendy squeaked.

The blood was running down Connie's legs and pooling in her sneakers.

Wendy dropped her flashlight. The beam cast tall shadows onto the trees behind Connie.

Connie looked down at her, her long blonde hair framing her face. "Mom?"

"Your mom's not here, Connie. What happened to you? Why are you bleeding? We need to get you to the nurse!" Wendy groped in the dirt path without looking and picked up her flashlight with unsteady fingers.

"It was an accident," Connie whispered, her little hands shaking. Drops of blood shook from her fingertips, as more streamed down the backs of her pale arms. *Where is it coming from?* Wendy wondered, but she was too scared to touch her.

"Help!" Wendy cried, even though she was too far from the cabins for anyone to hear. She staggered in the direction of the infirmary. A high-pitched moan escaped Connie, and Wendy turned back.

The little girl collapsed to her already-skinned knees. Wendy held a hand out, but withdrew it almost immediately.

"Stay here," she rasped, glancing between Connie and the path to the nurse's. "I-I'm going to go get help."

Wendy lurched down the path, the flashlight slipping in her suddenly sweaty palm. "Help," she cried, aiming the flashlight up and down the path, hoping to spot one of the counselors on their way back from the staff lounge.

The moonlight was gone, its brilliance smothered by clouds. Wendy's world condensed to the few feet she could see in her flashlight's beam.

"Help!" she cried again, but her words were drowned out by the rustling of leaves in the wind. The cold breeze snaked over her, icing through her panicked sweat.

Then it was as if a spider crawled up Wendy's back. She didn't hear anything, but her shoulders crept up to her ears, and her scalp tingled so much that she turned around.

Her flashlight beam fell on a woman a few feet away. She was pale, and her wide eyes bore into Wendy. She looked too old to be one of the counselors, and she didn't even have a flashlight.

Wendy's throat constricted, but she managed to croak, "You've got to help me; there's a girl back there—"

She cut her words short. The woman had closed the gap between them, and now stood inches from Wendy. She was staring at Wendy's red shoes.

The clouds above drifted on, and moonlight shone down upon them. Wendy didn't need her flashlight to see the woman anymore. Her breath caught in her throat.

The woman wasn't all there. It was as if she were outlined in smoke, the edges of her body dissolving into the air around her.

As she continued to gaze hungrily at the red shoes, Wendy realized who she must be. She leapt back and pointed her flashlight at Montague Mary as if it were a weapon.

The ghost lurched forward and grabbed Wendy's arm, her grip surprisingly solid.

"No!" Wendy screeched. She tried to yank her arm away, but Mary only tightened her grasp. Sharp nails dug into Wendy's arm until she cried out again, wordless, into the night.

Wendy wrenched her gaze from the ghost's grip, and terror fled through her as she locked eyes with the ghost, whose wide, searching eyes were framed with pale blonde hair. Mary tugged Wendy toward the darkness of the trees, and Wendy's legs seized up.

"Wait!" Wendy gasped. "Wait! I-I think I know where your daughter is!"

Mary ignored her, dragging her now since Wendy's legs weren't moving. Wendy had no doubt that once she left the bright moonlight and Mary pulled her into the dark trees, she was as good as dead. As dead as all those other girls who had worn red shoes on Montague Mountain. But there was one girl who wore red shoes that had started it all.

"Connie," Wendy cried. "Your daughter's name is Connie, isn't it?" She yanked on Mary's arm. "Isn't it?"

Mary's smoky outline waivered, and she looked down at Wendy with narrowed eyes.

“It's not me you're looking for,” Wendy pleaded. “It's Connie. I found her. I'll take you to her!”

“Connie?” the ghost mumbled, confused. She took another step toward the trees.

“Yes, Connie! She's back that way.”

Mary finally stopped.

“This way,” Wendy said, pulling Mary now. “This way!”

The ghost followed. Wendy had dropped her flashlight, but she could still see by the moonlight.

The little girl lay where Wendy had left her. Her eyes fluttered, and her chest barely rose with each strained breath.

"Connie?" Mary cried when she saw her. "Oh, Connie." She rushed forward and scooped Connie into her arms.

It was then that Wendy noticed where all the blood was coming from. A dark gash marred the back of Connie's head. Blood now coated the tips of Connie's long tangled hair, the light strands looking dyed black.

“Mom,” Connie cried.

Mary clutched Connie to her chest, her hand coming away bloody from the little girl's scalp.

"What happened?" the woman sobbed, rocking her daughter back and forth.

"I tripped, Mom," Connie whispered, her eyes closed. "It was an accident. I hit my head."

But she didn't say any more after that. She became limp in her mother's arms. Soon the woman was rocking a lifeless child. Wendy stood there, eyes wide, her mouth hanging open.

The woman turned to Wendy. "You found her. I've been looking for her forever."

Wendy didn't know what to say. Her heart beat painfully fast in her chest, and she could tell her arm was bruised from Mary's grasp. She stumbled back, afraid Mary might still try to take her.

"Thank you," Mary said. "I didn't know what happened to her."

She looked down at Connie and tucked a strand of bloody hair behind the girl's ear. Both Mary's and Connie's outlines wavered like smoke. Mary stared down at her daughter, tears streaming down her face. A small smile pulled up the corners of her mouth before she placed a kiss on Connie's forehead.

Then they were gone. Their smoky outlines blew away into nothing.

Wendy turned and ran. She sped haphazardly along the path, tripping on rocks and exposed roots. There was no way she was going back for her flashlight now. Her heart raced as fast as her legs.

She finally reached her cabin. Panting, she reached for the door knob, fear that it was still locked rising up her throat like vomit. It turned.

She let out a shaky breath as she ducked inside and locked the door behind her. She stumbled toward her bunk. For several long minutes, she sat on her bed trying to breathe normally, not wanting to wake the others. She was sweating, yet cold, and she couldn't stop her fingers from rubbing the bruises on her arm. The cabin was filled with the sounds of sleepy breathing and the constant chirping of crickets outside.

She reached down and untied her red sneakers with trembling fingers.

As she lay on top of her sleeping bag and stared out the window into the moonlight, she realized that she had nothing to fear from wearing those sneakers anymore. Montague Mary had found her daughter.

Maybe tomorrow Caroline would find her sleeping bag up a tree. Or, her sneakers hanging from the camp's flagpole.

Maria Carvalho

FULL MOON SEEN IN A DIFFERENT LIGHT

Diane gently set her large black telescope down in her backyard, anticipation making her downright giddy. She'd been waiting a long time for tonight's event: a supermoon for the ages, when the full moon would occur on the night it was the closest it would get to Earth until November 2040, over a decade away. And unlike the bitterly disappointing rainy night of the last supermoon, the sky was totally clear. It was a quintessential September evening in New England: crisp but not cold, the songs of peepers and crickets mingling with the shimmering confetti of late-season fireflies.

She positioned the wide barrel of the telescope and focused the laser pointer at the spot above the horizon where the moonrise would occur. The scope was powerful enough to afford her marvelous views of Saturn's rings and the cloud-band stripes of Jupiter, but the moon was still her favorite thing to look at. It went back to her childhood, when she'd spent many nights on the family farm lying in the fields with a pair of binoculars, mesmerized by the details of the moon's face. She'd always felt there was something magical about it and had the comforting sense that it was watching over her. Now, at twenty-five, she still had that sense of wonder and was amazed whenever she saw the fascinating details of the lunar surface through her telescope.

When she had finished setting it up, Diane went back into her small bungalow to retrieve the strange contraption she had purchased that afternoon. She had long admired the stately Federal-style home a few blocks away, and when she saw an estate sale sign in front of it as she drove past, she simply couldn't resist going in to take a look. As she'd browsed the Victorian furniture and ornate decorative items, she came across an antique telescope. In some respects, it had a traditional appearance: a long brass barrel with wooden inlays along the sides sat atop three wooden legs. But there were several things about it that were unusual. A brass compartment was mounted inside the space between the three wooden legs, and a brass lever—which looked a cross between a light switch and a joystick—was set into a recessed brass panel on the front of the compartment. Tarnished tubing, which might have been copper, ran from the top of the brass chamber to a small glass ring set atop the scope's main barrel. Diane was fascinated. She had never seen anything like it.

She had gingerly picked up the odd apparatus and headed toward the register at the front of the grand front parlor, where a petite middle-aged woman was handling sales.

"Do you know anything about this telescope?" Diane asked eagerly. "It's so odd-looking."

The woman smiled. "Oh, yes, I know all about this piece," she replied. "It was made by my great-grandfather, Thomas Conrad, who was the original owner of this house. My father told me all about him. He was a brilliant man who graduated from Harvard with a physics degree and had a distinguished career as a research scientist. He helped make advances in the new fields of the time, from electricity to radiology. He was an astronomy buff, too. After he retired—let's see, I think that would've been around 1920—he started working on a project in the basement. He'd lock himself in his workshop down there for hours on end, and according to my father, he wouldn't tell anyone—including his wife—what he was working on. He spent the better part of a year on it while his health grew progressively worse. The last time my father saw him, his grandfather told him that he was close to a breakthrough, and he promised to show my father what he'd been working on soon."

She suddenly paused, grinning sheepishly. "Sorry. This is probably way more information than you wanted."

Diane shook her head emphatically. "Not at all! It's fascinating. Please continue."

"Okay. Well, one winter night, my great-grandmother awoke quite late to find that her husband still hadn't come to bed. She went down to the basement, ready to give him hell for staying up so late working on that infernal project, but he wasn't there. She eventually found his body in the backyard, under the light of a full moon, lying next to this telescope. She had never seen it before; she realized that it must have been what he was working on in the basement.

She was, of course, devastated. She was sure that his obsession with this device had played a large part in his death. The next day, she asked her son to stash it in the attic, and she forbade anyone to use it. Her children and grandchildren followed her wishes, and it sat up there for over 100 years. But now we're selling the house, and I simply don't have the room to keep a fraction of what's accumulated here."

"That's so sad," Diane said sympathetically. "Your great-grandfather sounds like a fascinating man. I promise I'll take good care of his telescope."

The woman smiled gratefully. "Honestly, I don't know if you'll be able to see much with it."

"Don't worry—I actually have a great one already," Diane reassured her. "I just think this one is so interesting, and what an amazing story behind it! It will make a great focal point in my living room."

Carefully loading her purchase into the back of her little hatchback, Diane had marveled at the serendipity of it. What were the odds she would come across such a thing—and on the night of a supermoon, no less? It certainly was her lucky day.

As darkness began to fall, she placed the odd antique next to her modern telescope, excitement fizzing inside her. Minutes ticked slowly by until the glowing disk of the full moon finally began to emerge from behind the sapphire horizon. With her eye practically glued to her scope's eyepiece, Diane watched in reverence as the spectacular moon began to ascend. It appeared a bit larger than usual, but the most striking thing about it was its brightness—it was almost as if she were watching a sunrise. Rapt, she continued to stare through the powerful lens, drinking in every detail of the dazzling lunar surface. It was *amazing*.

Eventually, she pulled away from her telescope and looked directly at the supermoon, enjoying the magnificent sight. Diane's gaze wandered over her small but private backyard, now bathed in a luminous glow, until it came to rest on the strange old telescope. *Might as well give it a try*, she thought. She peered into the eyepiece at the narrow end of the long brass barrel, angling it until she could see the moon through the other end. It was a good thing she hadn't expected much, because the view was worse than if she had been looking through a cheap pair of binoculars.

She wondered whether the small glass ring on top of the scope's barrel provided a way to focus or zoom in, but there didn't seem to be any way to manipulate it. Then it occurred to her that perhaps this was the purpose of the brass compartment set into the base, since it was connected to the glass ring via the tarnished tubing. She reached down and pulled on the lever protruding from the front of the compartment inside the tripod legs, but it wouldn't budge. Using both hands, she pulled with all her might until it yielded. Then she looked back into the eyepiece, and much to her surprise, she saw a red circle of light perfectly outlining the full moon. *Interesting!* Perhaps Thomas Conrad had been working on a precursor to the laser focusing feature that was now standard on modern telescopes. But the quality of the lunar image inside the red circle of light was unchanged. Maybe Mr. Conrad hadn't had a chance to finish perfecting his invention before he died.

Diane's thoughts were interrupted by a series of whirring and clicking sounds emanating from the brass chamber in the old telescope's base. Then, without warning, a beam of green light burst forth from the glass ring. She shrieked in alarm, jumping away from the scope as the green light shot quickly away in the direction of the moon, then disappeared from view. *What the hell was that?*

Apprehensive but intrigued, she stepped back to the device and cautiously peered into the eyepiece. She found herself looking at the shape of a sphere that appeared to be made of crisscrossing lines, like lattice. She could just make out shadowy shapes that seemed to be inside the latticework sphere. Confused, she pulled away from the old telescope to look up at the full moon, but it didn't appear any different than usual. She looked back into it, but the crisscross sphere with the shadowy shapes had disappeared, and the full moon was back in its place, although it was no longer outlined by a red circle of light. The noises coming from the scope's base had ceased when the green light blasted out of the glass ring, and she saw now that the lever on the front of the brass compartment had returned to the upright position. Diane was utterly mystified. *What had she just seen? What exactly was this strange telescope meant to do?*

Her pounding pulse intertwined with the sounds of the crickets and peepers as she thought about what had just happened. That burst of green light had been like something out of *Star Wars*. Had it been a fluke? Would it happen again if she pulled the lever? What if something even more bizarre occurred? She knew the prudent thing to do would be to leave the device alone and have some kind of expert check it out, but her curiosity got the better of her. "May the force be with me," she said wryly as she pulled down on the lever again.

This time, it yielded without resistance. Looking into the eyepiece, she saw that the red circle of light was again superimposed around the moon. In short time, the whirring and clicking sounds came from the brass compartment. She didn't pull away when the beam of green light was fired from the glass ring in a trajectory toward the supermoon. After a few moments, the image of the moon she saw through the lens seemed to morph into the curious latticework sphere with the vague outlines inside it. She stared at it in wonder until, seconds later, the image faded and was replaced by the familiar face of the moon.

Mind racing, she thought back to what the woman at the estate sale had said about her brilliant great-grandfather. He had studied electricity and radiology. Was the green light that emanated from his telescope meant to show something specific on the lunar surface? And was the red circle that outlined the moon a kind of targeting system for the green light? But how did it relate to the odd gridwork sphere she had seen through the scope after the light was fired? Then it hit her: radiology. *X-rays.* Was it possible that the green light was revealing what was *inside* the moon? But that was a crazy thought. Diane knew that x-rays shouldn't be able to travel that far or get through Earth's atmosphere. Had the brilliant Thomas Conrad managed to figure out a way to propel them to the moon? If so, why would the x-rays show that there was some type of complex artificial structure inside of it? It didn't make any sense.

She wondered whether Mr. Conrad had been trying out his invention for the first time on that winter night under the full moon, just after he'd told his grandson he was close to a breakthrough. Had the light revealed the same latticework sphere she had seen—but he died before he could tell anyone? Whatever was going on, she was going to get to the bottom of it. She wasn't sure who she should contact, but she needed someone to examine the apparatus to determine whether what she suspected was actually true. And if it was, well…then that would mean the moon was not what it appeared to be at all.

Hands shaking, she reached for her phone, wondering who to call first. She paused to glance up at the glorious supermoon, wondering if she would ever look at it the same way again.

In the main monitoring room of the moon station, Sagia averted his three amber eyes from the grisly image of the woman's charred remains. "Our ancestors would be ashamed of us," he said sadly in the sing-song language of the Jakrins.

"Our ancestors would have understood that we had no choice but to protect ourselves," replied Geiwan, a respected elder. There were murmurs of agreement from the crowd gathered in front of the primary viewing screen.

The thirst for knowledge had always been an intrinsic part of the Jakrin race and was the driving force behind their society.

Throughout their history, the Jakrins had sent out research probes that travelled all over the universe and gathered data on any planets they encountered. The information was transmitted back to Jakri, where the planet's inhabitants eagerly reviewed and catalogued it in their underground cities. All of the data was housed in an immense electronic library that was the pride and joy of the Jakrins.

When one of the probes sent back information from a distant planet (which would eventually be called 'Earth' by its inhabitants), the Jakrins realized that they had a unique opportunity. The probe showed the existence of an intelligent species that, while still primitive, appeared to possess the potential for great advancement. Having only found civilizations on two other planets previously—both of which were already highly advanced—the Jakrins were elated. Here was a chance to watch the evolution of an intelligent species from almost its infancy.

When they reviewed the probe's data on the large moon orbiting the planet, the residents of Jakri decided it would provide the perfect place for a station where they could directly observe the development of the planet's inhabitants. The moon was close enough for video monitoring, but far enough away to ensure that the species they were observing would be unaware of their presence. Plans were devised to excavate a large portion of the moon, where a small-scale version of a Jakrin city would be built to serve as home to a permanent research colony. A giant sphere made from an interlocking framework of super-strong metal beams would surround the city inside the moon. It would be developed using the same methods that their ancestors had used to create the intricate web of underground cities on Jakri long ago, when the deterioration of the planet's surface conditions had forced its inhabitants to forge a subterranean existence.

Three enormous Jakrin ships containing materials, engineers, and the future colonists—who were picked using a lottery system due to the abundance of volunteers—were sent for construction of the moon city. To the occupants of the planet below, the ships looked like glowing triangles of colorful lights floating next to the moon. People around the world gazed upon them with a mixture of awe and fear, certain that the strange lights were gods. Ceremonies were held and sacrifices were made in an attempt to please the mysterious deities. The Egyptians, believing these new gods were children of Khonsu, their moon god, began planning construction of a series of colossal pyramids to pay them homage.

Almost two years after the ships arrived, construction of the moon city was completed. The engineers returning to Jakri were transferred directly from the new city onto the waiting ships, leaving the colonists safely installed in their new home. Robotic apparatus removed all traces of the excavation from the lunar surface before the ships departed—a precaution taken in case the simple beings on the blue world ever became advanced enough to visit their planet's satellite.

The colony inside the moon thrived. Their new city had everything they needed, from vast food-growing greenhouses to cavernous virtual reality halls for entertainment and exercise. Honored to be the first of their kind entrusted to carry out the most important research mission in their history, the colonists threw themselves into analyzing and documenting the avalanche of data pouring in from thousands of video feeds streaming images from around the world below them. They were baffled by humans' greed and their never-ending battles for power—clear markers of how truly primitive this species was—but inspired by the constant acts of kindness and love that they witnessed. All of their findings were sent to Jakri. In response, messages of thanks and encouragement flooded in to the colonists, who were considered heroes on their home planet.

And then the unthinkable happened. Six years after construction of the moon station, the colonists received a garbled communication from Jakri. Amidst the sounds of explosions and screaming, a frantic voice conveyed the horrifying truth: a massive asteroid had slammed into the planet and carved an immense chasm into it. Their delicate web of interconnected subterranean cities was collapsing, and their ships could not get free of the badly damaged underground hangers. There was no way for any of the Jakrins to escape the escalating devastation. The message had abruptly gone dead. It was the last time they ever heard from their home.

Stunned and devastated, the lunar colonists had mourned for Jakri. Everyone they had known and loved was gone—their entire civilization erased, the library with all their precious data from the reaches of the galaxy destroyed. They were completely alone now, the last of their kind. Bereft but determined, they vowed to carry on with their mission. They would begin building a new library consisting of all the information they gathered from the planet below. The Jakrin legacy would live on.

And for thousands of years, that's exactly what they had done. One generation after the next had observed in fascination as the humans continued to make mistakes and advancements, unaware they were being watched over.

Until Thomas Conrad had, shockingly, revealed the moon city's existence with his x-ray invention.

Sagia thought back to that day when the city's sensors had detected x-ray beams from Earth sweeping over the city. The Jakrins had stared at each other in disbelief. Humans had only recently discovered the existence of x-rays! The technology needed to x-ray the moon should have been hundreds, perhaps thousands, of years away.

"Where is it coming from?" his father had demanded, a note of panic in his voice that the young Sagia had never heard before. The x-rays' point of origin was quickly determined, and when one of the video monitors zoomed in on the location, they saw an old man on his knees, clutching his chest as he collapsed to the ground and lay still. He was clearly dead, and Sagia felt pity for him; humans were so delicate and had such a brief lifespan compared to the Jakrins. Beside the old man was an archaic telescope, but it looked very different than others they had seen. "He must have figured out how to make that telescope send x-rays to look inside the moon!" Sagia's father had exclaimed in amazement.

When the x-ray scope was carried into what was presumably the deceased old man's home the next day, the inhabitants of the moon city were greatly relieved—but the seed of fear had been planted. It was agreed that a defensive system needed to be developed in case the x-ray telescope was used again, or something similar was invented that could reveal the moon city's existence. For if the humans found out there was something inside the moon, they would surely come to investigate as soon as they figured out how to travel there. And by the Jakrins' estimates, humans were likely to develop that technology in the near future.

Sagia had been terrified by the possibility, imagining a fleet of ships from Earth arriving at his home and drilling into the moon to figure out what was inside of it. What if their city was destroyed the way those on Jakri had been decimated by the asteroid so long ago? And yet it seemed wrong to him to take any action against the humans, even in the name of self-defense. They were never meant to harm anyone on the planet. But he did not dare to express this opinion to his father or anyone else, and the Jakrins set to work on creating a laser that could be aimed with pinpoint precision to neutralize any future threats while causing minimal damage. And because the laser was invisible, no one on Earth would be able to determine who or what was behind it.

Decades had subsequently ticked past without any need to employ the laser. The x-ray device remained in the house it had been carried into, and no other threats arose. Even when the humans reached the moon with their Apollo missions, there was never any real concern; the moon city's residents knew that their ancestors had covered all traces of construction on the lunar surface, and the astronauts walking on it had no reason to suspect the city's existence. Even as the twenty-first century began, humans still had no way to determine the truth about what was inside their moon. Their ideas about its composition were pure conjecture based on laughably simplistic tools including gravitational readings from old weather satellites that they used to infer the moon's internal structure. The Jakrins were easily able to manipulate those readings to give the illusion that the moon was completely solid.

But today, everything had changed. The residents of the moon city had gasped when their video feed showed a woman carrying the x-ray device out of the house it had been in for so long. They tracked her movements, hoping she would not try or not be able to figure out how to use it. But she had succeeded in making it work, as evidenced by the sensors, which showed that x-rays were repeatedly penetrating the moon city. And for the first time, the Jakrins used the laser they had developed all those years ago to destroy the x-ray telescope and kill the woman using it before she could tell anyone what she had seen. They had taken a human life in order to protect themselves. It made Sagia sick.

Geiwan took Sagia aside. "I feel terrible about this too, Sagia. But we had no choice. Take heart from the fact that this invention was a fluke, the product of a human whose mind was generations ahead of his fellow men. Now that we've destroyed it, we will be safe for a long time. Perhaps there will never be a need to use the weapon again."

At an emergency meeting in a bunker under the White House, Secretary of Homeland Security Flaherty looked grim. "Madam President, we've confirmed that the source of the intense heat detected by our thermal imaging satellite was a laser fired from the moon. As I mentioned when we spoke earlier, the heat signature was on a trajectory to Connecticut. I just heard back from the team we sent to the location, and they found a badly charred body—apparently a random victim who had been alone in their yard when the beam was fired. Nothing else was hit except a metal object next to the victim. This was clearly a limited test of the weapon, most likely conducted to determine its range and accuracy."

"Who the hell built a moon laser without us knowing about it?" President Denney demanded.

"We can't say with absolute certainty, ma'am, but we suspect that ISIS is behind it," said Secretary Flaherty. "They are by far the most well-funded terrorist group, and both Homeland Security and the Department of Defense have heard rumors that they've been working on an advanced cloaking technology. That would explain how they constructed the weapon without detection. And as you know, in recent weeks we've been picking up increased chatter about a potential terrorist attack, but with no details on the target or method." He paused. "Madame President, whether it's ISIS or not, whoever is behind this weapon doesn't know that we were able to identify the source. The beam is invisible—it didn't show up on any satellite images—and we've kept our thermal imagery scan technology entirely under wraps. That gives us an advantage, but only if we act now, before they can launch a large-scale attack."

The president considered this. "Where are we with the risk analysis of using Armageddon?"

"Our scientists just finished running the computer models, and they show that the moon would be obliterated into small particles. The vast majority of these would be blown far enough away from Earth to be pulled into its gravity and form a ring. A small percentage of these particles may make it into our atmosphere and burn up, but the models show that any resulting elevation in the Earth's temperature would not be life-threatening," replied Secretary Flaherty.

President Denney nodded, relieved by the good news. "And what about the long-term risks? The tides, for instance?" she inquired.

The secretary shook his head. "The scientists have advised that the long-term implications are much more difficult to predict, ma'am, and the computer models do not agree with one another. The loss of the tides would certainly take a toll on plant and animal life, but to what extent is unknown. The ultimate effects on Earth's orbit and its axial tilt cannot be determined with any accuracy, but those effects wouldn't unfold for thousands of years."

"So…are you saying that if we do this, the planet may eventually become uninhabitable?" she asked tersely.

"That cannot be ruled out, Madam President. But we're talking about unknown repercussions in the distant future, and we are facing an immediate, catastrophic threat. The potential loss of life and devastation to the United States—and perhaps the entire planet—are immeasurable if we don't take action to protect ourselves now."

President Denney rubbed her temples, feeling the weight of the impossible position she was in. No one had ever contemplated using Armageddon on the moon, for god's sake.

Its development had been unplanned, the product of a breakthrough in physics by a genius who was a researcher for the Department of Defense. All work on the project had been done with the utmost secrecy. The resulting Armageddon bomb was half the size of a nuclear warhead but infinitely more powerful. It could never be used on the planet, but it would offer the perfect defense against any future hazardous asteroids on a collision course with Earth.

What if the computer models were wrong, and the moon's destruction spelled an immediate death sentence for Earth? And even if the short-term ramifications were not severe, would the planet become inhospitable to life far in the future? Yet if she didn't act now, she'd be allowing her country and the rest of the world to become sitting ducks for a weapon of mass destruction.

At length, she nodded resignedly. "Do it," she ordered. "And may God help us."

Stargazers around the world continued to revel in the sight of the stunning supermoon, oblivious to what was about to happen, unaware it would be the last time they'd ever see the moon gracing the sky. The people of Earth would never know the truth about the beings who had watched over them for so long. And in a cruelly ironic twist, the Jakrins would be erased without leaving behind a single shred of evidence that they had ever existed.

Leigh Statham

IN DESPERATE NEED OF A MANICURE

Drew pulled down on her bottom lip. Black dots of ink lay in the pink flesh like bugs burrowed in for the winter. The pain had decreased, and her lip was almost a normal size again, but the ink remained: numbers and letters scrawled upside down inside her mouth to make it easier for the cadets to read, easier to classify, easier to contain. F9803GH—she tried to memorize the sequence. She didn't know why, but it seemed like a good idea to know the code tattooed on the inside of your lip.

"Hurry up in there. Lights out in five," a rough male voice barked. His nightstick banged on the tiled entryway to the bathroom of her once-high-school-now-turned-detention-center. The cadets assured them all it was a contained protection zone, but Drew knew better. They couldn't leave and they were shuffled around like inmates.

This was a prison.

Talk spread of co-ed bathrooms in the new facility. That scared Drew more than anything else the other people gossiped about. The bathroom was her one refuge, the only place she could be away from the cadets, and if she could get a stall with a locking door, she could be away from everyone else as well. She let her lip fall back to her teeth and stared at her gaunt face. The flickering fluorescent lights cast a green glow on everything, including her hair, turning the once light brown to the murky color of stagnant water. She still remembered when girls her age would giggle into these mirrors and apply colors to their cheeks and lips. Makeup to even the adolescent skin tones, smooth the red spots into brown and beige and cream, lipstick painting their lips to draw a kiss from a boy. She snorted at the thought. How many of those bright red lips got more than they'd bargained for from those kisses? And even though she had successfully avoided any disease, her identifying tattoo made her lip redder and more swollen than any lipstick or eager kiss ever could.

Drew turned away from her ghoulish reflection and took a deep breath before heading into the hallway. Another night lay ahead with her yellow striped blanket on the floor of a classroom that used to be flowing with life but now occluded it.

The disease crept like a forest fire—the population, a stand of dead trees waiting to be picked off and destroyed. Luckily, just like the flames that licked the branches from trees, it tore through the community quickly. There was no drama, no zombified aunts and uncles stumbling around begging for a cure. One day your fingernails fell off, the next day you were dead.

Experts determined the epicenter to be Chicago, four hours north of their small Indiana town. Drew was one of the first to be identified as immune. Her whole family was wiped out in the initial wave of illness. She'd spent the first week alone in her house with their bodies, the smell intensifying as she alternated between sleep and utter despair. She'd kept checking her fingers habitually, willing the nail beds to give up their shields and confirm her imminent death as well. Eventually the cadets came through on random checks and found her emaciated and alone in a cloud of human rot. The bodies of her long-dead family members lying in their beds, decomposing and gaseous. Drew had covered them with sheets, their gray, oozing hands reverently folded over their chests, the skin swollen and slowly sloughing off, the nails sometimes still on the floor or bed. Her own nails were chewed to the quicks.

Three months later, living as a prisoner in her old high school, they still hadn't fallen off.

Drew made her way down the dark hallway. The glow of a rising moon came down through the skylight, trickled in from beneath closed doors, and left patches of silver on the dirty tile floor. She didn't want to go back to her assigned sleeping area. The old man in the corner stank like piss and cigarettes, even though no one smoked anymore, and everyone else snored. There were a few other girls her age, but she didn't want to know them. They were from neighboring towns, the same wide-eyed shock plastered to their faces as Drew saw on her own in the mirror.

The days since she'd arrived felt like an eternity, but she was starting to wake up from her fog. She was trying to accept the fact that she was still alive. She tried to convince herself that she had a life ahead of her, had choices—only none of that was true. Yes, she was alive, but there were no choices.

"Hey," a voice hissed from a classroom to her left.

The lights were off in the room. She couldn't quite make out the speaker's face, but the voice was young, familiar.

"Drew, is that you?"

It was a boy, someone she knew. She couldn't place the voice or the outline of his head in this strange setting.

She stepped hesitantly toward the speaker. "Yes, it's me. Who are you?"

"Hell, yes! I thought that was you. I saw you earlier today. Hurry, get inside." He reached out and grabbed her arm, pulling her into the darkened room.

Drew's heart began to race, the hairs on the back of her neck dancing and quivering. Fear gripped her as her eyes adjusted to the din, and she glanced around quickly. There was no one else in the room, just this boy and Drew—completely unprepared to defend herself. She backed away, shaking off his grasp but knocked into a desk. The loud screech, cutting the silence in the room and down the hallway, made them both jump.

"Shhh! It's me, Josh DeSpain. Geeze! You're going to bring the whole pack down on us."

"Josh who?" Drew said.

"From Honors Chemistry. Don't you remember me? Front row? Glasses?"

Drew felt like he was talking about another lifetime. When did she ever think something like Honors Chemistry would be a useful way to spend her time?

"Do you have the shocks or something? Did the cadets get to you?" Josh took a step closer to her, reaching out a hand. A beam of light from the room across the hall hit his face and revealed cracked, black glasses, freckles and messy blonde hair.

Josh.

She did remember him. He was a huge nerd, always knew all the answers. He'd said hello to her sometimes, but she ignored him. She'd been too busy daydreaming about cheer practice and hooking up with Joe Michelin.

"I remember you," Drew answered.

"Sweet. I knew you would. How could you forget DeSpain the Brain?" He chuckled.

"Right." Drew was still trying to acclimate herself to the old reality crashing into the new when he started rattling off his plans.

"So, I was getting ready to bolt this place, but then I saw you. I thought I'd see if you wanted to come with me," he said as he shoved his hands in his pockets and tipped his head to one side, looking from her face to the floor and then the wall.

Drew watched him speak, like she was in a movie theater and he was on the screen presenting some fantasy that she could slip into with buttered popcorn and a Coke.

"I heard a rumor that down the river, in Hamstead, there's a group of regular citizens running the show. I'm pretty sure if you stay here, they are going to turn you into a breeder, which wouldn't be bad if we were paired up, but, yah, didn't think that was your dream come true, so I thought—Hey! Why not spring her, too?" His smile was almost infectious. How could he be in a place like this and smile?

"Breeder?" she asked, finally registering his meaning.

"Yah, that's why they are keeping the immune locked up here. Going to try to get the population jump started again with a breeding program." He let his voice drop and sounded almost embarrassed this time. No jokes about the two of them hooking up.

Drew remembered a girl at school last year who got pregnant. Her friends all told her to have an abortion, but she insisted on keeping it. Her belly swelled over the next few months, stretching her clothes and slowing her stride. Her friends gradually slipped away and her boyfriend, an older guy, disappeared altogether. Drew wondered if the girl or her baby had made it. She wondered if the girl regretted being a breeder or if she'd had time to enjoy the tiny fingers and toes and cries in the night.

Drew would give anything to hear her little sister cry in the night now. Or to hear her father singing Simon and Garfunkle in the shower, or even to hear her mom yelling for her to hurry up, they were late for school. Instead, all she could hear were cadets down the hall rounding the last wandering souls up for bedtime check in and the beating of her heart in her chest.

"You think you can climb out?" Josh pointed to an open window to the courtyard. A chair was pushed up to the ledge.

Drew looked out the window and let the rush of his words settle.

She'd heard the same rumors; that the school was being prepped as a baby mill. The cadets were going to save the human race. That was definitely not something she wanted to be a part of, but until now, there had been no other option. Sure. She'd go with Josh the Brain Whoever and die in the woods. It was better than being forced to have sex with that smelly old man in her assigned bunk room.

"Why not, Josh."

He looked like his face was going to split in half, a huge toothy smile dividing it.

"Yes! I knew you'd come. I knew I'd be the hero in this story. As soon as I saw you, I thought: that is my calling in this messed up world, to save Drew Orwell. Thank God you're not totally nutso like the rest of them. Let's get going! I have a pack with some food and water. Can't waste any time."

He reached out for her hand, and she let him take it.

What did it matter? Live here, die there, it didn't matter.

He pulled her gently toward him, but she stumbled around a desk. Her hand slipped out of his; a strange pain pricked her finger. She stared through the shadows to the spot at the end where it hurt.

She looked at Josh the Brain. He was staring at his own hand. The light of the moon fell perfectly on his palm, illuminating a single fingernail.

Stephanie Bedwell-Grime

LOVE THY NEIGHBOR

Mabel fumbled for the keyhole in the darkness. Her fingertips touched cold metal. With her nail, she found an indentation. She shoved the key in what she thought was the right direction and heard it grind into the rusted lock. It turned, just barely and then stuck.

For a fleeting moment, the full moon escaped the heavy cloud. She glanced up at the light above the door, finding the old glass shattered. The broken bulb within hung like jagged teeth, its filaments waving in the wind. The clouds picked that moment to smother the moon's light again, leaving her in darkness.

Standing alone on the porch of an abandoned house in the dark was not the smartest idea. Wind ripped through the old neighborhood with little to stop it. Most of the porch lights were out, her neighbors having moved on long ago.

Once in a while, in the rosy glow of the setting sun, she could still catch a glimpse of the neighborhood's former grandeur. Stately old houses stood where they'd always been. Daylight revealed the cruel truth. Dried up lawns were taken over by weeds. Empty driveways collected trash and anything else that blew in on the wind. Boarded up windows covered broken glass.

Something crunched in the brush behind her. Likely an animal, but she didn't wait to find out. Leaning on the key with all her strength, she finally convinced the old lock to cooperate. The door swung open, and she tumbled inside.

Scrambling to her feet, Mabel slammed the door shut and eased the old bolt back into place. She stood in the darkness, listening. The heavy door muffled the sound of whatever was outside. Animal or human, unless it wanted to break a window, it wasn't getting inside.

She'd intended to come armed with a flashlight, but the batteries in her old torch had picked that night to die. An unforeseen complication, but she'd already promised her former neighbor's son that she'd go next door and fire up the furnace and turn on the lights. It seemed he'd finally sold the old place, and her new neighbors would be arriving soon. He lived out of town and wouldn't be able to do it himself. Would she mind? One last favor for an old friend? He'd already made the arrangements before he'd asked, playing on her loyalty to his late mother. It irked her that people found her so predictable and took advantage of it.

Her relationship with her neighbor's son had never been easy. Though Ada had given her child an angel's name, Zachariel, the kid had been trouble. His formative years had been a nightmare. With his father traveling most of the time, the discipline was left to Ada, who clearly wasn't up to task.

Zach had gotten himself kicked out of school. He'd snuck out of the house at night. He'd come home in the back of a police cruiser more times than Mabel could count.

As he grew older, his misdeeds became darker and more clandestine. Small animals began disappearing from the neighborhood. Lost cat posters appeared on lamp posts. Mabel voiced her concerns to Ada, but her friend had never been able to see her son's shortcomings. But when Mabel caught him torturing a squirrel, she knew the truth.

None of Ada's attempts to rein in her son had worked. Eventually, he'd grown from a troubled child to a troubled adult. And still Ada refused to see her son's darker side.

Isn't it wonderful how often he visits me, she'd remarked. Mabel knew those visits were only excuses to extort money from his forgetful mother.

Eventually Zach had moved away, leaving Mabel and Ada to continue their friendship in peace.

Feeling along the wall, Mabel located the light switch and flipped it on. The small click it made sounded unusually loud in the silence, but the lights didn't come on. Damn. Wanting to save on electricity, Zach had turned off the main power. Now she'd have to go looking for the breaker box.

Mabel's house was similar in layout to Ada's, but that didn't mean she could find the power box in a pitch-black basement. Still, she'd made a promise...

With a very unladylike curse, she felt her way along the wall to the kitchen and the door that led to the basement.

She moved across the floor with the confidence of someone who'd been in this kitchen hundreds of times. Only to collide full force with something large and heavy. Her knee throbbed with the impact. The idiot son had moved the table. Instead of against the wall where it had always been, it was now sitting in the middle of the floor. Now, why would he do that, besides to cripple an old woman in the dark? Maybe he'd done his best to stage the place. It had taken him forever to sell. She bent down to rub her knee. With a bang like that, it would be bruised and swollen tomorrow. But all she needed to do was turn on the furnace and the lights, and her job would be done.

Skirting the table, she walked more cautiously, hands out in front of her and feeling with her feet for any other obstacles that might cause her further damage.

She found the basement door without further incident. Her hand closed on the doorknob. It opened with a screech that made her jump. Apparently Zach hadn't sprung for oil for the hinges.

She put her weight gingerly onto the first step, gripping the banister so hard she could feel the grain in the wood. It creaked ominously, but it held, so she began moving slowly downward.

Anything could be waiting for her at the bottom of the stairs. She tried to blot that thought from her mind. Still, the house had been vacant for years. Squirrels, raccoons and even rats might be nesting down there, hoping to find a warm place to winter.

Nothing had come racing up the stairs toward her. She stopped on the bottom stair and listened into the silence. For a second, she thought she heard something rustling off in one of the corners until it fell silent. A squirrel or a raccoon she could handle. Anything bigger, not so much.

Best thing was to get the lights on, then she'd know what she was dealing with. If an animal had made the basement its home, it was the new neighbors' problem.

She moved out onto the open floor, hoping for her knee's sake that Zach hadn't left anything sitting in the middle of the basement.

It was hard to judge the distance in the dark. She didn't even know if she was moving in the right direction. She tried to keep the layout of her own house in mind and moved cautiously to where she thought the far wall and the breaker box would be.

The concrete wall seemed to rear up out of nowhere. She reeled back. Now she'd probably have a black eye to show for her adventure as well.

Again, she heard that rustling in the far corner. She had to find that power box, if only to be able to navigate her way out of there so she could tell Zach to handle it all himself.

Putting out her hands, she felt along the wall in what she hoped was the right direction. After a few minutes of fumbling, her hands closed on cold metal. She located the main power switch and threw it.

Light arced across the basement. There was only a bare bulb in the basement ceiling, but still the sudden light brought tears to her eyes. On the edge of her vision something moved. Something dark, skittering just out of view.

And then it vanished, leaving only an empty basement.

Mabel blinked at the spectacle. The basement had been choked to the brim with the remnants of her neighbor's life. Pretty much all of it. Tossing something in the garbage was an alien concept to Ada. Old clothes, old newspapers, old furniture, a forlorn Christmas tree from decades past had filled the basement to its rafters. She suppressed a smile. Must have taken Zach quite a while to clean it out. What she'd seen must have been a shadow. There was nothing left in the basement except for the wheezing old furnace.

She turned to study the furnace. Once it had been new. She remembered when Ada had bought it, how proud she was to have something so modern.

The basement hadn't been so cluttered then. Instead, the detritus of Ada's life merely clung to the edges of the floors, climbing the walls on occasion. Back then the new furnace had risen from the floor, a gleaming icon of modern invention.

Now the furnace lay beneath a thick layer of dust. Wires spilled from its insides across the floor. She could see where just about every working part had been replaced. Ada's son would never have paid to replace it, not when he could keep the appliance working with a cheap repair job.

Mabel crouched before the furnace. Well, it certainly didn't look so shiny new now. She peered at it in the dim light from the overhead bulb. Of course the pilot light was out. Nothing about this reluctant favor was going to be easy.

It took her a few minutes to find a box of matches. At first she'd feared she'd have to make the trek back to her own house, but it seemed Zach had left one useful thing in the basement after all. She crouched before the furnace again. Her bones creaked as she lowered herself. Every muscle protested as she maintained that position. It wasn't getting down that was hard, she thought grimly, it was getting up again.

The furnace loomed above her. She lit the match and fed it into the breach. She felt a breeze, and the flame died. There was only one window in the basement, same as at her house. She shot a furtive glance at the dark pane. Closed. Mabel reached for another match. This time the flame extinguished before she even got it near the furnace.

Mabel took a nervous glance around. She didn't see anything in the basement. Not even the shadow she thought she'd seen earlier. Her legs shrieked in protest for forcing them to maintain such an unusual position. One more. If this match didn't get the pilot light lit, she was turning around and going home to inform the no-good son he was going to need a furnace repairman as well.

She fed the match to the furnace.

To her surprise, the flame caught and the old furnace wheezed to life.

It began with a hiss and a flare. Then came a series of loud knocks as if something inside were trying to fight its way out. A plume of dust shot from the side of the thing, narrowly missing her face. Another loud bang and tepid air began wheezing through the vents.

Mabel gripped the sides of the contraption and crawled her way up its side until she stood on unsteady feet. One of her legs had gone to sleep, and she stamped it to bring back the feeling.

There. She'd gotten the furnace lit. The power was back on. She'd helped Ada's son out of a sense of duty to her departed friend. Now she was going home to sit in her own house. She cast a nervous glance around the basement. If the power went out or the furnace died, that was Zach's problem to deal with. She took a step toward the stairs.

And that's when she saw it. Curled in the nest of wires lay the dusty remains of a small animal. Mostly bones now, it had definitely been there for a very long time. She thought of all the neighborhood animals that had gone missing years ago. Is this where they'd ended up?

Ada's son had cleaned up the basement, hiding the evidence of his cruelty. With the furnace in such a mess, it would have been easy to miss something. Or had he left it as a last taunt, knowing that she knew his dark secret and there was nothing she could do about it?

Above her, the basement door slammed shut. The force shook the house and brought a shriek to her lips. Mabel limped toward the staircase, moving as fast as she could on legs that protested every movement.

Overhead, the single light bulb flickered and went out. Its filament glowed in the darkness before that meager light was gone as well.

Her shin hit the first stair, toppling her forward. She bit back a yelp as her hands hit the rough wood of the stair above her.

At least she'd found the stairs. If nothing else, that stopped her from wandering around in the dark. She bent to rub her shin before beginning to climb.

The furnace wheezed and grunted, spewing dusty air throughout the house. Beneath that sound, she thought she heard the soft sound of something breathing. She froze on the stairway, listening.

There was nothing down there, she told herself. She'd seen the entire basement in the light. Nothing but an old furnace the new neighbors would surely replace and the carcass of a long-dead animal. The sound she thought she'd heard was just the whisper of air in the ducts.

She lurched another step upward in the darkness, hands stretched before her to find the door. Yet there it was again, the soft sound of something breathing. Panting with anticipation.

Putting every ounce of speed she could muster into her aching muscles, she scrambled up another couple of steps. A thick sliver stabbed into her palm. She felt the stickiness of blood against her fingers. Below her, the panting ceased and then began again with renewed vigor.

Heedless of her bleeding hand, she crawled up another step. The door had to be there somewhere. She felt around wildly in the darkness. Her questing hands met only air.

Another drop of blood splashed on the wooden stairs. Ada's son would have to clean that up. No way was she coming back here. That is, if she made it out alive.

That thought brought her to her feet. Feeling ahead of her, she lurched for the top step. Her bloody hand closed on the doorknob. It spun beneath her hand, but didn't open. She raised her other hand and hammered on the door as hard as she could.

Down below her in the basement, the tempo of the panting increased.

It was the blood, she realized suddenly. The blood on her palm. She gripped the doorknob with her other hand. The knob spun a little before the friction from her good hand kicked in. And still it stuck. As though someone on the other side was holding it.

In the basement, the panting quickened with delight.

Mabel leaned on the doorknob, putting all her strength into making it turn. It stuck again. She shoved against the door, using her ample hips as leverage.

With a pop, the door sprang open, spilling her into the kitchen.

Cautiously, she got to her feet and took stock. The lights were still on in the kitchen. The old bulb in the basement had finally burned out, that was all. The ancient furnace wheezed on, circulating warm, dusty air throughout the house. She looked back at the blood on the basement steps. She shut the basement door, leaving a bloody smear against the white paint.

She was cut, bruised and every muscle ached. It was late, she was tired, she'd been terrified, and she wanted nothing more than a cup of tea and a biscuit before bed. Instead, she'd gone on this fool mission. And for what? As a favor for a no-good son who hadn't done a thing for his mother while she was alive. It should have been him down there in the basement.

And that gave her an idea…

Limping and dripping blood, she headed for the door, leaving the lights on. No more staggering around in the dark. Looking back, she noticed her bleeding hand left a trail of crimson droplets across the floor. Zach could clean that up. Once she was out of there, that was it. No way was she coming back.

She locked the door and left the key under a long-dead potted plant, as he'd instructed her to.

The short distance between the houses seemed to stretch forever in the darkness. Mabel took one last look at her neighbor's house and shuddered. She couldn't think about it right now, not until she was safely holed up in her own home with all the doors and windows locked and the lights on.

Blood dripped into her sink, leaving bright splashes against the porcelain. She ran her hand under the water until it ran clear and then extracted the large sliver with an ancient pair of tweezers. After dumping some disinfectant onto the wound, she wrapped it in gauze and went to boil the kettle.

Sitting at her own kitchen table, she took stock of her injuries. Blood from the cut on her hand leaked through her awkwardly assembled bandage. She had a wicked bruise on her knee and one forming on her cheek. And all of this for a son who'd considered his aging mother an inconvenience.

Mabel considered her adventure in the basement. She *had* seen something down there. Sure, age weighed on her the same as it had her friend, but she wasn't senile yet. Not like…

She thought back to Ada's last days. Ada's decline had been sudden and rapid. One day it seemed Ada had been full of life, the next bedridden. Mabel had brought soup and biscuits, but Ada had refused to eat a bite. She'd raved of things crawling the walls, of something evil lurking in the basement. Mabel had assumed she'd been delirious. Now she wasn't so sure.

Luckily, Ada had said, her son was there on one of his rare visits. He would take care of everything. The next day Zach had informed Mabel her help was no longer needed. Very soon after that, Ada died.

Mabel paused, the tea halfway to her lips. She put the cup down and reached for her phone. A landline, of course. She had no need to carry one of those small things with her. She didn't go anywhere, and she couldn't read what was on the screen anyway. Slowly, she punched in the number. Ada's son's phone picked up, but predictably, the call went to voice-mail. He'd just be expecting confirmation that she'd done his bidding like a good neighbor. Good old girl and all that. She had a surprise coming. She waited for the beep and left him a very different message. *Basement lights were out, no idea what the problem was. Something wrong with the furnace. Should probably check it out. Oh, and, cut myself in the basement. A lot of blood to clean up. I'm just an old lady. I couldn't possibly do it myself. You should probably see to it before the neighbors arrive…*

Mabel got up with the sun the next morning—just in case. She didn't want to miss a thing. She made tea and sat by her window, waiting. But Zach didn't show. Figures, she thought stirring her tea slowly, that kind of son wouldn't dirty his own hands. She stayed by the window anyway, watching, waiting.

By the time night fell, she'd eaten a sandwich and drunk countless cups of tea. She was just about to give up and go to bed, thinking Zach wasn't going to come, when she saw headlights light up her neighbor's driveway.

Mabel pressed her face against the glass and peered into the darkness. Sure enough, it was Ada's son. He got out of his car and reached into the back for a toolbox. Straightening, he cast an unhappy glance at her window. If he saw her, he made no outward sign, merely shrugged deeper into his coat and walked toward the house.

The sight of him brought a fresh wave of anger washing over her. The child Ada had longed for had turned out to be the greatest heartache of her life. Yet there he was. And Ada was gone. Ada had loved her son to the last, despite everything he'd done.

Mabel's conscience nagged at her. Zach was Ada's son, after all. No matter what she thought about him personally, she couldn't let him go into that house. Grabbing her sweater, she limped to the door.

The night air had an unexpected bite to it, a warning that winter wasn't far off. She stepped onto the uneven gravel and walked toward the house.

With the lights off, the going was even more treacherous for an old woman. She stopped at the end of the driveway. The full moon's glow cast Zach in shadow against the front door. The silver light illuminated the hard set of his mouth, giving him a determined, almost maniacal look. He appeared to be struggling with the lock the same way she had.

"Stop!" She felt surprisingly winded after the short walk. The breeze stole the sound of her voice. She tried again. "Stop. Don't go into the house."

He heard her this time but didn't turn to face her. "And why shouldn't I go into the house, Mabel?" He gave the door one more shove, and the old frame finally relented. The door popped open. Zach finally turned toward her.

Frozen in his cold stare, she hesitated. What could she say, really? She moved a few steps up the driveway toward him.

"Something's not right in that house. There's something in the basement." It sounded stupid even to her own ears, like the ramblings of an interfering old woman.

"There's nothing in the basement, Mabel. I had it cleaned out."

"I know. But—"

He came a few more steps down the driveway. He towered over her, far taller and more muscular than his father had been. She could understand why Ada had been intimidated by him. Mabel backed up a step.

"But what, Mabel?" She hated the way he used her first name. No respect. An undercurrent of threat ran beneath his over-use of her name.

This was a mistake. She should turn around and go back to her own house and lock the door. Instead, here she was in the cold, wearing only a sweater and trying to reason with her dead neighbor's no-good son.

Her mouth worked. No sound came out.

"I know what you're trying to do, Mabel." His voice dripped with scorn. "You're trying to stop me from selling this house, so you can keep it out of some demented monument to your dead friend. Well, she's gone, Mabel. She's been gone for a long time, or haven't you noticed that? This house has stood abandoned long enough. Finally, it has a buyer. And I'm going to make sure the sale goes through." He looked beyond her at the wan light coming from her own house. Somehow, he managed to turn that glance into a threat as well. "Now go home, Mabel, and stop interfering."

With that, she was dismissed. He turned and strode up the driveway, leaving her shivering in the cold.

"Don't," she said as he put his hand on the doorknob and shoved the door open farther. But he ignored her. The door slammed shut behind him.

She should go back to her own house and pretend none of this happened. Mabel stared at the closed door. But despite his many failings, he was still Ada's son and she had to stop him, if only for Ada's sake.

An icy wind circled down her back. Mabel pulled her sweater tighter. It wasn't meant for weather like this, but she'd only intended to be out for a few moments. It hadn't occurred to her Zach wouldn't listen to her. Then again, he'd never listened to anyone. With a sigh, Mabel tugged her sweater tighter still and limped up the stairs to the front door.

The doorknob refused to turn under her hand. Zach must have locked it behind him. She decided the likelihood of him opening the door if she knocked wasn't very high.

Mabel left the front porch and began skulking along the side of the house.

She'd gone no more than a few steps when her ankle turned on the gravel driveway. She bit back a yelp and kept limping forward until she reached the side window. Peering above the sill, she could see that the lights were still on inside. She watched Zach cross the kitchen floor and head for the basement.

Mabel hammered on the window. His head jerked up at the sudden noise, searching for the source of the sound. His gaze found her where she stood outside, her nose barely above the windowsill, and he cast a glance of pure annoyance in her direction before continuing down the basement stairs.

For a moment silence reigned.

Mabel imagined his trek downstairs. He must have reached the bottom of the staircase by now. First, he'd go to check the furnace. That would take him about—

A piercing scream split the air.

The scream was followed by an even more harrowing whimper.

Mabel ducked beneath the windowsill. She huddled against the brick, afraid to go limping back along the driveway. Something terrible was happening inside the house. How could she just sit there silently and let it happen?

A lot of terrible things had happened inside that house. Most of them committed by Zach. Ada never could see the dark side of her precious son.

Still, Mabel couldn't just leave, not knowing what had happened.

She peered back above the windowsill, but all she could see was the open basement door. Nothing else looked out of place. Slowly, still favoring her ankle, she crept back along the side of the house.

Zach would have locked the door, of that much she was certain. But when her hand closed around the doorknob's cold metal, the lock sprang open.

For a moment she stood on the threshold, afraid to take the next step and enter the house. She owed it to Ada, she thought, squaring her shoulders. She owed it to Ada to make sure her son wasn't lying in the basement injured.

The open basement door beckoned. Mabel limped toward it.

Warm air gusted from the vents. Whatever Zach had done, the furnace was working. She inched down the stairs, fully expecting to see him lying on the basement floor, bleeding the last of his life into the cement.

Instead she saw nothing, except Zach's toolbox lying open on the floor.

The old furnace chugged away, blasting warm air throughout the house. She searched every corner of the basement and found nothing. Not even the shadow she thought she'd seen earlier.

Hauling herself up the stairs by the banister, she left the basement to do a thorough check of the rest of the house. Her search came up empty.

Mabel pulled her sweater tighter about her body and headed back to her own home.

A couple cups of tea later, she surveyed the house from the safety of her living room. Horrible things had happened in that house. Over the years, the house had witnessed them all. Perhaps the old house had decided to settle the score.

But now the lights were on and the furnace was working. The house looked fresh and new, ready to welcome its new owners.

Lauri Hedman

FINDERS KEEPERS

"Hey there! Are you all right?"

"Yes. Yes, thank you for asking. My sandal just caught on a loose board. I'm fine, though." Darya readjusted the strap on her shoe and glanced at the basket in her hand to be sure nothing had fallen out. In the radiant moonlight, she saw that the face coupled with the voice was an affable one.

The teenager smiled. "Are you alone?" She pulled a cell phone from her jacket pocket and glanced at it, then frowned. "At almost midnight? A woman your age…alone?" The brilliant moon slid into a pocket of clouds casting about all sorts of ambiguous shadows.

"A woman of my age? Oh, the candor of youth!" Darya chuckled.

The girl was not alone. They were a group of five with rainbow shades and varying lengths of hair. Three, including the spokesperson, wore leggings and combat boots and graffiti-splattered t-shirts under leather jackets. The other two also wore boots but paired with dresses: a white, diaphanous one kissing the ground and a black, skintight one hugging the hip. They seemed a motley but oddly harmonious crew. Nothing to be feared. Darya did not ask why a group of young ladies would be gallivanting around on a nearly deserted beach at midnight. She had done that herself at their age. She understood.

She gave the girl a sincere smile. "Yes, I'm alone. I like to sit close to the sea when the moon is full and bright. I just let its midnight beams wash over me while I listen to the waves roll in. It makes me feel…whole…and, uh, *young* again."

This time they all chuckled.

"Well, just be careful, okay? You never know who's lurking about out here. And weird things happen, ya know."

"Oh, yes. I know. I've done this countless times. Have a good rest of night." Darya turned and continued toward the coast, knowing that in just a few more steps the irritable scritch of old boards would give way to the cozy squish of pliable sand. The girls' footfalls became fainter and Darya glanced over her shoulder—wishing them well—then turned her attention back to her own path.

After a few minutes she reached the end of the weathered boardwalk and set her basket at its edge. She tottered a bit as she lifted her right leg, reached around, and slid the leather sandal strap over her heel toward the center of her sole. With some difficulty, she tugged off the shoe and set it atop the blanket in the basket. She swayed a bit as she bent and pulled her left ankle to her right knee and jiggled off the other shoe. With a sharp exhale, she dropped it into the basket on top of its partner. Picking up her load again, Darya stepped off the boardwalk and, with a sigh of utter satisfaction, wiggled her toes into the somewhat itchy, slightly damp, shockingly cool grains of ancient earth. She stood rooted to the spot for a moment—giving thanks for sand, rocks, mud, trees, roots, life, all of it.

A gentle breeze ruffled its fingers through her long silver strands and she relaxed into its tender caresses. She continued on, her indigo sarong whispering against her legs. There must have been a broken, rough reed on her basket. Every once in a while it scratched against the fabric creating a delightfully syncopated rhythm in counterpoint to the now steady beat of the ocean waves which began to lull her senses. The silent but briny belch of the sea permeated the air. There were no lights along the beach, only the steadfast stare of the lustrous moon. And on she strolled.

Darya had lost count of how many sacred moon rituals she had attended and shaped during her seventy-three years. They had begun when she had blossomed into full womanhood—probably right around the age of the young ladies she had just encountered—and had continued with only occasional breaks. Her mother had a friend who considered it her calling to help young women find their way toward communion with their feminine forebears.

Sophia had introduced Darya to the ancient teachings, to the cyclical nature of life, and toward an intentional lifestyle which honored the goddess within and rejected the domination of one gender over or under or against another. Darya learned from other maidens how to embrace the feminine, from mothers how to create seductive and sacred spaces for its life-giving energy, from magas how to honor the thickening and the thinning, and from crones how to balance a pure heart and a strong mind. Never one for the rigid rules of religion or what seemed like the harsh eyes and hard hearts that shot arrows from behind them, Darya felt this way was more natural. Like breath. Like warmth. Like light.

She had wholeheartedly entered these stirring full moon ensembles with intention and reflection. The circles lit by multiple flames of female fire kindled her heart and set her ablaze. But at some point, a decade or two ago, she realized that she also required celestial conclaves like the one tonight. In order to fully honor her spirit, she needed these private trysts between her soul and the moon. They had become the holiest of holies—a place where only she and the great white orb convened. No one else was allowed to enter.

She had been visiting this particular beach on and off for a few years. It wasn't far from the condominium and was quiet and somewhat secluded but with enough nocturnal patrons to make it feel safe. They'd discovered it one night after Murdock—rest his soul—had taken a wrong turn between their favorite Indian restaurant and the condominium. He was adamant that it was the right way. When his blistering curses melted into a convulsive sweat, she had known something was very wrong. She had seen the entrance to the beach and suggested they stop for a walk. Within minutes, he was himself again. Within weeks, they were walking in an entirely different universe, one with a currency of suffering and uncontrollable inflation. That bloody tumor…

Oh, how she missed him! He had adored her. He was the only man she had ever known who respected the braid of reclusive privacy, emotional nudity, and fierce loyalty she had woven into her life. Some boys had attempted to shape her into the socialite they wanted to drape from their suited arms for a time. Others had tried, valiantly, to shame her for the regularity and intensity and "ridiculosity" of her emotions. Only Mur had understood it and had made it his life's mission to embrace and make love to that invisible braid tattooed indelibly on her spine.

She strolled closer to the waves, letting her soles rest on the firmly packed sand. The sea spray was invigorating. Its waves were cool against her legs. The water was not icy but not warm; it was cool to the touch, like a tile floor in the heat of July. She walked along, one with her thoughts, even as the moon's dark eyes followed her path. She was sure he was reading her mind, anticipating along with her a satisfactory ending tonight.

Finally, she came to her favorite spot. She walked away from the water toward an area of shrubs. She could spread her blanket there on dry sand and have a wide-open view of the ocean with the plants as a protective shield behind. She turned and maneuvered her sandals toward the side of the basket and set it down. Then she grabbed the blanket, gave it a sharp shake and let it fall to the ground. She moved the basket to the top of the blanket and began to empty it.

Darya dug little holes in the sand at each corner of the blanket and nestled a glowing LED candle into each one as she uttered familiar words:

In the dark of night, under Moon's rapt eyes,
I give thanks to East, South, West, and North.
Naked and true, without disguise,
I humbly summon powers forth.

May these words waken sleeping forces.

May the moonlight rouse the resting,
nudging awake the ancient sources,
while ocean waves are cresting.

I call upon fire, air, water, and earth,
may wisdom encircle me.
Let the orbit continue—life, death, rebirth—
manifesting destiny.

I submit to the shadow, embracing the light.
I wait for the day as I bask in the night.

Now, with the comforting flicker of the four candles, Darya sat down near the center of the blanket. She placed a wooden tray in front of her and then, one at a time, pulled seven crystals from a small velvet bag. She placed them in the shape of a half circle, like an empty bowl before her: black onyx, carnelian, citrine, peridot, sodalite, amethyst, and clear quartz. They were not evenly sized, mass produced, cheap, tumbled rocks. Each stone was unique with its own history and the ridges and cracks to prove it.

The last thing she pulled from the pouch was the precious pendant. Her wedding ring notwithstanding, this was her most prized possession. She loved it not because it was valuable in a monetary way, though she had paid a pretty penny to the artisan who fashioned the silver setting for the icy blue moonstone to her exact design and specifications. She treasured it, like most things, for the mysterious story surrounding the object.

When she was seven, her family had gone on holiday—one whole week in a slightly ramshackle cottage right at the water's edge. It was on a quiet island near Florida's west coast, and they had the run of the beach. She swam, made elaborate sand castles, collected shells, and explored every bump and barnacle. Her parents left her alone while they read thick books and nuzzled like lovebirds. On their last night there, while she was taking a bath, Darya planned a grand adventure for the next morning. She would wake up early, sneak out of the cottage all by herself, and watch the sun rise. It would give her plenty of words for the "What I Did This Summer" story her second grade teacher would surely expect.

And what an adventure it was! She managed to roll out of bed and tiptoe from the cottage without waking her parents. The squeaky screen door almost spilled the sea beans, but she was able to shush it. She was surprised at the moon; it looked like the top of a giant flashlight with a dying battery. Was every morning moon as dim as this one?

She walked in the dusky pre-day, sometimes giving a happy little skip and sometimes giving herself a reassuring hug. And just when she decided she had walked far enough and maybe should go back toward the cozy cottage to see the sun wake up, she spied something on the sand ahead. It wasn't moving. No, it wasn't alive. She would keep going, and if it suddenly moved, she would run.

It turned out to be a very flat black rock rimmed with thirteen burned out, drippy wax candles. And there in the center was a little whitish-blue stone. Glancing quickly around to make sure there was no one there, she reached for the gem. Instinctively she held it to the sky between her thumb and first finger. Even in the phantom light it had a brilliant sheen. There must be fairy dust trapped inside. Maybe the fairies had left it for her to find. Maybe it was a test and she should put it back. But finders keepers, losers weepers, right?

She was still deciding what to do when there was a loud splash. Darya spun toward the water and froze. There in the water, a little ways out, something was rising up. She squatted down to make herself small and squinted hard to see what was there. It was a woman. But she wasn't really swimming. She stood there, half in and half out of the water, her back to the beach, arms flung wide. She just stood there like a statue. The waves pushed past her, but didn't push her down, as they headed for the sand to make their jaggedy foam art. Darya stayed low to the ground now, gripping the tiny stone in her sweaty palm. The fairy dust would protect her. She decided to keep it.

And then, as a new line of white-crested waves rolled in, there was an ear-splitting roar. Darya gasped as some hulking thing rose up like a tall tower in front of the woman. It was a huge black creature. It grabbed the woman's shoulders and pushed her backward under the water. The shadow was there for a couple of seconds; then, it too, was gone. Darya's heart was pounding louder than the waves. It made her ears hurt. But she didn't run. She didn't move. She didn't blink.

The two rose above the water again. This time Darya thought she saw some kind of tentacles wrapped around the woman's neck and waist. The thing gleamed like it had been dipped in oil. No, not oil. It was only shiny in *some* places, like a dead fish that still sparkled in spots when the light caught it just right. But the burned-out moon wasn't giving enough light for her to see anything clearly now. The morning was dark, the water was darker, and whatever was in it was darkest of all.

There was more crashing and thrashing but no screams. The two disappeared beneath the roiling waves once more. Darya held her breath and waited. She waited more. But there were only waves—rolling in, rolling in, rolling in. There were only the waves and the silent moon.

She didn't know how long she had been squatting there, but when she finally stood, the moon was nothing but a faint white pearl in an opalescent sky. The sun was just starting to peek out across the top of the water. Darya looked hard but nothing floated on the surface. She put the stone in her pocket, closed her eyes, breathing in the light, breathing out the fear.

"Darya! Are you out here?"

She heard her father's strong voice and ran toward it. He was standing outside the cottage surveying the horizon, his morning cup of coffee in hand, smiling from ear to ear as she ran to him. "Hey! Careful, Princess. The coffee's hot. What are you doing out here?"

She stood as close to him as she could without touching.

"I wanted to see the sun rise."

"You could have told me. We could have watched it together."

"I wanted to do it by myself."

He laughed. "Well, that's my girl. Seven going on seventeen! How was it?"

She took a deep breath. "I paid so much attention to the moon, I almost missed the sun, but it was…The sky looks kinda like a seashell, doesn't it?" She didn't tell.

Almost every day for years and years, that secret would smash through her mind like waves on a troubled sea. Had there been an actual woman or had she just imagined her? If there was a woman, what was the horrible creature that destroyed her? Maybe it had been a man and a woman swimming together, playing or diving, and she took it for something else entirely. Maybe the misty morning shadows had fueled a little girl's imagination and fooled her common sense. But if something had happened—for real—

God, could she have somehow stopped it? She'd never spoken of it—not even to Mur.

She'd hidden the fairy stone for a long time. Sometimes she slept with it under her pillow. Sometimes she carried it in her pocket. Sometimes she set it on the windowsill, amazed at how it gleamed the most whenever the moon was at its fattest. Many years later, when Sophia taught her about chakras and energies and crystals, she learned it was a moonstone.

She had cleansed it. She had charged it with positivity and love and good intention. Eventually, just like the exhausted moon on that early summer morning, the shame of stolen things and hidden secrets faded away. Darya designed a setting for the delicate moonstone and dangled it from a silver chain around her neck and near her heart. She wore it often.

Now, overflowing with gratitude for amulets and fairy dust, Darya rested the pendant in the half circle on the wooden tray. Her gems were charging in the light of the moon. She began to charge her spirit with a bit of mediation. She sat quietly, calming her mind, recognizing thoughts as they floated past but not attaching herself to any of them. She sat on the blanket, one with everything, still holding the little pouch.

After a while she opened her eyes and gazed up at the magnanimous white circle. Full moons were a culmination, an invitation to release things no longer needed and to embrace what is new. October's full moon had many names: Hunter's Moon, Travel Moon, Dying Moon. Darya's favorite was Sanguine Moon for its double meaning. She set down the velvet bag, closed her eyes, and began to focus on her breath. She was mindful only of the air as it moved from nostrils to throat to chest to diaphragm and then that relaxing whoosh as it twirled away from her lips.

She was ready now for the "letting go." She opened her eyes and reached to the left of the tray before her, beginning with the onyx, she touched each crystal, in turn, with gentle fingers as she spoke these words:

"I release fear… frustration… shame… inaction… assumption… comparison… attachment."

Then she gave each gem a second touch, in the same order, and said, "I embrace courage… joy… peace… intention… truth… authenticity… freedom."

She reached for her basket, pulled a flask from it and let the cool, clear water trickle down her throat. She had brought some molasses cookies and chunks of papaya but she wasn't hungry. The water was enough.

She looked again at the glorious moon and how it lit the beach and caused the ocean—even in the dead of night—to sparkle and gleam. She didn't usually swim unless she was with the others, but the night was so bright and beautiful. She felt pulled to the water and wanted to be enveloped and buoyed up by it. She stood and unbuttoned her white shirt, untied the knot holding the sarong around her waist, and dropped both of them on the blanket. Glancing down at her sturdy, vein-crossed legs she giggled. Oh to be seven again, dashing along the beach, discovering fairy stones!

She squatted down and pulled her phone from the basket to check the time. Sunrise wasn't that far off. Like an enchanting first date, these nights with the moon passed far more quickly than she liked, and they seemed further and further apart. She gently tossed the phone onto the pile of fabric and headed for the water. It was a little chilly, but she would warm up.

She wanted to throw herself in all at once and not have to prolong the torturous temperature adjustment, but she had to get to a decent depth first if she wanted to avoid a sandy belly flop. So she sprinted into the water, shivering as a million icy prickles poked at her feet, her calves, her thighs. She gasped as the water reached her chest. Darya took a deep breath, squeezed her eyes shut, and plunged into the inky sea.

It was so much colder than she expected. She resurfaced, shaking her head and slicking the wet hair off her face. Suddenly, the sky darkened the moon in a charcoal shroud and Darya thought she saw a flash of lightning. Uh oh. It was definitely time to get out of the water and dash for home.

She leaned back and began a steady, fast backstroke toward the beach with chin pointed skyward, but there was an intense current. She didn't panic. She just flipped over and started the front crawl. The more she reached, the farther away she seemed to be. She was a pretty strong swimmer, but it felt like she wasn't making any headway. She stopped and began to tread water. The moon passed between the clouds, like a familiar face, in a gathering crowd of them before it vanished once more. Darya tried again. Not working.

She decided to just relax into a back float for a while. Maybe she was caught in a rip tide and she could float across and try again. The sky gave a throaty grumble. Maybe she would be able to touch bottom here. She forced herself upright and flexed her toes down. They hit sand. There. She stood up, saw the massive wave crest just a few feet ahead, and threw her arms wide to steady herself against them.

Darya held her breath as the liquid yanked her under. She struggled up and barely got to her feet again when a deafening racket paralyzed her. She wanted to cover her ears but couldn't move at all. The water was lead, pressing against her, holding her tight. There was a moment of eerie silence and then tingling; the tingling dread that rushed from her spine to her shoulders to the top of her head. Still frozen, her eyes stinging with salt, sinuses burning from their briny baptism, her jaw dropped slowly open.

Oh my god! It was massive: an obsidian monstrosity that reeked of rotting flesh. There was no face. Feeling utter dread, Darya stood immobile in the presence of the Dark One, the All-Knowing Keeper of the Ocean Depths.

She knew beyond belief now.

There was no resistance. He reached for her and plunged her below the surface. Instinctively, she strained to find air. The thing relented. As she breached the surface, she pushed her head back, stubbornly staring at the thing as she gulped air. It wasn't a he, but it wasn't a she. An *it* or a *they*, maybe. Whatever the hell it was, it could not be stilled, charmed, or conquered.

Its strong, sinewy cords reached slowly, deliberately, almost *tenderly* around her neck as they began to press and to pulsate.

The duo dropped below as the cold water hardened like sheets of ice around her. There was no air. Everything inside was flooded. She and the beast, cinched together, continued to descend the depths. It was pulverizing her. Her limbs were gone. Did she have skin? She was being crushed. Smaller, smaller, smaller. Finally, she was so infinitesimal, nothing could hold her.

Earth's light was dimming. Below was absolute darkness. But now, right now, she was among billions and billions of wee white specks. They were hovering all around her in glorious suspension. She was floating. She felt extraordinary, suddenly common and then one with them, suddenly nothing.

The golden orb of the sun winked at the moon as if to say, "My turn now." The moon was happy to acquiesce. There weren't too many folks milling about on the beach yet, but anyone could see that it was going to be a gorgeous day.

"Papi, mira!"

Seven-year-old Bella dashed toward her father, panting with excitement. "Can I keep it? ¿Por favor? I found it over there with some rocks and stuff. And, Papi, there's nobody around. *Nobody*."

Fernando reached down and took the treasure from his daughter's trembling hand. He rubbed a few moist grains of sand off on his shirt and held the pendant to the sky. "Wow, Princesa! It's really something, eh? Are you sure there was no one around?"

"Yep! I looked and looked!"

"Well, you know what they say: finders keepers, losers weepers."

John M. Floyd

LUCIFER

Esther Logan sat in a rocking chair on the front porch of their small house on the rolling plains. A full moon, unbelievably white, floated in the eastern sky, lighting up the fields as if in midday, and a warm spring wind bent the grass and riffled the leaves in the trees. Gazing into the peaceful distance, she felt a moment of simple pleasure. Esther didn't get much pleasure these days, or leisure either. As her grandma used to say, she was born tired and never got rested.

But at least Walt wasn't around. Esther wasn't sure where he was—he never told her anything. Which was sometimes just as well. This way she could hope he stayed gone all night. All day tomorrow, too, would be fine with her. Walt Logan was the sorriest excuse for a man she'd ever known, and she had only herself to blame for marrying him. Her first husband, Richard, had died suddenly and far too early, thrown from a horse during a trail drive, and Esther's ma had thought the only thing worse than having never been married was being an unmarried widow with a ten-year-old son to raise. Little had she known.

Esther touched the most recent bruises on her cheek and wondered how far she and Ricky—now almost thirteen—could get if they packed up and left now. Not far enough, she figured. And when they were caught and brought back it would be even worse for them both.

Esther looked out over the moonlit plains and whispered a prayer. "Give me a sign, Lord," she said aloud. "Tell me what to do."

But she saw no signs and heard no answers. What she heard was the pounding of footsteps on the hardpacked dirt of the side yard as Ricky came charging around the corner of the house. He leaped up onto the porch and stood in front of her, sweating and panting.

"What in the world's the matter with you?" she said to him. "Why ain't you in bed?"

Ricky took off his hat and blurted, "I caught him, Ma. He was in the barn."

"What? Caught who?"

"Lucifer. I locked him in."

Esther just stared. "Lucifer," she said, "is in our barn?"

Ricky nodded. "He almost got me. I left my pocketknife there this afternoon, and I was about to walk in and get it when I smelled something funny. I stopped, swung the door shut, and latched it just as he hit it from the other side, growling and snarling at me." He looked down at his hands. "I'm still shakin'."

Esther rose from her chair, her drying-towel from the supper dishes still in her hands. She stood there a moment and then sat down again. She opened her mouth to say something but couldn't seem to get it out. Her mind was whirling.

Lucifer was a legend in these parts, something parents told their kids to make them stay close, something you heard about but never saw. Some said he was a panther like those in the tales of foreign lands with jungles and elephants, others said he was a giant black mountain lion. The few who had seen him said he was four feet high at the shoulder and ten feet from nose to tail. Many had heard him scream in the night, a sound that chilled the blood, but never, ever had he been known to venture into a settled area.

But on a night like this…

Everyone knew bad things happened with a full moon.

Finally, Esther found her voice. "Can he get out?"

"No, ma'am; he's shut in tight. I even ran around back and made sure the other door was latched. He's pitching a fit and plenty mad, but he can't bust through that door. And I don't think he can chew or scratch his way out either." Ricky swallowed and added in a trembling voice, "What do we do?"

"I guess we wait for your pa to get back." She turned to look east, where the wagon-path entered a stand of pitch-dark trees. "He rode his horse into town a while ago, to do some business."

Ricky's face, usually so animated, went still. "He ain't my pa, and that ain't his horse. And I can imagine what kinda business he's doing."

Esther held her tongue, mainly because he was right. Walt was probably at the bar of the saloon, or in one of the rented rooms on its second floor. Finally she said, "Your stepdaddy, then. He rode your horse into town, and when he gets back—"

"What'll that be? Tomorrow?"

"When he gets back, we'll tell him about it." She rocked forward, took both Ricky's hands in hers, and said, "Right now we got bigger problems than Walt. This cat, this—thing—in the barn, he's killed half-a-dozen folks, and who knows how many head of livestock. Maybe Walt can knock a hole in a wall and stick his rifle through or something. Or go get more help."

Ricky fell silent then, looking out into the night as Esther had been doing earlier, and what he said next shocked her. He seemed to have read her mind.

"I think I should go out to the back pasture, catch Mary and Roscoe, and hitch 'em to the wagon," he said. "You and me could pack up and leave. I bet we could get to Dodge 'fore sunup."

"But what then?" she asked. Tenderly she touched his smooth cheek with her palm. "Even if he didn't come find us, what would we do? This is our home. I was born in this house and you were, too. You think your real pa would've wanted us to leave?"

"My real pa woulda killed Walt years ago, when we found out what kinda man he was."

She closed her eyes and sighed. "I made a mistake, Ricky, and I know it. But I'm telling you again, right now we got to think about what you locked in the barn. You understand? And as worthless as Walt is, he can probably handle this. He'll find a way to kill it—"

"If he ain't too drunk."

"—and when he does, maybe that'll change him. At least for a while. He'll feel like he's important, with people everywhere talking about him. The man who killed Lucifer. Maybe that'll keep him from thinking about you and me. We could both use a little of that, right?"

Ricky had gone quiet again. Probably thinking about how bad things were for their little family, for her to be saying such things. She felt herself wishing, for the thousandth time, that her precious first husband were still here.

Before she could come up with anything else to say, she saw her son look past her, and when she turned she saw Walt Logan loping out of the trees and down the winding path from town. He had to have been drinking, to be riding that fast in the dark.

He reined Ricky's horse in beside the front steps and sat there leaning on his saddlehorn, trying to focus on Esther. He was indeed drunk.

Before he could speak, she said, "Walt, we need your help. Something's—"

"Where's that little coffeepot you used to have?" he growled.

"What?"

"The fancy one with the long spout. I found somebody wants to buy it."

Esther felt her face grow warm. "That pot was my mother's, Walt. I can't sell it."

"Well, *I* can. I did. Fella in town's waitin' for me to bring it to him."

"In the middle of the night?"

"It's barely nine o'clock, Esther. Where's that coffeepot at?"

She stared at him. "Are you really going to do this? When I'm begging you not to?"

He spat into the dirt. "I'll ask you one more time," he said. "Where is it?"

Slowly Esther turned to look at Ricky. What she saw in his eyes broke her heart: it wasn't anger, or hate. It was just sadness. For her and for him, too. Both of them were helpless and hopeless. And then, all of a sudden, she knew what she had to do.

Maybe it wasn't bad, that big white moon. Maybe it was a sign.

She turned again to face her husband.

"It's in the barn," she said.

Estelle Rodgers

SUMMER CREATURES

The decaying skeleton still smolders with red starlight embers. It looms above the silver treetops and casts splintered shadows over festival entrails. Silhouetted black against the black sky, the ribcage of charred beams disintegrates atom by atom in the warm summer breeze. Tendrils of melted plastic dangle like mucus and severed arteries. Shreds of scorched paper and canvas drift on the air and cling lamely to a scaffolding spine. Fragments of smashed lamps glitter like rubies, emeralds, and sapphires in the moonlight. Flower petal confetti mixes with grey ash in a ghostly snowfall.

Beyond the threshold of the ruined stage stretches the ravaged clearing: a woodland pasture turned wasteland. The earth is marred with footprints, trampled tents, and myriad trash all pressed together into the foul mixture of mud and vomit and vile wine. Dead firepits pockmark the field. Stone circles, shrines, offerings, and wine vessels are scattered, splattered. A venerable old forest encloses the clearing with a company of towering pines, crooked oaks, and all their limbed, leafy cousins.

Those trees watched the stage burn earlier that night. When the full moon hung low in the sky, the trees were bystanders to the chaos. In the silver light and long black shadows they had leaned away from the raging flames as not to singe a single twig. The trees are cautious folk, after all.

The only break in the dense woodland is the clearing around the trail that leads back to the parking lot. From down that trail—a good twenty-minute walk in a hurry—comes the sound of human voices, car engines, and the weeping that follows in the wake of panic.

In an expansive gravel lot sit the beating hearts that escaped the fire—two hundred festival residents who are refugees from their own celebration. They huddle in the alleyways between cars and campers. Many are in their twenties or thirties, but many others have long gray hair to weave through flower crowns. There is no one who will admit to being younger than eighteen.

They are a panic-stricken menagerie of creative and whimsical creatures. Some have iridescent fairy wings or curling horns; some wear corsets or intricate braids. They are satyrs, mermaids, vampires, wizards. A witch in a flowing Anthropologie maxi dress wipes at her reddened nose as three polyamorous punks with matching tattoos comfort one another in long embraces. Everywhere makeup is streaked and eyes are bloodshot. People wander in search of lost companions, and their concerned, soprano voices accompany the forlorn, minor-key chorus of ghost murmurs.

Rows of drooping sunflower lights flicker yellow illumination over the scene as two white ambulances idle with their back doors flung open wide to receive patients. They treat burns, smoke-inhalation, cuts, poison ivy, and low blood sugar. But nothing in either truck can cure the curious pain and panic in the eyes that watched the stage burn.

A proud Engine Two gathers firefighter cygnets on its long back before rumbling down the uneven forest road. The fire was out by the time they arrived, anyway. Police cruisers park askew among the drunken ranks of camper vans, old trucks, and new sports cars.

At the edge of the lot stands Officer Maria Reyes. She bites the inside of her cheek as she listens to a distraught young woman give a strange statement.

"A goat?" Officer Reyes looks over her notepad. The girl she sees has hair in two short, brown pigtails and the same smokey pain in her eyes as the others. She is wearing only a halter sundress, hiking boots, and a seashell necklace.

"Yeah," the girl replies. "Or like, a sheep. It had big horns. It was white." Her voice shakes as she speaks. She sits with knees knocked on a felled log. She pulls a scratchy grey blanket tighter around her body. She meets Officer Reyes's eyes in desperation and whispers, "It looked at me."

"Uh-huh." Officer Reyes tries her best not to raise her eyebrows. Higher up in her notepad she has scrawled other words from other interviews such as 'Aliens?', 'Mind vortex', and 'One dragon'.

"It was real!" the girl says. "Everyone else was on drugs but I wasn't."

"I didn't say you were," Reyes replies in a level tone.

"But you're thinking it. All day people said they were seeing things because they were on LSD or whatever. But I didn't take any drugs. I saw a…a weird goat. I'll take a drug test. It was real. I'm not just trying to get outta trouble. It was real."

The officer nods and makes a few more notes. "I believe you. Sometimes goats come down from the mountains. Even weird goats. Don't worry, you aren't in trouble. What's your name?"

"I'm Liz."

"Okay, Liz, are you here alone? You have anyone we can call to come get you?"

"There's no service out here," she sneers. Abruptly she sits up and glances around frantically. "Selene!" She jumps to her feet and looks ready to flee. "I'm here with my friend Selene, but I haven't seen her since, like, seven! Oh, God!"

"What does she look like?" asks Reyes.

"She's my age. Eighteen. She's shorter than me, skinnier. She has all white hair, like, she dyed it silver. She's super pretty. She's my best friend." Liz looks touched by fresh fear. "Oh, God. Where is she? People were so mean to her. I hope…" She casts her eyes from face to face, scans the faintly glowing herd under pale electric light.

"I'm sure she's around here somewhere," Officer Reyes assures. "Sit tight. We'll find her. You want something to drink? Coffee?"

Liz glances at the officer, then runs off into the crowds, shouting. "Selene? Selene!"

"I could use some coffee." Reyes snaps her notebook shut. "I'll get me some coffee. That's awfully nice of you to offer, Maria, working so late. Nothing insane about this at all."

Steel travel mug in hand, she pours tepid coffee over her weariness. It is 1:43 a.m. She convenes with several other officers by their cruisers a little distance from the public. Each shares odd findings.

"My guess," says Officer Jenny Yoon, "is that they must've had some kind of unauthorized pyrotechnics show goin' on up here tonight. It's been a dry summer. All the flowers and tree branches and nonsense they had all over their stage just went up like kindling."

Officer Ray Ewing scratches under his tight collar with his cheap pen.

"That's a negative," he says. "I talked to the stage manager, and she said…" He flips to the page in his notebook. "She said, 'The moon and the stars are the most spectacular light show in the universe. We wouldn't be so audacious as to distract from it.'"

"So, is that a 'No'?" asks their Chief, Officer Helen Hastings.

"But, people said they saw fireworks," Yoon replies.

"People said they saw a *lot* of things," says Reyes.

Yoon snorts a little and long-blinks. "They sure did."

"Yeah, one lady reported animal abuse," Ewing adds, "but she couldn't tell me by who or even what type of animal."

"I meant more like they saw cows with human legs and eight-foot tall ghosts and…" Reyes trails off.

"Probably someone just tossed a joint, and wham." Ewing flicks his finger in pantomime.

Reyes eyes him with raised brows. "Someone tossed a joint?"

"Okay, a cigarette butt," he relents.

Hastings motions to the crowd as a whole to end the conference. "Let's worry about exactly what happened later. Just write down everything they say, no matter how looney it sounds. Some things are bound to match up eventually. More importantly, ask who's missing. The search team found a lot of people hurt or hiding in the woods, but they had a hard time searching in the dark."

Reyes raises her hand to speak. "I think I already have at least one confirmed missing."

Hastings nods and frowns. "I won't be surprised if there are more."

They disperse back out into the mass of shaken heathens.

The silver moonlight floods a pair of glistening lemon eyes with long pupils.

Maria Reyes is tall so she bends like a willow branch when she listens. She takes statements from five humans, two fauns, one displaced dryad, five fairies, and at least nine druids. Some seem reluctant to speak to her; she knows they're afraid she'll search them for drugs. Others excitedly relate astounding details, solicited or not.

"It came from the stars! It was the extraterrestrials!" A pug-faced man with gauged earlobes waves a crooked wand at the sky. "It was like a ball of white light. Felt like ya could reach out an' grab it!" He snatches at the memory with his free hand.

Several individuals have equally bizarre stories to share.

"I was chased by a centaur!" A round druid with pin-straight blue hair wipes at his running mascara. "It sounds ridiculous, but it's true! Don't look at me like that!" He shoves the woman beside him who looks embarrassed. "You saw it too!" He turns to Reyes beseechingly. "I'm not on drugs! Or the wine. I heard there was something in the wine. We're straight edge, anyway. We don't even do caffeine."

"Sometimes I drink a Corona," the woman confesses.

"Freddy!" The man looks sincerely hurt and has to resist giving Freddy a smack on the bicep.

"It was Pan!" says a hunched, hirsute old man with tiny round glasses and a long green beard full of glitter. He makes a circle in the air with two bony fingers. "It stands to reason! Tonight is a full moon, and you know Pan was in love with the Moon Goddess! Makes sense he would try to get her attention with his mischief. Although," the man lowers his hands and turns his eyes to consider, "he was fairly taken with just about any goddess. Or god. Or handsome young shepherd. Or his flock…"

Eventually, Officer Reyes finds herself speaking to a bare-chested young man who gives his name as Dirk Mossgrove.

"Mossgrove," she repeats. She imagines repeating the name in a beer. "That's a name you don't hear every day."

"It's my Pagan name." The young man is kneeling in a patch of grass. His curly brown locks are disheveled, his thick lashes are made thicker by eyeliner, and his arms and chest sprout copious body hair. He is lean with long muscles and wears a paisley skirt of pine green and tangerine that hides his legs and feet.

"My legal name is James Constantinou. But everyone calls me Dirk. Everyone here knows me. I had a show earlier tonight."

"I see." Reyes flips to a new page in her notebook. "So. What can you tell me about the fire? Any idea how it might have started? Is anyone you know missing? Any details you can remember might be important even if they don't seem like much right now." She chants the words with practiced repetition.

Dirk nods and glances around. He seems uncomfortable.

"Actually, I think maybe I do know how the fire started. It's pretty weird though."

Reyes stays as solemn as a funeral director. "I expect nothing less."

Dirk nods in agreement. "So, it's hard to find big Pagan events. Usually it's just small stuff, like eight or ten people, so events like these are great for my personal brand. Friday afternoon my friends introduced me to this guy Clark and some of his friends. Major negative energy on this guy. You can always tell who the 'posers' are, you know? Some people just get into Paganism because they think it's all orgies and drinking. Which I mean, sometimes, yeah, sure, but it has meaning, you know? It's about connecting with the earth and the elements, not getting laid. Whatever. Anyway…"

Dirk pauses in his story. He looks up at the stars for a moment, runs his hand through his hair, glances around. Reyes watches his behavior and is about to press when he continues.

"Anyway, it's a long story, but I think that Clark guy started the fire. He was acting all high and mighty, like he was better than us. He said we weren't 'real', that we didn't understand. He was acting like we weren't sincere. But he wasn't there. He didn't see it." Dirk drops his voice to a conspiratorial tone. "We invoked Pan."

He lets these words hang in the air for a moment. Reyes stares at him. He sits back and nods triumphantly. The officer begins to shrug her shoulders as slow as a sunrise.

"Pan! The god of wild nature and shepherds!" Dirk hooks his fingers over his ears into little horns. "We held a ritual Friday night under the full moon and we summoned him, a real god! Clark left early with some cute boy so he didn't even see it. But I saw it; it was real. It chose one of us! We told him about it the next day and he laughed at us, called us 'whacked out hippies'. Real hater."

"Invoked…Pan…" Reyes murmurs as she writes. "And you think this Clark burned down the stage why? That's a big accusation."

"He was super sketch. He said we would never understand the forest if we didn't understand fear, or something."

"Did you see him set fire to the stage?" she presses.

"Uh." Dirk hesitates and squints into the distance. "Well, no. I wasn't actually there when the fire started. I was at the lake." He pauses and sheepishly corrects himself. "I was in the lake."

"You were swimming at night? That's dangerous."

"No, no." Dirk hesitates again. He straightens and shifts, scratches his arms and head. "I was, uh, I was hiding."

"Hiding? From who?"

"From… Well, it turned out, I think we…" Dirk continues to squirm and scratch. "I think we pissed Pan off. This is gonna sound crazy, but I got chased by, like, a big sheep."

Reyes pauses and considers this information for a moment.

"A sheep? Like, a farm animal?"

"Not a farm animal! It was the spirit of Pan. Pan takes many shapes and can be in many places at once. He was huge and all white with a black face and yellow eyes!"

"Why do you think, um, Pan was mad at you?"

Dirk threw up his hands. "How should I know? After the ritual, that sheep was stalking the woods all weekend. It attacked a girl."

"What? Was she all right?"

"Oh, yeah, she was fine. Pan wouldn't hurt you; he's just a prankster."

"Huh."

Reyes tries to make sense of this story. She's puzzled and wonders where the LSD-fueled hallucinations end and the real events begin.

"Have you seen Clark out here tonight?" she asks.

Slices of red meat begin to rot in the warm summer air. Tiny black things with wings circle and taste the abandoned campsite. A kitchen knife reflects the trampled grass. It glows with silver light.

A young man is comforting a younger woman by wrapping one arm around her shoulder and replacing his hand on her knee every time she removes it. The pair sit on the lowered tailgate of a gleaming black pickup truck. She has wavy aqua hair and smeared raccoon eyeshadow. She wears a collection of beaded necklaces and bracelets, feather earrings, stud piercings, a lilypad tattoo, and a single silver toe ring. Her pupils are dilated. She repeats herself.

He is dressed in a pair of chestnut brown fur shorts. He wears shoes that make his feet look like cloven hooves. A pair of asymmetrical, spiraling ram horns protrude from his dark, messy hair, and he wears down-turned, peach-fuzz goat ears. Colorful tattoos of twisting ink vines, living tree roots, and the symbols that organize the universe reach up his arm, across his chest, and down to the girl's leg.

To Reyes, the girl looks a bit like a sexier Kira from *Dark Crystal* and the boy looks a bit like Tim from *Monty Python and the Holy Grail*, as portrayed by Jim Morrison.

"We all did it," the girl replies when Reyes presses about the cause of the fire. "All of us. All at once. We ignited our souls. We are all embers in the blood fires of life. Fleeting."

"Okay." Reyes draws a little spiral symbol in her notebook and nods sagaciously. "I should have known. Very common, really. You'd be surprised how often that happens." She turns her attention to the young man. "And what about you? Any idea what caused the fire?"

"It wasn't fire," the young man says. "I mean, it was. But it wasn't red and yellow and orange, and it wasn't hot. It was cold! It was like," he waves his clawed fingers around, "white and silver and purple. It was like a waterfall falling up. It was like moonfire."

"Okay. And what's your name?"

"I'm Clark."

Reyes writes 'Clark the Goat' in her notebook and adds another spiral symbol beside an exclamation point.

The girl turns slowly. She looks at Clark as if seeing him for the first time. Then she narrows her eyes until she is almost blind.

"What are you talking about?" she snarls. "What is *moonfire*? How high *are* you?"

"Babe!" Clark seems hurt. "You saw it too! You said it was beautiful!"

"Are you insane? It was horrifying. I was crying."

Reyes interrupts. "And what's your name, Miss?"

"I'm Wisteria Shadows at Dawn," she replies.

"What?" Clark withdraws his arm from her abruptly. He leans back from Wisteria, inspecting her face and outfit under the low, humming lights. Then he casts his eyes around the crowd as it churns under the night sky. He looks anxious. "Wait, you're not Selene!"

"Oh, screw you!" The girl shoves him and jumps off the back of the truck. She folds herself into the other shadows and disappears.

"Babe! Wait!" Clark scrambles after her with an outstretched arm. "Where'd Selene go? Come back!"

Officer Reyes taps her pen on her notepad twice. She purses her lips and glances around until someone else in the crowd makes eye contact. It's a mermaid sitting with her arms wrapped around the knees of her iridescent scales.

"Excuse me, Ma'am. Can I ask you a few questions?"

Selene is alive, at least. She clings to the body of the tree. Her fingernails are blackened and her face is smeared with dirt. Tears carve slick rivulets down her cheeks. The ground is far below. She is afraid her heartbeat is too loud.

Officer Reyes recognizes Liz near the foot of a trail and stops her from entering the woods alone.

"I have to go look for her! You have to let me go!" Liz demands.

"Please, just calm down," Reyes begins.

"I will not calm down! There is nothing to be calm about! My friend is still out there and she's in danger! You have to do something! That's your job, isn't it?"

Reyes holds her hands out as if warming them on Liz's fire. "Why do you think your friend is in danger?" she asks.

Liz leans in and lowers her voices. She hisses out her words. "She is a danger to *herself.* After all the shit that happened this weekend?"

"What happened?"

Liz raises her voice again and scrapes the air in frustration.

"Please! We're wasting time! She could drown herself! She could take a bunch of drugs! She could throw herself off that cliff! I don't have time to explain it!"

Reyes touches her fingertips together and adopts a compassionate expression.

"I understand you're worried about her, and I do believe you. I want to help you, and her, but before I can help, I need more information. We can't just go running into the woods and hope to randomly bump into her. Right?"

Liz draws a deep, ragged breath. She stares at the officer for a moment, half defiant and half relenting.

"Just let me go look for her."

Reyes shakes her head. "Nope. No way. We have all kinds of reports of a possibly rabid animal in the woods, and there's a lot of debris and broken glass. I don't need you turning into another missing person."

"Then will you go look for her? I'll come with you! I think I know where to start looking. I'll tell you about what happened on the way."

Reyes frowns and breaks eye contact for a moment, shaking her head.

"Please? She's my best friend and she could die. She might already be…"

Reyes leans back and shifts her weight.

"Aw, Jesus, kid." She sighs and glances over the crowded parking lot. Some cars start their engines, headlights blinding. Skinny searchlights pan over the woods as vehicles attempt to navigate an exodus. An EMT runs across the lot, waving his arms.

"You can't drive like that!" he screams.

Reyes pushes her radio to her mouth. She hesitates.

"Boss?" she says finally into the radio static. "Reyes."

"What's up."

"I have a young lady here who says she may know the whereabouts of one of our lost persons. She says this person may be a danger to herself. Permission to head back up to the campgrounds to take a look?"

There is a long silence while Reyes and Liz wait for a reply. Liz looks ready to run. Reyes stares up at the night sky. Part of her secretly hopes her boss says 'No' so she doesn't have to go into the forest at 2:30 in the morning.

Finally the foil-crunch voice returns. "Take Yoon and Ewing."

Liz nearly grabs Reyes when she hears these words.

"Oh, God! Thank you!"

"What's goin' on?" comes Ewing's distant voice through the radio.

"Takin' a walk in the woods."

Cold beams of LED light glide over the forest path, slicing moon shadows and casting branch silhouettes into the canopy. The three officers and stricken Liz are far from the yellow lot. Their eyes adjust to the well-lit night.

"We barely need the flashlights," Yoon mutters.

"We'll need them to find Selene," says Liz.

The leaves rustle and the air is dry and sweet. The natural perfumes of the warm summer night mix with traces of smoke and burned plastic. Their footfall is sharp and feels too loud. There ought to be a string orchestra rehearsal of crickets and peepers and cicadas, but there is only the sound of Liz's voice.

"I just saw Selene earlier tonight. On Friday, after we set up camp, we met…a guy. Clark. He invited us to a midnight ritual. Well, he invited Selene. He said they were going to invoke a Pagan god or goddess or something, but you could tell it was just an excuse to get naked. Selene wanted to go, but I could tell he was just trying to get with her. He kept telling her how pretty she was. He said he loved her hair and her name, he said he thought she was so beautiful. Laid it on real thick. Joke's on him."

Liz pauses in her story and calms her anger before continuing.

"So we went to the ritual. There were maybe ten people way back in the woods, separate from the festival. Clark left because Selene told him to fuck off. She was more interested in the ritual. Robes, hoods, some people were naked underneath. Then, when it had barely begun, this sheep, goat, something, just walked into the clearing. It wasn't afraid of us or anything. Of course, people were losing their minds about it. Saying it was a god. Some people tried to pet it. One guy got down on his knees and bowed to it. That pissed it off I guess, because it went crazy. It rammed the guy and knocked him out. I thought he was dead. He had a huge welt like a baseball on his head this morning; it was disgusting."

"He's lucky to be alive," Ewing says.

"Right?" Liz's voice is piercing in the silent forest. "It started chasing people! Some of us climbed trees, some people just ran off. It chased after Selene and knocked her over. It tried to hump her leg. She got away; she was okay, but then…God, people are such assholes. People saw it happen, then told the story all day today. This morning I saw people pointing at Selene and whispering. It was like being back in high school but with better beer. One lady even came up to her and asked her what it was like. If she felt blessed. Can you believe that? Like she thought Selene banged a Pagan god."

Behind them Yoon suppresses a sudden onset of choked coughing.

"If Selene rejected Clark, do you think he could have made the rumors worse?" Reyes says quickly, loudly.

"Probably," Liz mutters.

"I had a witness who said a man named Clark gave him spiked wine," says Yoon as she catches her breath and clears her throat.

"Oh, I met him," Ewing says. "Goat guy."

"You met him, too?" says Yoon, stunned at the coincidence.

"So did I, actually." Reyes recalls.

Liz gives a quizzical look but seems distracted. "Goat guy?"

"Yeah. Dressed like a goat from the waist down?" says Ewing. "Brown hair, horns, tail?"

Liz shakes her head. "Clark didn't have…" Her voice trails off. She glances around, then up to the infinite night sky. She gives a curt little laugh. "No, you're right; that's him. That guy would feel up a tree if it was curvy enough. Terrible swimmer, too."

The group walks into the clearing of the abandoned campground. The field is a moon-bathed cemetery with headstones of shattered tents and camping gear scattered askew. At one end of the field the carcass of the murdered stage is outlined in the white chalk of its own cinders. Its broken ribcage bones are sharp against the sky.

"After everything that happened Friday night, Selene was so humiliated," says Liz quietly. Each officer slides a beam over the debris until the lights have gone too far and the darkness consumes them. "After the sun set, she just…walked off."

"You didn't go looking for her?" asks Reyes.

"I did. There was a lot going on." Liz points toward the trees at the end of the field opposite the stage. "This way." She starts confidently toward the treeline. She is able to see her path clearly in the moonlight, better than by the shifting, glaring light of the flashlights. "I looked for her everywhere. I asked around. Some people were shocked to hear she was real at all. I even went to ask that-that Clark guy… But, I couldn't find him. And then the stage went up in flames, and we all ran."

They cross the field in single file.

Reyes shines her light toward their destination.

Ewing shines his light into the trees, vigilant for any bright spots of fleece.

Yoon shines her light in the direction of every small echo, every whisper of crumbling wooden frame, every imagined pair of yellow eyes peering back at her from the dark.

Liz leads them down a narrow trail. They pass a signpost pointing the way to the public bathrooms and shower building.

As they walk, the forest slowly creeps closer. The shadows become dense and the undergrowth thick and tangled. Red ivy gleams wet at their ankles, and they step their heavy boots carefully to avoid it. The forest is cool, dark, like a cave of black-leafed branches with a million bat-eye stars clinging above.

At last they reach the small clearing. At the center of a rock circle stands a simple table-like structure of found stones. On the slab tabletop sits a collection of flowers, crystals, melted wax candles, and a necklace with a charcoal amulet. A hair-fine wisp of smoke rises from incense. The ground is flattened and torn with many footprints.

There is blood.

It is splattered across the shrine and ground in erratic patterns. It pools in small depressions. It shines slick in the moonlight and black in the shifting shadows.

As they stare, a droplet lands on the stone table.

All eyes follow the three flashlight beams up into the trees.

Reyes stares at a screaming jaw of crooked cork teeth at the end of a long head. A ragged, white beard runs from a stained, wet chin to drooping ears. Watery frog eyes stare into nothingness. A pair of slender horns come to sharp points.

High up, forty feet in the air, the white and red creature is draped over a limb like a rug out for beating. Its stick legs jut down dead and rigid.

Another drop of blood hits the altar.

Ewing is the first to cry out. "Oh, what the fuck!"

"Is that a mountain goat?" Reyes mutters. She squints into the trees.

"How did that get up there?" Ewing can't look straight at it.

Yoon half recoils and half snorts with morbid laughter.

"Jesus! What happened?" Ewing goes on.

Liz rushes to the roots of the tree, cranes her head back, and screams. "Selene?"

High above, with her muscles locked tight, is just another tree branch. The flashlights catch her figure as searchlights would catch a prisoner at the moment of escape. Suddenly, there is a girl.

At the sound of Liz's voice, she stirs and looks down at them. Her silver hair is spotted with bits of nature. In one hand she clutches a knife with a shining blade. Her arm is blackened up to the elbow and dark blood splatters face and clothes. She shields her eyes from the intense glare of the three flashlights.

"Liz!" In the forest's reverent silence, Selene's small voice travels easily. "I stopped him," she cries. "He was after me, but I stopped him! Freaky bastard!"

"Come down!" Liz calls up. "I've been looking everywhere for you! I couldn't find you without a light!"

Selene seems to look through her. Her eyes flick side to side and her voice is manic.

"He was funny! Nice to me. He was sweet. He made me laugh." She sits back from the body of the tree and stabs the kitchen knife into the bark. She slices again and splinters rain to the ground as she speaks. There is a dull 'thunk' every time she attacks. "But, then he chased me."

Thunk.

"I thought I lost him!"

Thunk.

"He said he couldn't see me under the full moon. But he could smell me. Listened for my heart."

Thunk, thunk.

"He said I was invisible tonight because I *am* moonlight. Like a teardrop in an ocean. 'You can't tell the two apart,' he said."

Liz glances at the police and lets out a small, nervous laugh.

"Liz? Don't—the trees! Just-Just come down! We'll go home!" She is about to climb the tree herself.

Reyes puts a restrictive hand on Liz's shoulder and calls up to Selene.

"We're the police," she says. "You're safe. Nothing is going to hurt you. Can you climb down on your own? Are you hurt?"

"No, no." Selene's voice is calm but distant, as if she's only talking in her sleep. Suddenly she focuses and shouts. "What if he comes back?"

Thunk.

Behind Reyes, Ewing shines his light on the goat, then on the large kitchen knife.

"It's safe," he says. "No one down here but us. And we'll shoot any more goats that try to come after you." He and Reyes exchange a quick look, as if to say, 'Won't we?'.

Selene considers. She yanks the knife free. "Promise?"

"Yes! You're safe with us."

Selene's pale, muddied foot, raw and cut from her climb, touches the soft earth. The knife is upright in the ground beside the tree. The blade is half buried after the long drop.

"There," says Reyes.

Liz rushes to Selene and hugs her close. "Oh my goddess," she whispers as they murmur thankfulness to each other. She strokes her hair and touches her as if to confirm she never has to let go again. "Selene," she whispers. "Don't disappear like that on me again!"

All the vengeful intensity that coursed through Selene's veins when she was in the tree seems to evaporate. For the first time in many dark hours, she relaxes.

"Let's get back," Reyes goes on. "You all right? Can you walk?"

Selene nods.

"Great. And we'll have the EMTs check you out."

Liz grabs Selene by the wrist and pulls her hard. Selene yelps in surprise and stumbles after her friend, who drags her down the path so quickly she nearly falls.

"This way!"

In the sickly yellow parking lot it is past 3 a.m. Maria Reyes and her fellow officers are reunited with their duties. They inquire, listen, record. They are solemn. They no longer make doodles in their notebooks. No story is too outlandish or too strange. The humor in the peculiarity of the people has gone. Each silently wrestles with a knot of shame.

Far at the edge of the lot, where the charcoal trees lean in to listen, Selene and Liz sit side by side on a log. They are away from the crowd and away from the leering eyes of those who haven't forgotten the cruel rumors.

Liz has one arm around her friend's shoulder.

"I'm sorry about the goat," Liz says. "About everything. That was awful."

Selene nods slowly. Her head hangs, and she is scraping her shaking hands with an alcohol wipe. The stringent smell of the wipe mixes with the strong iron and copper smell of the mountain goat's blood and makes her eyes water.

"I'm sorry you were up there so long. I just couldn't find you," Liz goes on. "I'm so glad you're safe."

Selene looks up and gives her a weak smile.

"Don't beat yourself up," she whispers. "It's over. I stopped it. I'm okay. I'm just tired. Maybe a little scarred for life."

"I tried to look for you," Liz goes on. "I looked everywhere, all night. After the fire, I thought you would be here in the parking lot where I could see you."

There is a sound of crunching gravel. The two girls look up and see someone approaching. It's the shaggy young man wearing the long skirt. Selene remembers him from Friday night. He walks with a slight limp, and when he reaches them, he crouches beside Selene.

"Are you sure you're all right?" Dirk asks softly.

Selene raises her eyebrows, confused, but gives a small nod. Her mind is elsewhere. She is still in the tree. She is still stabbing, slicing at a goat as it clambers toward her, braying and snorting.

"I'm glad," he says. "Sometimes my tricks go… wrong."

Selene suddenly focuses. She sees him now. Blinking, she tries to comprehend. Her mind tries to catch up to this moment, to race from the tree to the lot in time to act.

"Your tricks?" she repeats on a rising tide of fury.

"I thought you would like it!" says Liz. "It was cute!"

Selene snaps her head and stares at her friend.

"What?"

"You liked it at first!" says Dirk. "You climbed on my back and we ran through the woods! We chased those awful people who teased you! And we drove that stupid boy right into the lake! He wasn't much of a swimmer." Dirk chuckles at the memory. "They might never find him!"

"They think they met him," says Liz.

"No, don't be upset!" says Dirk. He reaches for Selene. "Is that why you ran away? Some awful boy?"

As Dirk speaks, Liz smiles and places her hand on Selene's knee.

"What!" Selene turns between them. "Wait. What? How do you know—" She grabs Liz's hand and pulls it away.

"What did you think of the fire?" Liz asks. "Did you like it? I made it special just so I could find you! What a waste, huh?"

Liz smiles. Dirk smiles. Together they tilt their heads to the left. Their cheeks are soft taffy pulled back by invisible hooks and wires to reveal rows of human teeth.

"Oh! And I got you something!" Dirk gestures with a hand to something behind Selene. She hesitates, eyeing him with furious suspicion, then winces and turns.

Standing between the trees, just beyond the light, is Wisteria Shadows at Dawn. She sends Selene a giddy wave, steps closer, and kneels on the grass.

Selene is surrounded on three sides.

"I thought you might like me better like this," says Wisteria. Her voice is low and excited, like she's sharing a secret recipe. She tries to take Selene's hand but cannot catch it in time. "This way, we can be together. I know you don't like…" She glances at Dirk.

Selene stares in horror. Her hair flies as she looks from one face to the next, then back to Wisteria.

"Do you not like her?" asks Liz. "I can go get another. I can get anyone!" Liz and Dirk gesture toward the lot in unison.

"So long as it's a full moon," says Dirk.

"Did you like the tall woman with the red hair?" asks Wisteria.

Selene draws a long gasp. She grazes her fingertips over her brow. She sees yellow goat eyes in her palms.

"No!" she shouts, and tries to push them away. "You drowned that boy! You tried to—"

"Sh, sh!" Liz slaps a hand over Selene's mouth. "They'll hear!"

"His own fault!" says Dirk.

"Let's get away from this terrible place, my darling," say Wisteria and Dirk and Liz in a single discordant voice.

Dirk grabs Selene by the ankles. Wisteria grabs her by the wrists. Liz keeps her hand clamped tight over Selene's mouth and holds her head by a fistfull of snarled silver hair.

Selene kicks and jerks and tries to scream. She tries to bite, to contort, to growl. She tries going limp then suddenly flinging her body to the side. The three people who are not themselves, who are not three people, hold her tight.

A thing with six arms bends low and drags her. A being with six mismatched eyes glances behind, ahead, and above at once. An old creature with three smiling mouths carries Selene into the black woods.

Sharon Frame Gay

THE WITCH'S DAUGHTER

Legend was, Elsbeth, the woman who lived in the forest, was a witch. Hunched over, she walked with a knobby cane; her face burned and scarred, hands raw and blistered. She never spoke to anyone as she hobbled down the path each day with a wicker basket strapped on her back, picking herbs and plants for her potions.

The local children were afraid of her. They dared each other to dash into the woods and peer through the window of her small cottage. There were tales of bats, cats, and eye of newt, babies in cages, and fish out of water, dancing about the room.

Their parents were no better. They cursed and jeered, then later begged for signs and spells to fill empty wombs, heal illnesses, or find lost loves.

The townspeople called Elsbeth a witch. That made me a witch's daughter. I would tell you it was a strange thing, to be called this, except that I had known nothing else.

I knew her only as my mother, abandoned in these darkest of woods, me deep in her belly, secrets as vast as her expanding waistline.

Legend indeed. For I would always tell the story of how she raised me with only stones in the soup, and our breath for fire.

Mother named me Bliss on the day I was born. She told me that rays of sunshine lit the way to her birthing pallet as she lay there alone, giving me life. Later that evening, stars fluttered through the forest all the way from heaven, just to gaze at me, she said. We lived in the woods, a long walk from the nearest village. Although we were poor, I wanted for nothing. I grew up nurtured by love and happiness in our cottage deep in a hollow by a stream.

Our home was small, just one room, with a hearth, a window, and a door. Mother and I slept on straw pallets on the floor, close to the fire. We had a goat and an old cow who had seen better days, a kitten named Fern, and a half-blind dog who stumbled upon our cottage one day and stayed. I named him Wander.

Nights were peaceful because no soul dared brave the woods when darkness came. All we heard after twilight were the creatures who hunt, the owls and wild dogs, things that slithered and bumped against our door, but nothing and no one opened it.

Mother was crippled and walked with an old stick she carved from a tree limb. As a young woman, she met with an accident that almost broke her back, and she could not straighten. Her hair hung in snarled tendrils about her shoulders, face scarred and blistered from many burns that never seemed to heal. Her features were frightening and strange looking. But her eyes were the same brilliant green as mine. I thought she was beautiful. She laughed when I said this, throaty giggles transforming her into the lovely woman I imagine she once was.

How she came to live here, she would not say. It was a great mystery, and I begged to know. But she remained silent and turned away.

"Bliss," she said one rainy afternoon, "If I wanted you to know everything right here and now, I would tell you. You will learn all in good time."

The same townspeople who condemned us made their way through the woods to our threshold. They bought charms and brews and asked Mother to roll bleached bones on the hard-packed floor and tell them what their future held. She was paid with silver, or flour and meat. They scuttled away well before dark, clutching tiny vials of potions to their chest or swallowing herbs before they even reached the trail back to town. Mother laughed at their foolishness, then tossed their coin into a small pouch tied around her neck.

On the first night of every full moon, Mother left our hut when birds roosted and the forest cooled with approaching darkness.

"Never follow me, Bliss," she said each time. "For only bad will come of it."

I never did, fear pulsing through my veins as I worried each time until her return before dawn, the smell of night on her cloak. Then she would lie down and sleep for two days, breath shallow and wispy, sometimes moaning in her dreams. When she awoke, it was as though nothing happened. She returned to her potions and long walks in the glade.

I was eighteen and curious. I asked Mother over and over again to tell me where she went when the moon filled the sky, and what she did. Once, when I pushed too hard to learn the truth, she turned and hissed at me like a cat.

"Stay well away from me during the full moon, Bliss. It is all I have. All that keeps me going." And with that, she gathered her cloak around her shoulders and stepped out the door into the rain and bluster of an autumn day, whistling up Wander, strapping her basket on her twisted back.

Despite her warning, I learned the truth soon enough, and it changed our lives forever.

It was the night of the Harvest Moon. It shone through the trees and lit the paths in the hollow. Mother had been preparing for days, rinsing her hair with essence of flower petals and washing her meager dress in the stream next to our cottage. It dried, draped over a tree limb in the breeze, gathering the last rays of sunlight.

That day, I was instructed to go to the village to buy slabs of ham and a wheel of cheese. I dreaded going into town. Every time, the shopkeepers sneered and made me wait while they helped others. They shoved the food at me, snatched the coin from my hands. By the time I returned, it was sunset. When I stepped inside the hut, Mother was pacing nervously.

"What took you so long?" she asked, turning green eyes to me. "You must get ready for sleep, then I shall leave." She thrust a bowl of soup in my hands, scowled while I sipped it. "Hurry, Bliss!" she said, then turned toward the window, twisting her hands in exasperation.

I finished the soup, lay down on the pallet, rolled to my side and closed my eyes. Before long, I heard her bustling about. I caught glimpses of her packing a basket with food, braiding her long hair so it hung down her back like a thick snake. Then she tossed a shawl around her shoulders and slipped out without a word.

I leapt up, dressed, and curled out the door like smoke, closing Wander and Fern inside the cottage. Wander whined and pawed at the threshold as I stepped into the darkness.

In the distance, Mother limped down a worn trail through a stand of ancient oaks. I trotted behind, darting from tree to tree. Once, she stopped as though listening for footfalls. I fell to the ground, face in the leaves, heart pounding. In the distance, I heard the cry of an owl. Then silence. Mother turned back toward the trail and hurried on her way.

I followed for some time, matched my steps to hers as she hobbled along. Far ahead glimmered a light in a small meadow circled by tall trees. A fire. As we drew closer, it bloomed and glowed, as if it were a living thing.

Mother entered the clearing and glanced around. She took off her shawl, set the walking stick on the ground and tightened her grip on the basket. Then, to my amazement, she walked right up to the fire and stepped inside the flames! I stifled a scream, thinking of the burn marks all over her broken body. For a moment she disappeared entirely, then emerged on the other side.

I could not believe my eyes! There before me was a beautiful woman. She stood straight and tall, her face lovely and unmarred, no sign of the crippled, scarred woman I call Mother. She loosened her braid; hair flowed about her shoulders, gleaming under the moon's full light.

There was a rustling in the bushes and I ducked behind a gnarled oak, pulled my hood about my face.

"Elsbeth," a low voice said. "My love."

I edged around the tree, looked across the meadow. There stood a handsome soldier, his arms open wide. Mother ran right into them. He pulled her close, his hand tilting her face up to his. They kissed, then he removed his coat and spread it on the ground. She knelt before him, opened the basket and brought out food and ale.

I stared in astonishment. My mother, suddenly beautiful, was having a picnic under the Harvest Moon with a handsome soldier.

They finished their meal. Then without speaking, rose together and walked into the woods hand in hand.

I took one stealthy step, then another, into the clearing. The flames grew higher, reaching toward me. The heat was intense, and I heard voices coming from the depths of the fire. A spark flew from the blaze like a hornet, burned a hole in my dress, and seared my skin. I gasped in pain. Soft laughter rippled through the embers.

Frightened, I stepped back, but it was impossible to resist the voices. They pulled me closer, the heat unbearable. I fell to the ground, unable to run away. The voices grew louder, eager. I covered my ears with my hands, cried out in fear.

Just then a sharp wind whistled through the glade, and it broke the spell. The flames flattened and hissed. I crawled into the nearby bushes and collapsed. The fire murmured disappointment. Intense weariness overtook me, and I fell into a deep sleep.

When I woke, the sun was peering through a canopy of leaves. "Mother cannot find me here," I thought and turned toward home, glancing over my shoulder. I hurried down the path toward our cottage and flung myself through the door, tossed my cape on a peg and sat by the hearth.

It wasn't long before I heard familiar footsteps. Mother was home. The door swung open, and I looked up. There was the same scarred face and crippled body I knew so well. She smelled of smoke and mystery. Elsbeth undressed and knelt upon the pallet as if in prayer, closed her eyes and sighed wearily.

I pretended to stir the oats in the cauldron, turning away so she could not see all the questions on my face. Fetching a basket from the wall, I opened the door and took a step out into the new dawn.

Mother suddenly looked up, eyes wide, and stared at my dress.

"Bliss!" she cried. "What have you done?" Her finger pointed at the scorched hole in my skirt. I shrugged, nervous.

"Come here, Bliss".

I walked over. She reached for the skirt, brought it to her nose, inhaled the burnt fabric and groaned. It smelled like embers and wildflowers. Then she placed her face in her hands and cried.

"Mother, what's wrong?" I asked, guilt washing over me, for I knew I had done something terrible yet had no idea what it was.

There was a deep silence. Mother stood, walked to a chair, and sat down. It was only then I realized that there were fresh burn marks on her face and arms.

"Did you follow me?"

I did not know how to lie to my mother, so I turned toward her, hung my head. "Yes."

"What did you see?"

"Everything. I saw you walk into the fire. It transformed you into a beautiful woman. Then a man came out of the darkness and shared a meal with you. The two of you walked into the woods together."

Mother cried again. Soft little gasps that gave way to sobs. Startled, I threw my arms around her shoulders.

"What's wrong?" I asked.

She shuddered, turned her ravaged face to me, and said, "You ruined everything."

"I don't understand," I said, wringing my hands. "Please, I'm sorry! I won't do it again."

Mother rose, stepped toward the door. "I'll be back. Go nowhere. Wait here for me."

I sat down and stared out the window, heart heavy. Time went by, the forest quiet but for a few birds skirting in and out among the leaves. In the corner, Fern licked her paw, then curled up by the hearth.

Finally, I heard footsteps and stood to face the door.

Mother walked in with a smoldering stick in her hand. From deep in the charred wood, I heard faint voices. I could not understand what they were saying, but there were many of them. I stepped back, afraid.

"Sit, Bliss, for now that you have been touched by the fire, you have to know the secret. There is no other choice."

I stared warily at the stick. Mother tossed it into the hearth and it trembled, then sparks flew around the room. I ducked, shielding myself. When I looked up again, the fireplace was burning so brightly it was as though daylight had entered our hut.

"Now," Mother said. "I must tell you."

She pulled me over to the table, sat down, and stared deep into my eyes, flames reflected in hers like blazing emeralds.

"When I was young, I fell in love with a soldier. He had come to the village near my home on a mission with an army. My father told me to stay away from the soldiers, not to speak to any of them. I was already promised to a young man for marriage the following year. I wasn't happy about it, yet I had to obey Father. He was a cruel man, Bliss, and I feared him." She stood, began to pace the room. The flames in the fireplace followed her, back and forth, as though they were listening, too.

"The soldier and I began a friendship despite Father's wishes. His name was James. We were very attracted to each other. He was to stay a fortnight near our village. We met every day in the forest. Our feelings deepened.

Father found out I was spending time with James. He was furious that I disobeyed him. Angry, he locked me in my room so we could not see each other. I paced like a wild thing, distraught and trapped. Only the servants came to my door, day after day. They brought no news, and I feared that James was lost to me forever. I begged a trusted servant to give James a message. It was a great risk to all of us, and I did not know if James would ever get it.

One dark night, James climbed a rose trellis up to my window and slipped inside the room. I was overjoyed to see him again. We whispered in the darkness, sat by the fire and held hands. Then he took me in his arms, and we made love until dawn."

My cheeks burned as she told me this. I hung my head so she could not see me blush.

"When the fortnight was over, James did not go back with the army. Instead, he lived in the nearby village and continued to come to the window each night. We made plans to escape together, go far away from this land, marry." She sighed, her gaze misty with tears.

"During the next full moon, James came for me. I slipped out the window and into his arms. We started down the creaking trellis. Suddenly, it shook as though a mighty wind had knocked it about, and James and I tumbled to the ground. I landed on my back. Pain shot through my body. Father had shaken the trellis, pulled it from the earth in his rage, causing the fall. He stood over us, livid. He told me to stand up, cursing, curling his fists in the air. I could not move my legs. I called out to James, but there was no answer." Mother clasped her hands to her chest. "He lay dead, sightless eyes looking past me to the stars. His neck was broken."

Then Mother's face changed. She was furious, agitated. She dug sharp fingernails into her palms until they bled. The scars on her face reddened.

"Father carried me into the house and set me on a rug by the fire. My pain was excruciating. I begged to die with James. There was no future for me now, crippled and heartbroken. All I wanted was to be with James. Reaching down, Father slapped me, shouting that I had humiliated him. He said he would see me in Hell before he ever handed me over to James, even in Death.

"Then see me in Hell, because I curse you, Father," I screamed. "I curse you to the Devil's own fire!"

The flames in the fireplace reached out and snatched at him, hissing and licking at his arms, his legs, setting him ablaze. Father fell to the floor screaming, and I watched in horror as the flames consumed him. I could not help. All I could do was lie there and watch him die. I regretted the last words he heard from me. I didn't intend to hurt him. But the fire heard my curse and obeyed."

Mother wrung her hands, tears spilling down her face. She shuddered, then went on.

"Father was dead, his charred remains on the rug before the hearth. My James was dead. Deep in the embers, I heard voices. They were calling to me. I could not move away from them. Sparks leapt higher and higher until they reached my skirt, lapping at the hem until the dress burst into flames."

She halted, stared at the hearth, the fire glittering and casting shadows about the room. "I should have joined James and Father wherever our souls might take us, but the Devil had other plans for me, it seems."

She lowered her voice, shook her head from side to side in wonder. "I awakened here in these woods. I don't remember, or know how I got here. My belly was filled with you, and you grew despite my pain and the slow weariness of healing." She looked at me tenderly, took my hand.

"After you were born, I found myself called from my bed during a full moon. I followed voices down the path to the clearing. On the other side of the flames, I saw James, waiting for me in death. I wanted to join him for all time, but I had you, Bliss. I could not bear to leave you behind."

I stood then, touched her scarred face. "What happens, Mother?" I asked. "What happens with every full moon?" But I feared that I already knew.

Her voice was soft. I strained to listen.

"I walk through the flames. On the other side is James. We spend the night in each other's arms. My heart sings. We are so happy to be together, even in death."

"I can't leave you yet, Bliss, so in the morning when the sun comes up, I say goodbye to James and step back into the fire. The flames don't want to give me up, and I pay a price. They lick at my legs, lap at my face, mock me with their voices. Each month, each year, they grow hungrier."

"My love for you is stronger than the bite of the fire, but my love for James keeps me going back every time the moon gains fullness."

She hesitated, smiled. "James is your father."

I nodded, knees trembling, heart pounding. My father! I had seen my father in the glow of the embers for the first time in my life.

She kissed my forehead, turned toward the hearth. "So now you know. Following me may have broken the curse. Or made it stronger. The fire had a taste of you, and now the voices are getting louder. They are hungry for your soul, too. I am not sure it is safe for you here anymore."

"But Mother, this is the only home I know!" I cried.

She nodded. We sat at the table, our fingers touching. Hers were warm, smelled of charred flesh. We talked for hours. I wanted to know about my father. She was eager to tell me. Finally, weary, she limped to her pallet and lay down, tossing fitfully in her sleep.

Rising from the table, I flung upon the door and rushed into the cool afternoon. Wander bounded ahead of me as we ran down the path toward the meadow.

When I reached the clearing, the fire was gone, as though it had never been there. In its place were wildflowers and grasses, dancing in the breeze. Wander whimpered, sniffed at the ground, sat and cocked his head toward the far trees. It all seemed like a dream.

I returned home uneasily. There was nothing to do now but wait through the phases of the moon. The days spent themselves peacefully in the glade, the slight tang of autumn drifting through the trees. But inside our home, there was tension and a great sadness that belied the soft sounds of the birds and wind in the trees.

The next full moon was approaching. I sensed Mother's agitation as each dawn passed. The cycle was drawing down upon us, night after night. I wondered what Elsbeth would do. Would she return to the fire? Could she resist its spell?

Finally, when the moon had risen completely in the night sky and bathed the forest in its cold light, I turned to Mother and spoke.

"I'm almost a woman now, and I know what love means. I understand that your love for me and for my father brought you through the fire month after month. One day it will take you forever."

She nodded sadly. "I do it for you, Bliss, and for him."

I reached for her cloak, held it for her. "No more, Mother. I won't let you do this again. I want you to go to James." My breath stopped for a moment. I drew myself up with all my courage and stammered, "Forever."

Her eyes met mine. I saw hope and despair at the same time. Fear and relief. My heart ached to think of all the years she'd walked through the fire for our love. How she must have suffered.

"No, Bliss. I can't leave you. I won't go back tonight, or ever again."

"Yes, you will. Because I hear the voices in the flames, too, Mother. They're waiting for me as well." I hesitated. "It's also where I belong someday."

She cupped my chin in her hand.

"So," she said. "You now understand all of it."

I nodded. "We all died that terrible night, didn't we, Mother? I died with you, in your womb. But you couldn't bear to lose me to death, to have me perish before I had a chance to live, so you fight the flames over and over again. You defy the pact you made with the Devil during every full moon. You gave me life, but you never fully lived. We must go to the fire tonight, Mother. We must! It is your time."

I threw on my cape, tucked her arm in mine, and we walked slowly toward the light deep in the woods. As we drew closer, the burns on my leg erupted into blisters. My fingers held the stick that Mother brought from the clearing and it trembled in my hand. From far away, I heard the voices calling, as the moon lit our way.

"Come no farther, Bliss," Mother warned. She took the stick from my hand, stepped into the meadow. The fire burned even brighter than it had the month before. We heard the voices calling out. I felt a surge of longing, wanted to step forward too, but Mother stopped me with a kiss on my cheek. Before I could tell her goodbye, she walked toward the fire, and stepped inside. The blaze grew higher and higher, dazzling. I fell to the ground as a great whoosh of air sent sparks into the night sky like a thousand stars.

Then, Elsbeth stepped out into the evening on the other side. She looked luminous in the moonlight, as beautiful as she looked on the day she died. Out of the woods walked my father, and she ran to him. He gazed across the fire at me and smiled. I had a brief glimpse of all the love I had missed, all the years I did not know him. They stood together and looked long at me, as though etching me into their hearts. Then they walked toward the edge of the woods. Mother turned back one more time, hesitated. James gathered her close, and they disappeared into the dark.

The voices sighed, the fire went out. I sat in the meadow and watched the sun come up over the line of trees as flowers sprouted and bloomed from the ashes.

I knew the fire would call to me someday, and I would join my mother and father, but it was not time yet. Mother sacrificed everything so that I might live, and I owed her this lifetime.

This was just the beginning of *my* story. I would walk out of these woods, leave the legend, the curse, and the Witch's Daughter behind. Venture out to new lands and live my life the way Elsbeth and James would want me to do. I knew that one day they would be waiting for me once again across the flames.

There is no greater love, I thought. Then I stood, dusted off my skirt, and turned toward home, Wander leading the way.

Max Sparber

THE CINDER BULL

McCracken nudged the searchlight with his foot. It moved, but just enough. The muted edges of its beam caught movement between a row of cattle cars: the heel of a boot.

There was never much useful light during McCracken's shift, even when the moon was full, as it was tonight. The bosses were stingy and limited nighttime illumination to a military surplus searchlight. The light was old and dim, throwing a paltry beam from the engine house to the switching tracks, offering scant visibility on the main line.

This left too much darkness in the yard. It left places where a clever jack might hide. An ambitious hobo could tuck himself into the brush alongside the tracks and wait for the opportune moment.

No matter. McCracken knew what to look for. He was old, but not so old that his eyes couldn't pick out movement from a distance. He knew when a tramp was creeping behind a rail car, like now.

Bos should know better. But, McCracken reasoned, if they knew better, they wouldn't be bos.

This yard, McCracken's yard, had a reputation in the tramp world. Hobos had their own language, and in their language this was a *bad road* and McCracken was a *yard boxer*. He was a *cinder bull.*

He was, they said, a man who liked to kill hobos.

If McCracken had cared to argue the point, he would have said that it wasn't about liking or disliking. There was no emotion in it. It was a job, and this was a time when you did your job right the first time and without fuss.

The old searchlight was rickety, but McCracken knew how to wield it like a razor. Perched on a wooden stool on the engine house porch, he could nudge the lamp with the toe of his engineer boot and it would move imperceptibly. He could follow a tramp's movement with just the lightest touch. He could see what he needed to see with just the fuzzy line of the spotlight beam, the place where light faded to darkness.

The bo would never know the light had caught him. He wouldn't know that he had been spotted until knowing made no difference.

In this way, McCracken followed the tramp behind the cars. The man staggered and shuffled. It used to be that hobos took care to move with light feet, but McCracken had seen more and more of these stumblebums, drunk on sterno, looking for a car to sleep in.

He'd put a few of these wretched men under the oily dirt of the train yard.

Anyway, if McCracken wanted to argue about his reputation, he'd mention that he was licensed by the state, and his license included using however much force he deemed necessary. The sap was not a subtle instrument, but was meant to inflict damage, and sometimes it would split a head or burst an organ.

McCracken didn't care to argue the point. As he figured it, a reputation for murderousness made his job easier.

Should anyone request it, the county could investigate a death. Nobody ever requested it, and so, come sunup, McCracken would just write a report and enlist help from an unhappy yard employee. There was a half-acre at the end of the yard where they planted unlucky tramps, which they did without concern or ceremony.

McCracken inched his spotlight again. Directly in front of him, McCracken had left the door to a cattle car open. Not open much, but enough that a man could slide through. The hobo now reached this car.

An experienced tramp would know this to be a trap and wouldn't go near it. He would, instead, locate the darkest corner of the train and fold himself under it, setting a board on the steel rods that hung beneath the older cars. There he would wedge himself behind the wheels, where he would be hard to see and harder to dislodge.

McCracken had a pointed stick for this circumstance. If he couldn't poke the tramp out of his hiding place, well, McCracken was still strong enough to reach under, grab fabric, and drag a man out.

But the bos with the boards were lifers. They had spent decades crisscrossing the country going from one itinerant job to another. They knew the path and knew where it wasn't safe. They knew which yards had brutal guards and which had hobo graveyards. They didn't come to McCracken's yard anymore. Not with his reputation.

There was a new group. Jobs were scarce and so there came a flood of young comets, cats, dingoes, fakirs, and other amateur hobos. These men were new to the road and didn't know which yards were safe and which were bad. They didn't know enough to be cautious.

The amateurs always went for the open door on the cattle car, into the trap. Like this bo.

In preparation, McCracken put his hand out to his left, a move so practiced he did not have to look. There, hanging from a nail, was his nightstick.

McCracken nudged his spotlight again, sending just a sliver of light through the louvered side of the cattle car. It lit gently, like a trench lamp opening.

The car was now just lit enough that McCracken could see a silhouette through the slatted walls. The figure pulled itself aboard the car and then stood for a moment, glancing about. Then the silhouette crossed to a corner of the stock car.

There was some fabric there, probably burlap sacks hung by ranchers to feed traveling cattle. Hobos liked to use these for bedding. The silhouette draped the fabric around it like a blanket and sat down.

As soon as the hobo was seated, McCracken moved. With a single, fluid motion he swung the spotlight fully onto the car, lighting it up. He snatched his billy club and his posterior left his stool. He ran toward the cattle car with a ferocious yawp.

McCracken had done this many time before. The hobo would be temporarily blinded by the spotlight and panic.

McCracken relied on panic, as it made hobos foolish and reckless. McCracken had once seen a panicked hobo leap from a moving train directly in front of an oncoming train. Falling beneath it, the hobo had been tossed for several miles, losing his limbs along the route.

McCracken knew how this panic played out in the yard. When a hobo was hit with McCracken's spotlight, he would make a blind run for the door. When he found it and leaped out, McCracken would already be there, his nightstick slicing the air.

The entry to the cattle car was about waist high for McCracken, so his first blow would typically catch a tramp on his shins as he leapt to the ground below. Then McCracken would strike again, this time at the head, as the hobo staggered to his feet in pain.

Most times, the hobo kept going, rabbiting into the woods and leaving blood and teeth behind. Sometimes they just collapsed, eyes open and staring insensibly.

McCracken brought the fallen men back to the engine house, doused them with a water bucket, and menaced them for a while. Usually that was all that was needed, but sometimes McCracken had to bust a finger to make a point. And his point was simple: Don't come back.

This was how things went with the bos that woke up. Some never did. These McCracken buried with the help of a grumbling yard joe.

This was how panic usually played out in the yard, but not always. Sometimes, the hobos remained in the train rather than fleeing it.

This happened now. McCracken reached the door, breathing hard from his sprint, arm raised with club ready, and found an empty door. The bo should have popped out but didn't, leaving McCracken's arm hanging in the air, giving his sap no target.

This only happened with the dedicated booze artists and dipsomaniacs. They were often so soused on squeeze as to be unaware, and McCracken would find them sprawled on the floor of the stock car, sometimes in their own sick.

These were the worst. Alcohol made them numb, and so McCracken had to put extra effort in. Some scarcely noticed when he mashed noses or brought blood from eardrums, but McCracken knew his job. He always made his point in the end.

McCracken peered in the stock car. There, in the corner, under burlap, was a man-sized lump.

McCracken liked to make a lot of noise in these circumstances. A cornered hobo could turn swiftly and surprisingly violent—McCracken had a scar under a rib where he had once taken a knife from a tramp feigning sleep.

The cinder bull pulled the entire cattle car door open, bringing forth an ear-splitting metallic scream. Then McCracken pounded the walls of the car with his sap, which boomed like a sledgehammer striking a metal drum.

The lump did not move.

McCracken pulled himself into the train and stood up. He walked toward the figure slowly, still pounding on the wall. The noise was terrific, but still the lump did not move.

He stood above it. Perhaps the lump was already dead. There had been an epidemic of hobos getting their hands on industrial alcohol poisoned with methyl alcohol and chloroform. Hobos who drank this often crawled into dark places and curled up, to be found the next day, hands clutching stomach, faces contorted in pain, bodies stiff.

McCracken gave the lump an experimental whack with his sap. The blow landed with a practiced cruelty, the sort of experienced blow that would contuse muscle and splinter bone.

The lump did not respond, so McCracken struck it a few more times. If the hobo wasn't dead when McCracken started, the hobo was certainly dead now.

McCracken pulled the burlap from the figure, expecting to see a smashed face staring blankly back at him. Instead, there was just more burlap. He dug through the sacks, confused.

It was impossible that he had just been flogging fabric. McCracken knew the feel of a body when his stick struck one, and there had been a body. And yet there was nothing but burlap sack piled atop burlap sack.

McCracken pressed his tongue to the back of his teeth, thinking, and then made a frustrated "tsk" sound. It was impossible that the hobo had left the stock car without McCracken seeing.

From behind him, McCracken heard the unmistakable sound of somebody climbing into the car. McCracken turned.

The hobo squatted just inside the door, hands pressed against the ground, like a dog might sit. The man was dressed in soiled rags and a filthy fedora, his hair long and tangled, his mottled face partially hidden under a massive, matted beard.

The hobo stared at McCracken, eyes dim and yellow. His mouth moved, opening and closing with a smacking of his lips.

"Connecting train 48," the hobo said, his voice hollow and remote. "Albany to Ashtabula."

The hobo rose, standing upright, but oddly. His shoulders lifted too high, up around his ears like he was shrugging, and his arms hung loosely at his side. McCracken's tongue darted back and forth across the back of his teeth, an unconscious gesture when he was confused.

The hobo moved, an act that seemed to take some effort. He shuffled forward, still staring at McCracken with his yellow eyes, his jaw still working, opening and closing his mouth like a puppet might. "26 daily continuing," the man said. "Utica to Elkhart."

McCracken watched the hobo approach. When the man got close enough, McCracken brought his sap up and then down in rapid motion, striking the corner of the hobo's left knee at a vicious angle.

This sort of blow would separate ligament from bone, leaving the leg useless and bent slightly sideways. In McCracken's entire inventory of nightstick attacks, this was the one that consistently produced the greatest response, the most satisfying and hideous cries of agony.

The hobo's knee bent inward, as expected, but there was not the cry, nor the fall to the floor that always followed.

McCracken glanced up. The hobo continued to stare at him and then resumed shuffling forward, the left leg wobbling in a grotesque way as the man put pressure on it, making an audible grinding sound.

McCracken smashed his stick along the hobo's head, hard enough to pop the man's hat off. The side of the head, above the ear, crushed inward like a rotten melon, leaving a visible dent.

The hobo continued forward, still staring at McCracken, mouth still opening and closing. "Pittsfield eight ten Buffalo eleven fifty," the hobo said.

Behind the hobo, McCracken caught movement. He looked over the tramp's shoulder and saw another man climbing aboard the train. This man was likewise in rags, with a bare, bald head and sickly, yellowed eyes. The man saw McCracken, and the man's mouth fell open.

"Passaic and then to Port Jervis," the new man said.

McCracken frowned. He put his hands on the ragged coat of the hobo in front of him and pushed the man backward, toward the train door.

McCracken was still strong enough to throw a man off a train, and so he shoved the hobo into the bald man, scattering both into the blasted tall grass outside the stock car.

Then, in the full moonlight, McCracken saw what was outside the stock car and froze in place.

There were at least a hundred of them, many right outside the door, all in ragged coats and battered hats.

All staggered toward the stock car, staring at McCracken with sallow, glassy eyes. All had mouths that opened and closed as though uncontrolled, all muttering. "Susquehanna," one said. "Depew," another said. "Through Sleeper New York Bradford," said a third.

They surged toward him.

McCracken unpeeled himself from where he was standing and grabbed the stock car door. He pulled it hard, dragging the heavy steel door along its track. Several hobos, reaching into the cab, were dragged along with it, and then they all jammed up at the end in a clump of foul smelling fabric, straw hats, and muttering mouths.

If McCracken was going to get the door closed, he was going to need to clear those hobos out. He kicked at the nearest, shoving the tramp with his foot, but the crowd behind was thick. The hobo fell back and then was pushed forward again, returning to his place at the door.

McCracken knew he was starting to panic, and he knew how dangerous that could be.

So McCracken inhaled and exhaled. He pressed his tongue against the back of his teeth.

He considered what he knew and what he didn't know, and he threw away what he didn't know, as there was no time to make sense of it.

McCracken knew that there was something wrong with these men. He knew they were coming at him. And he knew that it was safest to assume the worst and act accordingly.

He looked at the vast gang of hobos pushing their way toward the door. He looked at the hobos blocking the door from closing.

Then he made a decision. He reached into his engineer boot. McCracken pulled out a blade with a wooden handle.

He stood and set about his grim task. This was now the job, and he intended do the job right the first time and without fuss.

He walked down the line of hobos pressed against the doorway of the car and plunged his knife into each one, just below their neck and above their collarbone.

There was a blood vessel there, a thick one, and McCracken knew that once it was opened, a man would go down in seconds and would be dead in a minute.

The blood came, and in the gauzy shine of the spotlight it looked wrong: thick and black.

The hobos stared at him with yellow eyes as they drained, mouths still moving, still muttering train numbers and destinations. Then each slumped in turn, like deflating paper bags.

Behind them, the other hobos continued to push forward. McCracken watched them and wiped his knife on his shirt.

The hobos began climbing over the bodies. McCracken expected that. When the next row reached him, he stuck them one by one, expertly finding the place between the throat and the collarbone, letting the thick black blood ooze out.

McCracken was old, but he could still fight for as long as he needed to. He was ready to cut down row upon row of these ragged men, even if they piled up at his feet.

McCracken would fight even if they scrambled over each other, even if that pile grew, even if he had to stand atop bodies.

The next row of hobos climbed atop their dead and staggered toward McCracken. Behind them, in the light of the full moon, there seemed to be no end. The air was filled with the muttered names of whistle stops and weigh stations, routes and timetables, spoken by thousands of hoarse, distant voices.

An unhappy yard employee found McCracken the next day and sprinted into the engine house to alert the boss, who came out and looked in the stock car and then shook his head.

The yard boss wrote up a report and then he and the miserable yard joe buried what they found.

The boss's report was the words of a bewildered administrator. He noted that the cause of death was unknown, since McCracken was found in an empty car. There was speculation that McCracken must have been inside when cattle were loaded on or off.

This happened every so often, the boss noted. A yard employee was in the car at the wrong moment and was trampled by the stock. Put 12 cows in a car, that's 24,000 pounds of cattle, and a man does not want to get caught in an enclosed space with that much tonnage.

But the boss also wrote that it was unclear when cattle and McCracken might have been in the car at the same time. And McCracken was experienced. He had been one of the oldest hands at the yard. The boss noted that it didn't make sense that McCracken had gone like this.

Moreover, as the boss wrote and underlined, nobody could explain how McCracken had been crushed against the ceiling.

These frustrated notes were put on file in the engine house office, should anyone request to see them.

If someone had cared to, they could have asked for an official investigation.

But nobody ever did.

Amanda J. Evans

MOONLIGHT MAGIC

My mother warned me about magic under the full moon. Of creatures that lurked in the shadows of the old oak trees. Their razor-sharp claws that could slice through skin and bone, and a scream so terrifying it forced the soul from the body. I asked her what happened to the bodies and their detached souls. She said I never wanted to know. I should have forced her to tell me.

Sarah's tap tap tapping of her perfectly manicured nails went through my brain. "Will you please stop," I snapped.

"What?" She stood poised at the entrance to my bedroom, door swung open, as she tapped her fingers against the frame.

"That bloody tapping. It's driving me mad."

"Oh." She curled her fingers into her fist. "Sorry." She shifted her weight from foot to foot, mouth open as if to say something.

"You could help."

"I could." A grin spread across her face and she shook her head. "But I don't think I will."

"Please," I begged looking around at the mess. "You know what she's like. We're not leaving until it's done."

"Fine," Sarah said, glancing at her phone screen. "But only because I don't want to be late. What is it with you anyway, Cass?"

"Huh?" I lifted my head from the pile of clothes I was sorting.

"Your mom's a clean freak and you…well, look around; you're a bit of a slob."

I followed her gaze. Sundresses, shorts, and t-shirts covered most of the fawn carpet. College books sat piled high on the small desk in the corner. A few of them splayed open on the floor where they'd fallen earlier. My bed with its flower-patterned duvet was in disarray, and I still hadn't opened my curtains. "It's homely."

"Yeah, right," Sarah muttered stepping inside and closing the door. She toed the pink, daisy-covered sundress, like it might infect her. "What's with all the summer clothes anyway?"

"I needed somewhere to hide everything," I said, shoving the black, leather-bound book into my bag and reaching for the pillar candles.

Sarah shook her head. "It's nearly winter."

"Exactly. Mom's not going to look through my summer clothes at this time of the year."

Sarah's phone chimed and she tapped the screen. "Hurry up, Alice is waiting. I've told her we'll be there in five. You know, you really need to reconsider moving in with us. You can't stay here forever."

"You know I can't. Mom needs me."

"You need to live your life, too."

I closed my bag and placed it on the floor. "I will when she's ready."

"It's been five years, Cassie. She can't live in limbo forever. Look around you. Nothing's changed." Sarah motioned to my room. Pink and girly, a reminder of how things used to be. I pushed the memories away. Mom was all I had now, and she needed me more than I needed my freedom.

"Mom, I'm off now," I shouted on the way down the stairs.

"Everything in its place? Balance is essential," she said as she stepped into the hallway.

I sighed. My mom, immaculate in every way. Her pristine navy dress kept clean by the apron she wore over it. Her chestnut hair pulled back into a neat bun at the back of her head and her makeup flawless. She looked exactly the same as she had five years ago.

"Yes, Mom," I mumbled, meeting her at the bottom of the stairs.

"Wait there while I check."

I huffed and folded my arms. Sarah pretended to inspect her nails as Mom brushed past us and disappeared upstairs.

"Off you go," Mom called a minute later. "Be back before eleven."

"Bye, Mom," I called, racing towards the front door.

"Bye, Mrs. Pierce," Sarah shouted.

"Come on, you," I said, shoving her out the door.

"What?" She glared at me. "I'm only being polite. I'm the only one she lets in, remember."

Just as I was about to shut the door, Mom called out again. "Be safe." I poked my head around the door and caught her smile.

"I will," I said, shaking my head. She still treated me like I was fifteen.

The park was quiet when we arrived. Swings at a standstill, not even a breeze to make them sway. No screams of delight as little kids flew down the slide. Even the walking track was empty. I looked over my shoulder, scanning the park as we walked.

"What are you looking for?" Sarah asked.

"Nothing, just keeping an eye out for Alice."

"Are you afraid of the dark?" Sarah teased.

"Of course not."

It wasn't that dark anyway. Lampposts lit the way every couple of yards, and the full moon glistened, casting light over the black water of the lake. No swans or ducks tonight. No children throwing crumbs. No chirps or tweets of birds in the trees. In fact, there was no sound at all.

My foot snagged on the side of a rock and I stumbled forward, grabbing onto Sarah to stop myself from falling flat on my face.

"You all right?"

"Yeah. Didn't see the rock."

She stifled a laugh. "Alice said she'd meet us by the entrance to the woods. She's probably wondering what's keeping us." Sarah checked the time on her phone as she picked up the pace.

The light from the screen reflected off her face. She was the pretty one in our group. Blonde curls framed her face and fell halfway down her back. High cheekbones, full lips, and deep brown eyes completed her look. She didn't have to try. Even dressed in black jeans, flat boots, and a loose black top, she looked great. I looked down at my own attire. Same clothes, but I looked totally different. Short and stumpy was how I'd describe myself. My chestnut hair never shone like Mom's. It dangled limply past my shoulders and never changed, no matter how much I styled it. I'd gripped it back in a ponytail before we left the house.

"You're very quiet. Are you nervous?" Sarah asked, disrupting my thoughts.

"No, just thinking."

"I'm excited. I can't wait to see what happens. It's not every day you get to become a witch and cast spells. You know, if this works, we can do so many things. Free drinks at the bar, perfect hair every day, any man we want. It'll be great."

I laughed. "You know that nothing is going to happen. There's no such thing as witches, or spells for that matter."

She stuck her tongue out at me. "Spoil sport. Let me dream about Scott Grayson falling at my feet and begging me to go out with him."

I laughed and she joined in.

At the end of the pathway that ran parallel with the lake, we took a left turn towards Oak Woods. It was darker now, the lampposts left behind.

Sarah pulled out her phone again and switched on the flashlight. An owl hooted, making us both jump as fallen leaves crunched under our feet. My breath came out in white wisps. "Is it just me or has it gone cold?" I pulled my jacket tight.

"It is a little chilly," Sarah said, rubbing her arms. "I should have worn a jacket."

The trees loomed above, branches moving, leaves rustling. A creaking, moaning sound came from in front, and I stalled.

Sarah walked past me, following the small beam of light from her phone. I focused on her silhouette, forcing one foot in front of the other.

It wasn't my idea to come out here. I'd found the book among Dad's things in the attic. He was a professor of the occult before he vanished five years ago. Since then, Mom's refused to change a thing. She was always on guard, watching, and being totally over protective. Sarah had spied the book over my shoulder and insisted on looking at it. I'd tried to stop her, but once she got an idea in her head, that was it. She took the book and thought all her Christmases had come at once. "We have to try it. It'll be an adventure," she'd said.

Trudging through Oak Woods in the pitch dark wasn't my idea of fun. Of course, she'd roped Alice into it too, convinced her it'd be exciting. A branch snapped under my feet, and Sarah shushed me. "I want to sneak up on Alice, and that's not going to happen with you making all that noise."

"I can't help it. I can't bloody see where I'm going."

"Shush; we're almost there."

The trees blocked the light from the moon, cocooning us within their prison. The trail through the woods was just around the next corner. "Try to be as quiet as you can. I'm turning off the flashlight so Alice won't see us. I can't wait to see her face. She's such a scaredy cat."

"You sure that's a good idea?"

"You're no fun, Cass. What's gotten into you tonight?"

"Nothing," I mumbled. But there was something. A dread gnawed at me from the inside, and the closer we got to the woods, the worse it became. It wasn't Alice that was afraid; it was me, and I had no idea why.

Sarah turned off the flashlight and stopped. She looped one arm through mine. "Quiet as you can," she whispered.

Darkness closed in as I tried to adjust to the loss of light. I blinked a few times and focused on where the path turned. One hand brushed off the bushes as we tiptoed along. Sarah giggled every couple of feet as we crept up on Alice. A twig cracked under my feet, and a beam of light pointed in our direction.

"Who's there?" Alice said.

"It's just us, Alice," I said.

Sarah squeezed my arm, hard.

"Ouch." I glared at her.

"Sorry. I just wanted to see the look on her face. I didn't mean it."

"What took you so long? I've been waiting for ages, and it's freezing," Alice said, rubbing her arms. She wasn't wearing a jacket either.

"Why aren't you wearing a coat? I asked.

"Thought I'd dress the part," she said, doing a spin.

I laughed. I couldn't help it. Alice wore a long, floaty, black dress and stripy tights.

"You know, if we were going to be witches and all. You like my hat?" She pulled a hat from behind her back and placed it on her head.

Sarah broke into a fit of laughter. "Good God."

"It's great." I managed to say between giggles.

"Let's get going. I don't want to be out here all night." Alice linked arms with Sarah and turned towards the woods.

"Wait for me," I said, linking in with them.

It was a narrow, twisting path, winding through the woods. The moonlight was obscured by the tall imposing trees on either side. During the summer, the green-tinged sunlight cast shadows on the path and the air was heavy with blossom fragrance. How I wished it was summer again as we walked almost tiptoeing along. Using the phones as flashlights, we followed the pathway towards the clearing at the centre of Oak Woods.

"Have you got everything?" Alice asked as I dropped my bag on the ground and started to unzip it.

"Yep. Place these in a circle around me," I said, handing over the pillar candles. "Make sure you make it big enough for me to move around in."

"Where do we stand?" Sarah asked as she looked around the clearing.

I hadn't thought about that. From what I'd read in the book, the person casting the spell sat inside the circle. There was no mention of anyone else. Not that anything was going to happen anyway. Sarah waited for me to answer. "Erm…I guess you can sit or stand wherever you like."

"We'll sit under that tree across from you," Alice said. "The roots are huge, plenty of room for both of us, Sarah. And we can see everything."

Alice walked towards the tree, glancing behind her every couple of steps.

"You okay?" I asked.

"Yeah; didn't think it would be this dark or quiet though."

"The clouds are moving quick enough and the moon is full, so there'll be plenty of light in a minute or two."

"Come on." Sarah clapped her hands. "Candles are done. What does the book say to do next?"

I pulled the book from my bag and opened it to the page containing the spell. "A bit of light, please."

Sarah shone her phone over the page, and I read down through the instructions. They were written in an ancient language, but after spending most of my childhood shadowing Dad, coupled with his subtle notes in the margins, the spell seemed pretty straight forward. "You need to place the bowl with the dried herbs in the center of the circle."

"I have them here," Alice said, taking a small wooden bowl and a handful of withered-looking leaves from her bag. She placed them in the center of the circle and stood back.

"Now I light the candles and say the words." I positioned myself on the ground inside the circle. It was cold and damp, a chill seeping into my bones. Pulling the lighter from my pocket, I lit the first candle.

Alice sucked in a deep breath and grabbed Sarah by the arm. "We better move out of the way."

They shuffled over to the oak tree and sat on the gnarled roots protruding from the ground. Sarah kept the light from her phone turned on. I glanced over at them before lighting the remaining candles. Shadows danced on the ground as I held the book open on my knees. "You ready?"

"Do it. I want to see what happens," Sarah said.

Alice huddled in close to her.

"You ready, Alice?"

"Yes—just do it so we can get out of here. This place gives me the creeps."

Sarah laughed. "You're such a chicken."

"You know I don't like the dark, not since you all left me out here when we were playing hide and seek when we were ten."

"Oops. Forgot about that," Sarah said as she linked arms with Alice.

"It'll be fine. Nothing's going to happen," I said, trying to reassure them both. The thing was, Dad believed in this stuff, and Mom's stories played in my mind. I shook my head and focused on the book. My hands trembled as I read over the words. Sucking in a deep breath, I started at the top of the page.

"O great spirits of the ancestors, hear me now and assist in this spell. Bring forth your essence and instill me with your power, so I may conjure the elements. O great ones…"

A branch snapped and Alice squealed. "What was that?"

Sarah's gaze met mine. "It was probably just an animal, Alice. It's fine."

"Cassie's right," Sarah said as she released Alice's vice-like grip on her arm.

I continued. "I command you. Wind from the north, wind from the south, the east, the west, gather your strength. Hear my words. Come forth now." I paused, stuck on the words that followed. I wasn't sure what they meant, and I couldn't translate them.

"What's wrong?" Sarah asked.

"Nothing. It's just these next words. I don't know what they mean."

"Just say them like they sound."

I brushed my hand over the page, finger underneath each word as I pronounced them. I had no idea what I was saying, but it sounded musical on my tongue. My heart thumped in my ears as a breeze fluttered around me. The last part was easy. "Fire, earth, water, air, elements of power, hear me. Take this offering. Give me your power. Give me your strength, reveal the truth, reveal it now. Show yourself."

I stumbled on the next word. It was underlined three times. Did that mean to say it three times? I couldn't translate it either, and there were no notes in the margin. I cast a glance at the girls. Alice shivered and the light from Sarah's phone revealed a big grin on her face. I fumbled over the word and completed the spell. "Show yourself spirit, and let us be one. I command, and so it shall be."

The book slammed closed and a sharp gust of cold air swept through the clearing, snuffing out the candles.

Thunder rumbled in the distance, and fat drops of rain hit my face. I struggled to pull the lighter from my pocket. "Sarah, shine the light over here."

There was no answer.

"Sarah?"

Alice shrieked, and I managed to light the candle in front of me. "Alice, Sarah?" I looked in their direction. Two shadows hunched over beside the oak tree. "Shine the light," I yelled.

"She can't," Alice blubbered. "She's…"

"What?" I scrambled to my feet.

Branches cracked and leaves rustled behind me. "Who's there?" I spun on my heels, peering into the darkness. Heavy, fat raindrops turned into a torrential downpour, soaking my face. Thunder erupted again, followed by a flash of lightning. It was enough to show me my friends. Alice gripped Sarah's arms and shook her.

"I'm coming over to you."

"I can't wake her up," Alice sobbed. "She just fell over."

"It's okay." I took in a deep breath and reached for one of the candles. I lit the wick and cradled it in my hand, protecting the flame from the wind and rain. One foot in front of the other, I stepped outside the circle.

A high-pitched scream tore through the clearing, and the hair on the back of my neck stood. I froze. "What was that?"

Alice screamed again, and I forced myself to move. The wind whipped my hair across my face and icy rain pummelled my body.

"What's happening? What did you do?" Alice trembled beside Sarah's unconscious body.

"I didn't do anything. It's a freak storm. We have to get out of here."

I reached out for her arm and pulled Alice to her feet. Her hair was flattened against her head, hanging limply down her back. Her blue eyes wide as her gaze fell on Sarah.

"We need to get her up," I said, grabbing one of Sarah's arms.

"Did we do this?" Alice stuttered.

"No, it's a freak storm."

"The weather man didn't say anything."

"Of course he didn't. That's why they're called freak storms. No one knows when they'll hit." I tried to make my voice light, but even I was trembling inside.

"Sarah," I said, tapping the side of her face. She mumbled. I gripped her arm, and Alice and I pulled her to her feet. "Come on. Wake up. We have to go," I said as she blinked her eyes and staggered.

"What happened?"

"You passed out. I couldn't wake you," Alice said, wiping her hand across her face. "I thought you'd died or…" She stopped and peered over her shoulder. "Did you hear that?"

"Hear what?"

"I heard something moving."

Sarah and I looked at each other. "Let's just get out of here. We're all soaked through." I reached down and grabbed my bag. "Are you okay now?" I asked Sarah.

"Yeah, just a little dizzy."

I threw my bag over my shoulder and we started to move. "We can call a taxi once we get back to the park."

A strong gust of wind blasted me as I stood out from the shelter of the tree. Rain assaulted my face, and I lowered my head. "We'll have to run." I aimed the beam of light from the phone towards the opening in the trees. "Grab onto each other."

"What about the candles and stuff?" Alice asked.

"Leave them. I'll come back for them tomorrow."

Thunder boomed in the distance, and a flash of light lit up the small clearing again.

"Where's the exit gone?" I gasped as large brambles and bushes blocked the pathway back to the park. "There's nothing here."

"It's there; look," Sarah said, pointing her phone to my right.

We turned. The ground squelched beneath my boots, already muddy from the downpour. It was one of the things I hated about living in this part of the country, especially in late autumn. You never knew what the weather would throw at you.

The three of us gripped hands as we edged forward, the small beam of light from the phone leading the way. We'd only taken a couple of steps when Alice cried out.

"Something bit me." She reached down and rubbed the bottom of her leg. "Look." She held out her hand. It was covered in blood.

"Bit you? Are you sure you didn't catch your leg on one of the brambles?"

She started crying. "I felt it—teeth sinking into my leg. I want to go home now."

Sarah looked at me and then back to Alice. "You take Cassie's hand. I'll go behind."

Alice limped behind me as we made our way towards the opening. Her clammy hand slipped, so I squeezed it tightly.

"Almost there," I said to reassure her.

The rain stopped and the wind died down to a gentle breeze. The air smelled of damp, and I pulled in a lungful.

"About time," Sarah said. "At least now, we might dry off a bit before we get home."

I pushed forward, my focus on the gap between the trees and our freedom. "Just a little farther and we're on the park trail," I said to Alice. She'd stopped crying, but her snuffles and hiccups told me she was anything but fine. "How's your leg?"

"It stings like mad. I probably need a shot. Who knows what bit me."

"I think we're going in the wrong direction," Sarah said.

"No, the clearing is right ahead," I said, shining the light. In front of me stood a solid barrier of trees and brambles. I shook my head. "It was there a second ago." I stopped and turned. We all stood in a line. Alice shivered.

Sarah looked dumbfounded as she lifted her phone and shone it around in a circle. "We're still in the center of the clearing. We haven't moved."

"Don't be silly. Of course, we moved."

"I'm not joking, Cass. We're still here; look." Sarah aimed her phone, and the circle of candles was right in front of us, along with the book I'd left there.

"The storm must have confused us."

"It's the spell. We're trapped." Alice started crying again.

I wrapped my arms around her. "There's no such thing as magic or spells, Alice. We're not trapped. I promise."

"At least the rain has stopped," Sarah said. "We may as well gather up this stuff before we leave."

"Good thinking. You start gathering the candles, and I'll grab the book."

"Don't leave me on my own," Alice sobbed as I stepped to the left.

"I'm just going to grab the book. Have my phone. You'll be fine."

"No," she cried, grabbing my arm.

Sarah met my gaze and shrugged.

"I'll gather everything. You stay with Alice," I said.

Alice grabbed Sarah's hand and pulled her close.

"I'll just be a minute and then we can go home." The book lay closed on the ground. It looked undamaged. I stepped into the circle and bent to retrieve it. A gust of wind caught the cover and the pages flipped open. The candles flared to life and flames shot into the air.

"Cassie!" Sarah screamed as a deep moan reverberated around the clearing.

I spun on my heels. A black mist circled the ground, moving up and around me. Sarah screamed again, followed by Alice.

"Are you guys okay?" I called, trying to peer through the inky shroud. I was blind. Reaching to the ground my fingers found the book, and I slammed it shut. The flames quashed instantly and the veil that blocked my vision receded. Sarah and Alice stood with their arms wrapped around one another.

There was something behind them, a thick blackness. "Stay there. I'm coming over to you."

I fumbled with the last candle, my hands slippery with the cold sweat covering them. As I shoved it into my bag, I saw something move out of the corner of my eye. I looked, but there was nothing there.

I slung my bag over my shoulder. "Let's get out of here."

Sarah didn't reply. Alice didn't either. They both stood motionless. The clouds parted and moonlight filtered into the clearing. Alice's body trembled, her knuckles white where she clung to Sarah's arm. Sarah's mouth was wide open as she stared at the thing in front of them.

"A dog. It's just a dog," I whispered as I moved one foot and then the other. It turned its head towards me and growled. Its fangs dripped with saliva, snout sniffed the air, and its eyes glowed bright red. I jumped backwards and my feet sank into mud. The animal jerked its head back to Sarah and Alice and crept forward.

"Get away from them," I screamed, tugging at my legs. My feet wouldn't move. I yanked as hard as I could. Nothing. The dog circled the girls. Alice's sobs cutting through the silence.

"Get a branch or something, Cassie," Sarah said as she inched backwards. The dog snapped its teeth and growled.

"Cassie!"

Snapping out of my stupor, I searched the ground for something I could use to fend off the dog. There was nothing close by. The animal turned as I struggled to free my legs.

"I can't move. My feet are stuck. Don't let him see your fear. He'll attack if he thinks you're afraid."

"We *are* afraid," Sarah shrieked.

This is it. He's going to attack. We should never have come here. Panic seeped into the pores of my body. Beads of sweat formed on my forehead, and my chest hurt from the thumping of my heart. *The Candles. I can throw the candles.* I dropped my bag on the ground and pulled out the first candle.

"Get away from them," I roared and threw it as hard as I could. It bounced off the dog's head. He yelped and moved back a step. I grabbed the next one and threw. I hit him in the back. He cried out, snarled, and dug at the ground. With the third candle gripped firmly, I aimed and let it fly. It hit him square between the eyes, and he shook his head and roared. I leaned forward grabbing another candle, ready to throw it. "Get away from them."

He turned and started creeping towards me, slow movements, one paw in front of the other. *What do I do now? I can't move. Don't show fear. Dogs can sense fear, remember. Just act brave. You can do this.*

I threw the candle, putting all my strength behind it. It hit its target, but the dog shook its head and continued stalking towards me. "Run," I yelled to Sarah. "Get something to hit him with. I'm running out of candles."

One paw scraped the dirt and then the other. The moonlight glinted off the razor-sharp points of his incisors. My heart raced as I tugged on my legs trying to release them. Sarah looked at me. "Run."

The dog was closing the gap. He stopped and sniffed the air. Something horrid filled my nostrils. Gone was the damp earth smell left by the rain. In its place, putrid rotting air. My stomach lurched. The dog placed his paws in front of him and groaned. *What is he doing?* He looked at me and lowered his head. I bent over. There was only one way I'd get myself out of the mud.

I unzipped my boots and slowly removed them from my feet, leaving them stuck in the muck. Sarah and Alice searched the tree line for the way out. I crouched low and then jumped as high and as far as I could. My feet hit the ground and I ran, bits of pine cones stabbing and cutting into my soles. Snarls and snapping teeth sounded behind me.

"Run," I pumped my legs.

Alice screamed and stopped dead. Sarah grabbed her by the arm and pulled. "Move or die," she screeched as the dog leapt in front of me. I stopped. Sarah hadn't found anything to fend him off with. He lunged, and I watched as he sunk his teeth into Alice's leg. Her scream ripped through the air.

All I had was my bag, so I gripped the strap and swung it with all my might.

"Let her go," I said as it connected with his head. He let go and turned to face me. Blood dripped from his teeth. His eyes glowed. Sarah grabbed Alice and pulled her towards the trees and the gap; the pathway out.

An icy wind swept across the clearing and the moonlight faded. Clouds raced across the sky. Crouched down, my legs ready to jump out of the way, I waited for the attack. He used his tongue to lick the blood from his fangs as he pulled a paw across the ground. My eyes followed the razor-sharp claws. His head dipped low, and I sucked in a deep breath. *Get ready.* I wanted to turn, to make sure Sarah and Alice had made it to safety, but I couldn't risk taking my eyes off him. The longer I held him here, the farther away they could go.

"Come on, then, what are you waiting for?" I shouted.

He shook his head as if laughing at me and turned to look behind him. I thought of Alice limping away, Sarah trying to drag her to safety.

"Come and get me, coward."

He didn't move. I had one chance at this. I could make a run for it, get to the nearest tree, and pray I climbed it quickly enough.

"Well done, Bradley."

I flinched as a woman's voice came from the tree line. The dog whined. "Yes, okay. Go find them, but no snacking just yet." She stepped into the clearing.

The dog lifted its head and sniffed the air before bounding off in the direct Sarah and Alice had fled.

"Sarah, run!" I screamed as loud as I could.

"It's no use," the woman said.

The clouds parted and moonlight filled the clearing. Walking towards me was a woman dressed in black. Long black hair flew around her face as the wind picked up. She smiled and stepped closer. "You have something that belongs to me."

"I…I," I stuttered, desperately trying to spit the words out.

"Come now, hand it over and you can go."

"What?" I gasped.

"My book, silly fool. Did you really think you could hide it from me?" She grinned and I saw the yellow, stained teeth that filled her mouth. "Give it to me now, or I'll have Bradley retrieve it after he tears you to shreds."

I lowered my bag to the ground and reached inside. My hand found the leather grimoire and I pulled it out.

"Give it to me." She thrust her hand out, and I stepped back.

"Leave my friends alone and you can have it," I said, trying to steady my voice.

"Don't threaten me. I can snap you like a twig."

I recoiled at the image, and she laughed. "You have no idea what you've done."

She was right. I had no idea and I didn't care. I held the book up, the cover cold beneath my touch. "You can have it, but call your dog off first."

"You think you can bargain with me? I hold all the power." With that she raised her hand and thunder boomed. "Give me my book."

I extended my arm slowly, blood pulsing in my ears. I hadn't heard any screaming. Sarah and Alice must have made it out. The woman stepped closer and then stopped abruptly. Her hands reached out, feeling the air around her. "Think you're clever, do you? A barrier won't save you."

Barrier? I looked down at my feet. I was standing inside the circle I'd cast the spell from. *Magic's not real.*

"Step outside the circle. Give me my book, and you shall live. Your friends too."

I do have power. As long as I stay inside this circle, she can't touch me. I grinned. "Call off your dog first."

She laughed.

"What's so funny?" I asked, feeling braver now that I knew I was safe.

"You think Bradley's a dog. How stupid the young are today."

I swallowed. I wasn't going to ask the question that sat on the tip of my tongue. I didn't want to know what he was. "Call him back, and I'll give you the book."

"I want your word, witches honor," she spat.

"Huh?"

"Your coven's oath. Recite it now, and I will summon Bradley."

"Listen, lady. I've no idea what you're talking about. I don't have a coven or oath or whatever it is you're looking for."

"Don't lie to me, witch." Her posture straightened and she started mumbling. Lightning flashed in the distance and the wind picked up. "I will destroy you where you stand."

"I'm not lying, and I'm not a witch. I found this book in my father's belongings."

She tipped her head, finger poised at the side of her lips. "Father, you say. That wouldn't happen to be Stephen Pierce?"

I gulped. "How…how'd you know?"

"How's he been since?" She shook her head and laughed. "That's right, you wouldn't know."

"Know what? What did you do to my father?"

"Fiery, aren't we?" She tapped a finger against her chin. "I'll tell you how to find him if you give me my book."

My head throbbed. Was she saying Dad was alive? Did she know where he was? Tears stung my eyes as I remembered the man who had tucked me into bed and read me stories every night. Tales of magic and mayhem, evil demons and sorceresses of light. The story of Shebha and how she could only be banished by the full moonlight. Could his tales have been true?

"Stop stalling. Give me my book and I'll give you your father. Do we have a deal?"

I snapped my head up and swept a hand across my face, removing the tears.

"You'd like to see him again, wouldn't you?" She smiled, showing her rotten teeth again.

I knew she was lying. Dad was dead, but I allowed hope to blossom, just for a moment. "My father is dead. You can't give him to me."

"Oh, but I can. Stephen's not dead, merely," she paused for a moment, "misplaced."

"Misplaced. What's that supposed to mean?"

She read the confusion on my face. "He wasn't quite quick enough. Pity really. He was a great adversary. His soul is mine now."

"You're a liar," I shouted, clutching the book tight against my chest.

"Am I?" She placed her hands out in front of her and mumbled. The air sparked.

Think, Cass, think. I chewed on the inside of my cheek as I tried to remember the story Dad had told me, the one of the full moon, Shebha, and trapped souls. He'd told it so often I stopped listening. Mom's warning filtered through too, and the dots connected.

"Shebha," I mumbled.

"Ah, you do recognise me. Are you ready to make a deal? My book for your life and your father's soul. All you'll need is his body to restore him." She inclined her head and reached out her hand.

Shebha, Shebha, Shebha. I needed to remember that story. Dad's smiling face surfaced, his animated actions, and the different voices he'd used when telling the story.

Shebha had been the most powerful witch in the land, revered and coveted by every king. They sought her out, but she favored Philip. She gave him riches beyond his wildest dreams as well as something she gave no other—her heart. When Philip chose Madeline, a princess of royal blood, as his bride, Shebha was distraught. She vowed to have her revenge and end his bloodline. She succeeded with the use of dark magic, but in doing so, corrupted her own soul.

She was imprisoned by the witches' council in a realm where she could do no harm. Years passed and Shebha grew stronger within her prison world. She created creatures that could traverse worlds and do her bidding. Eventually, she gained enough strength to break the confines imposed on her during the night of the full moon. A spell created by a powerful warlock was the only thing that could restrain her. The spell disappeared, and it was said that Shebha kept it safely hidden inside her grimoire.

I raised my hand the book still within my grasp. I had the power to stop her.

"Are you ready to trade?"

"I need proof that you speak the truth, that my father is…" I stopped. I wanted to say alive, but I knew that wasn't true.

She huffed. "Fine, if we must."

She mumbled and the wind howled. A gust swirled in front of her. My hand covered my mouth as tears fell. Dad was inside the wind. His mouth was moving, saying something, but I couldn't hear him. I focused on his lips. He was calling my name and something like *louder*. I watched as he repeated the word over and over, until I had it. I moved my lips in sync with his, and he smiled. Shebha stopped mumbling and he disappeared.

"There's your proof, now give me my book."

I clutched it to my chest. "How do I save him?"

She laughed. "That's for you to discover." She stretched out her hand. "My book now."

The ground shook, and I nearly dropped it. I couldn't give her the book. I had to do something. "My friends?"

She raised her head and sniffed the air. "Safe, for now."

With nothing to lose, I whispered the word my father had said. As it left my mouth, my ears started to ring. Everything became louder. I could hear my own heartbeat, the sound of cars on the road miles away, movement in the trees. Shebha's gaze locked with mine. I could hear her heart beating too, thump, thump, thump. The air around me fizzed and all the hair on my body stood to attention.

"Cassie, don't move, just listen to me. I'll help you." Dad's voice came from behind me. "She can't see or hear me, only you can."

"What are you doing?" Sheba asked.

"Nothing. I'm just making sure I've given my friends enough time to make it back to town. You can have your stupid book then."

"Clever girl. Bradley return, let them go." As soon as she spoke, Bradley emerged from the trees and sat by her feet. "Next time," she said, patting his head.

"Cassie, listen. I need you to do exactly as I say. She can't step inside the circle. You're safe. I want you to drop the book and then open it to the second to last page. That's the spell to banish her. Recite it as soon as the moon peeks through the clouds. She won't be able to stop you. Wiggle your little finger if you understand."

I wiggled my little finger.

"Okay, when I tell you, drop the book."

"Your friends are safe. Give me my book. I grow tired of waiting." Shebha paced in front of me.

"Now," Dad said.

I reached my hand out, pretending to give her the book and let it fall to the ground. "Sorry. My hands are slippery," I said, wiping them on my jeans as I bent to pick it up.

"Close it, you foolish girl."

The clouds parted and a shimmer of light streaked into the clearing as I opened the book to the second to last page.

"Now," Dad said.

Book in hand, I read the first words. "O great ancestors." The moonlight increased.

"Stop," Shebha shrieked. Bradley rose to his feet and gnashed his teeth.

I continued. "Hear my plea, banish this evil in front of me. Take her back to her prison world. Bind her power."

Shebha screamed as mist rose up from the ground surrounding her. Bradley lunged at me. He struck the air in front of me hard and evaporated.

"Let her be no more, great ancestors. By the power in me, I ask your assistance, so let it be." I stopped and took a deep breath. Shebha raged in front of me, but the mist was receding. "It's not working, Dad."

"You're not finished. The inscription around the edge of the page. You need to say it now. Hurry."

I turned the book in my hands and recited the Latin phrases written around the edge of the page.

"No," Shebha yelled as the words flowed off my tongue. My body trembled, and I felt the energy drain from me. I finished the last word, and my world went dark.

When I opened my eyes, Dad stood over me. "You did it. You freed me."

"Dad." I shook my head, blinking repeatedly. "It's really you."

"Yes, love. I'm here."

"Shebha?"

"Gone."

"Dad, what happened? How?" I asked, pushing myself into a seated position.

"I don't have much time. Your mom will explain everything."

"Dad!" Tears spilled onto my cheeks.

"I'm sorry, love. I have to go now. My soul is no longer trapped. It's time for me to move on. I'm so proud of you, and I'll always be watching over you."

His face shimmered and he started to fade.

"No," I sobbed as I lunged forward to touch him. My hands met only air, and he disappeared.

I cried and cried until there were no tears left. Then I screamed. A scream that sounded so familiar. The scream I'd heard from my mother the night my father vanished.

I sat in the circle in the clearing of the Oak Wood and watched as the moon played hide and seek with the clouds. I couldn't go home now, couldn't face the hurt in my mother's eyes. I'd had the chance to save him, and I'd failed. I kicked out my feet. Something moved. The book, Shebha's book. I wrenched it off the ground. There had to be a spell in here to bring him back. There just had to be. I sucked in a deep breath as I opened the cover.

A hand touched my shoulder. "Dad?" I gasped as I looked up.

"No, Cassie. He's gone."

It was Mom. I curled in on myself. I didn't want to meet her gaze, to see the look of disappointment in her eyes. She sat beside me and wrapped her arms around me. "You freed him. I felt it, and I heard you scream."

"I'm sorry, Mom. I couldn't save him," I sobbed as I let my head fall against her chest.

"Shush, it's okay." She stroked my hair. "You did save him, more than you know."

Mom sat with me until the sun rose, both of us silent in our grief. The heaviness in my heart weighted on me as we trudged home. "Where is he now?" I finally asked as Mom pushed open the front door.

She looked at me and smiled. "Everywhere. Now he's everywhere."

In the days that followed, my pain lessened and my smile when I thought of Dad grew. He'd stolen the book from Mom and cast the spell under the full moon light. He didn't have magic though, so all he'd managed to do was release Shebha and her creatures. He refused to give her the book, so she trapped his soul and waited.

Mom kept everything exactly the same. She said it was so he could find his way home, so she could try to release him. Saving him was impossible. Without his body, his soul had to move on.

"Why didn't she take the book?" I asked Mom.

"She couldn't. It had to be given to her."

"And now?"

Mom smiled. "Let's just say the world is a safer place, thanks to you. But never cast a spell under the full moon light because you never know what you'll unleash. The full moon holds the power of both good and evil, and only trained witches can control it."

"I won't," I said and meant it.

"In time, you will," she smiled.

"What's that supposed to mean?"

"You've awoken the witch within. It's time to start your training. The balance between good and evil is a burden all witches bear, and you, Cassie, are a witch."

I looked at her and she smiled.

"This is just the beginning."

Lawrence Salani

THE WATER'S EDGE

Placid and timeless, a stream meanders through a small suburban town. While the afternoon sun hovers high over the horizon, the vegetation along the river bank glows a beautiful emerald and viridian hue and blue sky reflected over the smooth surface coruscates under the afternoon light. The sun slips lower, and the landscape lends itself to more somber tones. Shadows cast by the last rays of the setting sun play eerily on the dark, murky water and form strange shapes within the underbrush and foliage growing wild on the surrounding land. The sound of lapping water lethargically drifts among despondent willow trees lining the grassy shore, as reeds along muddy banks sway gently in the soft evening breeze.

As oncoming twilight darkens the sky, and night enfolds the lonely rivulet, a soft moan gently permeates the deathly stillness. The sound gradually becomes louder, then drones amongst the deepest shadows before fading into the deathly silence.

Over the still lagoon, a full moon casts its pallid reflection, illuminating the surface with its soft effulgent glow. Below the ostensible stillness of the black, mirror-like water, something flickers and swirls menacingly. Although not disturbing the water's surface, the movement becomes more discernible and gradually forms a multitude of sad, wretched figures cascading and entwining in the darkness below. Their distorted faces look up from their cold, watery grave and moan an insidious song of death to the moon.

Tangled among reeds and debris, a strange object, covered in decaying foliage and algae, floats unnoticed and unseen within the stagnant water. Indiscernible, it has lain there for some time, its rotting flesh nourishment for animals living along the mud-covered banks. But if one gazes intently at the abnormal form, soft, insipid moonlight gently outlines the decaying corpse of a man.

Within the thick vegetation lining the shrouded bank, a black silhouette stands before the tortured faces as they plead for release. The form is one with the thick darkness until an old woman slowly emerges from the shadows, allowing the pallid light to outline her ancient contour. Time and hate deeply line her face, and within her green eyes burns a pernicious evil glow. Myriad faces beneath the water wail a song of mourning to the wan moonlight, but their torment goes unheard, for the ghostly form only smiles at their bitter anguish. Throughout the long night the crone-like figure watches over her treasure, like a miser lecherously gloating over hoarded gold.

Although early morning light gradually disperses the darkness, a dismal emptiness remains. An ominous atmosphere clings to the shadows, and sunrise, as it glistens upon the murky, green surface of still water, has a mesmerizing effect. The stillness is uncanny, for not even the sound of birds singing in the trees or frogs croaking along muddy banks can be heard. A fetid stench creeps throughout the area; once wholesome air is now tinged with a damp, sickening taste of death.

Only the unwary visit the deserted banks of the stream, for the smooth surface reflects cerulean sky during daylight hours, and lush vegetation imparts nothing of the horror lying beneath the lustrous water. And as a new day begins, happy voices are heard drifting along the morning breeze.

"What a great day," said Conrad before kicking aside a small clump of lantana branches blocking his path. "The sky looks so vast and clear. There's not a cloud in sight." His stocky build seemed to move effortlessly along the weed-grown path. Brushing his long, brown hair from his eyes, he looked ahead, hoping to see a clearing or even glimpse some water.

Conrad had recently moved into the neighborhood from the city. Outdoor activities always fascinated him, and the stream looked like a wonderful spot for fishing. He had planned to relax for some time; however, because of work constraints, finding time was always difficult. Now that Justin had arrived from out of town for the day, Conrad thought some fresh air and sunshine would be a good way to entertain his friend.

"I hope the fishing is good," said Justin while looking up at the clear sky and walking listlessly behind. Fishing had never interested him, but Conrad had been very convincing, so Justin accompanied him more out of friendship than any desire for fishing.

"We'll soon find out. The stream isn't far from here," replied Conrad, leading the way towards the reed-covered banks. A few minutes later, they broke through the wild scrub and on to a grass covered clearing.

The creek wound like a sheet of glass through the distant vegetation. "This certainly is a good spot," Conrad said as he seated himself on the grassy shore and looked over the placid rivulet.

"Yeah, it's so quiet." Justin seemed entranced by the surface of the creek; his unblinking dark brown eyes were transfixed by the shimmering light on the smooth water.

Conrad sat quietly and consciously listened for any sound, but only a deathly silence crept over the languid lagoon. "Now that you mention it, it is abnormally quiet. There doesn't seem to be any birds about." Conrad quickly dismissed the matter and pointed downstream. "What if you try fishing down there, near the bend in the creek, while I try farther along the bank?"

"That sounds good to me." Justin picked up his rod and trudged along the shoreline. Conrad watched from his position beside a large willow tree until Justin stopped before the slight curve in the stream. Conrad waved to his companion before casting his line into the water and making himself comfortable beneath the tree.

Peaceful and dreamlike, the atmosphere made time stand still. Conrad found himself drifting into a surreal lethargy. But, as he sat before the placid water, a strange shadow suddenly appeared on its surface just below a great bough of the tree he was seated under. The indefinable form swayed gently from side to side.

At first, he thought it a trick of the light, but, as he concentrated upon the area, a black, hazy silhouette, as if something were hanging from the branch, appeared before him. Quickly, he turned away. When he looked back again, the odd, blurry shape had disappeared; however, a strange feeling, as if he had entered another world, overwhelmed him. Corruption and death drifted over the putrid water while sorrow and misery clung to the mud and rotting debris along the shoreline. Blackened trees growing along the adjacent bank gently swayed as they forlornly reached for an unwholesome, sickly brown sky. Exposed, thick, finger-like roots slithered snakelike as they sucked abhorrent nourishment from the filthy water and wallowed in the disease filled mud and soil along the water's edge. A profound depression overcame him, for life no longer held any promise of happiness; the mournful specter of death filled his being with unbearable black misery and hopelessness.

On the opposite bank, trees reflected on the water's surface began to mock and taunt; claw like branches—twisted and gnarled—reached perniciously towards him. The murky, green surface looked warm and inviting; its magnetic pull offered solace and joy away from the wretchedness that surrounded him. Conrad stood and walked towards the beckoning water.

Then, suddenly, something from within his sub-conscious broke the spell holding him entranced! Realization suddenly gripped him. He stepped back a few feet from the bank, and the despondent feeling quickly vanished. Dread filled him as he looked upon the turbid water, for remnants of the depressing sensation that had overwhelmed him still lingered within his thoughts.

"You must be more careful." A thin, sardonic voice, coming from behind startled him. "A nice looking young man like you could find himself in trouble."

He quickly turned and was confronted by an old woman. She wore a long brown dress and ragged black jumper. Her face was the texture of wrinkled parchment, and her piercing green eyes looked at Conrad with a malevolence that sent a slither of fear through him. The whole aspect of the figure was one of hopeless destitution.

"How's the fishing today?" she asked, as Conrad sat bewildered before her unsure of what to say.

"Not too good. I've been here for an hour and haven't had any luck." He rose from his seated position by the stream and approached the woman, but, as he drew closer, an unpleasant stench assailed him. At first he thought it may have been her unwashed clothes, but this was something more; it smelled like rotting carrion; the smell of death.

"You should not be here. Don't you know this place is cursed?" When the woman looked into Conrad's eyes, a strange premonition overcame him; something abnormal lay within her gaze. It penetrated his being, his very soul.

"What do you mean cursed?"

"Death lingers within the water of this lagoon. Cannot you feel its presence? Cannot you feel the magnetic attraction?"

Conrad looked towards the water as she spoke, and the odd, morose feeling he had experienced previously overcame him again. Life began losing all meaning. A sad wretchedness blanketed the lagoon; a stagnant, unhealthy atmosphere surrounded him. This time, it took all the resolve he could summon to break the spell.

"What's happening?" he whispered, then turned to confront the old woman again, but there was nobody there. He moved away from the area near the willow tree and sat on the grassy slope above the bank. Everything seemed normal, the beautiful blue sky, the emerald green vegetation, and the shimmering mirrored water's surface. The old hag had left. Perhaps it was for the better, for he needed time to think. The serenity of the spot was more than he could possibly want, so why was it affecting him in such an adverse manner? Perhaps, the dismal silence was affecting him badly; not even the rustling of trees could be heard.

But what was that sound? Puzzled, he strained to listen. There it was again, a distant buzzing noise. At first, he could not determine the direction of the buzzing, but when he stood up he could hear it plainly. The noise emanated from a cluster of thick, green foliage growing abundantly about fifteen meters from where he stood. Carefully descending the bank, he tentatively approached the mass of reeds. The sound grew louder; it was now only meters away. Using his fishing rod, he moved a clump of the green bulrushes to one side, and, suddenly, a stream of large blow flies assailed him.

"Filthy things!" he exclaimed as he brushed them aside, "but why are there so many and what are they doing amongst the reeds?" He moved closer—walking into the shallow creek water and mud—trying to see more clearly. Upon moving aside another clump of reeds, the rank smell of death filled the air. To his horror, floating amongst the driftwood and rotting vegetation was the partially decomposed body of a man!

Astonishment and sickening revulsion overwhelmed him as he gazed upon the carcass. Quickly scrambling back up the embankment, he stood on the grassy slope looking at the place where the body lay, and began retching uncontrollably. The sickening stench of death filled his lungs; its greasy, repulsive touch crawled over his skin. Gradually the spasms subsided, and he stood upon the bank looking bemusedly into the lagoon.

Then, suddenly, he remembered. "Justin! Where is Justin?" Conrad looked towards the bend in the creek, where he had last seen him, but he was not there. Dropping his fishing rod, he began walking quickly downstream. As he neared, he noticed a black figure standing on the bank looking towards the middle of the stream. At first he could not recognize the dark silhouette, but as he drew closer the figure became more distinct. It was the old hag. Conrad followed her gaze and saw Justin in the water up to his waist.

"Justin!" Conrad screamed "Stop. Oh, please stop!" But Justin seemed in some sort of a trance and was oblivious to his warnings as he continued wading farther away from the bank. Conrad began running heedlessly, stumbling and tripping on rocks, clumps of grass, and fallen branches in his haste. By the time he reached the bend in the stream, the old woman had gone, but Justin was still struggling desperately to reach the centre of the stream.

"Justin. What are you doing?" Conrad screamed as panic grew within him, for he knew Justin could not swim. "Wake up. For God's sake, wake up!" Justin's head began bobbing in and out of the water, desperately gulping the air before submerging below the surface again. Conrad rushed to the water's edge, but stopped suddenly before jumping in. A strange premonition overcame him. The water was alive; something lurked beneath its opaque surface; something dangerous crawled amongst the mud and slime, ready to rip and tear and pull him under the placid exterior and into unimaginable horror below. Conrad stood helplessly watching Justin thrash about wildly as his head appeared intermittently above the water.

The creek finally engulfed him. And when the noise of Justin's splashing stopped, and the surface gradually regained its mirrored sheen, Conrad sat forlornly on the bank pondering the events that had just transpired. He needed a few lucid moments, for his mind could not accept the fact that the creek had swallowed up his friend. Foreboding and silent, the stream lay before him mocking his anguish.

"Now that's a shame." The high, thin voice startled Conrad, who quickly turned and confronted the sound. The old hag stood behind him again. A mocking smile lined her wrinkled face, as she looked towards the turbid stream. "Oh, he will pop up again somewhere, but his soul has been absorbed by the water."

Conrad felt an overwhelming hatred for the woman. Her mocking smile was more than he could bear, but his anger dissipated when he looked into her emerald eyes. An intense feeling of hopelessness and depression filled him. The muddied banks only held the misery of the damned while the willow trees despondently moaned to a blackened sky filled with agonizing pain and sorrow. An incredible, empty bitterness engulfed his being. Above the creek hovered the brooding specter of death, but within the warm, inviting surface of the lagoon there was succor from the pain and torment he felt. He yearned for its gentle embrace to fill the hollow darkness within his heart.

Something screamed within his being; intuition, a subconscious caution, an intangible warning awoke him from the spell holding him captive. When he turned around he was alone; the old crone had disappeared again. On the river bank, Justin's discarded rod lay in the mud amongst the driftwood, and, suddenly, memories of the past events surged back into his mind.

Unable to comprehend what was happening, he walked dismally beside the water's edge, through the overgrown grass and foliage, and back along the path from which he had come. There were houses nearby where assistance could be found, but something was wrong. The wretched silence and the accursed stillness of the trees and shrubbery began affecting his mind. In his haste he must have become disorientated, for the area no longer looked familiar. The sudden spike of fear he felt sent a frenzy of emotions streaming through his body. He began to scream loudly, but his cries were absorbed by the thick, vacuum-like atmosphere of the lagoon. In any case, there was no one to hear; only the voiceless willows looked on while the placid, shimmering water began entrancing him with its bewitching beauty. This time, he needed all his inner strength to break the spell holding him entranced. Then he began running.

He ran oblivious of direction; everything seemed to whirl around him. The trees were alive, reaching out for him, their exposed roots moving and sliding, burrowing snake-like into the muddy soil. Numerous times he fell, bruising and scratching himself, picking himself up again, and running frantically in any direction.

When sanity finally returned, he found himself standing beside the large willow tree he had been fishing under upon his arrival. Again, the strange shadow shimmered beneath the bough that grew over the stream. More a blur than a shadow, the shade emanated an intense sensation of malice. Curiously, he moved closer to the muddy bank, and an unclean, diseased sensation crept over his skin.

The object swung gently before him like a dirty, black rag. And as he stood dumbfounded before the uncanny shape, it suddenly materialized into a rotting corpse dressed in ragged clothing. The head of the body was facing away from him; however, as he stood fixed in wonder, the corpse slowly turned until the features of the old hag became visible. Wild, straw-colored hair clung grotesquely to her face, and her bluing tongue hanging limply from her mouth gave her a more frightening appearance. As Conrad stood disbelieving before the gruesome sight, the eyes opened and the mouth began moving. The familiar voice awoke him from his stupor.

"Come, join us beneath the waters. Submit to your longing and let it grow; let it fill you. Abandon your doubts and feel the warmth of release."

A sudden warm breeze enfolded his body as she spoke, and lulled him into a sense of comfort and safety. Then a soft lament filled his mind; a song of misery and despair; an unrestrained murmur of voices drifted over the still water and chorused through the wooded landscape.

"You old witch, who are you?" cried Conrad as he backed away and fell cringing on the grassy bank above the stream.

Filled with uncontrollable fear, he closed his eyes in an effort to shut out the horrid, bloated face, but upon opening them again, the old hag stood on the bank behind him.

Unhallowed thoughts burrowed into Conrad's mind, filling him with unfathomable anguish. Black, charnel feelings burned inside his heart until the touch of death seemed more a blessing than a curse.

The voice again coursed through his head, "Feel the warm, soothing water. Succumb to its call."

When Conrad turned and confronted the figure, a great anger swelled inside of him. He rose from the grass-covered bank and, with arms outstretched, dashed toward the hag in an effort to assail her.

A malicious grin lined the old woman's face as Conrad tried to grasp her. Overwhelming pain seared through his body when she clenched his wrist. Wild, insidious laughter drowned out his futile screams as he fell to his knees before her. Looking up from within his agonizing pain, the last thing he saw before succumbing to oblivion was the hatred that lurked within her penetrating, green eyes.

Conrad was awoken by a dull, throbbing ache in his skull. Sitting up, he held his head, hoping the pain would dissipate, and then looked towards the great bough that hung over the water of the lagoon. The area beneath the branch was empty, and only a deathly quiescence filled the air. Fragments of the past occurrences began forming within his mind. The old hag! Where was the old hag? He looked around, fearing she would still be there, but only his fishing equipment lay on the deserted river bank. Rising and regaining his composure, he made his way back along the track from which he had formally come.

The sky was tinged by on-setting nightfall. A pale, full moon drifted eerily amongst a crimson sky on the horizon. Fear that darkness would fall caused him much anguish. This time, however, he managed to find the track he was looking for.

The stream meandered through the outskirts of the small town before making its way to the ocean. A row of houses lined the main road nearby, so he approached the first he came to, an old timber dwelling with a dark green tin roof.

Conrad knocked several times before receiving a barely audible response from behind the locked door.

"Who's there?"

"Look, I need help," Conrad replied, his voice quavering slightly. "I need to use your phone to call the police."

The door handle began turning, and Conrad saw a grey haired, spectacled face peering out of the darkened gap as the door slowly opened. "Why, what's happened?"

"I think my friend has drowned, and there is a body floating in the creek. It looks as if it has been there for some time; it's badly decomposed."

The old man opened the door and stepped out onto the verandah. "Don't tell me you were over by the creek!"

"Why? What's wrong with that? We just went there for some fishing," replied Conrad, somewhat astonished.

A puzzled expression spread over the old man's face. "You're not from around here, or else you haven't been living here long. Don't you know the place is cursed? Nobody goes there. Since the suicide, about ten years ago, there's been a lot of trouble along that stretch of water."

The old man stepped out farther onto the verandah; a look of anxiety replaced the perplexed look on his face.

"Look," the old man said, "I've been living here all my life. My parents lived in this house, and now I live here alone. An old woman's body was found hanging on one of those trees along the banks of that stream, and, since then, a shadow has been cast over the area. There is something that's not quite right, and various deaths over the years have increased the menacing atmosphere that lingers over the lagoon."

A curious feeling of weakness spread through Conrad's body. Desperately, he grasped at the door frame in an effort to retain his balance. The old man noticed the sudden change in his complexion. "Are you all right?" he asked.

"Yes, I'm fine." There was little else Conrad could say.

"Quick, you'd better come inside. There's a full moon tonight," said the old man as he looked toward the red streaked sky beginning to turn violet along the horizon. "The bad aura that lurks around the creek seems greater when there's a high tide."

The old man ushered him inside and allowed him to use the phone. The body floating among the reeds was of a local man who had been missing for some time, and Justin's body was found near the spot where he had disappeared.

After the death of his friend, a noticeable change took place in Conrad's character. A subtle feeling of sadness lingered over his face, and he brooded constantly over the occurrence of that day. The aversion he felt to creeks gradually increased until he had a phobic repugnance to any pool of still water. The events of that day seemed unreal. Some days he began to forget and imagined it may all have been a dream and that Justin was still alive. But those thoughts were quickly forgotten when he looked at *the livid, red hand-shaped scar on his wrist where the old hag grasped him that day by the creek.*

As a full moon hovers above the lonely, darkened lagoon, a pale, deeply lined face stares over the water's surface. A new face has been added to her brood beneath the shimmering, mirrored water. Their despair fills her with delight as she listens to their song drifting upon the night air; a soft lament melts into the darkened spaces between the twisted trees that agonizingly reach for the radiant globe. While she looks towards the black, contorted silhouettes growing along the distant banks, her eyes gleam maliciously in the moonlight, for she is one with the darkness. Again, she looks towards the multitude of faces and feels their sorrow and despair. The ecstatic feeling courses through her heart filling her ancient body with fire.

On the horizon, the first rays of sunrise begin to tinge the night. She knowingly watches, for the daylight will bring more fools curious to know her longing and feel the fetid touch of death. As the strange figure melts into the thick shadows, the sound of water lapping the decaying banks drifts into the fading darkness, and an eerie stillness falls over the turbid stream.

Edward Karpp

MOONFACE RETURNS

2016

The first thing Alyssa did when they arrived at the cabin was to ask which bedroom was hers. The second thing was to run to that room and climb onto the sheetless bed. The third thing was to look at the papers posted on the cork bulletin board above the headboard.

"What's that, Mommy?"

"That," Stephanie said, "is Moonface." She pulled the pushpin out and held the drawing up so Alyssa could see it better. It showed the figure of a person; the proportions of the limbs and body looked realistic but the head was a perfect circle, colored yellow, with no facial features.

Stephanie anticipated a handful of questions her daughter might ask in response to the name and the picture, but the one she asked was not among them.

"Was he here last year?"

"Yes, his picture was right here. You didn't see it because you've always slept in Mommy and Daddy's bedroom at the cabin."

She nodded.

"Aunt Christina drew that picture. When we were a little older than you, we slept in this room every summer."

"And now I'm sleeping here every summer," she said proudly.

"That's right."

A serious look came over her face. "Is Moonface a real person?" she asked.

"Tell you what," Stephanie said. "I'll let you know when the sun goes down."

Alyssa slid off the bed feet-first and jogged out to the front door of the cabin to retrieve her suitcase. Stephanie stepped into the main room to watch Alyssa wheel the case across the wood floors and into her bedroom. Joshua trailed after their daughter, lugging a much larger suitcase and a duffel bag. He dropped the bag in front of the door to the other bedroom.

"Anything else out there?" Stephanie asked.

"Just dinner," he said. They had picked up fast food from a drive-thru a half hour ago, a short break from the Memorial Day weekend traffic. After Joshua retrieved the paper bags, he put the food on plates for the microwave.

"Hardly a gourmet dinner," Stephanie said as they ate their burgers and fries. *But kind of a tradition*, she thought, remembering the McDonald's a hundred miles away that, years ago, was the closest fast food place with a drive-thru.

After dinner, Alyssa asked, "Is the sun down yet?"

"Let's go see," her father said. He opened the door and the three of them stepped out onto the porch. Gold Rock Lake was down a trail to the right; Stephanie could just see its silvery glinting surface through the pine trees. Above the trees, the evening star hung in a deep blue sky.

"A little longer," Stephanie told Alyssa, whose shoulders slumped. "Just enough time to unpack."

Alyssa was excited to unpack. Stephanie couldn't tell if it was because of the novelty of it all, or because Alyssa wanted to learn more about Moonface. After making the bed, Stephanie helped Alyssa hang her shirts in the closet and place her folded pants and socks and underwear in the dresser drawers. Alyssa pushed the drawer shut and asked, "Is the sun down enough now?"

"I believe it is," her mother said. "Let's go."

Instead of going to the porch again, Stephanie led Alyssa and Joshua to the short hallway that doubled as a laundry room. Opposite the stacked washer and dryer stood a narrow white door that Stephanie had called the secret door as a child.

"Are we going up to the loft?" Alyssa asked.

"You have to be very careful," Stephanie said, turning the small oblong knob and pulling. The door opened with a squeal. Behind it were dim, steep steps, somewhere between a staircase and a ladder. "Let's let Daddy go up first, and I'll go up after you."

At the top, Joshua pushed open the trapdoor, climbed into the loft, and pulled the chain to turn on the bare lightbulb. He turned to help Alyssa up, then offered his hand to Stephanie, but she brushed it off with a smile.

The loft was one open room under a slanted ceiling. At its highest point, the ceiling was seven feet high, but just above the trapdoor it was only four feet high. One round window was set into the wall at the front of the house. Stephanie took Alyssa's right hand, then Joshua took Alyssa's left hand. They walked to the window. Their reflections looked back at them.

"Honey, I think you'll need to turn off the light for a minute," Stephanie said. Joshua walked back toward the trapdoor and pulled the chain. The reflections disappeared and the moon appeared, white and just shy of full.

"If you look to the right—that's this way," Stephanie said, pointing, "you could see Gold Rock Lake if it weren't so dark. We just call that the big lake. Now look the other way, to your left."

Alyssa stepped closer to the window and peered to the left.

"There's another lake over there, the little lake. Do you see it? The reflection of the moon over there?"

Alyssa smiled. "I see it!"

"That little lake is almost a perfect circle. Now, the story we heard when I was little was that you had to wait for a full moon. And when the moon rose far enough, the reflection of that full moon would reach the center of the lake."

Joshua whispered, "Are you scared, sweetie?"

Alyssa gave her father an incredulous look. "Why would I be scared?"

Stephanie continued, "So when the reflection of the full moon reaches the exact center of the little lake, that's when Moonface is allowed to appear. He rises out of the water with the moon's reflection for his head, and he walks through the woods."

"How big is he, Mommy?"

"Well, the moon's pretty big, isn't it? I'd say his head goes up to the tops of the trees. But he only stays until the moon goes down. He has to get back to the lake and wait until the next full moon."

There was silence as the three of them stared out the window. Moonlight shivered on the surface of the lake.

"Will he come out tonight, Mommy?"

Joshua patted Alyssa's shoulder. "Honey, it's just a story."

"Aww," Alyssa said.

"Aww," Stephanie repeated. "Anyway, the moon's almost full, but it's not quite full. Even if he weren't just a story, we wouldn't see him tonight."

Joshua turned the light back on so they could climb downstairs, then he pulled the chain again and climbed down after them.

In their bedroom after Alyssa was asleep, Joshua pulled on sweatpants for bed. "I'm not sure you should be telling her scary stories."

"I don't consider it scary," Stephanie said. "Not at all. It's just a story we told as kids." She pulled the comforter back and slipped into bed. "She wasn't scared."

"You're right about that." He started to pull on a t-shirt, but she put up her hand to stop him.

"Hold on," she said, grinning. "You know, you're still looking pretty good without a shirt on."

He returned the grin and jumped playfully onto the bed. The springs squealed. She shushed him so they wouldn't wake Alyssa and then she wrapped her arms around him.

2017

Light from the sunrise was streaming through the east-facing window as Stephanie came out of the bedroom to make eggs. Alyssa would be up soon now that light was coming into her room. At six years old, she was sleeping better than ever, almost never waking up in the middle of the night.

Stephanie walked past the barstools and into the kitchen. For a second she watched Joshua, sitting at the desk at the far end of the main room, concentrating on writing final exams on his laptop. One more year until tenure. Then she started scrambling eggs just as she heard Alyssa's bedroom door creaking open.

After breakfast, Joshua went back to his finals and Stephanie convinced Alyssa that it would be fun to dip a toe into the big lake. This involved changing into her swimsuit and blowing up her water wings. They took the dirt path from the porch to the lakeside, where there was about fifty yards of natural beach with fine gravel. The water slipped back and forth, tumbling the smallest pieces of gravel over and over. Stephanie kicked off her flip flops and stepped into the ice-cold water. Alyssa followed with an exaggerated shiver.

"Does Moonface live down there?" Alyssa asked, pointing to the middle of the lake.

"That's the other lake, remember, honey?"

"Oh, yeah. I had a dream it was the big lake."

Alyssa splashed in the water for a few minutes, getting her calves wet. Stephanie took pictures with her phone and tried to text them to Joshua, but as usual, there was no signal. When Alyssa was done splashing, Stephanie dried her legs with a towel and they watched a motorboat trailing skiers speed across the middle of the lake. There were a dozen piers and a boat launch on the other side of the lake near the general store, but this side was much less developed, more natural, with only a handful of rustic cabins.

On the way back up the path, Stephanie saw someone approaching her family's cabin through the trees from the east. A big man who looked to be in his forties wearing a fishing cap. "Good morning," Stephanie called.

The man stopped and turned toward them. "Morning," he said. "I was just coming by to introduce myself."

As they walked to the cabin, he told them his name was Mark Cabot. He was the deputy police chief of Somerset, about a hundred miles away. His family was renting the next cabin over, and his wife and son and daughter were unpacking, but he wanted to be neighborly and invite them to a barbecue tonight, if they didn't have other plans. They'd brought steaks.

They reached the porch, where Joshua was sitting on the bench, laptop on his knees. He closed the computer and shook Cabot's hand when Stephanie made introductions. "Mr. Cabot invited us for a barbecue tonight," Stephanie said. "It'll be a chance to meet our new neighbors. They have kids a little older than Alyssa."

"Sounds great," Joshua said.

"Perfect."

After they stepped inside, Stephanie told Joshua it would be good to have a policeman next door. She told him about the fire that had destroyed the cabin on the other side when she was nine years old; they'd called 911 immediately but the response had been too slow to save the structure.

Just before lunchtime, they drove around the lake into town. At the general store, Alyssa unbuckled her seatbelt and hopped off her booster seat, eager to see what toys and treats were in stock this year. Last year she had come home with a herd of plastic dinosaurs, a plush raccoon, and half a dozen other treats Stephanie couldn't remember.

"Good to see you, Stephanie." The cashier at the checkout was Rachel Washington, the daughter of the store's owners.

"Hi, Rachel." Stephanie guided Alyssa to the checkout counter while Joshua looked for a bottle of wine to bring to the barbecue. "Alyssa, you remember Rachel, right? We grew up together."

"You gave me my raccoon."

"That's right, sweetie. Why don't you look over there and see if something strikes your fancy?"

Alyssa rushed to a display rack with plush animals and tourist items. Stephanie asked Rachel about business, as she always did, and Rachel said it was picking up. It looked like the lake would be more crowded this Memorial Day than last year. Rachel thought it was probably because the economy was forcing people to take vacations close to home.

"Mommy, this postcard is about Moonface."

Stephanie glanced over at the postcard rack, where Alyssa pointed at a card with a picture of the moon hanging above its reflection in a lake. Alyssa pulled it off the rack to look at it more closely.

"Moonface?" Rachel said.

"She likes a picture my sister drew when we were kids, so I told her the story."

Rachel nodded but looked skeptical. "That brings back memories," she said. "That story scared the life out of me when I was in elementary school."

"You know, I never thought of it as a scary story." Stephanie felt defensive, but she tried to control the feeling. "It's just a legend like…I don't know, Paul Bunyan or something."

"More like the boogeyman, warning kids away from the little lake. Remember when that toddler drowned? That place is dangerous. Did you know that over the years more people have drowned in the little lake than the big lake?"

Stephanie thought, *Wouldn't the story make kids want to go down to the little lake at night to see if it's true?* She needed to change the subject. She started to ask about Rachel's parents when Joshua interrupted, holding a bottle of red and a bottle of white.

"Steak would be red wine, right?" he asked.

"Yes, Mr. Two PhDs."

They bought a bottle of red and some other groceries—bananas, apples, bread, batteries. Rachel didn't charge them for the postcard.

At five-thirty they locked up the cabin and headed toward the property to the east. A low hill and a stand of pines hid the Cabots' place from view. The path they took led to the one-story cabin's extensive back deck, which faced the big lake. Mark

Cabot was already grilling on a barbecue built into a stonework wall; the smell made Stephanie's stomach rumble. Mark waved to them to come up the back steps onto the deck.

A ten-year-old boy chased a seven-year-old girl through the French doors and onto the deck, shouting something about sleeping bags. When they saw the visitors, they smiled and the boy apologized for being loud. Stephanie said it was fine. The boy was Todd and the girl was Madison. Their mother, Sandra, told them to get ready to eat and they rushed back into the house to wash their hands.

They ate at the two picnic tables on the back deck. The steak was the best Stephanie had ever tasted, a fact she announced three times during the meal, and one that put a beaming smile on Mark's face. She also remarked on the Cabot children's impeccable dinnertime behavior; she quickly felt guilty that this observation would draw comparisons to Alyssa's behavior, but Sandra said Alyssa was being just as good if not better. However untrue—Alyssa had reached for the food aggressively, had chased a butterfly around the deck, and had excitedly described Moonface after the children had been asked not to be so loud—Stephanie felt better after hearing Sandra's comment.

As the sun set, Stephanie handed Joshua her beer bottle to finish, then helped Sandra and the children clear up. Mark and Joshua stayed on the deck. Stephanie had expected the two men would have nothing in common, but it turned out Mark had been a part-time instructor at his local community college for many years, and Mark and Joshua bonded over their shared frustration with campus politics and bureaucracy.

In the kitchen, Sandra took a pile of plates from Alyssa and suggested the kids pick out a game to play on the living room rug. They walked into the other room. The light snapped on and Stephanie heard Todd quietly listing games. They settled on Uno.

"She's adorable," Sandra said.

"She'll be a handful in about fifteen minutes. She had a long day."

"It's so quiet out here. I slept like a baby last night, except for the squirrel on the roof at midnight. Is it always so peaceful?"

"Stop! Stop!" It was Todd's voice from the living room. Stephanie and Sandra hurried to the doorway. Alyssa was standing at the tilting bookcase stacked with games, pushing it with both hands to keep it from falling over on her. A few board games had fallen off a shelf and were scattered on the floor. "No!" cried Todd.

"It's all right, honey," said his mother. She pushed the bookcase upright.

"I'm sorry!" Todd sounded earnest, but Stephanie couldn't tell if he was being sarcastic. She knelt down to clean up the games on the floor.

"I was just looking for another game," Alyssa said, shrugging her shoulders, as if Stephanie or someone else had accused her of causing trouble.

"No harm done, but I think it's time for bed," Stephanie said. "Maybe we'll see Todd and Madison tomorrow. That would be nice, right?"

Alyssa nodded. "Yeah."

Madison was sitting on the rug, looking back at the doorway between the living room and the kitchen, a doorway that looked almost black except for the faraway outline of the moon through the kitchen window, and the dim shapes of Joshua and Mark outside.

They walked back through the woods, the three of them holding hands, Joshua navigating their way through the trees using a sliver of moonlight from behind them. Joshua commented that Stephanie was right, the steak was very good, and the Cabots seemed very friendly. Alyssa said she left her postcard, which she wanted to show them, back in her room, but maybe she could tell them more about Moonface tomorrow.

Stephanie said nothing but recalled the fearful look on Madison's face as she stared at the dark doorway, a look no child should ever have.

2018

On Saturday morning, Mark Cabot knocked on the cabin door. He had grown a mustache in the intervening year, a mustache that looked grayer than the hair on his head. Stephanie told him they would be happy to come to dinner again this year, and Mark told her he remembered how much she liked the steak. She warned him that Joshua was flirting with vegetarianism this year, but they would be over at five-thirty. "More steak for you," Mark said.

Stephanie attributed the little things that were going wrong—like almost running out of gas on the way to the lake—to Joshua's stress about his tenure confirmation. His department had voted in favor of tenure, but not unanimously, and he was worried he hadn't made a good impression on the provost. She kept telling him not to worry, it would be over soon and his department was lucky to have him.

They repeated last year's trek to the general store for a bottle of wine, but the cashier was a teenage girl who said Rachel was upstate and would be gone most of the day. Alyssa chose an activity book from the magazine stand, though Stephanie thought it looked too young for her.

Back home, Joshua got frustrated that Alyssa was drawing a Moonface picture at the kitchen counter next to a manuscript he was editing. Alyssa was confused about why he didn't want her to draw the creature. "I had a dream he saved the animals from a forest fire," she explained. In the picture, Moonface stood above the trees, carrying a rabbit and a frog. Joshua apologized to Alyssa, but he said nothing to Stephanie all afternoon.

The steaks at the Cabots' place were good but not as good as last year. Joshua ate half a steak while explaining he was in the process of changing his diet. Stephanie decided to wrap up the uneaten half in tinfoil rather than finish it. Mark was quieter this year. Stephanie thought his mood might be a reflection of Joshua's, but it was probably completely unrelated. Stephanie talked more with Sandra and learned that she volunteered at a food pantry almost full-time back at home.

While clearing the plates and silverware, Alyssa gasped. She had cut the side of her thumb on a steak knife. There was only a little blood. Stephanie rinsed Alyssa's thumb in the sink and Sandra provided Neosporin and a Band-Aid.

The kids played at the kitchen table, and this time there were no accidents or arguments. Todd and Madison seemed even better behaved than last year, if that were possible: They answered questions, asked permission to get up from the table, and let Alyssa pick the games.

The walk home seemed easier this year because the moon was brighter. Joshua was silent. Stephanie asked Alyssa if she had a good time and she said yes. She asked about her thumb. "It hurts more now," Alyssa said.

Joshua closed and locked the cabin door behind them while Stephanie looked through the toiletry bag for liquid pain medicine. "It's not here."

Joshua said, "I'll run out to get some."

"No," Stephanie said. "I'll go. You stay here with Alyssa."

He protested, but she insisted. It might give her a chance to see Rachel. She took the keys and drove around the lake, passing an SUV sitting on the side of the road, its brake lights bathing the pines red.

A college boy was at the register in the general store. He thought Rachel was visiting family and didn't know when she would be back. Stephanie paid for the medicine and climbed back into the car.

The full moon was higher on the drive back to the cabin. The idea that Moonface was anything but a children's story still seemed ridiculous to Stephanie, but picturing shadowy arms rising above the tallest trees made her shiver.

The SUV was gone. She didn't see any taillights or headlights on the drive back.

She parked in front of the cabin. The front door was open. She set the emergency brake, grabbed the medicine, and ran to the front porch.

She called Alyssa and Joshua's names, but nobody was inside. Nothing looked disturbed, though the secret door was ajar. She climbed up the steps, her heart pounding. Moonlight streamed through the round window, revealing a pale empty loft. She pulled her phone from her jeans and tapped Joshua's number. The signal showed one bar but it refused to connect.

If the moon hadn't been full, she wouldn't have noticed the movement in the distance outside the window. She ran to the window to be sure it wasn't just branches swaying in the wind.

Small figures moved at the edge of the little lake, walking toward the black water.

"Oh, God, no," she said. She barely felt herself scrambling down the steps and over the porch and down the dirt path to the left of the cabin. She didn't feel the twigs snapping against her face as she pushed through them.

She stopped at a clearing, unsure which way to go. Instinct dragged her to the left. The dirt turned soft and wet and the trees gave way to marsh grasses. "Alyssa!" she called. She pushed through the grass, wondering how she'd lost the path, and her feet splashed into the lake.

She couldn't see anyone or hear anyone. "Alyssa!" she called again. She splashed forward into the lake. Dragged her hands through the water. "Alyssa!" The darkness of the lake surrounded her. She trudged deeper, reaching outward as far as she could and then down into the water.

Her right foot slid and she spun around. The moon was bright above the trees and she saw Todd there, drenched and sitting at the trunk of the tallest tree.

She swam and trudged and clawed her way out of the little lake, through the grass, to the base of the tree. "Are you all right?" she asked. He nodded. "Where are your sister and Alyssa?"

"I don't know. It was dark and I couldn't see. We had to do something to help Madison. He was hurting her."

An image of Moonface holding the little girl flashed in front of Stephanie's eyes. She dismissed it. "Where?"

"My house," Todd said. "Madison broke a lamp and he was punishing her. He wouldn't stop. I came to your house and asked for help. They called 911 but nobody came."

Stephanie took his hand and guided him to the path, pulling him back to her cabin. They climbed the porch stairs. "Joshua, my husband. Where did he go?"

"After he called 911, he went to help Madison. We were hiding upstairs. Alyssa said she knew how to get help so we went to the lake."

"Where is she?" Stephanie asked, her voice breaking.

He just shook his head.

"I need you to hide in the loft again, and close the door. Can you do that?" She pointed him to the secret door. She used the landline to call 911 and gave them the address. The operator said the call had come in a few minutes ago and help was on the way.

Stephanie retrieved her father's shotgun from the back of the closet and the shells from the combination safe. Loading the shotgun felt awkward; she had fired it exactly two times, on a hunting trip with her father twenty years ago.

She locked the front door and quietly made her way over the rise toward the cabin next door. Every footstep crunched pine needles and dead leaves. She stopped when she could just see the top of the cabin's roof. Nothing was moving there. She crept closer. All the lights were on inside, the back door wide open, and she could see Joshua lying on his back at the foot of the steps leading to the deck.

She ran to him, stooped down. His head was bleeding but he was breathing. He opened his eyes and she squeezed his hand. She heard faint sirens, too far away.

She peered into the house from the back steps. No movement inside. Through the open French doors, the kitchen looked emptied out, with no sign of the table or chairs.

Joshua tried to turn over, then fell back. "I didn't see Madison," he whispered.

"Where's Alyssa?"

He shook his head, looking confused. "She was hiding in the loft."

Stephanie crept up the steps, the shotgun barrel wavering in front of her. The sirens sounded no closer. The top step creaked. She moved to the side of the doorframe, peered into the kitchen.

This is crazy, she told herself. *The girls aren't in there.*

Blood smeared the kitchen walls. From this angle, she could see Sandra prone on the floor by the sink. Stephanie took one step inside. Sandra wasn't moving at all and her head, though mostly hidden in darkness, seemed bent back too far. Stephanie swung to face the dark empty doorframe leading to the living room.

Suddenly a pale light swept through the entire cabin and the floor shook, as if a train were passing just yards away. In the light, Stephanie saw more blood on the living room walls, and the room was scattered with what looked like wrinkled piles of fabric. On the far side of the living room, something slid down the wall, trailing blood.

There was movement to Stephanie's left. She swung the shotgun toward it. The bay window was shattered and a shape was slipping through, leaving the cabin. It didn't look like the picture. There were more than two arms and two legs, and each of the glistening black limbs had multiple spindly joints. Then it was gone, along with the light.

Voices cried from outside. Recognizing Alyssa's scream, Stephanie was outside instantly, but only Joshua was there, pointing up at the trees. She turned around.

Alyssa and Madison sat on the roof of the cabin, soaking wet and shivering, pressed against the shingles at the intersection of the roof and the gable above the bay window.

The sirens grew louder and red lights swept through the trees. Stephanie laid the shotgun on the ground. Tears streamed down her face. "Alyssa, I'm here," she called to her daughter. "Please, please be all right."

She knelt in the dirt, surrounded by the sounds of truck doors opening and slamming shut. Then she was driving behind the ambulance and the paramedic van and the police car, her hands trembling on the steering wheel, following the convoy to the hospital twenty miles away. She looked out the side window and saw the trees flowing by to her left. The full moon hung behind the trees, keeping pace with her car, and she knew everything would be all right.

Linda A. Prince

ALISTAIR'S SHADOW

It was Thanksgiving when his grandmother revealed to the family she'd been battling cancer for most of the year. That night, she sat at the end of Alistair's bed and held his hand. "Sugar's bad for you, kid," she said. "And I don't like to coat things in it." At twelve, Alistair had never witnessed the end of a person's life and couldn't believe something so intangible might take hers. "Stop feeling sorry for yourself and try to feel sorry for me," she said.

She left him to sleep, but memories played through his mind like clips from a projector reel. His grandmother had signed him out of school more than once, claiming a family emergency to the front office, only to have a proper date for her Cribbage club. The other ladies were so charmed by the boy who sat quietly behind them that they failed to notice the discrete signals Alistair was sending his grandmother.

"Claire, you ol' serpent, you won again," her friend had said as she pushed towards Alistair's grandmother a pile of bank envelopes, mini bottles, and grocery coupons. "That young date of yours is quite the rabbit's foot."

"Maybe he should stay in school next week," Evelyn said, eyeing the others, then turning her gaze to Alistair. His grandmother shrugged and opened a tiny bottle of tequila.

Helping her cheat was fun, and she always spent some of her winnings buying him ice cream or taking him to a matinee. They never seemed to enjoy the same activities, but they compromised, and they loved each other's company. It was unsettling for Alistair to think it might end.

When sleep came he saw her again in what didn't feel much like a dream at all, through the glass doors. She sat on her back porch, and the wicker chair groaned under her weight as it often had. She was dressed like she was going to lunch with friends in her polyester pant suit and vibrant silk scarf. She gazed across the backyard and was still.

Inside, Alistair felt the night breeze on his face as if a freezer door was opened. Outside, a man appeared beside his grandmother, and not so much a man as a shadow of one. Large and wispy, loosely formed, enough to suggest limbs of a human, though at times, the arms would blend with the torso or the two legs would brush together in the breeze, becoming nothing more than a single extension of that torso. It was a misrepresented shape designed by a heavy-handed charcoal artist. Only the eyes were consistent, though merely two holes where the head would be, and apparent only by the back-glow of a distant streetlamp. The light which shone through determined where the shadowman directed its attention. It stared directly at Alistair's grandmother, yet she didn't seem to notice *him* at all.

The next morning his father explained that while Alistair slept, his grandmother passed away in her favorite spot on the wicker chair of her back porch. She'd been suffering longer than she'd let on and knew nothing could be done. The medicine she'd been prescribed was only a tactic to stall for time or mask the pain, and soon they would run their course, so she stopped taking them.

Alistair hauled two suitcases across campus and was nearly at the dorms to meet Jordan when he saw a girl some ways ahead. He tried though couldn't seem to look anywhere but where she sat among a small group outside the student union. They sat in the grass with open books around them and across their laps.

She was the only one reading. Without taking her eyes from the page, she pulled her hair atop her head and tied it into a loose bun.

Her hair made him think of espresso and then about asking her to get coffee with him, which brought an image to his mind of the two of them talking over coffee and laughing about something one of them did or said.

Closer now, there seemed no way of getting through the throng of conversing girls without drawing attention to himself and essentially creating an audience for what could be a crushing rejection. She didn't look his way as the wheels of his luggage bag scuffed and rattled along the pavement. He kept his eyes to her and hoped she might see him, but she was the only one who didn't.

"That's Gwen," Jordan said when Alistair described her faded, lime-green flip flops and weather-beaten messenger bag. Jordan tossed a burrito in the microwave and studied the timer. "She's from Savannah," he said, watching the seconds pass. "Likes some writer. Something-something-Wallace."

Alistair looked to the mirror above the dresser. Years of insomnia had brought a pallor to his face and robbed his eyes of soul.

"David Foster Wallace," Alistair said.

"She likes his philosophy on something. Fate, I think. Or timing."

"Free will." Alistair unloaded clothes into a drawer. "You two talk a lot?" The microwave beeped, and Alistair turned to see Jordan tear into the wrapper.

"We met during orientation," Jordan said through a mouthful of refried beans. "I asked her about the book, and she talked about Wallace…Davis…for a while. Don't remember what she said, but I remember the flip flops. She kept sliding her feet in and out of them."

Alistair grimaced as a piece of burrito fell from his friend's mouth. "Gross."

Jordan shrugged. "Not really. She has nice feet. I probably won't hook up with her, though, if that's what you're worried about."

Returning to the mirror, Alistair was not surprised to see a shadow against the wall behind them without anyone there to cast it. The form extended to the ceiling and then vanished as if into a vacuum. He waited for the presence to return because it always did. No matter where or how far he moved, it was a matter of minutes, or sometimes years, before the shadow came to him.

His parents had been convinced a brief stint of childhood therapy would cure him of the hallucinations, and Alistair never had the heart to tell them how futile it was. He'd never spoken about his visitor again except with Jordan, but he soon worried how his friend perceived him and opted not to mention it ever again if only to seem normal.

Alistair spent the next three weeks looking for a reason to say something to Gwen, but it seemed she was always in a conversation or face-deep in a book. It wasn't until he walked the campus yard that Gwen saw Alistair, too. Her eyes followed a rogue frisbee as it whizzed by and caught him in the throat. She hid her mouth with both hands, and whether she stifled her shock or her laughter, he was content to know he finally had her attention.

As she approached, he crossed his arms only to uncross them and let them hang before sliding his hands into the pockets of his jeans.

"I didn't mean to laugh," she said.

Alistair freed his hands and crossed his arms again, but nothing he did felt normal. "You're still laughing a little."

"Got a little cut, huh?" she said and briefly touched her fingertips to his throat.

"It actually worked out pretty well," he said. "I just signed a contract for a neck modeling agency. This thing's insured for ten-grand."

She laughed again and Alistair reveled in the sound.

"Maybe you could use some to buy me a drink," which she followed with an inhale and a look to say boldness was new to her.

"For ten-grand? I could probably buy us *both* a drink."

It seemed Gwen's entire body exhaled when she did, and for a moment, Alistair forgot he was bleeding.

Nearly three months passed, and the streets were bright now with strings of holiday lights lining the night sky. Store windows had been frosted by snow from a spray-can, and ice skaters were illuminated by a stretch of sequined pine trees surrounding the arena and reflecting the ice beneath them.

Gwen had become an unfamiliar fortune in Alistair's life, and he'd yet to do or say anything to scare her away. They learned more about each other every day, whether they were being open or quietly paying attention. When he asked if she was happy, she took his arm and said she was, but there were things she didn't know because he didn't tell her. Her mind was better for it.

They lost themselves in the crowd of people. Some tumbled while others flaunted their skill, eager to lap amateurs like Alistair who didn't glide but lunged and grasped at the air around him.

"Am I slowing you down?" he asked when Gwen circled him to keep pace. "You're a prodigy ice skater, aren't you?"

She pushed off and glided away on one blade, then turned and coasted forward to pass him. He pretended to curse the air as she spun and skated in reverse with the eyes of a puppy but the grin of the Cheshire Cat. And when the shadow-man loomed behind her, she was skating backwards toward it. Lights which once flickered now flashed belligerently. The shadow's form was constant, though everything else was a rapid series of stills, but it was Alistair who'd stopped while the motion around him carried on.

"Gwen, stop," he called to her. "Come back this way." He waved her in, but his voice was no match for carols blasting from the speakers, and the figure towered behind her now.

Alistair pushed off but couldn't make the distance she'd put between them before the shadow overtook her. He picked up speed and charged through the current. The shadow billowed as oblivious skaters skimmed by and, at times, straight through it.

Seconds away, someone rammed Alistair's side and sent him to the ice. He made a frenzied attempt to get to his feet, but the shadow was gone, and the lights returned to a subtle flicker. He spun to find Jordan there, head back and laughing maniacally into the sky.

"Gwen's gone," Alistair said when he regained the breath knocked from him. "Dammit, Jordan, it was here. It was right *here*."

Jordan stopped laughing and shook his head.

"I'm not fucking around, Jordan, she's gone."

"She's right there, man," Jordan said.

Alistair followed his friend's gesture over his own shoulder and turned to see Gwen mid-twirl a few yards away. What he saw, what Alistair had always seen, wasn't haunting him anymore. It seemed, instead, to toy with him.

Alistair hated the way Jordan stared at him now so void of expression as if he blamed Alistair for dragging this boyhood nightmare through both their lives. Alistair looked down to avoid his friend's gaze.

"You aren't wearing skates," Alistair said. "What are you even doing here?"

"On my way to the airport. Just wanted to stop by and let you know. I'm guessing you aren't going home for Christmas."

Alistair shoved his hands into the pockets of his jeans and watched his breath escape into the chilly evening. "Nope," he said. "Not a good idea."

"Right," Jordan said. "Because your life is really getting back to normal now."

Alistair felt his face twitch as the air turned colder between them.

"That came out wrong. I just…I don't know what to say anymore, man."

"I never asked you to say anything."

Jordan took a deep breath and a quick glance around as though he searched for something else to say. "I got a cab on the way, so…"

Alistair gazed over Jordan's shoulder to see Gwen moving towards them. "I don't think it'll ever be normal," he said. "Or maybe this *is* normal."

Jordan threw his head back. "Don't be such a defeatist, man. My cab's here. It's Christmas. Try not to feel so sorry for yourself, okay?" He slapped Alistair's shoulder and, with a goofy smile, waved goodbye to Gwen before sliding to the end of the ice on the soles of his tennis shoes.

Gwen stayed in Alistair's dorm for the first time and fell asleep in his arms, though it always took longer for him to close his eyes. There were times the shadow came and left like a glitch in a lucid dream.

The steady rhythm of Gwen's breath was what lulled Alistair to sleep, and his dream brought a wakefulness he'd come to know well. As he stood in the darkness of a new nightmare, he realized how little those changes meant to whatever it was haunting him. He ran his hand along the skin of his arm, and the familiar sense of air having suddenly chilled it warned Alistair the shadow was there with him, but he only saw his friend before him.

Jordan sat in the backseat of a yellow cab and gazed through the windshield where Alistair stood on the other side facing in. Jordan's expression began to morph into one of horror, but the changes were slow and subtle. When Alistair saw the fear in Jordan's eyes, he also saw the smoky figure standing just outside the car. The dull glow of the lit 'TAXI' sign made the always-reforming silhouette noticeable against the surrounding void, in the same way common fog is made sinister by the light of an expiring lantern.

Alistair feared the shadow-man, and though he slept, he felt dread prick his skin and cramp his muscles. He strained his throat to call out to Jordan who sat oblivious to Alistair's presence, to Gwen who slept, oblivious to Jordan's fate. Alistair knew even if he found his voice, nothing he could do or say could prevent what would transpire next. He wasn't there, not really, and he had no say in this inevitability. The shadow-man didn't see Alistair. It never took the absence of its eyes off Alistair's friend in the backseat whose blood then trickled across his face from a place with no wound.

Alistair was elsewhere in bed in some dorm room sleeping soundly while panic anchored in his gut. In his dream, he did nothing. He could only watch, and he watched the cab jolt up and over. The abrupt motion shook the unseen ground at his feet, and the yellow cab was suddenly gone, as was Jordan and the dark form who'd taken him.

He woke with his arms in Gwen's grip. She'd stirred him from a half-sleep as he cried out in a room not so dark as where he'd been. A full, white moon loomed outside the window and cast a faint glow along the edge of Gwen's face, though she remained mostly in the dark.

"What the hell was that?" Gwen asked. She had yet to let go of him, and her restless eyes were not lost in the lack of light.

It didn't take Alistair long to reassemble the scrambled images he carried from the dream. "It's Jordan," he said. He repeated with more despair, "It's Jordan. Gwen, I think he's dead. I think Jordan's dead."

Alistair ran his fingers through his hair and down his face, his skin now sensitive to the touch as blood rushed to the surface. Gwen took on the disquiet of the small room, too palpable to be disregarded, and she looked him over as though searching for an injury.

"Okay," she said after she calmed herself. "It was a bad dream. No one's dead."

Her tone wasn't disparaging unlike his mom's when he made the mistake of relating his dream after his grandmother's funeral. "Okay," his mom had said, but with more judgment than he believed could fit into such a small word.

There was no answer when he called his friend and no answer when he called Jordan's family. It was late into the following day when he heard from Mrs. Baker. They suspected Jordan's cab driver had underestimated the black ice on their way to the airport only a few miles from the university. The driver behind them saw the car spin and hit a broken guard rail. It flipped two or three times down the embankment, the driver attested, and landed upside down. Jordan must have been thrown from the backseat and, while Alistair slept, Jordan was crushed beneath the weight of a yellow cab.

Jordan's funeral was more difficult to bear than the others, and Alistair was determined to go through the motions as he'd learned to do, and to grieve later without spectators. When they arrived at the church, he introduced Gwen to his mom. He shook Mr. Baker's rigid hand and avoided eye contact with Jordan's mother whose face was swollen red behind her veil. Alistair told them all how sorry he was for their loss and that Jordan was a great friend. And "no, it wasn't fair" and "yes, he *was* too young," and "yes, all things aside, I'm doing fine."

By the end, Alistair was drawn into a factory line of hugs as he said goodbye to family, friends, and strangers, and all the while he pretended the svelte shadow of a man hadn't materialized at the corner of the sanctuary to watch him.

At the center of the courtyard where there was no shade, ice had already melted on the stone bench, and it dampened the seat of Alistair's suit and the jacket he laid down for Gwen. There was something unfamiliar about the campus as if the absence of students was not the holidays but an apocalypse. They were not there when it came, and now only he, Gwen, and the groundskeeper existed.

Alistair liked the idea of a new beginning and though he wanted Gwen to share in the theory, he wanted her to believe what was behind his silence was grief and not a daydream. Grief was there, somewhere in him, but it had churned for so long with everything else, and he couldn't feel it any more than he could feel anger, or paranoia, or guilt. What he *did* feel was a storm. It built slowly and without forecast, and he wouldn't trouble Gwen with what he couldn't, himself, make sense of.

"Jordan was there when my grandmother died," Alistair said. He rested his hands on the cold surface behind and looked out across the yard where the groundskeeper scattered salt along the walkway because he didn't realize there was no one left to appreciate it. "His own grandmother outlived him."

"Death doesn't care about age," Gwen said. Her icy tone bothered Alistair for only a moment. She'd never been anything but rational. It was the balance he needed.

"I used to tell my grandmother everything. Guess Jordan took her place after she died. Always unloading my problems on them. I wish I'd have done more for *them*. In all the years I'd known Jordan, I don't know if he ever complained about anything."

"Maybe he was the kind of guy who felt better just listening to someone else's problems," Gwen said, and had her hand on his knee been an invitation to share with her the parts of his life he'd shared with Jordan, Alistair couldn't accept it. Instead, he extended an arm and drew Gwen in, and in the bitter cold where they sat on damp stone, Alistair hoped Gwen felt as warm in the embrace as he did. His eyes swelled with heat, and the tears rushed before he could will them back. His voice cracked without saying a word, and Gwen's hold grew firmer as his grief took over in soft, raspy breaths as if she also knew he might disappear in shame if she were to let go.

Alistair lowered his head against her chest. He'd not cried in front of another person for twelve years, but she'd somehow torn down the wall without trying, and she was the only one he would ever let in. "Gwen," he whispered against the breast of her black coat.

"Hm?"

"If someday I were to ask you to marry me, would you say no?"

There was silence, and he was tempted to pull away to read the look on her face, but he felt her chin tighten above his head and imagined she must be smiling to herself in the dreamy way she did when she read. "I won't say no."

She'd kept her promise, and they'd been married for seven years when their daughter Madison turned six. He spent those six years in a state of paranoia for his daughter's sake. The entity still came to him in dreams, always accompanying someone whom Alistair loved, or was acquainted with, or, in recent cases, only met in passing. Upon waking, he'd learn it had already taken them. But after Jordan, he didn't have to sleep to find it. It lurked in his peripheral. It mumbled behind his ear, raspy and garbled, more like an echo of sounds in his head than any language he'd heard. He believed his mind was going or perhaps gone already.

Alistair convinced Gwen to make a life again in Charleston, and they rented an old townhouse near Harbor Bay on the outskirts of downtown. With the tranquility of life by the water and the wave of tourists brought in by the heat of summer, Alistair hoped to regain some sanity.

The moving vans were gone and half the boxes were unpacked when Gwen and Madison took a break to see the bay. Alistair turned the volume up on Sinatra and arranged the framed photos along the mantle. Among them was one of him and Gwen standing outside the courthouse, each with a hand to hold their marriage license. The next frame held Alistair's parents beaming with a month-old Madison in his mother's arms.

Alistair lifted a third photograph from the box, and behind the glass was him and Jordan. Jordan's hand rested on Alistair's shoulder for support as their bodies bent with laughter over something. There'd been plenty of photos that day, as if the university wasn't a few hours from home, but it had been their favorite so Alistair placed it on the mantle with the others, and there it sat as a reminder of the darkness which trailed Alistair like his own shadow.

A few hours passed after Gwen and Madison rushed inside from their adventure, and daylight receded behind billowing shades of charcoal and olive storm clouds. Alistair pretended to look through the last few boxes while stealing long glances towards the couch where Gwen read to Madison, who seemed spellbound by the view from the bay window.

Alistair thought of the times his mom told him to count his blessings, and here were two in front of him. He wondered if sleep might come easily in the new home despite the recurrent rattle of the house. Perhaps the torrential rain and jarring thunder would deter his visitor, though Alistair found no logic in it. There'd been months at a time without a trace of a shadow, but he was only asking for *this* night. Were the request granted, he might have believed he'd regained some control, but the storm only got angrier as they slept.

Rain pummeled the house and muffled the relentless bass drum of far-off thunder. Alistair wedged himself into bed with Madison turning and thrusting herself between him and Gwen. She grew still for a few minutes until lightning cracked the sky and lit the room with a rapid flash, and she opened her eyes with a tiny gasp.

"It won't get you in here," Gwen said, sitting up on her side of the bed as she stared out the window with eyes as wide as her daughter's. Alistair wondered if she was saying it aloud to make it true for herself.

"Here." Alistair pulled the blankets over Madison's face. "Safety fort." He gave her a quick tickle through the fabric, which brought a shrill giggle from her side of it. Alistair turned off the lamp and, like a blind cavefish, hunted Gwen's mouth without a light to guide him. When he kissed her eye instead, she laughed and found his lips with hers.

"Sweet dreams," she whispered by his ear, and though it was a nice sentiment, the words rarely mattered.

That night was no exception. As sleep took him, Alistair found himself in the archway of the den where Madison stood a few feet from the bay window, beguiled by sudden flashes in the dark of debris and limbs as they struck the panes and disappeared with the blaring wind. The window clattered in its frame as if a lunatic were fighting his way in. The wind was incessant, and rubbish swept with the current against the glass exterior.

Madison had yet to see her father standing at her side as she lifted her little arm and extended all five fingers toward the window. It was as if she'd been watching the slender shadow who stood there long before it appeared to Alistair. Alistair strained the muscles in his body to shield his daughter but soon remembered he had no body to move and no voice to be heard. He was just inside the doorway, and at the same time, paralyzed beneath the bedcovers where, beside him, his wife and daughter slept. Alistair recognized the wintry air of the shadow's presence, but he also felt the mattress at his back. He heard the wind pick up somewhere in the back of his mind, but also heard breathing from Gwen's side of the bed. He watched as his daughter reached for the shadow-man but also heard his daughter rustling in the sheets beside him.

In both realms, Alistair willed himself to make words, to warn his wife or threaten the shadow whose arm now raised slowly toward Madison's like a wilted branch of dense smoke. He heard himself bellow *Gwen*, but she didn't stir. *Gwen.* It came from somewhere outside him, or too far inside him to be heard. In recognizing the difference came a sense of reality, which pulled his consciousness toward the bed where his physical body waited.

The stirring of Gwen's grip around Alistair's arm lurched him from the den and into their bed. He threw the blanket back.

Madison wasn't there.

Within seconds, he was in a sprint through the hall until he grasped the frame of the den's archway. He saw Madison facing the bay window, which shook violently against the storm. The warning sirens outside bled through the hollow screams of a nearing tornado, and Madison turned her watery eyes to Alistair as he charged towards her, clutched her small body through her nightgown, and tore her away in the instant a branch of driftwood propelled through the glass pane like an artfully pitched spear.

Alistair returned to the archway where Gwen reached out with shaky arms. Madison embraced her mother's legs, and Alistair spun back to see where the bough pierced through the wall opposite the window.

He turned down to his daughter, up at Gwen, then back to the wall. "The bathtub," he said over the piercing whistle from the hole in the glass. He couldn't take his eyes from the branch protruding from the wall, and his legs weakened as it became clear the outcome had he not been warned by the shadow or had Gwen not woken him.

He heard Gwen shouting for him from the back of the hall, and before he could crumble under the weight of reality, what remained of the glass shattered inward. The entire room seemed to shift backwards as objects from inside and outside swept by him. Behind the movement, even in the darkness, the dark figure faced the archway, its empty sockets aimed directly at Alistair.

Alistair turned and staggered towards the bathroom where he draped his body over Gwen and Madison. Gwen held their sobbing daughter against her body and looked up at Alistair with bewilderment.

"It'll be okay," he said. "I promise." And though he trusted his own words, Alistair knew the only way to keep his family safe was to share with Gwen the secret he'd kept so she would be there to wake him.

Lauren E. Reynolds

A MOST MAGNIFICENT MASQUERADE

A most magnificent masquerade was being held in their honor, for tonight was theirs and it was glorious. Seven strangers whose faces held no meaning to one another exited their cars and carriages with proud regality and into the welcoming arms of their awaiting benefactors, like kings and queens to the rapturous shouts of their subjects.

And why wouldn't they? Were *they* not royal in the eyes of these beautiful yet simple creatures? Were *they* not the masters of them—these willing servants—who were oh so ready and oh so eager to make their every whim, wish and dream a reality? Oh, others had come, and others had tried; others had fought and quested and sought, and others had failed: no glory for them. No, they were destined to forever work and scrap and struggle for their wishes and would never know of the dauntless, blissful peace of a life where all their dreams came true—not like *them. They* were the Seven; *they* were the Chosen; *they* were the Blessed—the *Fae*-Blessed—for the fae had chosen *them*, and tonight was theirs.

The golden October moon overhead shone down on them in a resplendent ostentation of greatness, guiding them and their light-hearted entourage across the meadow to the beautiful, castellated palace of their host. It came alive as they approached—as if their very presence had transformed it. It shimmered like a jewel in the velvety darkness.

Freshly furnished and fully restored, it was a marvelous structure—a creation designed after their host's own outrageously eccentric and augustly splendid taste. Finely-pointed spires rose in marvelous towers to challenge the sky, while mortared walls rose in splendid barracks; wings and flying buttresses laced between them in a vaulting web, and the ceiling above transformed into a series of magnificent arches, crowned with glittering pinnacles. Stained-glass windows sparkled like jewels against the luminous, holy white color of the stones, and multi-colored celebratory banners hung from the torrents. The citadel itself blazed with the light of thousands of crystal chandeliers, and through its lancet windows, music—more beautiful than any heard before—was issued forth with beckoning sweetness.

The Seven Chosen quickened their pace, impatient to join the revels and eager to take part in the voluptuous spectacle held in their honor. The enormous oak doors swung dutifully open as they approached, and euphonious sounds and riotous elation rushed out to greet them as they crossed the threshold into a fairytale.

In a swirl of smoke and twinkling light, their old identities were whisked away, and each was arrayed in shining garments; the women were resplendent in shimmering gowns and jewels while the men were handsome in bright, linen tunics with long cloaks tossed dashingly over one shoulder. Faerie folk, gorgeous in a myriad of costumes and sparkling masks, drew them into the festivities, and at once, fond cries met them on all sides. Wherever they walked, the fae gathered around them, bowing in low, graceful angles, kissing their hands, and murmuring their gratitude. The party accepted it all expectantly, and the company scattered throughout the reverie.

And what a voluptuous reverie it was—this marvelous masquerade. Beyond the entrance hall was a ballroom of breathtaking grandeur as bold and bright and beautiful as the assembly of the court. Dressed for fun, frolic and folly, the vast floors were of a smooth ivory that would not be out of place on an English rose, inlaid with vines and rivets of gold, whereas the ceiling was a magnificent dome of stained glass between golden geometric panes. Marble pillars wrapped in vines of crystalline roses curved into lovely flying buttresses lost in the recesses; crystal chandeliers floated among them, gleaming with lights like falling stars trapped in cages of glass. Cast-iron candelabras, lit with thousands of candles, were scattered about, casting shadows that danced about the walls. Long, low banquet tables groaned under the weight of all matter of delicacies, misting the air with the spice of all things sweet and savory; plates and cups of gold and silver glittered with jewels alongside all things delicious and imaginable.

Music fluttered about in tumultuous tunes; the very air reverberated with wild abandon. For this evening, their host had provided all the appliances of pleasure: masked mimes acting impoverished skits; flexible acrobats performing daring gymnastics atop long, large tables and swinging from trapezes overhead; opera singers singing in high, sweet voices; and an orchestra playing a juxtaposition of classical music and wild folk tunes. There were ballet dancers spinning in elegant pirouettes; jesters jumping in amble jets; folk dancers stepping to the fiery tempos of the mandolin players; and servants twirling and spinning about in their own vibrant dance between couples engaged in fiery waltzes, carrying trays and offering glasses of champagne, fine desserts, and savory hors d'oeuvres. No expense was spared, no extravagance too gaudy, no service nor entertainment too bizarre, and no magnificence too unusual.

Most marvelous of all were the rooms. There were seven main ones—one for each Chosen—connected and conjoined at sharp turns, the irregular angles forming an octagonal shape around the center ballroom. They were just as one might've expected from their hosts, who were notorious for their passion for the august, their preference for the bizarre and peculiar, and their unique eye for color and effects. Unlike the long, straight vistas of the mortal castles, to enter each room, one had to pass through the others before it, and each room was a vision—composed in uniform splendor, the eye embraced one room at a time, creating a novel effect. To the left of each entrance stood a pair of grandly decorated folding doors extending from floor to ceiling, ascertaining that the whole of the ballroom and its entertainments were vibrant and visible and scarcely impeded. Mounted into the opposite wall were tall, stained-glass windows whose brilliant colors glittered between the curled black panes in a marvelous gothic effect.

It was in these rooms that the Seven found their places of honor. Much like the stained-glass windows, the colors and brilliance of their finery varied in accordance with the splendid decorations and prevailing hues of the chamber in which they'd claimed as their own.

The seventh room was a light blue; its aquamarine windows sparkled and bathed the cerulean walls and furnishing with azure light. The room's occupant lounged lazily on a cyan couch in a powder-blue tunic and a cloak trimmed with gems of agate, secured in place by a zircon brooch. Faerie women surrounded him, offering grapes and wine and giggling and hanging off his every word. He grinned the way one would think a Cheshire cat would grin—all charms and sweet words. It was the way he'd used to charm girls and teachers and friends alike to do his bidding—the kind that perfectly masked a careless attitude and indifferent nature. Obviously, years later, he was still thinking back smugly to when he was young and popular.

"I asked for this," he bragged, thinking of his wish for eternal wealth so he'd never have to work another day in his life. "I charmed a wood spirit with my manner and grace…" The entourage of fae women nodded politely, only half-interested, and continued feeding him grapes and wine and handing him things he did not want to get up and reach; they were completely aware that he'd grown as graceless and frumpy as the old cyan couch that consumed the heart of his splendid room.

The sixth room was orange in its ornaments and tapestries and as obnoxious as its tenant, whose tangerine dress and thick, tiger-striped fur coat blazed as boldly and as unignorably as the black planes and citrus glass. She swaggered oafishly about, scrutinizing the lavish decorations with her gaunt fingers, glittering with orange-gold rings set with huge orange topaz and large tiger's eye stones. Her courtiers trailed her every step, removing her giant, plumed hat, massaging her fat feet, and offering her trays of the most perfectly prepared food for her sample and approval. She only half-enjoyed the pampering, preferring instead to indulge her attention in the giant jewels of her rings and the large, topaz necklaces that noosed the heavy folds of her fat neck.

"I deserve this, you know!" she bragged, ravenously devouring the delicacies they brought her. "My parents were so cruel, you see, spoiling my sister and always making *me* work for things!" she whined as if still hurt by the injustice of it despite the shameless luxury she now lived. "Did you know that, when I was eighteen, they would not buy *me* a new car, but they agreed to pay for *her* to go to some fancy college? The nerve!"

They all nodded, pretending to agree as she continued on about how a handsome faerie understandingly offered her heart's desire, and that when she decided one wish was not enough, avariciously asked for her every pleasure to always be fulfilled. She laughed as she finished the tale, oblivious to the way their eyes rolled.

The fifth room was a splendid, vivid blue; the walls were a cool ultramarine, the carpets and tapestries a deep navy, and the windows a bright sapphire that shone upon the cobalt casements. The lady of the room was a pretty woman with an obvious pride in her torso; she spun about in a voluptuous gown of royal blue satin stripped with diamonds that bared her shapely shoulders and generously accented her bosom. She swept forward, her eyes darting between the handsome fae men assembled in the hall as if she had her choice of them.

They swooned about her, loving her the way men never had when she was young and bitter and ugly. Now, she was beautiful with mermaid hair, a voluptuous figure, luscious lips, and vivacious eyes—and no one would *ever* mistake her for her sister again. The thought passed her mind with bitter spite, but then she laughed about how, with a little fae magic, she had become romance personified, and laughed again as the men hung onto her every word and smile. Let her sister have that worthless, freckled, old face and the attention of that stupid, small town—

she could have any man she wanted, and these fae men were devoted entirely to her. She never noticed how their eyes wandered or the distance of their smiles.

The fourth room was a brilliant red, with its crimson walls and curtains falling like bloody waterfalls about the glittering, garnet glass, casting a blazing vermillion upon the russet carpets and the intricately carved, tinted-red wooden desk and chair—the only pieces of furniture that embellished the room in lieu of the usual couches and comforts. At that very desk sat the master of this room, imperial in a tunic of fine, scarlet brocade along with a cuirass so fine and polished, it shone garnet in the flaming, raging, red light; his mantle was bathed in the deepest, darkest of bloodiest red and was thrown militaristically over one powerful shoulder. He commanded his court with a ruthless efficiency and stern eyes that glittered with an underlayer of violence. The soldier fae that surrounded him remained humbly silent, and the women were respectfully submissive in their service, as though he were a king to be respected and feared, but not loved—and that was how he wanted it.

Power was what he had wanted—what he had wished for that day he'd unknowingly rescued a fae—and power was what he had received. Bitterness was all he felt when he recalled that frustrated man, who worked and worked as hard as his father and his father before him—and just like them, all it earned him was scorn. Now, *he* was above them all, just as *he* was above these simple creatures, whose very existence was to serve him; violence would be their punishment if they disobeyed. In his fist, he clenched a crystal glass until it shattered, sending spikes of pain and rivers of blood on his fingers. He furiously demanded another one, smiling at how they flinched from his anger. The fae served him obediently, though they smirked and snickered beneath their masks of fear.

The third room was a bodacious and voracious gold; the yellow color gilded the walls and upholstery and bathed it in splendid flares of lemon light betwixt the amber panes of the saffron stained-glass windows. The host of the room was equally splendid in his long-sleeved, mustard-yellow tunic embroidered in topaz and his crown of golden eagle feathers that plumed his golden hat like the Jack of the notorious tale. He dazzled the fae company gathered about him with coin tricks and cards; they were all eager to play a game with him, all eager to challenge him, and all eager to lose to him, for he won every hand, every roll of a die, and every spiral of a coin with a magic that had nothing to do with his gambling skills. He flipped a golden coin into the air to the delight of the lovely faerie ladies; they fluttered their lashes as he explained how he'd won it in a bet he'd made with a faerie lord. Lady Luck had chosen him that day, and now she was his avatar. He had it all now, thanks to that wager: a full partnership, a gorgeous wife, a darling baby, a fine house, and all the money he could ever want—a splendid reward for that single moment of greed. If only he'd seen the smirks on their faces every time he threw the dice.

The windows of the second room glistened an envious emerald and jade, bathing the viridian walls and celadon porcelains with different shades and hues of green; the polished floors were a smooth, green jasper, and courtiers danced about their lady hostess in grass-green skirts. This lady certainly wasn't idle, for she spun about in a gown of deep green satin—to the wonder and amazement of all—until the emerald firelight was in her dress, hair, and eyes. Avian faerie terpsichoreans entertained her: two dancers fluttered about daintily on the tips of their toes like robins; couples, grouped and separated by gender, met in elaborate glissades like long-legged flamingos in courtship; sprites rollicked about on their colorful wings like hummingbirds gamboling from flower to flower; and a flock of swan maidens did a graceful pirouette in a grand ballet so elegant, the lady watched green-eyed in the emulous emerald firelight. Then, it was her turn, and all gasped in enviable wonderment upon her talent.

They saw that she had talent—that she *was* talent—and when a rival had challenged that, *stealing* her throne and her place of honor and glory, and usurping the destiny that was rightfully hers, *they* had granted her wish and had given her one last dance—and that dance had become the first of many more. Now, she was the envy of the troupe—the star that no one could make fall—and she would mercilessly clip the wings of any who dared to soar above her. She laughed as she recalled her youth and danced in elegant circles around her court, unaware of the boredom hidden behind their awed smiles and the way the dancers checked their steps to spare her ego.

The first and final apartment—and thus the one all the others had to pass through—was majestically shrouded in velvet curtains of royal purple; the sparkling glass of its window reflected deep shades of amethyst, which lit and adorned the orchid walls and plum carpets in violaceous hues. The lord and master, himself, was royally dressed in a splendid, purple tunic, cloaked by a dramatically long mantle of amaranthine silks hemmed with mauve; necklaces, rings, and bracelets inlaid with jewels of sparkling amethysts adorned his neck, wrists, and fingers. He sat in a throne of the deepest, darkest tanzanite, ageless and beautiful, and smirked with prepossessing pride as the other six were forced to pass through his realm and gaze upon his regal glory; all about him, complaisant faeries permeated and honored him with true, eager encomiums.

Yes, he thought vainly. All of this was his, for he was the greatest, the best, and the *First*. His youth and magnificence would never fade, never change, and never decrepitate or deteriorate as he'd feared all those centuries ago when the fae had come to him during his fit of inconsolable rage—in the days when his inevitable decline had plagued him day and night. They'd promised him relief from his fears—promised him youth and beauty, ageless and eternal—and the freedom to indulge in his narcissistic, Hellenic desires guiltlessly and without consequence. It was *he* and *him* they had chosen—yes, he was the *First* Chosen—and he had been untouchable since that night—not by man, nor law, nor Death, herself. He indulged and enjoyed it all with splendid vanity, completely immune to the solemn lassitude kept well-hidden in the sagacious eyes of his faerie attendants.

Yet it was between this first room and the seventh, beyond the majestic wonders of the ballroom and the glittering stained-glass windows and their vantage points, that there was another room—an eighth room, which each of the Seven had failed to correspond with. This eighth room—a secret room, glimpsed only from the outside through the adjacent pillars and buttress halls that shadowed the flanks, betraying nothing of its secrets and less of its majesty—was a locked room, concealed behind its own set of simple, separate doors of strong oak. It was also between these doors that, like some dark prophecy foretold, a grandfather clock, more massive and monstrous than any seen before, stood.

The instrument was a beast of ebony and dark wood, with its massive pendulums swaying ever so slowly like the ungula of some enormous monster. A fat, forlorn-looking face of polished porcelain, round like the moon, swollen to fullness by the stolen sunlight, was orbited by five wrought-iron hands. The metal was twisted and forged into elaborate swirls and shapes of various lengths, tracking minutes and hours, as well as days and months and years, and even the phases of the moon; its carved gibbous phases glittered like two eyes partially closed in sagacious scrutiny, and the full moon glowed like a sovereign jewel upon its crown.

And yet, for all its beauty, it seemed to be broken. Oh, it certainly ticked and it certainly chimed, and its pendulum certainly swung to and fro, but its hands did not seem to properly record the time—rather, they seemed to move backward in their own method of calculation, counting down a span of seven years. Furthermore, each month was represented by a different-colored moon, but unlike the true year, this clock started with the month of November and ended so that the month of October rested right above the number twelve.

Worst of all was its sound: when the minute hand circumnavigated the face, its brazen lungs announced the hour with a heavy, monotonous clang so clear and loud, deep and sonorous, that it commanded everything around it to stop. With each echo of the hour, the musicians, singers, and dancers froze and silenced in paralyzed respect, so much so that even the Seven were forced to cease their pleasures and pay silent homage to the powerful, riveting voice of this strange, clockwork god. Then, when the roaring echoes of the clock's foreboding speech lapsed into silence, a light-hearted laughter followed, and all liveliness returned until the next circumnavigation of the minute hand.

Despite this inconvenience, however, it was a most magnificent masquerade. The company of seven enjoyed themselves immensely, immersing themselves in the entertainment provided and indulging in their hearts' unruly desires in the rooms chosen and designed specifically and specially for them. They gazed through the grand, open doors and upon the fury of entertainments and amusements taking place in the ballroom as if it were all some great, grand show crafted entirely for them to watch and engage. It all continued until, unlike the hours before, the clock's five elongated hands met and aligned in perfect sync, announcing in true, undeniable power the twelfth hour of the full moon on the last day of the October of the seventh year.

With that first echo, the revel stopped: the acrobats ended their show, as did the jugglers and mimes, who had stopped in their movements; the singers and musicians became silent as the servants retracted their trays, and the courtiers closed their mouths and bowed their heads. All service upon the Seven had ceased in such sudden abruptness, it was as though some powerful enchantment had been cast upon them. The clock's brazen sound had enthralled them with such a powerful sense of dread that the whole blissful company had been drained of all their joy and replaced with a lassitude of the most severe gravity.

With the second chime, the food and tables were cleared away, vanishing in puffs of light and flashes of smoke. Following the third chime, the faeries all rose in perfect unison, as if obeying some silently conveyed order. With the fourth chime, the guests were ushered from their seats to their grave displeasure: the lazy charmer groaned at being forced to move; the obese woman in the tiger-striped coat screeched in insolent indignation; the beautiful woman shrieked at being abandoned; the powerful man raged violently when his intimidations failed; the man in yellow complained when the games were forfeited with no winner; the dancer with the green light in her eyes snapped at being ignored; and the ageless youth in splendid royal purple became baleful and cross when his person was forgotten.

At the fifth chime's command, they were ushered from the sanctuary of their personal, private rooms and through the doors of the ballroom, where all the company had gathered before the two locked doors on either side of the booming clock. At the sixth boom, the doors unlatched, and with the seventh, they burst open in command of the clock's thunderous voice. Permitted by the eighth command, the faeries marched in perfect, silent unison through the doors; following the ninth echo, the Chosen were forced to accompany them despite their protests, growing more vexed when their grievant aggravations went unattended.

They entered the room, and their protests ceased.

With the tenth echo announcing their arrival, the Seven cast their eyes upon an incomparable garden; there was nothing tamed, manicured, nor systematic—no, this was nature in its rawest, wildest, and most savage form. A carpet of dense grass covered a bed of soft earth, and the trees had long since run wild, now overgrown with tangles of ivy and elder and frosted thickly with silvery-green moss. The enclosure wall was a ruin of grassy weeds, burst to life with colorful, orange milkweeds and tiny dandelion suns, and the pillars and buttresses were covered in tangled vines of climbing roses, moonflowers, and fuchsias. A tiny stream slithered through the forest like a garter snake, feeding into a small pond dense with cattails and duckweed; algae floated across its surface like a green gauze blanket decorated with lily pads. Frogs croaked and hopped about the slime-covered rocks; dragonflies hummed contently; birds sang from the branches; and butterflies fluttered about like silent whispers. The air was spiced with the smell of flowers and the pungent taste of mold, leaves, and dirt.

Illuminated by the golden radiance of the moon above, the wild, majestic beauty of the garden in its truest, most primal form was undeniably magnificent and stunning—so much so that the company of seven despaired. Their eyes flashed in envy as they surveyed the landscape with covetousness, insulted beyond all other offenses that such a place had been kept a secret from them.

Then, as if to strike them for their arrogance, the clock bellowed its loudest, eleventh chime, commanding the attention of all upon the doors the Seven had not noticed earlier, sitting between two trees twisted together to form an arch and atop a staircase of tree roots woven through the dirt. With that final, foreboding chime, the double doors opened, and there she was.

She was a vision—something half-dreamt that had found its way into reality—and the visual impact of her was truly stunning. All watched as she descended the steps with a fluid, alien grace, her hair streaming about her in flowing waves and her feet barely touching the ground; wherever she stepped, grass, shrubs, and flowers of all kinds would bloom and grow in her place. Her features were that of a woman, and yet not, for she appeared unusually ethereal and alien-like: the oval of her face was a marvel of faerie beauty; her body was a tall and willowy landscape of curves and hollows balanced far too smoothlyto be real; and her skin, milk-smooth and pale with a touch of gold and cream, was inhumanly perfect. Her garments consisted only of a sleek, elegant dress of gray and silver that curled and swayed with a life of its own as if made of smoke, shimmering like mists rising at the foot of a waterfall. And there, trailing behind her…Were those wings? Or was that simply the moonlight illuminating the magnificent, graceful elegance of her in a way the sun could never hope?

She was terrifying and mesmerizing in her beauty, bright, like a devouring star. There was something enthralling about her—her lovely smile, her too bright eyes—something soft, sweet, fragile, and inviting that beckoned and drew all to look upon her until she took up the totality of their vision.

Her eyes and lips were a cold and terrible smile. It was *dazzling*.

It hurt to look upon her, but so graceful and lovely was she that they could not look away, even as tears came unbidden to their eyes. Then, to their own secret horror, the company of seven found themselves smiling back at those cruel eyes and that cold smile, longing for her face to lighten with approval.

"Welcome, Chosen!" she said in a lilting voice, and the seven shivered with delight as she addressed them. "Welcome, Seven!" Her voice was a lullaby, melodious and mellifluously sweet; when she spoke, it was a song, duple in its tempo, harmonious in its chant, and foreboding in its prophecy:

Seven summons to the Fae Queen's court.
Seven summons to herald thou art.
Seven glories and seven ruins.
Seven gathered before the Hunter's Moon.
Seven promises have been made...

Her smile curled as shadows crept about the court; the very air seemed to darken as the wind picked up with a piercing, howling moan. Overhead, the fat, full moon glowed, then darkened to a dusky harvest-gold, then a burning, devouring ochre, and then finally a deep, dark, bloody red.

...Seven debts and seven tithes must yet be paid.

She laughed a jagged, grating sound that filled the air with a cruel mirth; the fae joined her in a vociferous cacophony, and the illusion broke at once. A shadow swept across the garden, and all around them, the magic of the masquerade shattered like glass, evaporating like smoke as the laughing fae abandoned their facades, no longer finding a use for beautiful faces.

Whatever the company had once seen as divine or ethereal, they now saw as savage and grotesque. The faes' smiles became lipless and rowed with shark's teeth; fangs protruded from their lips, sharp and yellow and dripping with venom. Their eyes became beady like berries, elongated with slit pupils, or black like the shimmering night, and their hair transformed into wisps of smoke, thorny branches, or coarse seaweed. Their skin became bark or scales or slimy with brine; soft, dainty hands became long, gaunt fingers, sprouting claws and talons. Cloaks of fur transformed handsome men into ferocious beasts, and gorgeous women became long-limbed and hollow-backed; bursts of light became tiny-winged creatures with pointy teeth, and monsters made of trees emerged from the throng. They were phantasms, gruesome yet gorgeous, grotesque yet glamorous, and frightening yet fantastic. All of them cackled until the wind echoed with jagged laugher like vultures descending onto a corpse; all of it mingled together in a vociferous, cacophonous chant.

Crom Cruac. Crom Cruac. Crom Cruac.

They were voices of the wind—phantasms prophesying death.

Crom Cruac. Crom Cruac. Crom Cruac.

They chanted in harmonious summons; antiquarian, long-forgotten voices rose from beyond the barrier of this world and the next.

Here, he comes, the Hunter born,
A prize and penance for every scorn.
Two worlds like golden apples upon the branch,
Eclipse the other in perfect tranche,
One of shadow, fantasy and might,
The other, reality, lies and light.
The Conquer Worm for whom we bring
A sacrifice for every dream.
Until his hunger has been soothed,
Come forth! Keeper of the Hunter's Moon!

The earth shook as the very earth convulsed beneath their feet, cracking open and bucking apart, roaring up and down in a rolling wave, suggesting something moving below, something Herculean—something alive. Awakened from the dream and now trapped in the nightmare surrounding them, the Seven ran, shrieking and screaming as they barreled away from the garden, the queen, and the cackling, monstrous faeries.

The ground continued to quake beneath them, and from the black, earthy depths beneath, the company of seven glimpsed the glittering, gruesome plates of some massive, living creature slithering beneath. Soon, everything began to fall apart: the stained-glass ceiling and windows faded in color and broke; the walls, fallen pillars and ruined buttresses cracked, dulled, and crumbled; the floorboards splintered, pitched, and rolled; and the doors and decorations blackened and decayed—only the ticking clock remained pristine. And yet, the locks and bolts held strong; no matter how fiercely they banged and screamed and pounded and pleaded, the doors would not obey, and the only sounds that remained were the cruel laughter of the faeries and the ominous chimes of the clock.

The floor burst, and like the Kraken from the deep, the mysterious creature rose from the earthy depths with an eerie silence that was more dreadful than any scream. Gargantuan and glistening, the mighty worm beast moved its glittering, grotesque plates over its meaty, pink flesh; there was neither a head nor a tail—no beginning and no end. Heavy and swollen, it moved toward them with a wet, silent splosh of its massive weight, and a thousand eyes like a galaxy of cold glittering stars had their gaze upon the Seven. So beautiful, so bright, and glistening were those star-like eyes that, all at once, the company stopped.

Their fear was forgotten, and their terror transformed into enthralled desire. Captivated and conquered, they stepped closer in hortatory obedience, drawn like moths to the cold, beckoning light of those eyes. So enticing were they that they did not see its mouth parting nor the gaping maw of circles upon circles of pointed teeth until it dove and devoured them all.

High above, the Hunter's Moon glowed, bright and bloody; a satisfied witness as the castle reverted to a ruin of fallen buttresses and broken terraces. The stones were once again frosted with silver-green moss, and the glass dulled and faded with dirt and age as the floorboards rotted away; only the smooth black earth remained. Standing alone in the vacant ruins of the once great castle, the ebony clock clicked its final chime. Then, its gears turned, and all five of its hands swayed and reset, the longest hand finally resting on the number seven, and slowly, slowly, they began to count backward once more as the faeries departed this world for their own, eager to plan their next magnificent masquerade.

And pleasant is the faerie land,
But an eerie tale to tell,
Ay, at the end of seven years,
We pay a tithe to Hell...
—Young Tam Lin

M.E. Shotwell

A SAILOR'S CURSE

It's a little known tale, one you may not have heard if you've never stepped onto a ship, or spent time at sea, or sat alongside a sailor at a pub who's had one too many a drink. Even if you have, it still may not have crossed your ears. That's because anyone who sees it doesn't live to tell the tale. Well, most anyone.

Perhaps it's best to start in the middle of our story. For some knew of the tale to begin with, else Jimmy Bennett wouldn't have known the grave error he made that night. *HMS Westcott*, a 136-foot frigate, set sail across the Atlantic. Jimmy had experience on the converted naval-turned-commerce ship while docked—swabbing the decks, loading salted meats and grains, unloading empty kegs and crates. But this journey was his first on the water. And he couldn't have loved it more.

The first four weeks at sea brought no trouble at all. Of course, Jimmy was mocked, yelled at, and slapped quite a few times for not knowing what to do, or knowing what to do and doing it wrong, or knowing what to do, doing it right, and still getting a whipping for existing. It was the way of life for a lowly cabin boy. It didn't faze him one bit. He was a cheerful, positive lad, with nothing to lose and everything to gain. He learned through his mistakes and cherished having a family on the ship. Even if they were a bunch of wretched men.

On the fourth Sunday night, Jimmy found himself doing what he did every night: polishing the bits of brass scattered throughout the main deck. His favorite was the captain's wheel. Not all ships had wheels of brass, and not just anyone could touch it, either. He, along with the captain and quarter master, was the only soul allowed to lay a finger. And a finger he did not lay. Not without his polishing rag between skin and metal. The day had been scathing, the cloudless sky offering no repose from the sun. However, at night, that very night, the lack of clouds helped the temperature drop into a comfortable coolness.

Jimmy finished up the wheel, the full moon highlighting his work. It formed a perfect circle, a beacon outshining the pinpoints of stars in the sky. After buffing out the last spot, he reveled at the full moon reflecting back, the orb illuminating his face. He smiled at his work and leaned in for one last check. The moon's crisp edges blurred, and the circle appeared fuzzy in the brass. He turned around, staring at the real thing, not a cloud to be seen. His heart skipped and he held his breath.

He dared to look again at the reflected moon. A fog rolled in over the water's surface beneath the hazy light. Mesmerized, Jimmy leaned closer, squinting to make out the image. The mist thickened, blocking the moon in its full glory. Then something dark appeared. A black, curved mass broke the surface and retreated. A hump. It rolled in the water as it neared. Behind it, a second hump. The something slithered along the water's surface, approaching the ship. It brought a tightness in Jimmy's chest and a chill to his skin. He startled when old Hoggins pulled on his shoulder.

"What you doin' there, starin' with your loose jaw?" He stood two inches shorter than Jimmy, his hunched back and rickety legs giving him the air of a skeletal demon in the moon light.

"Sorry, sir," Jimmy said. "Nothing. Just polishin' brass, that's all."

"You didn' see her, did ya?" His single bottom tooth whistled the 's' in his speech.

"What are you talking about?" Jimmy glanced at the water's surface without moving his head. No clouds obscuring the moon. No fog. No black monster.

"Don't listen to that ol' coot," Jericho, the rigger, interrupted. "He'll tell you tales of demons and water fairies and unicorns coming out of your arse."

"Not true," Hoggins said. "I only tell true tales."

"And what's it this time?"

"Not so good, I'm afraid." Hoggins smiled a toothy grin and shook his head. "He's cursed us all."

"Cursed?" Jimmy found it hard to swallow the spit down his lumpy throat.

"You saw the fog, didn't you?"

Jimmy's eyes widened despite his efforts at keeping a straight face.

"What are you rantin' on about?" Jericho said. He shoved the old man.

"Quit your fussin'," he replied, shooing the younger and taller sailor away. "'Tis a full moon tonight."

"Yeah, what of it?"

Jimmy stood next to Jericho, riveted.

"*A full moon's light—a sight to see,*
But one not worth the agony.
Its reflection brings a curse—
The beast of death, along with worse."

"The beast?" Jimmy asked.

"Sea dragon. The devil's snake. Goes by lots of names, but only one purpose. You saw it, didn't you?" He poked Jimmy in the chest. "First the moon goes hazy. Then the fog appears, followed by the beast itself. Rolling through the waves on its way to you."

"That's a load of bollocks," Jericho said. "Tell him, Jimmy. Go on, tell 'im you ain't seen nuffin."

Jimmy stood frozen, mouth sealed tight and eyes wide.

"Looks like he did," Hoggins said. "We're all doomed. Just as well. I lived more'n long enough. We got three nights. Two more if you count this one. Enjoy 'em." He patted Jimmy on the shoulder and hobbled away.

"Don't believe nuffin he said," Jericho said, shaking his head. "Go on, finish up here."

"But I did see—"

"It's all up 'ere, lad." He tapped Jimmy's head. "Now go." He slapped Jimmy on the arm.

Jimmy abandoned the rest of the polishing and moved deep into the hull of the ship, down two levels to the berth deck where the men slept. His position didn't afford him a swaying hammock, but that night, it wouldn't have made a difference. He tossed and turned on the floor, images of the slithering humps consuming his dreams.

He awoke in the middle of the night, startled by the blackness of the sea monster overtaking him. The rocking of the ship calmed him, reminding him of his place on the ship in reality, instead of the torturous predicament of his nightmare. He switched laying from his left side to his right. He forced his eyes closed. He opened them at a sound, scanning the space, hammocks swaying with limp, slumbering bodies. The noise came from a sailor, across the room, whispering in his sleep. His arms jerked in small movements and he mumbled. Jimmy sighed. At least he wasn't the only one with bad dreams.

He closed his eyes and relaxed his body again. Within seconds, a shout jolted him to his feet. The whispering sailor now stood screaming over another crewmember, stabbing his stomach with a long pipe. The victim cried out at each blow.

"Someone stop him!" Jimmy shouted, knowing it was against his rank to attack a superior crewman . Two other crewmen wrangled out of their hammocks and pulled the attacker off the victim. It was Jericho, wielding his rigging marlinspike, soaked with blood.

"Snakes! Snakes! I seen 'em!" he shouted, as the two men wrestled for the weapon. They managed to get Jericho into their arms.

"Run for the doctor!" one of them shouted.

Jimmy ran astern, where the doctor's status afforded him private quarters. He burst in. "Doctor Thornton!"

"What is it?" Thornton sat up and rubbed the slumber from his scruffy face.

"Come quick! There's been a-an accident." Jimmy led Thorton through to midship. The doctor stood over the injured man, his hands bloodied as he inspected the body. He checked his eyes, neck, and chest. Thornton turned around.

"He's gone." He looked at the two men holding back Jericho. "What happened here?"

The man burst into tears. "I swear, on my life, there was snakes. They was comin' at me. I got 'em off and stabbed 'em."

"And where are these snakes? Hmm? Do you still see them?"

"No, sir," Jericho said. "I swear on me life, they was there."

Thornton checked Jericho's eyes. "Make sure he's secure for tonight. I'll inform the captain at dawn. We'll await his order until then."

"No, no. Don't tie me up. I won't hurt nobody."

"We know you won't," one of the men said. "Cuz you'll be tied up."

"No! Please. It's the curse!"

"Cover up his trap, too!" a sailor in a hammock shouted.

"Here, here," another joined in.

Jimmy returned to his corner, on edge. Jericho fought his restraints, moaning and crying, eventually tiring himself out and falling asleep. It didn't seem fair to Jimmy. Every time he shut his eyes, he saw the fog. The humps. The beast. And in the other corner, someone fresh off of killing a man slumbered in peace.

He had barely enjoyed two winks when dawn arrived. True to his word, Doctor Thornton informed the captain of the slaughter. Captain Mallack wanted Jericho off his ship, preferably at the bottom of the ocean. Most of the crew agreed, apparently, for they cheered and hooted when Mallack expressed his view. Thornton managed to talk him out of it. Instead, Mallack ordered Jericho to be lowered with the jolly boat.

"Please, Cap'n, I swear I did'n know what I was doin'," he said. "Don't put me out there. It's the curse. It made me do bad things."

"All the more reason to separate you," Captain said. "Be happy I'm keepin' you alive."

"That's the thing," he said. "I'll die down there. The beast is comin'. I'll be first to go."

"I don't want to hear any more talk of a curse," Captain said. "Send him off."

The jolly boat hit the water's surface. The crew gave the rope slack to keep the boat far enough away from the stern but not too far to cause noticeable drag on the ship. Jericho shouted from his sea prison for much of the next hour until everyone went on their way of daily chores and workings of the ship.

Jimmy spent the day half-focused, grateful for the endless list of tasks he had to accomplish. They helped to keep his mind off the curse and witnessing Jericho kill a man. Word spread of the curse, including its originator, and sailors took every opportunity to let Jimmy know. The harder Jimmy worked, the more the crew abused him, leaving him weak and soulless by supper.

As the sun drew a close on the heat of day, the crew took turns eating. When it was Jimmy's turn, he waited for the other four men in the group to take their fill before grabbing a biscuit and half a scoop of beans. The men sat in a cluster, and Jimmy stood off to the side. The last thing he wanted was to be tortured while eating.

"You know," the first man said, yanking off a bite of beef, "if it's true, then tonight is the second night."

"Better watch your back, then," a second quipped. The other two crewmen laughed.

"I 'eard from ol' man Hoggins the beast will swallow every last one of us," the third said.

"You can't believe a word that stick of wrinkles be sayin'. Think abou' it," the fourth said. "If the curse is true, and the beast eats everyone…" he leaned in to the other three, "how would we know 'bout it in the first place?"

"Someone found a way to survive it," Jimmy said. He gulped, the dry biscuit trailing down his throat. The four men turned to him. The words had escaped without his control.

"Got somethin' to say, have ya?" the first man said.

"Um, no, I—" Jimmy froze.

The first man broke into a chuckle. It grew into a thunderous laugh. He pounded the table with his fist, and the other three sailors joined in with laughter. Jimmy's face rushed with heat. He didn't care to finish his food anymore. He wanted to crawl into his corner for the night.

The same man took another spoonful of beans. "You're as good as dead, anyway," he said. "Either the beast will get ya, or one of us will first." He grinned, baring his gold front tooth. The others chuckled. The first man coughed amid his laughter. He coughed again, Jimmy perking up. The man's face turned red, eyes watering. The second man coughed, followed by the third and fourth. All four sat red-faced, struggling for air, veins threatening to pop out of their faces.

Jimmy's heart met his neck. He dropped the biscuit and beans and ran up the ladder to the top deck. Captain Mallack had his quarters built behind the wheel, and Doctor Thornton usually dined with him. He knocked on the most ornate door on the ship. Thornton answered.

"Who dares interrupt my supper?" Captain shouted.

"It's Jimmy, sir. The cabin boy. Four men are choking. The doctor must come quick!"

Mallack waved off Thornton, and Jimmy rushed the doctor down to the deck below. Jimmy's hands and feet slid down the ladder, skimming the rungs. The four men sat at the table, eyes wide and mouths open. Foam dribbled down their mouths. Blood trickled out of the first man's nose.

The doctor assessed them, as he had done Jericho. He put his hand on a dish. "What is this?" He smelled it. "Did you give them this?"

"What? The beans?"

"Those aren't beans." The doctor placed the bowl in Jimmy's face, and in it lay a gray lumpy powder. "It's rat poison."

"What?" Jimmy's stomach turned. "We…we were eating beans."

"Did you eat any?"

He shook his head. "I—" He ran over to his spot, the biscuit partially eaten and rat poison untouched. "I didn't have the chance before all this happened."

"You mean you didn't have a chance to kill yourself?" He pointed to the seated men. "They're all dead."

"I don't understand. They were beans." Jimmy teared up. Jericho was sentenced to the jolly boat for killing one man. Here lie four dead men. "I didn't do this, Doctor."

"I believe you, Jimmy," he said. "But I'm not so sure the other men will feel the same. I think it best if you leave this room. Find a secluded spot, and try not to be seen on your way. Stay there for a while, at least until word spreads to you. Act like you know nothing. Do you hear?"

"Yes, sir," Jimmy said.

He was willing to follow any orders if it meant keeping his life. He went farther down the belly of the ship, to the lowest deck, housing most of the cargo. He shimmied through to the stern and ducked behind two stacked crates. Waiting was excruciating as the footsteps of busy men sounded above. He waited and waited, picturing the crew carrying the bodies upward. Surely they would bury them at sea. What he wasn't so sure of was whether or not someone would make his way down far enough to find him. But the longer he waited, the more the sway of the ship lulled him to sleep. He had barely shut his eyes when someone shouted.

"Who's there?"

"What?" Jimmy stood, wiping his eyes. He poked his head out from the shelter of the crates. "Jimmy, sir."

"What are you doin' down 'ere, boy?" The man reeked of liquor. "Men are dying, and you're off taking a nap, are we?"

"Sorry, sir," Jimmy said. "I must've dozed off during a break. You said somebody died?"

"You don't know?"

"No, sir."

"Four of 'em," he said. "The damn curse if you ask me."

Jimmy shook his head. Silence was perhaps his best friend.

"Ay, weren't you the runt that saw the beast in the first place?"

"Jimmy!" Thornton shouted from above.

"I best go," Jimmy said.

"Go on, git up there." The sot swatted Jimmy as he passed.

Jimmy went up the ladder to the scene of the poisonous dinner. The bodies had been cleared out and the table wiped up. The doctor rushed to him and pulled him aside.

"I've been looking for you all night," Thornton said.

"What do you mean, all night?"

"Anyone question your whereabouts?"

"No, sir," he said. "I've only seen one person so far."

"Good. Because the men are uneasy. Some are refusing their posts. They think the curse has taken over the crew."

"Doc, it's time," a voice came from above. Thornton pushed Jimmy to the ladder. Light came through the hatch of the top deck. The morning sun was blinding as he lay topside. Impossible. How was it morning? He had only been asleep a few minutes.

Jimmy stood in the middle of the deck, the bright sun's heat striking. The crew stood silent, forming a circle along the ship's perimeter. The four laid corpses were covered in sail cloth and tied with rope. Captain Mallack stood with his hat to his chest. Doctor Thornton slipped behind the captain while Jimmy moved backward through the tail end of the crowd. He felt the jab of elbows in his ribs and whispers of insults in his ears as he walked by the crewmen.

"May these fine men find peace at sea," Captain said. He nodded, and two men picked up the first corpse at the head and feet. They swung it over the side, the body hitting the water with a splash. They proceeded with the next body, and a faint voice carried over the ceremony.

"You'll all be next," the voice said. It sounded stronger. "'Tis the curse! There's no escaping it!"

"Someone needs to cut the rope to that jolly," one man said. Jimmy held his breath at the realization. Jericho was still alive, dangling behind *HMS Westcott* in the jolly boat, and frightened as ever.

"He's right, ya know," a second sailor said. "None of this matters. We're all dead on this ship."

"It was him," a third said, stepping closer. It was Quarter Master Rogerson, the second in command. He pointed to Jimmy. "He's cursed all our souls."

Jimmy shook his head and crouched back. Rogerson attacked Jimmy, the second crewman intervening, fighting him off.

"Enough!" Captain Mallack barged into the scuffle. The attacker huffed and puffed, glaring at Jimmy, then switched his anger to the captain.

"What say you about it?" Rogerson said.

"About what?" Captain said.

"Ain't nothing we do on this ship can be done no more. The beast is comin' for us."

"Don't be ridiculous," Captain said. "Your orders are your orders."

"Not no more," Rogerson said.

The two other crewmen stood next to him. Three more joined the group.

The captain put his hands on his hips. "Am I to believe you wish to lead a mutiny, Quarter Master?"

Three men stood behind the captain. Doctor Thornton and Jimmy kept their distance from the growing divide.

Captain Mallack chuckled. "A mutiny, over a flight of fancy? Some taboo spell on the ship?"

"It's real," Rogerson said. "The ship is cursed. And we ain't doin' nothin' no more. A man can't eat or sleep without dyin'. You think I'll stick my neck out for anythin' more dangerous than eatin' or sleepin'? No, sir."

Captain scanned the group. "And you all feel this way?"

Rogerson looked at his followers. They nodded. "Aye."

"Very well," Captain said. "As I wish no more bloodshed, here is my proposal. No duties."

The men smiled, Rogerson breathing a sigh of relief.

"For today," Captain added. "When you see nothing will happen, and that there is no curse, you will return to your duties tomorrow morning, double-time. Agreed?"

Rogerson assessed his followers. "Aye," he said. The captain turned away and Rogerson's lip curled up, his eyes narrowing. "There will be no tomorrow, besides."

Captain Mallack stopped in his tracks.

"Today is the third day," Rogerson said. "The day of the beast. Migh' as well enjoy my last hours." He chuckled.

Mallack shook off the comment. "As for the rest of you, move!" He clapped his hands at the willing crewmen. "She doesn't sail herself."

The crowd broke up. The compliant men tended to their duties, covering what they could for the resisters. The defiant group, under Rogerson's leadership, sat along the edges of the ship at the stern, chatting about this and that—families, women, death. Jimmy avoided trouble as much as possible. It helped that Doctor Thornton occasionally passed him, whispering areas to go to where no one would bother him at various points in the day.

The day carried on smoothly, all things considered. Jimmy spent most of his time below deck. Toward the start of dusk, when the sun touched the horizon and the sky changed to orange, Jimmy sought fresh air. He listened for the threats and insults from the seated cowards, but instead heard them propose opening a barrel of whiskey for their final evening.

"Aight, you lazy gents," one man said. "It's enough you ain't workin'; it's another to steal the drink."

"Bugger off," a resister said, sitting on the floor of the deck with the others. "Maybe you won't notice your impending death while you toil away on this ship."

The working crewman kicked the seated defector, who winced and fell back. Another man stood and punched the kicker. The fight escalated, a fourth throwing a punch.

"Sail, ho!" the lookout shouted from the crow's nest.

Rogerson got between two of the fighters, holding up his hands. "Sail ho, he says! Sail, ho!"

The men stopped fighting, standing upright.

"Sail, ho!" the lookout repeated. "Port side!"

Both workers and defectors rushed to port. "A ship! A ship!" a man cried.

"That's it," Rogerson said. "Get the lanterns. Let 'em know we're friendly."

"I'll wave the white flag," another said.

"We don't know they're friendly, though," Jimmy said. Again, the words came out before he thought to stop them.

"Perhaps we'll send you out first, then," Rogerson said.

Jimmy shook his head.

"Then best get out of the way. Rather die from pirates than from the beast." He pushed Jimmy, who lost his balance and fell to the floor. The men laughed and moved to execute their plan.

Jimmy regained his composure and made his way to the captain's quarters. It didn't matter if the doctor was there or not to buffer the violation of protocol of a lowly cabin boy summoning a captain. Men were abandoning ship. Surely the captain would want to be made aware.

Jimmy knocked. No answer. He opened the door to the captain lying in bed.

"What is the nature of this?" Captain Mallack tucked his shirt into his pants and put on his hat. "How dare you come in here—"

"They're abandoning ship, sir," he interrupted. "Another vessel was spotted. Portside."

Mallack rushed to the porthole across the room. "Out," he said. "Now!"

Jimmy hurried out and stood midship, awaiting the captain's arrival. The men waved lanterns and a white flag, making as much noise as possible. The vessel had halved its distance from the last time Jimmy sighted it. It was a hair smaller than the frigate, and it flew a flag he'd never seen before, with black and white stripes. But the oddest part was the crew. It had none. Only one soul, at the wheel. He wore a black hat, black overcoat, and black trousers. Surely one man couldn't maneuver a ship that size on his own.

Captain Mallack appeared and fired off his double barrel pistol. The jeers from the revolters ceased as they stared at the captain.

"All men who abandon ship will be shot," Captain said. "By me."

"Don't think you got enough barrels there for us all, Cap'n," Rogerson said.

The captain aimed the pistol in between Rogerson's eyes.

"Go ahead," he said. "We're all dead men any which way."

Mallack hesitated. One of the dissenters wrapped his arms around the captain's legs, pulling him down. Others rushed to him, delivering blows and kicks.

Doctor Thornton screamed for them to stop.

"Do something!" Jimmy yelled at him. Surely no one would fight the doctor.

But the commotion over the captain died down as quickly as it had started. The attackers backed off. Doctor Thornton rushed to the bloodied body. The captain's eyes were closed, his face unrecognizable.

"No," Thornton said, closing his eyes and shaking his head. "He's gone." He inhaled and stood, facing the quarter master.

"That's right," Rogerson said. He wielded the pistol in his hand, addressing the entire group. "I'm the cap'n now. And we board that ship." He swung the gun to Jimmy. "Except you, cabin boy. You stay."

Jimmy held up his hands and stepped back. There was no use in fighting a losing battle.

The foreign ship glided closer, the wooden vessel lining up along *HMS Westcott* portside to portside. The vessel was plain, showing no adornment or carvings or brasswork, as if stripped down to its bare bones. The figure in black made a small movement—a hand in the air, palm facing inward, and flicked his fingers toward his face. An invitation. A minor gesture to welcome them aboard.

The anxious men set up the bridge to the ship, two planks side by side, to board. Rogerson, holding the pistol, smiled at Jimmy as he waved the crew to leave, one by one. Jimmy considered fleeing. Rogerson might shoot him no matter what he did. Instead, he stood still, shocked at the crew. For how was he, a cabin boy, to handle being on board, alone?

"—dead!" Jimmy turned astern, the shout pulling him out of his fright. He disregarded Rogerson and ran to the stern. Jericho stood in the jolly boat, waving his arms and shouting. "It's a trick! From the curse!"

Jimmy looked at the crew of *HMS Wescott* gathered on the deck of the strange vessel. They smiled and danced, relieved by their escape from the curse. Something didn't feel right. Their jubilation, the dancing and jumping…it should've been loud. But their feet didn't pound the deck. No shouts of joy accompanied their smiles. No cheering or chatting carried over the bridge. There was no sound at all.

"A trick," Jimmy said. He looked at Doctor Thornton, the last left to board before Rogerson. "Doctor!" he pleaded. "Don't get on. It's a trick."

"What do you mean, Jimmy?"

"Shut your yappin' and get on with it," Rogerson said. He pushed the barrels of the pistol into Thornton's ribs. The doctor complied and stepped on the plank.

"Don't do it!" Jimmy yelled. "I don't know what's happenin', but I know it's not what it seems."

"It's coming!" Jericho yelled.

"Enjoy the rest of your evenin'," Rogerson said. He stepped onto the plank and faced Jimmy. "Don't try to make a run for it. I'll go down with ya before I let ya step aboard."

Jimmy backed away from the plank. Thornton made it to the other side but didn't look back at him. That was it. He was alone.

"Get here, boy!" Jericho screamed. "For the love! Slide down and cut the rope, or we'll both perish!"

Jimmy snapped out of his hopelessness. He ran to the back, the man waving him over. Something with a higher pitch carried over Jericho's shouts. Screams. Terrifying, guttural screams.

Jimmy didn't know where the screams came from or if Jericho was crazy or sane. All he knew was what his gut told him.

"Hold on!" he said.

Turning away from Jericho, he hurried below deck to the galley. He stumbled through the meal supplies and grabbed the first knife he saw. He ran back up to the top deck.

The screams escalated, rivaled by splashing.

Jimmy took off his shirt and wrapped it over the rope tethering the jolly boat to the frigate. He stuffed the knife through a loop in his trousers and held onto each end of the shirt. He stepped over the back of the stern and closed his eyes. The shirt caught on the rough edges of the thick rope. He swung his body, propelling the shirt forward, until it reached a steep enough slope to gain momentum. He slid down the rope to the jolly boat. Jericho grabbed Jimmy's legs and helped him safely land.

"Give me it!" Jericho pulled the knife from Jimmy's trousers, cutting the fabric loop. He sliced the rope, back and forth. Jimmy turned around. The mystery ship was no longer there. The sea roiled, men screaming, reaching at the air, flailing to the frigate. A black mass weaved through them. The water churned purple.

"Hurry!" Jimmy said.

"I'm trying!"

The rope threads broke in phases, the thick cord resisting the knife's lacerations. The last of the overboard crew ceased to struggle, their bodies—what was left of them—floated at the surface. The front hump of the beast disappeared where the hull met the sea.

"Where'd it go?" Jimmy scanned the surface. Jericho paused, knife frozen in his hand.

The frigate rocked. The beast appeared starboard, two humps rolling through the water. "What's it doing?" Jimmy barely breathed.

"I'm not waitin' to find out." Jericho sliced through the rope, a large chunk of threads disconnecting. The ship rolled to one side, the vessel creaking amid the choppy water.

"It's sinking," Jericho said.

The water line rose up the hull. The boat tilted more, the weight of the mast knocking it completely over on its side. Water rushed into the hollow vessel. The force of the sea's suction pulled on the rope threads, shifting the jolly boat.

"Hurry! It's going to take us!"

Jericho sawed and sawed until finally the last thread ripped away. The pulling stopped and they drifted away from the sinking frigate. Wood snapped, jagged shards of the feeble lumber splitting alongside the sleek blackness of the beast.

Waves washed over the last glimpse of the boat. The blackness cleared and the ocean calmed, as if nothing had ever been there.

"Is it coming for us?" Jimmy shivered on the bench in the boat, picturing the beast crushing their vessel, dragging them down and tearing them to pieces.

"Don't know," Jericho said. He turned around and seated himself across from Jimmy. "I don't think so. You see, I saw it coming from here. I saw the beast. I saw what the crew was doin'. They was droppin' to their deaths, one by one, before I realized they was seein' things. Things not there. Like I did with the snakes."

"It was another ship," Jimmy said. "Another ship with only one man on board." He shook his head. "I thought it was odd. And yesterday—" Jimmy teared up. "Yesterday, I almost ate rat poison thinkin' it was beans. Four men ate it. They all died."

"I seen it," Jericho said. "Don't know why they was dead. But I saw 'em overboard."

Jimmy nodded. "So what do we do now?"

"Look out for each other. For trickery. Try to survive 'til we hit land. Or another ship."

"And how do we do that?"

"We hope for a miracle," Jericho said.

Jimmy and Jericho drifted at sea. With no oars, they were at the ocean's whim. They lost track of time, amid the heat of day and stormy nights. It wasn't until six weeks later that the jolly boat washed ashore. It was found by a husband and wife in a small fishing village.

In it, a young cabin boy lay, curled up, sunburned, clothing in tatters, face sunken and hair overgrown. Over the next several weeks, they nursed the lad back to health. And, when he was able to tell his story, tell he did. Of his journey. Of his partner's death somewhere in the middle. Of the fog. Of the beast. Of the sights of crazy men. All from a curse under the full moon light.

AUTHOR BIOS

STEPHANIE BEDWELL-GRIME is the author of more than thirty novels and novellas and numerous shorter works. She has been nominated for the Aurora Award five times and has also been an EPIC eBook Award finalist.

LAURA CAMPBELL is an award-winning, internationally-published author from Houston, Texas. Along with writing, her jobs have included managing the snake exhibit at a nature center, Medical Research Compliance, and assisting with offshore drilling litigation. She lives with her husband, Patrick Campbell, and children, Alexander and Samantha, along with a host of natural 'pets' who inhabit the back yard.

MARIA CARVALHO is a multi-genre author who lives in Connecticut with her husband and son. Her published short stories range from YA fairy tale to adult science fiction. Her 2013 children's book *Hamster in Space!* remains a current indie bookstore bestseller. A reading addict, Maria plans to finish all of the books on her 'to-read' list by the year 2347.

CANDICE MARLEY CONNER, an avid reader of fairy tales, takes turns with her Mermaid Girl and Dinosaur Boy on who plays the villain. Evil cackles have been mastered by all. Her family loves exploring watery, magical places be it beaches, swamps, rivers, even mud puddles. A member of SCBWI, her debut picture book releases with MacLaren-Cochrane Publishing in 2019.

LIZ DELTON most often writes fantasy with a dash of science fiction, and when she's not writing, she's doing something else with her hands (sewing, woodburning, painting, you name it). Her first books include the YA fantasy series, the Arcera Trilogy, which is available now in its entirety.

JENNIFER R. DONOHUE grew up at the Jersey Shore and now lives in central New York with her husband and her Doberman. Her work has appeared in *Daily Science Fiction*, *Syntax & Salt*, *Mythic Delirium*, *Escape Pod*, and elsewhere. She blogs at *Authorized Musings*, where she shares fiction and the tribulations of the writing life, and tweets @AuthorizedMusin.

AMANDA J. EVANS is an award-winning Irish author writing paranormal and fantasy romance. Growing up with heroes like Luke Skywalker, her stories focus on good versus evil with a splice of love and magic thrown in. Her books have all won awards. The latest, *Hear Me Cry,* won the Book of the Year Award at the Dublin Writers Conference 2018.

TONY EVANS is a crafter of horror and dark fiction, father, and wildlife biologist. He enjoys all types of horror, but prefers stories about dark entities, demons, and other supernatural boogers that may be hiding under the bed or in the closet. Growing up in eastern Kentucky, his work is strongly influenced by Appalachian folklore.

JOHN FLOYD has work in more than 250 publications, including *Alfred Hitchcock's Mystery Magazine*, *Ellery Queen's Mystery Magazine*, *The Strand Magazine*, *Woman's World*, *The Saturday Evening Post*, and *The Best American Mystery Stories*. A former Air Force captain and IBM systems engineer, John is also an Edgar Award nominee, a three-time Derringer Award winner, a three-time Pushcart Prize nominee, and the recipient of the Edward D. Hoch Memorial Golden Derringer Award for lifetime achievement. His seventh book, *The Barrens*, is scheduled for release in fall 2018.

ROB FRANCIS is an academic ecologist and writer based in London. He started writing short fantasy and horror in 2014, mainly on the train to work and in the early hours of the morning. Since then he has had around thirty short stories published in various magazines and anthologies, both online and in print. Rob lurks on Twitter @RAFurbaneco.

SHARON FRAME GAY grew up a child of the highway, playing by the side of the road. Her work has appeared internationally in many anthologies and magazines, including *Typehouse*, *Gravel*, *Fiction on the Web*, *Literally Stories*, *Lowestoft Chronicle*, *Thrice Fiction*, *Literary Orphans*, *Indiana Voice Journal*, *Crannog Magazine*, *Halcyon Days*, and others.

AARON GUDMUNSON is the author of the novels *Snow Globe, The Slingerman,* and *Emma Tremendous* (as A.D. Goodman) and the collection *From the Dusklands*. His short fiction and essays have appeared in numerous publications, including *Apex*, *Dark Moon Digest,* and *Dead Harvest*. Aaron can be found online at www.aarongudmunson.com or on Twitter @AaronGudmunson.

LAURI HEDMAN, by day, is an energetic customer service supervisor constantly amazed, horrified, and fascinated by humanity. By night, especially when seduced by the moon, she weaves words into sonnets and stories. This is her first work in print; hopefully it will not be her last. Lauri currently resides in Florida with her son and a well-mannered cat named Thor.

EDWARD KARPP is a new horror writer with stories published in *Thuggish Itch: Viva Las Vegas* (Gypsum Sound Tales), *Schlock! Horror!* (Hellbound Books), and more upcoming anthologies. In his day job, he is a college dean. His not-entirely-serious writing about misunderstood movies can be found at Senseless Cinema (www.senselesscinema.com), where he writes under the pseudonym Dr. Pseudonymous.

RED LAGOE is a horror/suspense writer and part-time substitute teacher. After leaving the nine-to-five, she found that the best way to avoid the domestic humdrum was to pursue her passion for writing. When Red's not creating, she can be found dabbling in her other love—amateur astronomy. For more about Red, visit: www.redlagoe.com.

MADISON MCSWEENEY has published horror, sci-fi, and fantasy stories in publications like *Rhythm & Bones Lit, Unnerving Magazine, Women in Horror Annual Vol. 2,* and *Dark Horizons: An Anthology of Dark Science Fiction.* Her poems have appeared in *The Fulcrum, Bywords,* and *Cockroach Conservatory,* and she blogs (mainly about music and genre fiction) at madisonmcsweeney.com. She lives in Ottawa, Canada.

D.K. MOK is a fantasy and science fiction author whose novels include *Squid's Grief* and *Hunt for Valamon.* DK has been shortlisted for five Aurealis Awards, two Ditmars and a WSFA Small Press Award. DK lives in Sydney, Australia, and her favourite fossil deposit is the Burgess Shale. Connect on Twitter @dk_mok or find out more at dkmok.com.

ANDREW NELSON is a data architect, specializing in high performance computing and distributed systems. He loves to hike, master video games, and spend time with his three children. An avid reader, writer, and viewer of all things speculative, fantasy, and horror, he is uniquely qualified to survive any upcoming zombie apocalypse—even with those three kids in tow. His work also appears in *Dark Magic: Witches, Hackers, & Robots.*

LINDA PRINCE holds an MFA in fiction writing and is a member of the Hub City Writers Project. She writes primarily about

America's Southeast where a dark twist compels her characters to defy their own morals, or even question their own sanity.

LAUREN REYNOLDS, inspired by her love of telling stories and making books, decided early that she wanted to be an author: she was eight years old. Years later, she is a writer and poet, publishing her second short story, inspired by her own love of dark fantasy and mystery and the tales of Irish faeries her grandfather and great-grandmother delighted her with as a child. She currently lives in Maryland with her family and is eagerly working on her next story and many, many others she hopes to one day share with the world.

ESTELLE RODGERS is an artist living and working in the Greater Boston area. She writes novels as a hobby and 'Summer Creatures' is her debut short story. When she isn't writing, she enjoys sewing, painting, and travel. She does not enjoy cooking, yoga, or romantic comedies.

JENNIFER LEE ROSSMAN is the kind of person who wakes up from dreams about horrific wolf monsters and says, "Well, that was delightful." She is also a science fiction geek from Oneonta, New York.

LAWRENCE SALANI lives near Sydney, Australia with his wife and child. He has been interested in horror since childhood, and he draws inspiration from pulp horror writers of the past. His interests also extend to fine arts, drawing and painting. His stories appear in *Danse Macabre*, Edge Publishing; *Darkness Ad Infinitum*, Villipede Press; *Gothic Blue Book 4*, Burial Day Press; *Dark Magic*, Owl Hollow Press; and *Dead Steam,* Grimmer and Grimmer books.

KATIE SHERMAN is a journalist and an award-winning author who covers fine food and parenting—two things rarely related—in Charlotte, NC. She has an MFA in fiction and an affinity for Southern Gothic literature, cider beer, Chicago, and morning snuggles with her two daughters. Katie has published extensively in literary magazines across the country.

M.E. SHOTWELL grew up in northeast Ohio, so it was only natural for her to pursue marine biology. After 83 years of studying, she turned to writing as a creative outlet. M. E. loves incorporating her science background into her fiction. When adulting, she's a wife to husband Matt and mother to three dragons, well, "children" on good days.

MAX SPARBER is an author from Minneapolis. His speculative fiction has appeared in *The Best of Strange of Strange Horizons: Year One* and *People of the Book: A Decade of Jewish Science Fiction and Fantasy*. Publications in 2018 include having stories anthologized in *Fangs and Broken Bones*, *Strangely Funny*, *Sanctuary*, *Black Buttons Vol. 3*, and *Ye Olde Magik Shoppe*.

LEIGH STATHAM is the author of four young adult novels, several short stories, essays and poems, some of which have won awards. She lives with lots of children and animals in North Carolina and only eats Brussels sprouts roasted with bacon.

More information about the authors and links to their social media profiles can be found online at owlhollowpress.com.

EDITOR BIOS

EMMA NELSON has an MA in American Literature, with an emphasis in folklore and cultural studies. She writes and edits in a broad range of genres and topics, but her most recent writing can be found in *Channeling Wonder: Fairy Tales on Television* and *The Routledge Companion to Fairy-Tale Cultures and Media.*

HANNAH STILES SMITH is an educator, has a BA in History, and has worked for years as an editor, helping bring fabulous books to their full potential. She spends her spare time escaping between the pages of a book, and a foray into publishing seemed like the best way to channel that energy. She lives in rural Virginia with her husband and four rambunctious children.

For more information and to discover other books by
Owl Hollow Press, find us here:

Website: owlhollowpress.com
Twitter: @owlhollowpress
Facebook: Owl Hollow Press
Instagram: owlhollowpress

Made in the USA
Middletown, DE
08 November 2018